Praise

Face ... .

"This is a typical Ali Vali romance with strong characters, a beautiful setting (Nashville, Tennessee), and an enemies-to-lovers style tale. The two main characters are beautiful, strong-willed, and easy to fall in love with. The romance between them is steamy, and so are the sex scenes."—*Rainbow Reflections*

The Inheritance

"I love a good story that makes me laugh and cry, and this one did that a lot for me. I would step back into this world any time."—*Kat Adams, Bookseller (QBD Books, Australia)*

Double-Crossed

"[T]here aren't too many lesfic books like *Double-Crossed* and it is refreshing to see an author like Vali continue to churn out books like these. Excellent crime thriller."—*Colleen Corgel, Librarian, Queens Borough Public Library*

"For all of us die-hard Ali Vali/Cain Casey fans, this is the beginning of a great new series...There is violence in this book, and lots of killing, but there is also romance, love, and the beginning of a great new reading adventure. I can't wait to read more of this intriguing story."
—*Rainbow Reflections*

Stormy Seas

Stormy Seas "is one book that adventure lovers must read."—*Rainbow Reflections*

Answering the Call

Answering the Call "is a brilliant cop-and-killer story...The crime story is tight and the love story is fantastic."—*Best Lesbian Erotica*

Lammy Finalist *Calling the Dead*

"So many writers set stories in New Orleans, but Ali Vali's mystery novels have the authenticity that only a real Big Easy resident could bring. Set six months after Hurricane Katrina has devastated the city, a lesbian detective is still battling demons when a body turns up behind one of the city's famous eateries. What follows makes for a classic lesbian murder yarn."—*Curve Magazine*

Beauty and the Boss

"The story gripped me from the first page…Vali's writing style is lovely—it's clean, sharp, no wasted words, and it flows beautifully as a result. Highly recommended!"—*Rainbow Book Reviews*

Balance of Forces: Toujours Ici

"A stunning addition to the vampire legend, *Balance of Forces: Toujour Ici* is one that stands apart from the rest."—*Bibliophilic Book Blog*

Blue Skies

"Vali is skilled at building sexual tension, and the sex in this novel flies as high as Berkley's jets. Look for this fast-paced read."—*Just About Write*

Beneath the Waves

"The premise…was brilliantly constructed…skillfully written and the imagination that went into it was fantastic…A wonderful passionate love story with a great mystery."—*Inked Rainbow Reads*

Second Season

"The issues are realistic and center around the universal factors of love, jealousy, betrayal, and doing the right thing and are constantly woven into the fabric of the story. We rated this well written social commentary through the use of fiction our max five hearts."—*Heartland Reviews*

Carly's Sound

"*Carly's Sound* is a great romance, with some wonderfully hot sex, but it is more than that. It is also the tale of a woman rising from the ashes of grief and finding new love and a new life. Vali has surrounded Julia and Poppy with a cast of great supporting characters, making this an extremely satisfying read."—*Just About Write*

Praise for the Cain Casey Saga

The Devil's Due

"A Night Owl Reviews Top Pick: Cain Casey is the kind of person you aspire to be even though some consider her a criminal. She's loyal, very protective of those she loves, honorable, big on preserving her family legacy and loves her family greatly. *The Devil's Due* is a book I highly recommend and well worth the wait we all suffered through. I cannot wait for the next book in the series to come out."
—*Night Owl Reviews*

The Devil Be Damned

"Ali Vali excels at creating strong, romantic characters along with her fast-paced, sophisticated plots. Her setting, New Orleans, provides just the right blend of immigrants from Mexico, South America, and Cuba, along with a city steeped in traditions."—*Just About Write*

Deal with the Devil

"Ali Vali has given her fans another thick, rich thriller...*Deal With the Devil* has wonderful love stories, great sex, and an ample supply of humor. It is an exciting, page-turning read that leaves her readers eagerly awaiting the next book in the series."—*Just About Write*

The Devil Unleashed

"Fast-paced action scenes, intriguing character revelations, and a refreshing approach to the romance thriller genre all make for an enjoyable reading experience in the Big Easy...*The Devil Unleashed* is an engrossing reading experience."—*Midwest Book Review*

The Devil Inside

"*The Devil Inside* is the first of what promises to be a very exciting series...While telling an exciting story that grips the reader, Vali has also fully fleshed out her heroes and villains. *The Devil Inside* is that rarity: a fascinating crime novel which includes a tender love story and leaves the reader with a cliffhanger ending."—*MegaScene*

By the Author

Carly's Sound

Second Season

Love Match

The Dragon Tree Legacy

The Romance Vote

Girls with Guns

Beneath the Waves

Beauty and the Boss

Blue Skies

Stormy Seas

The Inheritance

Face the Music

One More Chance

Call Series

Calling the Dead

Answering the Call

Forces Series

Balance of Forces: Toujours Ici

Battle of Forces: Sera Toujours

Force of Fire: Toujours a Vous

Vegas Nights

Double-Crossed

The Cain Casey Saga

The Devil Inside

The Devil Unleashed

Deal with the Devil

The Devil Be Damned

The Devil's Orchard

The Devil's Due

Heart of the Devil

Visit us at www.boldstrokesbooks.com

ONE MORE CHANCE

by
Ali Vali

2020

ONE MORE CHANCE

© 2020 By Ali Vali. All Rights Reserved.

ISBN 13: 978-1-63555-536-3

This Trade Paperback Original Is Published By
Bold Strokes Books, Inc.
P.O. Box 249
Valley Falls, NY 12185

First Edition: October 2020

THIS IS A WORK OF FICTION. NAMES, CHARACTERS, PLACES, AND INCIDENTS ARE THE PRODUCT OF THE AUTHOR'S IMAGINATION OR ARE USED FICTITIOUSLY. ANY RESEMBLANCE TO ACTUAL PERSONS, LIVING OR DEAD, BUSINESS ESTABLISHMENTS, EVENTS, OR LOCALES IS ENTIRELY COINCIDENTAL.

THIS BOOK, OR PARTS THEREOF, MAY NOT BE REPRODUCED IN ANY FORM WITHOUT PERMISSION.

Credits

Editors: Victoria Villaseñor and Ruth Sternglantz
Production Design: Stacia Seaman
Cover Design by Sheri (hindsightgraphics@gmail.com)

Acknowledgments

Thank you, Radclyffe, for the opportunity to keep telling the stories that crowd my head, and thanks to Sandy for all you do for everyone in the BSB family. I appreciate all you do to keep me on track even when I turn in the wrong thing.

A big thanks to my editors, Victoria Villaseñor and Ruth Sternglantz. Victoria, thank you for your ongoing lessons that make the writing as well as editing process fun. Ruth, with your help, the final product is something I'm proud of. You two are the best team in the business. Thank you to Sheri for another great cover.

Thank you to my beta readers Cris Perez-Soria, Lenore Benoit, and Kim Rieff. You can't know how much I appreciate you all.

To the readers: You know every word is written with you in mind. Thank you for all the encouragement to keep going.

This book was tough to write in that it deals with domestic violence, which is a subject not easy to talk about. Abuse isn't ever acceptable and something no one should have to endure. If you need help, reach out to the National Domestic Violence Hotline at 1-800-799-7233. Their motto is "You aren't alone," and if you call, their volunteers are willing to listen as well as reach out to our local program that can help you. I'm pledging a portion of each sale to my local program for all they do in the rebuilding and saving of lives.

Thanks to my quarantine partner, C. You do make every adventure fun. *Verdad!*

For C
and
The Brave Women Who Leave

CHAPTER ONE

"Fuck, fuck...fuck!"
Desi Thompson Simoneaux watched her husband Byron run his hand through his greasy blond hair and mutter some more. He'd been in a mood from the time he'd come home after losing at the casino—again. When he needed to vent, she was always his favorite target. Normally she braced for it and managed to hold it together until he was done.

This time, after his fist connected with her temple, her scream had made one of their neighbors call the police.

She pressed her fingers to her split lip, but the blood trickled through. The number of cops outside had increased when he'd refused to open the door, and the backup that showed up only enraged him more. Their front yard was lit up with blue flashing lights. "Please, Byron, you need to let them in. You know I didn't call them, and I won't say anything." She just wanted this to stop.

"I told you to shut up." He slapped his forehead as he screamed, and Desi thought he'd finally snapped. The thought made her shudder.

Maybe this nightmare would finally be over. Byron glared at her as if just noticing her, and she brought her hands up to protect her face as he moved toward her. The sudden shock of pain made her cry out, and her legs buckled. Byron had kicked right below her left knee, and she had no doubt her leg was broken.

She was going to be sick from the excruciating pain, and all she could do was concentrate on her breathing. There was no holding back her cry when he followed with three kicks to her midsection and ribs, and she stopped breathing when the pain became excruciating. The attack stopped while he walked to the door.

"No, please," she begged, when she realized he'd gone for the baseball bat propped against the doorframe, but doubted he could hear her over his swearing. The door splintered and crashed open, and two police officers tackled Byron before he could swing at her head. It was a shock he hadn't finished what he'd started. He'd always promised he'd gladly do the time if he knew she was in the ground by his hand.

"Ma'am, can you hear me?" One EMT knelt beside her and started cutting her jeans to expose her leg while the other began hooking her up to machines. That one placed an oxygen mask over her face. "That will help with the pain while we do what we need to do, and I'm going to check your other injuries. Just stay calm and hold still, okay?"

"Don't say a goddamn word, Desi. You hear me?" Byron was still yelling as he struggled with the police. "Not one fucking word."

"Why don't you give it a rest, asshole," the police officer cuffing Byron said. "Go with that right to remain silent thing we told you about."

"Ma'am, can you hear me?" the EMT repeated.

"It hurts," was all she was able to say. His voice sounded far away, and all she could hear was the pounding *thud-thud* in her head.

"I know, but we're here to help." He shined a light in her eyes. "Let's get a blanket on her and up the O2. She's going into shock."

Desi closed her eyes and prayed to die for the first time in her life. If she had to stay trapped in this hell, going on wasn't worth it. Perhaps the worst thing that could've happened was the police getting there too early and not letting Byron send her into oblivion. She closed her eyes and let the tears fall. How had life gotten so bad?

"We need a room, Sally!" the EMT yelled, slamming through the metal doors of University Medical Center in New Orleans as he and his partner ran in with a stretcher.

"Follow me." Sally, the charge nurse, moved quickly ahead of them.

All Dr. Harry Basantes could see from where she stood, scanning the large board that listed all the patients in the ER, was the blond hair of whoever was moaning on the gurney. Whatever had happened, the sickly green colored sheet the EMTs used was slowly turning red. She stayed out of their way, waiting for the crew to get the patient settled.

"Get a doc in here. We didn't want to medicate her, figuring she was going be worked up for surgery, but she's fading fast." The other EMT held an IV bag as high as he could get it. "I've done this for a long time and seen some sick stuff, but this one is going to haunt me for a while," he said after they'd worked together to slide her over to the hospital bed.

"What the hell happened?" Sally asked as she slammed her hand on the button on the wall above the bed to call for more staff. "Car accident?"

"Not that I wish an accident on anyone, but it might be easier for her to recover from if that's what this was. We waited an hour outside this shithole of a place while the police got her asshole husband away from her," the EMT said as the triage nurses moved from the next bay to take over. "He was about to hit her in the head with a bat, but I think the leg damage is from his steel-toed boots. I'd guess her face is thanks to his fist."

The EMT stepped aside to let a nurse in. "The skin is pierced just below the knee, and she's been getting quieter and paler. Probably shock."

"Poor darlin', but we're in luck. God just finished up in the OR. I paged her when y'all called in," Sally said. "She looks like my daughter Mindy," she said, looking at the woman on the bed.

"Dr. Basantes is available?"

"Today is her surgery rotation here, and if anyone in my family got hurt like this, there isn't anyone I'd trust other than Harry."

Harry was waiting for the crew to finish settling the patient. Hearing Sally's assessment made her warm. It was good when people knew you were the best. She motioned her residents to stay put and stopped directly behind Sally. "Taking my name in vain again, Nurse Hardass?" Harry whispered in Sally's ear, making her shoulders hitch.

"Doc, I was comparing you to God—how can you take that wrong?" Sally turned and gave Harry her best smile. "Besides, you know damn well I'm the only one in the building who's not afraid of you, so cut the bull and get in here."

"Let's see what we've got, folks," she said to her students.

Her attention went directly to the patient's injuries, and the noise and chaos of the ER faded away as she concentrated on what needed to be done. "Get the mobile X-ray unit in here, order a blood workup, and get her to surgery as soon as you're done," she said as she scribbled in the chart Sally had placed on the small table next to the bed. "No dawdling, people," she barked when her team didn't move fast enough.

"Ma'am," Harry said, finally glancing up at her new patient. When she looked at the tearstained face and watery green eyes, memories of high school came flooding back, and she clutched the side of the bed to regain her mental balance. "Desi?" She said the name like a prayer.

"Harry?" Desi wiped her face, her hand shaking, and an expression of surprise seemed to replace the pain, if only for a second. "What are you doing here?"

"I'm the surgeon on call," Harry said, trying her best to bleed the emotion out of her voice. There'd been plenty of time through the years for touching reunions, so they weren't going to waste time on that now. "You have an open fracture just below the knee, and it will require surgery. I'll know more once I see your X-rays." *Once the fracture's reduced, you can walk out the door like you did a very long time ago, only this time it won't matter.* She shook off the thought and tried to keep her expression impassive.

"Harry, please—" Desi said, but Harry raised her hand.

"I've ordered something for the pain, and once I get a look at your films we'll talk about the next steps." Harry placed the chart under her arm and waited to see if Desi had any questions.

"You're a surgeon?" Desi's eyebrows came together in apparent confusion, and the sweat on her brow prompted Harry to inject the painkiller into the IV line.

"Actually, I'm the janitor, but we're a little shorthanded at the moment, so the state expects everyone to pitch in." Harry laughed bitterly, but Desi didn't join in. "Look, if you want someone else, it won't hurt my feelings. Say the word." The radiology tech arrived and started setting up. "I'll be back once he's done."

Harry walked out, not giving Desi the chance to respond. She ran her hand through her hair, and then grunted at the return of her old childhood habit. Sally stared at her, then at her hand, but didn't say anything as Harry leaned on the counter to finish writing out orders for Desi's care.

The sight of her old friend had been a punch to the gut, and it wouldn't be a bad idea to get someone else to take her case. They had a history she'd tried to bury, but it was something that refused to die or be forgotten. Why the fuck couldn't she just forget her and move on?

"You okay?" Sally asked softly.

"Fine—let's go with that."

She hadn't said the name *Desi* out loud in years, but damn if she didn't find at least a minute of every day to think about her. It was doubtful Desi had given her and what they'd had together a second thought since those caps went flying into the air at graduation. How on earth had Desi ended up in this kind of mess?

"It's not often that we see the legendary Dr. Basantes in the ER with the huddled masses. What gives, Harriet?" Dr. Kenneth Reynolds asked, startling Harry out of her memories. He drummed his fingers on the countertop and laughed when she glared at him.

Kenneth was one of the few people she'd kept in her life since childhood, and the chief of pediatrics was her best friend. The nurses had nicknamed them the dynamic duo when they'd started their residencies, and for a long time the rumor had been that there was a romance to go with the friendship they obviously shared.

"Don't call me that, or I'll tell Sally what Tony calls you when you're at home. Got me, sugar pants?" Harry rubbed her temples and sighed.

"Okay, no need for bitchy." He put his hands on her shoulders and laughed. "Sounds like you've had a bad day. Does someone have their leg coming out of their ass or something? It'd take something that drastic to lure you down here with the little people. Usually your eager minions bring the patients to you." He didn't take his hand off her shoulder, and she could tell he was worried about her despite his teasing. "I thought your days of trolling the ER for interesting cases were over years ago."

"Did you learn that diagnostic technique in medical school? For your information I'm not that out of touch, and I was paged. No trolling involved." She handed the chart off to the waiting nurse. "This time, though, I should've left at lunch and started cultivating a gambling habit. You aren't going to believe who's lying behind curtain number three."

"Do I win a new washing machine if I guess right? Old Betsy is about to call it quits. I've had that washer since we were in college," Kenneth said wistfully as if he'd momentarily forgotten what they were talking about.

"If I bought you a new washer would you shut up?"

"Don't think I won't take you up on that. Those front loaders are damn expensive." He took a rubber duck out of his lab coat pocket and squeezed it a few times. "Whoever it is must be freaking you out since I can never sneak up on you. Wait, it's not your stalker from a few years ago, is it?"

"Please, don't jinx me by mentioning that crazy ass. No, it's Desi

Thompson. Of all the places in this city I could've run into her again, it's here."

"Is she visiting a friend, or is it something else?"

Harry thought of what she'd read in the file. "Broken leg and, from the look of her, probably some other things." She glanced back at the triage bay and fought the urge to call one of her partners to handle this.

"She's in luck then. You're good with broken bones, unless you forgot to pay the club dues and they've taken away your scalpel and special decoder ring."

"Cut the shit for a minute, will you? I'm bigger than you, so I can make that leg-out-of-your-ass thing a reality."

"You want me to go home and pick up Tony?" Kenneth asked, referring to his partner of fifteen years. "He's better equipped to deal with stuff like this. My forte is runny noses and nasty scrapes suffered on the playground. Major drama is more a Tony thing."

"I'm fine," Harry said, trying to convince herself. "She'll most likely want someone else to do this. We both know she overwhelmingly proved she doesn't need or want me for anything."

"Just go in there and do your job, pal, and when you're done, I'll take you home and treat you to a home-cooked meal. You know Tony's red fish stew is to die for, and he's been chopping stuff since early this morning. Pretend she's one of the hundreds of nameless faces who walk in here every day, and put those memories of yours back in the box."

"That's your advice?"

As she asked, a patient with an ear hanging by a small piece of cartilage was wheeled past them into the bay next to Desi's.

"That proves my point. Just another typical day in the ER in the great city of New Orleans," Kenneth said and slapped her on the back. "Just do your job, Harry, and the rest will stay buried if you let it."

"That, buddy, is easier said than done." She was an idiot for still having feelings about this shit in the first place. She'd learned from Desi that giving too much of yourself only ended in pain. It was a lesson she'd never forget.

CHAPTER TWO

Hey, I'm Sally and I'm going to be your nurse. Dr. Basantes will be back shortly for your consult. You know, the decision is up to you. I don't usually give my opinion, but there's no better orthopedic surgeon in the city. If she's available, don't turn her down."

"I'm sure it's her who'd rather not deal with me," Desi said with a raspy voice. Sally covered her with a warm blanket before hanging some smaller bags to add to her IV. "Thank you."

"Do you know her?" Sally sounded curious, but all Desi did was stare at Harry's back.

"I did, a long time ago."

"She's got a loud bark, but she cares about her patients. I don't see that changing today, no matter what your history is." Sally combed Desi's hair back and smiled. "Close your eyes and try to relax. Is there someone I can call for you?"

"My sister, please." She couldn't stop the tears, but it wasn't from the pain. Harry's expression was all she needed to see to realize she'd never be forgiven for what she'd done.

"I'll take care of it if you give me the number," Sally said as she placed the X-rays where Harry could see them. "Doc, your pictures are back."

Harry nodded at Sally, then accepted a hug from a guy before turning back to whatever was on the desk in front of her. "Jesus, what's she going to think of me?" Desi whispered, never feeling as much shame as she did in this moment. She closed her eyes and remembered the first time they'd met.

It was the first day of third grade, and the bus stop was crowded with children. Desi did her best to ignore them.

"They probably got lice," a tall redheaded girl said with a sneer.

"Yeah, and where'd you get those shoes? The garbage?" the brunette with her said.

"Don't listen to them, Rach." Desi put her arm around her little sister Rachel and moved farther away from the older girls who'd tortured Desi all last year. With Rachel starting kindergarten, they had two targets now.

"That's where they got those clothes too." The redhead shoved Desi down this time, and Rachel started crying when she fell on her. She looked to the street when she heard a car door slam and a tall girl ran toward them.

"Leave them alone." The bullies listened when her new defender clenched her fists. "Are you okay?" the girl asked, offering her hand.

"I'm okay." Desi helped Rachel up and rubbed where her elbow had scraped the sidewalk. "Rach, you okay?"

The woman in the car had stood back but came closer when she seemed to notice the tear in Desi's shirt. "Are you two waiting for the bus?"

"Yes, ma'am." She put her arm around Rachel again and she could tell by the way her shoulders were shaking that she was still crying.

"I'm Harry and this is my mom, Rosa." Harry had a big smile and was so much taller than the other kids around them. "I know you aren't supposed to go with strangers, but you should ride with us."

"Your name is Harry?" She held Rachel tighter against her but didn't move away from the new girl. "But you're a girl."

"My name's Harriet, but Harry fits better. Would you come with us?" Harry held out her hand.

"I don't know. My dad might get mad."

"Do you live around here?" It didn't sound like Harry was one to give up easily. "What's your name?"

"We live way that way, and I'm Desi. This is my little sister, Rachel." She watched Rachel slowly extend her hand when Harry offered hers again.

"Want to walk over and ask your dad?"

"He's sleeping." The last thing she needed was to wake him. "Are you sure, ma'am?"

"Let's get you all over there, so you're not late on your first day," Rosa said, "and we'll introduce ourselves to your dad later." Rosa opened the back door of the nice car and made sure everyone buckled up. "Once we see where your house is, Harry and I can pick you up from now on."

"It'll be great, you'll see." *Harry held her hand and she'd been right.*

That had been the beginning of their friendship, and they'd only gotten closer through the years. Harry and her family had been the best thing that had happened to both her and Rachel, and she'd felt cherished like never before.

Unlike the kids at the bus stop, Harry had never noticed their secondhand clothes or the shoes with holes in the soles. They began to spend every weekend with Harry's family, and Rosa and Francisco, Harry's father, indulged them the same as Harry. It was the safest she'd ever been, but those memories had faded under the cruel reality she was living.

She was brought back to the moment when Sally gently wiped away a tear and then handed her a tissue. "She's going to think you need a friend, and Harry's a good one," Sally said.

"That I already know."

"You can fall off the crazy cliff later, idiot. Let's hear the verdict and get the hell out of here," Harry mumbled to herself as she walked back to Desi.

She explained what needed to be done to her residents when she stepped up to the light boxes and studied the X-rays. The pain medication had wiped the horrifying expression of pain from Desi's face, but Harry felt scrutinized. Desi's beautiful green eyes continued haunting her.

Harry studied her old friend as she prepared to tell her what needed to be done. Time hadn't been kind since they'd last seen each other. The lines around her eyes were deep, like she worried constantly. She was pale and thin. But it wasn't any of her business, right? Just another patient.

Once they'd graduated, Desi had disappeared as effectively as cold July days in New Orleans. All their plans and dreams had gone with her, and Harry had been left hurting and had never understood what she'd done wrong. She'd tried for months to get Desi to talk to her, but Desi had made it clear with her silence that they were done. No explanations were necessary. Once again, she tried to put that memory aside and focus on the moment.

"You're going to need surgery to repair your leg," she said as a conclusion to her diagnosis and treatment plan. Desi had closed her eyes when she'd started talking, and she assumed it was so she wouldn't have to look at her, but her chest was moving too rhythmically. The meds had knocked her out. In sleep Desi's youthful beauty returned, and it brought her back to all the times she'd sat and stared at this woman she'd loved.

"Great, she's sleeping. Did you talk to her?" she asked Sally.

"Yes, and before she passed out, she asked that you do her surgery. If you know her, do you have her sister's information?"

"Her name is Desiree Thompson, and I knew her a very long time ago. Her sister is Rachel, but I wouldn't have the first clue as to how to get in touch with her. I didn't think they even lived in the city anymore."

It was their senior year of high school, and it seemed like it could be the best year ever.

"Harry, hurry up. I don't want to be late. You could skip your classes for the rest of the year and pass, but I suck at math." Desi walked backward so they could look at each other while they headed to the other side of the large campus. "You know more than the teacher, and the cat knows more than me, so I'm screwed."

"You give the cat too much credit. Geometry and poetry are more his thing."

"Funny." Desi stuck her tongue out, then hopped away when Harry made a grab for it. "You're coming over later, right? It's only our first week, but I don't want to fall behind."

"I've been helping you with your homework since grammar school—nothing's changing." Harry walked slowly so Desi wouldn't have to jog to keep up. "After we're done, I'll take you and the shrimp out to dinner. We have to celebrate our first week."

"You don't have to do that." Desi stopped when Harry took her hand to keep her from running into the wall.

"It'll hurt my feelings if you say no."

Desi smiled and gazed at her like she wanted more than dinner. "I'm not saying no."

"Good, and you can pack a bag for the weekend once your dad says it's okay that you and Rachel come with me." She let Desi go, not wanting to make her uncomfortable, but man, she wanted so much more. "Wait for me by the car."

They rode to Desi's house, and Harry took a seat on the porch swing. It was Desi's favorite spot and hers too, considering it gave her a perfect view of Desi's backside as she stared into the refrigerator. They could be doing much more interesting things than math, and the more Desi stared at her like she wanted her undivided attention, the more she needed to touch her.

"Do you want something to drink? We have water or water." Desi didn't move from that spot, but she bent over as if studying the bottom shelf. The shorts she'd changed into had Harry's full attention.

I swear she does that on purpose. "Water's good." She took Desi's book out and looked at the notes she'd taken in class. "Hey, Mr. Thompson," she said when she heard the telltale whistling.

Clyde Thompson didn't own a car, so he walked from the corner bus stop, and you could always hear him coming. "Hey, Harry. Must be learning a lot from that pile of books you got there."

"I'm trying to teach Desi word problems in math, sir, so it's going to be a long afternoon." She rocked the swing and tried to keep a smile. Clyde wasn't exactly a friendly person, and there was always something a little off about him, though he never did anything that was out of line. That she knew of, at least. "Would you mind if I take them for a burger later, then to my house for the weekend?"

"That'll be good. I've got some double shifts this weekend. Make sure they do their homework."

"No problem, sir." She watched Desi come out with a glass and walk carefully around her father. They didn't have a close relationship, and she understood part of it.

Clyde was a proud but distrustful man who hadn't been happy when Harry's mother had knocked on the door the day she'd met Desi and Rachel. He seemed like he had no clue how he'd ended up with two daughters, but it wasn't because he'd wanted them.

She and Desi sat on the swing while Rachel lay at their feet until all their work was done. "Are you hungry?"

"Yes," Rachel said loudly, then hitched her shoulders, not wanting to wake Clyde.

"Grab your bags so we can head home after." They packed into her small car and headed to the back of the Quarter. Port of Call was their favorite burger place, and they joked over the baked potatoes and huge burgers.

"Harry, have I ever told you how happy I am that we got bullied the day we met?" Rachel held up the last of her burger and winked. "You were worth the abuse."

"I'm glad too, and if you're finished, we'll go for beignets." She paid the bill and headed back to the car her parents had given her the year before. Desi practically sat in her lap with her arm around her shoulders. There was no chance she'd speed when they sat like this.

"In case you were wondering," Desi whispered in her ear, "I'm happy about meeting you too."

Jesus. She either had to find a way of telling Desi how she felt, *or it was going to be a long year.*

Taking care of Desi and Rachel had always been a privilege, and when it stopped so abruptly, it had come close to breaking her. Of all the scenarios she'd come up with as to when and where she'd see Desi again, she'd never imagined this.

The reality of the situation wasn't lost on Harry as she scrubbed in. One of her nurses was prepping Desi for surgery, and Desi seemed to be stubbornly fighting the drugs meant to relax her. They'd had to wake her to get her to sign the consents, and now she looked scared and lost as she stared up into the bright lights of the operating theater. Another nurse checked Desi's IV before coming over to Harry and holding up the gown that went over her scrubs.

"What are you in the mood for today?" Tyler, a young man in the observation room above them, asked through the intercom.

"I seem to remember Miss Thompson liked Madonna way back when, so cue it up, my man." Harry moved over to Desi.

"I'll have to dig deep, but I think I have one of her tracks."

The nurse put her gloves on and moved into position so they could start. Harry bent down and spoke softly in Desi's ear. "I want you to take slow deep breaths and let go. Hopefully, we'll be out of here in less than three hours, and I promise it'll be all right, so relax."

Desi nodded briefly and closed her eyes. Harry waited for her team to finish their jobs and for the residents to place all the X-rays up for reference.

"Doc, when you're finished, there's a detective here to see you from the NOPD," the lead surgical nurse said.

"Tell him if he wants, I'll call. I don't know how long this is going to take, and from the look of that fracture, we'll be here a while."

"He said he didn't mind waiting."

"What'd you do now?" Harry teased the nurse.

"Cut the wisecracks, comedian—it's about her and her injuries."

"I never did ask her how she got here, and I didn't see it in the file. Was it a car accident?" she asked as she made the first incision.

"This was no accident. Her husband did this to her, and the screams must've been loud enough that one of the neighbors called the police. Apparently, it was a bit of a showdown, and when the police got in, it looked like he was about to finish her off." The nurse shivered as if horrified at what had happened. "Any longer with that animal, and there would've been no need for us."

Harry had to take a minute to beat down her anger. In her mind Desi would always be the sweet girl from high school, not someone's punching bag. "What happened to you, Desi?"

CHAPTER THREE

The surgery went smoothly, and Harry was pleased that there wasn't as much ligament damage as she first suspected. She felt comfortable with the initial prognosis she'd given Desi. With physical therapy and time, Desi would heal completely. After she got Desi into recovery, she headed to the waiting room to speak with the officer who'd been there for two and a half hours.

"Dr. Basantes?" He jumped to his feet and stuck his hand out as soon as she'd cleared the door.

From his rumpled appearance, Harry guessed the officer had spent the time sleeping in one of the plastic chairs while he waited. "Yes, and you are?"

"Detective Roger Landry, Doctor. I know it's been a long day, but I was wondering if you'd mind answering some questions about Desiree Simoneaux?" He ran his hand down his jacket as if trying to smooth it out. Sadly, only a can of gasoline and a fire would get those wrinkles out.

"Simoneaux," she repeated softly, trying to figure out where she recognized the name from.

"Doc?" Detective Landry said as if to get her attention.

"Sorry, I'm not sure what I can tell you aside from what Desi's injuries are, but ask away."

"We'll start there, but there's a lot you can help me with." He asked her about hospital security.

"You think she's still in danger?"

"From what I could find out so far, Mrs. Simoneaux never pressed charges against this asshole, but Byron Simoneaux isn't exactly a stranger to law enforcement. If he makes bail tonight, I don't want to give him the chance to come over here and finish the job."

The name finally clicked. "She's married to Byron Simoneaux? If I remember right, his dad owns a mechanic shop and gas station in Mid-City. That's who you're talking about?"

Roger wrote some more notes as she spoke and nodded. "That's him, and it sounds like you're familiar with him."

"Not really, he's a name and face from a very distant past." Harry exhaled deeply and ran her hand through her hair again. "From the little I do remember about him, I'm just surprised that's who Desi ended up with. I never realized they were close."

"I'm sure given their history together, if she had a do-over, she'd make different choices, but tonight's reality is what we have to deal with. From what I read of Simoneaux, when he gets out, he's going to come looking for her. He said as much when they took him in. If he stops at his favorite bar first, then it's anybody's guess what he'll do, so I need to set up some extra security if that's okay. You have more than Mrs. Simoneaux to worry about, and I don't want any patients or staff getting caught in the middle of this."

"Tell you what, Detective—why don't I have Desi moved to another hospital once she's out of recovery? I'll have one of the services move her over to Baptist under a different name and into a private room." She scrolled through her contacts on her phone to find the information she needed. "The security over there is better."

"If you give me the information, I'll assign a couple of patrol officers to be there too, at least for tonight."

"I'm sure our guys would appreciate it, but like I said, I'll take care of it after that. If you need to talk to her, it'll have to wait until tomorrow. I don't know how these things work, but she's pretty out of it right now and will be for quite a while."

"Thanks, Doc. I'll see you both tomorrow. It's a shame what that asshole did to her. The boys in the precinct tell me this wasn't the first time, but like I said, she's never pressed charges no matter how many trips they make out there. Sometimes the fear overrides the pain of the beatings," he said as he handed her his card and shook her hand again. "This time I'm hoping she'll think before giving him a free pass, and maybe we can nail his ass to the wall. If she doesn't, there might not be a next time."

"Have you contacted her family? I knew Desi in high school, and she lived with her father and sister."

"I'll check into it and let you know." He pocketed his small notebook and turned to leave. "Thanks for everything, Dr. Basantes.

I'm sure it was a comfort to Mrs. Simoneaux to see a friendly face. It's going to help put this nightmare behind her."

She made the arrangements for the transfer, then called Kenneth and explained to his partner Tony what was going on. She was going to settle Desi for the night before doing rounds. "She'll be in for at least a week, so having her at Baptist will make it convenient for me to supervise the recovery." It would also make it harder for her personally, but she wasn't going to think about that now.

"Do you want Kenny to meet you over there? He called a few minutes ago, and said he's on his way home. I could get him to take a detour," Tony said.

"Don't bother. I'm sure he's ready to get home after wiping snotty noses all day. Sorry about dinner, but I'll call you guys tomorrow." Harry tapped her phone against her chin and fell back into her chair.

The quiet let her think about this whole situation. The truth of what happened to Desi so long ago wasn't a mystery anymore. She'd left her for the biggest asshole they'd gone to school with, and Byron Simoneaux obviously hadn't improved with age. It killed her that Desi had gotten hurt, but she was pissed the reason she'd left her was for that loser.

Harry took a deep breath and headed to recovery. The right side of Desi's face was bruised from her jaw to her temple, but she seemed to be resting comfortably. "What the hell were you thinking?" She crossed her arms over her chest and closed her eyes for a moment. The long day was starting to catch up to her. As soon as it was safe to move Desi, she could put this behind her and have someone else do the follow-up.

"Want us to page you when her room is ready?" the nurse asked.

"I'm having her transferred once she's out of recovery." She glanced at the radiologist's report and found some good news in all this. Her ribs were bruised but not broken. "This is a domestic violence incident, and we don't need to make it easy for her husband to try something else before we move her."

"You got it, Doc. Makes you wonder what happened before this asshole got ahold of her that made her take this abuse." The nurse jotted in the chart oblivious to her glare.

"Yeah, that must've been an even bigger asshole." *Or a complete idiot—it's a toss-up at this point.* She left to do rounds.

"Page me when she's ready to go. Everything's set at Baptist." She did her rounds but remained distracted by thoughts of the past.

They had been nearly all the way through senior year when things started to go sideways.

"Okay, tell me what's wrong." They were lying side by side in the backyard where no one could see them from the house in the darkness. It was past midnight, and they wanted to talk but not wake Rachel. They'd been out here awhile, but Desi hadn't said anything.

"Nothing." Desi's voice cracked, and she started crying, meaning it was something.

"Hey." She wrapped her arms around Desi, not worrying if it was inappropriate. "Please tell me."

"A year seems like a long time, but it's not." Desi turned her head and tried to muffle her crying against Harry's T-shirt. "I'm so scared about what happens when you leave for school."

They'd researched all the scholarships and grants, but none of them would cover everything, and they couldn't count on Clyde for a penny toward college tuition. Desi had started worrying about it over the summer, and it wasn't getting better.

"I told you—"

"Harry, I can't let you pay my way through school. It's too much."

"You could come with me, get a job, and save. Baton Rouge is close enough that we can visit Rachel on the weekends." She rubbed Desi's back soothingly. "If I get a job too, we can swing it." She glanced down at Desi when she didn't say anything. "What?"

"Daddy won't agree to that. He needs help with Rachel and the house. Without me there, Rachel will be all alone, and—" Desi stopped as if a fist of fear had closed around her neck.

"I can't help you if you don't talk to me. You know you can trust me."

"I trust you with my life, but I can't. Please, Harry, I can't."

"Okay." She didn't want to push, not yet. "Rachel's a couple of years behind us. We'll both save until she's done, and if I push it, I'll be back in the city for medical school. Once I am, I'll get a place big enough for all three of us, but until then, I'll be here every weekend and holiday."

"You mean it?" Desi lifted onto her elbow and looked down at her. "This has me so scared. I don't want to lose you." Desi traced her lips with her index finger. "I'm terrified you'll forget me."

"You can't lose what belongs to you," she said, kissing Desi's palm while praying she hadn't screwed up. "Haven't you figured out by now that I'm in love with you? That means not leaving you behind."

"You do?" Desi's voice was soft with wonder.

"I've loved you since the third grade, but now all I can think is how much I always want to be with you." She pressed her hand to Desi's cheek, relieved to see her smile. "If you need more time…" She was thrilled when Desi shook her head and came closer.

"I love you, and I want to be with you forever, but I've been afraid to say it out loud."

Harry moved slowly and rolled Desi to her back. "That's the best thing I've ever heard." The opportunity she'd waited so long for was here, and she wasn't going to let it pass without acting. She lowered her head, and Desi rose up to meet her, and the kiss was so much better than she'd ever fantasized about.

That simple act shattered the last secret between them. Now all she had to do was convince Desi to open up and tell her the rest of what scared her. No one was this skittish about their father unless there was something to fear. Even after all these years, she knew something about their father wasn't right, though Desi had never said a word about it. There was no way she could leave for LSU if Desi and Rachel were in danger.

"What are you thinking about?" Desi lay back down but interlocked their fingers. "You kissed me, and you can't take it back."

"That's not happening." She kissed Desi again. "I'm thinking of ways to get you alone now that I know kissing is okay."

"Really?"

"We can take our time, but you drive me a little nuts."

Desi laughed as she brought Harry's hand to her breast. "I thought you weren't paying attention, and I'm lucky our refrigerator still works. How you haven't fallen off the swing while you were staring at my ass is the true mystery."

"You little tease." She could feel Desi's nipple harden under her palm, and Desi's hand tightened on her back.

"It's only teasing if you plan to stop." Desi moved to take her nightgown off. "I don't want to stop."

"Are you sure?" She pulled her shirt over her head and tossed it aside.

"Baby, we've waited long enough." Desi put her hands on her shoulders and brought their naked chests together. "And I've dreamed about us like this."

There was enough light for her to see the small bow at the top of Desi's underwear, and whatever reservations she had were gone. "I want you so bad."

"I'm yours—always have been." There was no hesitation when she put her fingers under the white panties and tugged them down. "Are you sure no one can see?"

"Not unless they come looking for us, and my parents are sleeping. Dad's got early rounds tomorrow." She got naked and put her hand at the top of Desi's sex. "I love you."

"Then prove it."

Those words were too much, and she had to touch Desi the one place she hoped she'd only share with her. The wetness made her groan. "Tell me if you want me to stop." She stroked Desi's clit, but the light pink nipple so close to her mouth was too tempting.

"Uh, Harry," Desi said in a harsh whisper when she sucked her in, "do something, but don't stop."

She slid to the edge of the blanket and almost dove forward when Desi spread her legs. This was her first time too, and she wanted to please Desi and not disappoint. It must've felt good from the way Desi was thrusting up into her mouth and holding the sides of her head to keep her in place. She was never going to get enough of Desi like this.

"Oh…oh, Harry…so good." Desi jerked twice more, then went rigid. "Jesus, we shouldn't have waited this long." They both laughed when Harry moved back and covered Desi's body with hers. "We're doing that again, right?"

"Whenever I get you alone. It'll be tough waiting now that I know how sweet you taste." She kissed Desi, but she was wound so tight she was about to unravel. Desi kept one hand in her hair but the other trailed slowly down Harry's side, then between them.

"Are you mine?" Desi hummed when she touched between her legs, and she was so ready.

"Always."

For the next nine months, they made plans for the next year, and for all the ones to follow. While they waited for Rachel to graduate, they would have to live for long weekends and school breaks at LSU. Despite her father's money, Harry was going on both athletic and scholastic scholarships. She was as good on the softball field as she was at solving math problems and had been heavily recruited.

"And I'm yours for as long as you want me," Desi said.

"Death is the only way I'm letting go."

CHAPTER FOUR

"Harry?" Desi said without opening her eyes. Someone rested their hand on her forehead to keep her from moving. "Where am I?"

"Try not to move around too much." A woman's voice, one she didn't know. "Relax and lie still, and to answer your questions, you're in recovery." The woman's voice was mellow and soothing, and Desi forced her eyes open. "How about some ice chips to soothe your throat?"

"Did I lose my leg?" Her throat was sore, but she was numb everywhere else.

"Dr. Basantes did your surgery, and your leg is exactly where it was before." The woman checked her vitals and raised the blanket to look at her leg. "You still have everything you had, plus some new hardware."

"Is Harry still here?" The more awake she became, the more aware she was of the pain wracking every part of her body.

"I'm going to page her, but we need to clear you from recovery first. Dr. Basantes ordered you transferred, and she's going to take care of you." The woman smiled and covered Desi's hand with hers. "Can I get you anything while we wait?"

"Where am I going?" If they were sending her home, she wouldn't live out the night.

"To a private room at Baptist. You'll be more comfortable if you don't have to share a room, and it'll be safer." Two men entered and the nurse moved away to meet them before she could protest. There was no way she could afford top-notch care. That would be something else for Byron to get angry about.

She took some deep breaths when she saw Harry walk in. Their first interaction had been awkward, and she couldn't blame Harry for being so standoffish. What she'd done to Harry and how she'd been forced to do it would never be forgivable.

Seeing Harry again magnified the life she could've had that was stolen from her. Harry had been imprinted on her heart from grade school on. Her love for her had been so deep that not having her in her life had left a void nothing could fill. Her memories had been the one thing she could hang on to as Byron beat her, and no amount of suffering could make her let go of them.

"How do you feel?" Harry asked, her attention on her chart.

"Okay, thank you." She couldn't take her eyes off Harry, who hadn't changed all that much from the last time she'd seen her. Actually, she was even more attractive now. "I'm so sorry." Her eyes filled with tears, but she was so lethargic she couldn't wipe them away.

"Don't." Harry finally glanced up. "I don't want to be rude, but we're way beyond that. Right now, concentrate on getting better." The aides brought the stretcher over when Harry motioned them closer.

"I don't have the greatest insurance, so maybe I should stay here," she said as they prepared to lower the sides of the hospital bed. She coughed as the prickle in her throat got worse and was grateful when the nurse fed her some more ice chips.

"Don't worry about it, and the detective assigned to your case agreed you'll be safer at Baptist," Harry said as she grabbed a corner of her sheet. "Ready on two, and try not to bump her leg and mess up my beautiful work."

She couldn't help the small groan as they slid her over, but she bit her lip as Harry walked alongside her as they started out. Harry was on her phone with what sounded like someone at Baptist, and it seemed like she was coming with her.

"Take it easy," Harry said to the medic when they reached the ambulance. She injected a syringe full of something before they lifted her up. "This will help with the pain from all the jostling."

"Don't worry, Doc, we'll go slow," the medic said as he stepped up to sit next to Desi.

"Move over," Harry said. "I'll ride with you guys and save myself a trip to the parking garage." She strapped herself into the small hopper seat. "If you close your eyes, Desi, it'll help with motion sickness."

She should've closed her eyes, but she couldn't stop staring at Harry. Surely, once she was settled, Harry would disappear. She couldn't risk it, and though Harry didn't look at her much throughout the ride, she tried to do all she could to memorize every aspect of her face, just in case it took another sixteen years before she saw her again. It didn't take long for the doors to open, and the difference between the chaos of University Medical and the calm of Baptist was palpable. There were no crowds, no screaming kids, and no heavy police presence. Baptist was Uptown, where the streets were wider and the homes were larger. This was completely removed from her daily existence.

"If you roll through the ER, we can transfer her there and save you the trip upstairs," Harry said, standing where she couldn't see her.

"We don't mind, Dr. Basantes. The coffee up there is better than anything we're getting tonight."

Desi watched the numbers over the elevator doors, and then she turned her attention to Harry when they stopped on the third floor.

"Hey, Dr. Basantes," one of two attractive nurses said. They both were in dark blue scrubs and seemed more interested in Harry than her, but she couldn't fault that.

"You have a room for me?"

"Everything's ready and set to your orders," the other nurse said. "Are you okay? Do you need anything before we move you?" she asked Desi.

"I'm okay."

"You can head back to the station—I'll handle this." The shorter of the two inched closer to Harry. "You know, Harry, a girl could get her feelings hurt waiting for you to call."

"This isn't the appropriate time for that, and get it through your head—I'm not interested." Harry's voice was clipped and cold. "How about you head to the desk and let Savanah handle this?"

The nurse gave an unattractive pout and did as she was told. Harry didn't seem to notice, and Desi admitted to a certain satisfaction at seeing her dismissed. She had no right to feel that way, but still.

They settled Desi gently onto the bed, and Savanah excused herself to get another IV setup. Harry adjusted her leg, taking her time until she seemed satisfied.

The nurses and techs appeared to get the message once Harry was done, and they stepped out, leaving her alone with Harry. "How long do I have to stay?" The warm blanket Savanah had covered her with had helped with the pain, but the shame of being in this position made her keep her gaze on her folded hands.

"I can't give you an exact timeline. It depends on how well you heal, but plan for at least a week." Harry stood by the ledge of the window and wrote in her chart as she spoke. Desi guessed it was so she didn't have to make eye contact. Granted, she was the one with all the regret, but Harry was still full of anger. Desi'd had to sacrifice their dreams, and she'd paid dearly for it. She'd never blame Harry for being angry.

"Okay." It was all she could think to say.

"I realize I'm the last person you want to deal with, but I hope you realize the seriousness of the situation. Your recovery will take time, but you *have* time, and you have the chance to recover. You give this guy another opportunity, and surgery won't be able to fix you. These things only escalate, Desi."

She twisted her fingers in the blanket, trying to fight the paralysis that stemmed from embarrassment. "I don't want to talk about it, and you're better off not getting involved. Not that I don't appreciate you helping me, but maybe you should go."

"You certainly made your wishes clear, *Mrs. Simoneaux*, so no need to explain. I'll have someone from our practice take over your care starting tomorrow. Good luck."

This was the first time in their history Desi had ever experienced Harry's anger aimed at her, but she knew better than to get her hopes up that Harry would care again. She couldn't let Harry back in and expect to survive the loss when Harry realized how broken Desi was. Once the door closed gently, she blinked rapidly as her tears started again.

There was no comparison to Byron's fists, but all of Harry's clipped words had been like painful blows that had driven her out into the cold. She'd survived before, and she would again, by accepting that nothing was going to change. The old saying about making your bed was familiar, but no one had told her it was a bed of nails that got sharper as the years passed.

❖

Harry walked out clenching her fists, then thought of the optics and took a breath and flexed her hands open. The notion that she'd left all the hurt and anger in her past was a joke, and all it had taken was being this close to Desi to bring it screaming back. She needed to get the hell out of here and back to her life. This had nothing to do with her.

She punched the elevator call button, ready to go home, stand in her shower, then go to bed. Her day had started at five, and she'd almost gotten out the door before Sally had called about that last emergency. Today was a lesson in saying *no* every so often.

The realization that her car was still at University didn't hit her until she was outside. "Son of a bitch, this damn day is never going to end."

"Need a ride?" Kenneth said in an exaggerated sultry voice as he walked up behind her. "Going my way, handsome?"

"It depends. What's it going to cost me?" She relaxed for the first time in hours. Kenneth and Tony had been her roommates in college and had kept her sane through those years and beyond.

"Your appetite. There's a fried oyster po'boy and a beer waiting for you." Kenneth opened the passenger side door and bowed. "My fabulous spouse made one of your favorites even though he's been slaving in the kitchen all day long on something else, his words, not mine. He's never done that for me, which must mean he really loves you, so it'll be dangerous to your health, and mine, if you even think of turning him down."

"I need to pick up my car first, buddy."

"Already done, so get in. Tony got the thrill of driving your girlfriend home, and he even sprayed his favorite air freshener all over the place."

She got in, let her head fall to the headrest, and closed her eyes. She hadn't been this mentally fatigued since her residency days.

"It's going to be okay, Harry—just have faith."

"I love you, bud, but faith can fuck itself. She married Byron Simoneaux." She raised her voice on the name. "Can you believe that? She married that bastard to be his punching bag, and that obviously was better than being with me." She looked out the window, wanting to simply go to bed and forget this day ever happened. "Unbelievable."

"Harry, I hate to bring up your mother, but keep in mind what she's always preaching. There are two sides to every story, and I don't think this one's going to be that simple. Give her the chance to explain, and if it turns out to be simple, I'll apologize over a steak."

"Not everything in life can be fixed with meat. Most things, but not everything." She laughed and punched his arm. "Thanks for being a good friend."

"I'm the best, but you do help with Tony, which keeps me off his shit list. That means I'll do anything for you."

Kenneth and Tony spent the rest of the evening cheering her up and offering advice. She ate and fell asleep on their couch where her subconscious didn't give a damn what Desi had done. Desi was waiting patiently for her like she was most nights, making promises she had no intention of keeping. In her dreams though, it was easy to believe Desi. Dream Desi, though, was whole, safe, and completely hers.

It was Harry's first year of college, and it should have been the start of a fantastic adventure. Instead, it was a nightmare.

"I don't get it," Harry said as she slammed the phone in the kitchen down. It was the only one in the apartment she shared with Kenneth and Tony. "She won't return my calls or answer the letters I've sent. That's the last call I'll make, since I woke her father up for the tenth time. Clyde works three jobs, and I don't want to keep bothering him."

"He didn't give you a clue?" Tony asked.

"It's not like I can say, *I'm in love with your daughter and we've been making plans for the future for years, but now she won't even talk to me.* Where the hell is she?" Harry rubbed her chest like someone had kicked her.

"Maybe she changed her mind, and this is her way of telling you she doesn't want to see you anymore," Kenneth said and stopped talking when Tony pinched his arm hard enough to remove skin. He rubbed at it and glared at him.

"We're going home in two weeks, so wait until then to try again. I'm not saying Kenny's right, but if he is, you'll know for sure, and you can stop torturing yourself. No matter what happens, buddy, we'll be here for you," Tony said as he knelt in front of her and cried with her.

"I don't know what I'm going to do if she doesn't want to see me anymore. Desi's been a part of my life for so long that I'm not sure I know how to live without her."

"I'm sure it'll work out, but no matter what, Kenny and I will help you through it. You're not alone, Harry, and you never will be."

Harry wanted desperately to believe that, but deep in her soul she knew she was losing a huge part of who she was, and if Desi left her, *her heart would never be the same.*

CHAPTER FIVE

D r. Basantes, could you answer some questions for me and my family?" the elderly woman in the waiting room asked.

Harry had already explained the hip replacement she'd just finished on the woman's husband and what they could expect as far as recovery, but it seemed the woman needed more reassurance. Harry's six residents and three nurses stood by the rolling cart loaded with charts and waited, all of them knowing not to interrupt no matter how long it took.

Putting people at ease was something she'd learned from her father. She remembered the lecture she'd gotten from him as she followed him around the hospital during his rounds. "It takes no extra effort to be nice, Harry. Remember that when you have patients of your own. These people are scared and full of questions. I don't ever want to hear you blew anyone off because you didn't feel like talking or taking the time to walk them through something. You do that, and you'll need a surgeon once I'm done with you," Francisco Basantes had joked with her.

The woman and her three children all hugged her when she'd run through it all one more time, and she shooed her group to the elevator to start rounds. She laughed at the expressions of the patients when so many people in lab coats walked in, but it was the only way for the young doctors to learn.

"All we have left is Desiree Simoneaux, Dr. Basantes," one of the nurses said as she handed her Desi's chart.

"Thanks, I'll see her today, but bring Dr. Ruben up to speed when he makes rounds this afternoon. He'll be taking over her case." Harry looked at her watch and saw it was noon. "I'll take care of this one myself. Grab lunch, and I'll meet all of you for clinic this afternoon," she said to the residents, all of whom took off before she changed her mind.

The Baptist cafeteria was pretty good, but Harry left the hospital and headed to the diner she liked a few blocks away, where she picked up a couple of burgers and a vanilla milkshake for Desi. After waking up on Kenneth and Tony's sofa, she'd headed home for that shower she'd craved. With a little time and distance, she was more clearheaded about the situation—the best plan was to see Desi one more time and explain what came next with a new doctor. She could be nice and not put her heart at risk again. After what Desi had been through, she didn't need Harry's anger piled on too.

"I see you're not into hospital food," she said when she stepped in after knocking. Desi was sitting up in bed staring out the window with a melancholy expression, and the sunlight streaming in accentuated the slight red in Desi's hair. With the bruised side of her face away from her, Desi resembled that beautiful young woman she knew once. It tugged at her heart, and she took a breath to steady herself.

The hospital tray sat ignored, and Desi quickly wiped her face with the backs of her fingers. "Hey," Desi said and smiled. "I didn't think I'd get to see you again." More tears spilled from her eyes, and her lips were tightly pressed together.

"I wanted to check on you before handing your care over to Dr. Ruben." Harry dropped the bag on the nightstand so she could clear the tray. "How are you feeling? How's your pain?"

"I'm okay, and it's bearable. Thank you for everything you've done, but I don't want to keep you." Desi never looked up at her, and her words were a clear dismissal.

Walking away would be so much easier than she'd imagined, but there was still one thing. "What exactly about me do you find so hard to tolerate?" She tried to convince herself she didn't care, that the question was just to satisfy her curiosity. "If you don't want to answer, don't—I get the message."

"You wouldn't understand, and it's embarrassing to admit that I wish the police had waited before coming in. I'd be better off if he'd finally gotten the chance to kill me." The tears ran down Desi's face, but she made no move to wipe them away.

Christ. How had their lives diverged so completely that Desi would rather be dead? Harry's anger softened. "In my line of work, I never wish for death, no matter what. All life is worth living, and if you're at a point that you feel otherwise, you need to change the things that bring nothing but pain." She held out some tissues, thinking of someone to refer Desi to who could fix the parts of her she had no skill with. "Start by remembering the person you are at your core—you can't have changed that much."

"Life isn't that easy, Dr. Basantes." Desi laughed but it rang of disillusionment. "And I'm not telling you to go because of the reasons you probably think."

The expression on Desi's face when she finally glanced up was so broken that Harry wanted to put her arms around her, but she wasn't exposing herself like that again with this woman.

"You have a life, and I doubt it has anything in common with mine."

Harry moved the cheeseburger closer and opened the package. "That makes me think you didn't know me years ago, and you don't know me now. But I'll honor your request to be left alone." Desi's tears started again in earnest but all Harry wanted was to run. To offer comfort now was to start taking bricks off the wall she'd meticulously built around her heart, and she'd worked too hard to make it impenetrable. "Would you like the staff to call Rachel and your father? I'm sure they'd want to know what happened and where you are."

"Clyde died of lung cancer five years ago, and Rachel still lives with me, so I'm sure she'll be here when she can. I talked to her briefly yesterday." The way Desi wiped at her cheeks followed by the small bite of food seemed like a strategy to stop talking.

The news about Clyde came in a flat tone, but the information about Rachel was the first sign of life in Desi's voice. "Are you sure you don't want me to call her?"

"Are you talking about me?"

The young woman at the door with the red hair that was in no way a hue found in nature was leagues away from the Rachel she remembered. It was as if Rachel had thrived while Desi had gone in the opposite direction. Whatever the hell this was made absolutely no sense.

"Harry!" Rachel flung herself at her and Harry's arms automatically came up and held her. "I couldn't believe it when Desi told me you did her surgery. Thank you for taking such good care of her." Rachel stood on her toes and kissed her cheek.

"You're welcome, and if you stick around, you can meet her new doctor. He'll be taking over her care." She looked at Desi one more time before leaving, and she noted the way Rachel looked between the two of them. Still, there were no answers coming to the questions that had nagged at her like a swarm of stinging insects. *Not your business anymore.*

Harry walked to the sunroom at the end of the hall, glad it was empty as she sat and closed her eyes. She had another ten hours of work, so it was time to concentrate on the rest of her day. Her patients needed her head to be clear and her hands to be steady, so she tried her best to focus.

"Leave it alone and in the past," she whispered as a mantra to get her head right.

❖

"Aren't you going to say hello?" Desi pushed the tray away and held her hand out.

Rachel sat on the bed and took her hand. "Look at you. You're a mess." She raised her other hand and went to touch her cheek but stopped as if not wanting to hurt her. "He did a real good job this time, didn't he?"

"Not right now, okay?" She sighed when Rachel squeezed her hand.

"It has to be now, babe. What's it going to take for you to see reason and leave this asshole? I swear if you say a pine box, I'm going to lose it. Jesus, babe, there are police outside your room to make sure he doesn't come after you again." Rachel stood up and started pacing as if not able to contain her anger. "For once, take what the universe and fate have thrown at your feet."

"Please tell me you don't mean Harry." All those fantasies she'd had of Harry coming and saving her died the second she saw her in the emergency room. There was no room for her in Harry's world any longer, and she was left with nothing. The anger that seemed to consume Harry wasn't anything like Byron's rage, but it also meant there'd be no going back to what they'd meant to each other. "This is embarrassing enough without her knowing the truth of how pathetic I am."

"You can't stay with him, Desi. It's time to say enough." Rachel sat next to her again and put her hand on her shoulder. "You've sacrificed enough."

"Do you remember what happened the last time I tried to leave? He's never going to let me go." He'd threatened to kill Rachel if she tried to run again. It didn't matter if he was in jail—Byron would have his brother or father do it to kill the small piece of her heart that was left.

"You don't think I know why you've put up with this shit for as long as you have?" Rachel exhaled forcefully and started crying. "That I don't know what Clyde threatened? Our bastard of a father did this, but he's in the ground where he deserves to be, and it's my turn to take care of you. That begins with you pressing charges, and the two of us finding a new place and starting over."

"I won't gamble with your life, sweetie. I'm stuck, but you're not. It's time for you to make a life for yourself."

"You must not think very much of me if you can seriously say that." There was anger mixed with incredulousness in her voice. "You've had your reasons, and I love you for them, but this is it. There'll be no more pain and violence."

"I'm sorry for all this, and it's not that I don't want peace, but I'm scared."

"This time it's my turn to be brave, and if I get my wish, I won't be doing it alone." Rachel smiled and winked at her. "With any luck, Harry is single and as chivalrous as she always was."

"The last thing Harry wants to do is take on my boatload of problems, and she's still angry. She made that very clear when she handed me off to another doctor."

"Of course she's mad. She loved you. She made plans with you, and you disappeared without any explanation. You know I love you, but if you'd done that to me, I'd be pissed too." Rachel squeezed her hand, her expression resolute. "I appreciate everything you did for me, but you are not throwing away this chance. You know I'd never leave you in that hellhole, so taking a chance now sets us both free."

"I chose to do what I did, and I also knew the consequences of those choices. The last thing I ever thought was that Harry had been waiting all this time for an explanation. I figured she'd forgotten me." She sighed from the frustration of making Rachel understand. She'd given away her one opportunity in life to be happy for her sister.

Rachel put her fingers under her chin and forced her to look at her. "Tell me your choices haven't cost you *everything*, starting with the one person who mattered most. If you give me an honest answer, I'll do whatever you ask, but you have to be honest."

"Do you think if I had a do-over, I'd pick differently? I wouldn't—because I love you, and you have a chance to be different than me. If I'd picked what I'd wanted, there was no way I'd ever forgive myself for what Clyde had planned for you. That would've scarred you so deeply there'd be no chance of you being the amazing person you are." She spoke with conviction to get her point across. "You're free to make whatever life you want, and if you do that, it'll all have been worth it. I've told you that over and over, but you refuse to go."

"I love you as much as you do me, so we're not having that argument again. I go where you go, and you decided to stay with that asshole, so I stayed with you. And I'm with you now, for whatever comes next." Rachel's hair fell forward when she bowed her head. "There's nothing in the shadows that can hurt either one of us, babe. Not anymore. We can both have something new—you just have to want it badly enough."

"If I've learned anything, it's that life isn't that simple. I know my place, and there's no escape." She closed her eyes and turned her head. Her job now was to cut Rachel loose from this hell. "Could you give me some time? I'm tired." And she was. Tired of living, breathing, and being a punching bag for every man in her life. If there was something to look forward to, it was that once Byron found her, it would be over. Perhaps if any of the Bible stories were true, she'd find peace in the next life.

❖

Harry didn't have to open her eyes to know who was hugging her from behind. "How have you been, really?" she asked. They'd been in the same city all this time, but worlds apart.

Rachel took the question as an invitation to sit in her lap because that's where she landed. "You still smell the same, Harry." Rachel rested her head on her shoulder and pressed her nose to her neck.

"That's because I'm a creature of habit. I'm the same old boring Harry."

"If that's true, you're like an answer to a prayer. That old Harry was the one bright thing in our lives when we were children because you loved us." Rachel kissed her cheek and held her. "Thank you for taking care of Desi yesterday. The police had plenty of questions for me, so I'm glad you were there when I couldn't be."

"I was just doing my job."

"I don't quite believe that was it, and my goddess, I've missed you."

She tugged on Rachel's hair gently and allowed herself to

remember the happiness Rachel had brought into her life from that first day. Harry'd never questioned Rachel's tagging along with her and Desi, or that she'd be a part of their future. Losing Desi had only been compounded by losing Rachel along with her.

"I missed you too." She held Rachel, enjoying this solid reminder of simpler times. "But my part is done. You need to understand that Desi has a long recovery ahead, and she's going to need you to get back on her feet. She should also start therapy to help with what got her here."

"You're done? You're joking, right?"

"Rachel, there's no going back for me. She's had all this time to set things straight, and she hasn't. Neither of you has." She stopped talking when Rachel sat up, and from her expression, she knew she sounded childish.

"Listen to me, okay? Nothing that happened was your fault, and it was all so incredibly unfair to you."

"I'm sorry, squirt. This has nothing to do with blame or fairness, but it's done."

"You might not believe me, but it's not Desi's fault either, and you need to give her the chance to tell you herself. Maybe you don't think she deserves that, but she's been through hell, and I'm begging on her behalf."

"You don't have to beg." She kissed Rachel's forehead and smiled. "I don't have it in me to blame her for anything, and I didn't realize it until now. She has the right to live whatever life she wants. Desi doesn't owe me anything."

Rachel took her hand and threaded their fingers together. "Desi thought she had no choice, and she hasn't forgotten you. In truth, she's gotten hit plenty because she can't forget."

"Believe me"—she shook her head, trying to clear the sight of Desi in the emergency room—"I've spent hours since yesterday trying to put together the girl I knew with the woman in that hospital room. Nothing I come up with computes."

"Harry, her story isn't mine to tell." Rachel cupped her cheek. "I didn't understand what she did either, and I spent a long time being angry at what she'd done to you and how she'd done it. You were so good to both of us, and suddenly you were gone because she broke it off."

"You live with her, though." She gazed at Rachel, and her old friend couldn't keep eye contact. It reminded her of Desi and how she acted. "Why haven't either of you left? This attack was brutal, and from what I understand, Desi came close to not making it. The fact that she wishes Byron had finally finished her doesn't make sense either. Do they have children?"

"No, thank God, and I've tried for years to get her to leave, but Clyde and Byron were impossible to fight, and there was no way I was going to leave her to deal with it on her own. It's been years of terror, and it's going to take a lot of love to build her back up."

"Hopefully she listens to you and doesn't go back."

"Please." Rachel moved her hand from her cheek to the side of her neck. "She's *never* going to ask, but she's going to need you. Promise you'll at least try."

"She doesn't act like she wants me around, and she seems to have been through plenty already. The last thing I want is to force her into something else against her will."

"You and Byron are the definition of opposites. If you're still pissed, then think of it as doing it for me because you love me." Rachel scratched the back of her neck and kissed her cheek. "Think about it before you disappear. You'll regret it if you don't find out the truth." Rachel gave her a soft smile. "It's so wonderful to see you again, Harry." She left, her short heels clicking down the hallway.

Harry sighed and picked up the phone. "The smart play, Basantes, is to walk away." That'd be the best for everyone, but she wasn't exactly rational when it came to the Thompson sisters. "Hey," she said when her friend Dan Ruben answered. "Thanks for agreeing to take on the patient we talked about, but I'm keeping the case. It's more complicated than I thought."

That was such an understatement it was almost laughable.

CHAPTER SIX

Desi leaned her head over the side of the bed as far as she could so Rachel could wash her hair in the plastic tub. They hadn't really spoken after Rachel had gotten back until she took the supplies out of the bag she'd brought. It wasn't hard to sense the disgust Rachel was feeling.

"I know you don't want to talk about it, but what happened?"

"Nothing special—you know it never is. He was screaming about his father, and he'd headed to the casino after work." She closed her eyes as Rachel rinsed the shampoo out and shivered at the memory of Byron coming through the door.

Years with him had taught her the signs when he wasn't in control. Those lessons had been numerous in their time together, but at times there would be long stretches of only verbal abuse. That's when she knew he'd found someone else to spend time with and would only come home for clean clothes and food. Each reprieve always felt like a godsend, and each time she'd hoped he'd find someone he wanted to leave her for. He never did.

"I had dinner ready, but I forgot his beer. He started in on me, and my scream from this"—she pointed to her face—"got one of the neighbors to call for help." She rubbed the area where the stitches were starting to itch. Her lip was still too tender to touch.

"How did he break your leg? The officer said something about a bat." Rachel worked in the conditioner and it felt heavenly.

"They stopped him from hitting me in the head with the bat, but my leg was from a kick with his boot." These conversations always made her despondent. Their talks should be about their kids and spouses, and not how she'd survived one more assault. "It's hard to believe I'm still here."

"Maybe this is the universe's way of telling you that you're running out of chances, and it's time to go." The conditioner rinsed out, and Rachel very gently towel-dried her hair. "This doesn't have to be your life."

After lying in bed staring at the ceiling, she'd come to the same terrifying conclusion. "I know I should leave, but where am I going to go? I have a high school diploma and no job experience. And I'm thirty-three—no one's going to hire me." She swallowed the lump of despair. "And he could still come after me. Us."

Rachel combed her hair out and took some more things out of her bag. This was a routine they'd run through plenty of times over the years.

"Let's worry about getting you healthy before we find you a new career." Rachel tilted her head back again and put some moisturizer on her face and some balm on her chapped lips. "Come in," Rachel said when they heard the light knock.

"Good morning, Mrs. Simoneaux," the man said as he took a small notepad out of his coat pocket. "I'm Detective Roger Landry, and if you're up to it, I'd like to ask you some questions. I spoke to your sister last night, but your statement is important going forward."

"This is the first time a detective has cared anything about all this." The police had come out to the house over the years, beat cops who stared at her in shock when she'd refused to press charges.

"The brutality this time rises to attempted murder." Roger didn't get too close but came in and closed the door. "Your cooperation is crucial if we're going to make a case stick."

"It's good to know you're not here to tell us how hard it is to hold Byron, so we should let it go. That's happened before," Rachel said.

He shook his head. "My partner and I are going to work hard to make sure Simoneaux does some serious time for this. If you'll feel more comfortable with a female detective, that can be arranged."

Desi spoke in a monotone, trying to remember everything Byron had done before the pain made her shut down. "He was out of control and kept screaming for me to shut up when the police arrived. All the flashing lights in the front yard made him nuts."

"Dr. Basantes's testimony about the extent of your injuries combined with the fact that he was about to strike you in the head with the bat will put him away for a very long time." Roger closed the notebook and rested his hand against his side. "But we can't do that without your cooperation."

"Would he ever get out?" Caging Byron like an animal would seal her fate when they released him.

"Hopefully, not for years." He reached out his hand slowly and took hers. "Help us put him away. After seeing your home and knowing what he did, it's easy to see that you won't survive another attack like that."

"Who's going to believe me? I've never pressed charges before, and that will make people think I probably deserved it." She wanted to forget about everything and be left alone, but this time that wasn't going to happen. What Roger and everyone else didn't understand was it didn't matter whether Byron was locked up or not. Unless his brother and father went with him, nothing was going to change. She and Rachel wouldn't be safe.

"It's going to be hard not to believe you once the court sees you. Is this the first time he's put you in the hospital?"

"Hell no." Rachel gave Roger a list that wasn't complete. Desi flinched at the oral history.

"That shows a pattern of abuse," Roger said. "We have your medical records, your neighbors' recollections, and the list of times units were sent to your home. With your testimony, we think we have enough to convict this bastard."

"Can you promise Rachel will be safe from the Simoneaux family?"

"We'll get you both a restraining order today. Simoneaux's father posted bail, so that's the first order of business. We've placed officers outside your door to make certain he can't get anywhere near you. If you're concerned about his family, I'll get them on the no-fly list too."

"Okay," she said after a long pause. "I'll press charges." The idea of taking this forward was terrifying, but the thought of going back to the chaos of her life was sickening. Everyone was right. Something had to change.

"Can we take our stuff out of the house?" Rachel asked. "We don't need much, but we're not going back there, ever. I'll get a new place set up while Desi is recovering here."

"I'll call you after I deal with Simoneaux and give you an escort over there." Roger said to Rachel, as he squeezed Desi's hand before stepping back. "I'll be there for you, no matter the time. Don't forget that."

"Thank you," Desi said, having a hard time breathing. The fear of the future was almost scarier than the fear of Byron.

"It's good that neither of you are going back to the house. Wherever you go, I'll need a contact number, but I promise to keep it out of the report as a precaution. I'll keep you posted on everything—you have my word."

It was real now, and it didn't seem like there was any way to go back. Her problem wasn't letting go, but where to go from here. Her heart knew exactly what its choice was, but Harry was never going to forgive her, much less consider what they'd once had. She was so tired of fate taking the things that mattered to her most, but in this case, she deserved the pain. All of Harry's animosity, aloofness, and bitterness was well earned.

She might finally find her way to freedom, but the cost had been far too high.

❖

Harry stood at the nurses' station with her residents around her when she noticed the detective from the night before leaving Desi's room. The guy seemed to be in a constant wrinkled condition. He'd changed clothes, but he didn't look any neater.

"Good morning," she said when she shook hands with him.

"Hey, got a few minutes?"

"Take a coffee break, everyone, and I'll page when we're ready to continue," she said to her people. "Let's take one of the consultation rooms," she said to Landry and pointed the way.

"She's willing to press charges, which will be a way of keeping her alive," he said as a starter. "Once the time comes, I'll need you to testify to her injuries."

"That's not a problem—I've done that a few times." She stared at him and guessed there was plenty more he wanted to say. "Anything else?" she prodded him.

"Her sister Rachel mentioned last night that you knew them."

"We were friends in grade school, but I haven't seen either of them in years. Actually, yesterday in the emergency room was the first time since our high school graduation that I've run into Desi." She twirled her pen through her fingers to keep them limber. It was a habit she'd picked up from her father.

"I don't have a right to ask, but neither of those girls looks like they can afford a place to go once Desi makes it out of the hospital. Rachel says she'll find a place, but it's not likely it will be something secure. All I can do is put them in a shelter, but that's not a long-term solution. Putting them in protective custody isn't an option because it's a domestic abuse case, and I won't get the okay for something like that because he's not a high value criminal."

"I'm not sure I know where you're going with this." The thought of Desi and Rachel in a shelter, especially in Desi's condition, was awful.

"They need a place where it won't be easy for Simoneaux to track them down, and that might be with you. If you have room for them, would you consider letting them stay?"

"Nope." Even if this guy didn't know their complete history, this was a lot to ask someone. "We didn't end on good terms."

"Was it bad enough that you're planning to beat the shit out of her?" Landry asked and seemed totally serious.

"What? No," she said indignantly.

"If you decide she isn't worth your time or care, that's exactly what's going to happen to her if this guy or his family find her. This isn't something I can force on you, obviously, but please think about it."

"There's got to be someone else," she said, not ready to give in.

"They have no family, and if it's a friend they have now it'll be only a matter of time before Simoneaux finds her. And next time, it might be Rachel in his crosshairs too."

She laughed as she shook her head. "You're almost as good as my mother in laying on the guilt, Detective."

"These girls have been through enough. I think they deserve every break they have coming. If you can think of anywhere else they'd be as safe as they'd probably be with you, then I'm all ears."

She thought quickly, searching for an option, and came up blank. Damn it all. "Okay, I can't imagine they'll want to stay very long, but I have room."

"You're one of the good ones, Doc. Do you have any parking tickets or anything I can help you with to return the favor?" He grinned and his shoulders dropped slightly.

"I'm one of the law-abiding citizens you don't have to worry about, but thanks."

"Then maybe I'll stop by and get my knee fixed to give you some business."

"That I can help you with."

"How long does she need to be here? I want to have the legalities clamped down before she's discharged, and it would be good to have her in a monitored location until I can get him back in jail."

"It's going to be at least another week or so, but I'll call you when I know more," she said, taking one of her cards out. "Here's my information if you need to get in touch."

He flicked the card and shook her hand again before leaving. How in the hell she'd gotten herself into this she'd have to unpack later, but there was no going back now.

"Hey," she said when Rachel opened Desi's door for her. "I wanted to let you know that I won't be transferring your case to my colleague, and I talked to the detective. He says you need a place to stay."

"Yes," Rachel said quickly, as if trying to shut Desi down before she said otherwise.

"We'll think of something, but thanks," Desi said, glaring at Rachel.

Harry ignored the warning bells going off in her head and plunged forward. "You don't have to say yes, but I can't let you out of here if there's a chance you'll end up coming back in worse shape...or dead. Forget about our past, and think about your future, Desi. No matter what I did to make you change your mind about us," she said, dropping her crossed arms so she didn't appear confrontational, "don't let it cloud your judgment."

"I screwed up, but you don't need to take on my problems. If something happened to you..." Desi clamped her mouth shut and her eyes got watery.

"Let me worry about Byron, and let me take care of you until you can do it for yourself. You're in no condition to be able to defend yourself, and Landry thinks it would be good for you to be someplace Byron won't think to look. With someone who knows you." She couldn't bring herself to say *with a friend*.

"Are you sure?" Desi's voice was barely audible.

She wasn't in the least bit sure, but they didn't need to know that. "Rachel, I'll leave you directions to the house, and you can help get it ready for your sister." She smiled at Rachel's excitement and turned to Desi. "The rest we'll figure out as we go, but at least you'll be safe."

"Do you still live around here?" Rachel asked.

"I bought a place close to where Mom and Dad used to be. They're retired and living in Florida. There's plenty of room, and it's almost finished. Tony's been helping me redecorate."

"Tony Martin from high school?" Rachel asked.

"It's Tony Reynolds now, but one and the same."

"He made my prom dress in the tenth grade, and no one would've figured it didn't come from one of those boutiques on Magazine Street," Rachel said, coming closer to her. "Is he a decorator?"

"He's actually a nurse, but he's happier with a paintbrush in his hand. It's something he started when you two took those classes in high school. He married Kenneth Reynolds, and Kenny gives him the freedom to do whatever makes him happy."

"Wow, they're still together?" Rachel asked, putting her hand on her arm. "What a great love story."

"It's one he loves to tell, so don't ask if you don't really want to know," she said, glancing at her watch. She didn't want to talk about love stories from high school. "I'll stop by later and drop off a key and the codes to the gate."

"If I'm not here, leave it with Desi. The detective offered to give me a ride to the house so I can pack."

"Be careful, and make sure you wait for him. Anything either of you need before I go?"

"Will I see you again today?" Desi asked timidly.

Harry opened her mouth to refuse, but Rachel was staring at her with a pleading expression. Damn it. "How about in an hour? I have to finish my rounds, but then I'll stop by for another milkshake since the nurse told me you hardly ate anything. Do you want chocolate or vanilla?"

"Vanilla," Desi said and smiled.

The smile, though, looked forced and scared. That beautiful girl she once knew had been buried under the fears and scars of the woman cowering on the bed, who seemed afraid that any misstep would end with the worst of punishments. It was heartbreaking.

"Vanilla it is." She left before she backslid another inch. Not that there was much further to go. She felt marginally better when she saw Tony waiting.

"Did you think you could hide from me forever?" Tony asked. He was standing by the elevator with his hands on his hips and a tapping foot. She'd known him long enough to recognize his annoyed-with-the-world posture.

"Rounds isn't hiding from you, sunshine." She had to finish with her patients so she could head back to University Medical and do the same over there. "Want to wait a few minutes and ride with me to meet Kenneth?"

"No, I know what's happening with Kenneth. He's bitching about a new washing machine. I want to know what's going on in here." He tapped the side of her head.

"Once I figure it out, I'll be happy to lie on your crushed velvet couch and talk about it." She walked into an empty patient room so the whole hospital didn't overhear everything about her personal life.

"What's got you so mad? And don't deny it. I saw your hands clenched."

"The detective talked me into letting Desi and Rachel stay with me. They aren't safe to go home, and while I understand that—"

"You don't want them in your house," he finished for her.

"That makes me sound so heartless, but yes. Everyone should be able to forget first loves and high school crushes as soon as they start college and leave all that shit in the past." She was such a fucking idiot for wasting this much emotional angst on a woman who hadn't given her a second thought.

"I've prayed you would—forget, I mean—and move on. Desi Thompson made you skittish about commitment, but that's understandable. That connection you made lasted a lot of years, honey, and the years that followed came with no explanations." Tony hugged her and kissed her cheek. "I know you're pissed, but you've got a good heart. Maybe this is what you need."

"Thanks, but I'm not sure about the good heart."

"I am, so tell me what I can do."

"Keep that velvet couch on hold, and tell me if my guest rooms are ready. The only room I've been in upstairs is mine." She glanced out the door and spotted Rachel waiting for her.

"Rachel," Tony said, holding out his hand. "How'd you like to go shopping? Dr. Harry needs new bedding, and you might as well like what I pick. It sounds like you're staying for a while."

After a quick hug, Rachel agreed, and Harry shook her head at the ease with which Tony navigated socially awkward situations. She might not get any answers anytime soon, but she'd bet everything she owned he'd have the whole story before they got to the pillowcase section of the store. As much as she wanted that story herself, that would mean opening up again, and that wasn't something she was prepared to do.

CHAPTER SEVEN

Harry came back as promised with a milkshake and started a routine that they followed for the next week. Morning rounds and the snack break erased some of Desi's hesitancy around her, but only a little. Rachel had been right—whatever had happened to Desi, it had left her broken and compliant. They chatted but stayed far away from the subjects they both knew needed to be broached.

"I think you're ready to be discharged in the morning," she said as she sat next to the bed. "You have some more bed rest ahead of you, but you'll be more comfortable when you aren't being disturbed all night by nurses and attendants."

"Are you sure you want us there? We won't be in your way?" Desi's questions were hesitant, as if she didn't know if she had the right to ask them. Harry was getting used to Desi not making much eye contact.

"Rachel and Tony have broken me in—I'm used to having houseguests, so no worries." It turned out Rachel was unobtrusive and spent plenty of time working, so it hadn't been all that difficult having her there. There'd been no word from Landry, and she wasn't sure what that meant. "I know you don't like talking about it, but have you heard from the detective?"

Desi sucked on her straw in an obvious delaying tactic. "He called yesterday and said they haven't found Byron yet. They think he skipped bail."

"Are they looking for him?" There wasn't a future for her and Desi, but she did want Desi to have a future.

"He said they are. Maybe I should go somewhere else." Desi put her shake down and pressed her hands together. "You don't deserve to be dragged into this."

"No, what you need to do is put a fire under these guys." This was ridiculous. Byron deserved to be caged and beaten for what he'd done. The plastic surgeon who took care of the cut on Desi's temple had mentioned some of the other small scars on Desi's face to her. None of that mattered—Desi was still beautiful. But Byron's abuse had lasted long enough.

"No one pays much attention to these cases, Harry. It's my fault, after all."

"I have a friend in the DA's office who handles almost all the domestic violence cases." She softened her voice because Desi didn't need her anger, even if it was on her behalf. "If I call her, would you talk to her?"

"Do you think it would help?"

"Serena can walk you through the process, so you'll know what to expect. Roger can make promises that Byron will go away for a long time, something he deserves, but it'll be Serena who'll actually make it happen." She leaned forward and rested her hand on the bed. Close enough to touch, but not actually crossing that line.

"You don't think he'll go to jail?" Desi rubbed her hands together in a nervous tic kind of way.

"I don't know more than what Serena has told me, but the most important factor to the success of any case is you. Getting away from him is something you have to want and something you have to follow through on."

Desi looked at her and didn't waver. "Is that something you think I don't want?"

"Only you can answer that." She almost turned her head, not comfortable with the sudden intensity of Desi's gaze. That was so strange, considering she'd lived to bask in Desi's attention. "It's been a long time since we've seen each other, so I can't begin to guess what's in your heart and mind."

Desi took a breath and it started her tears. "God, you must think I'm so pathetic."

"Let me finish." She took a chance and held Desi's hand. "I don't think you're pathetic—I never did—but I do think you need to decide what happens next. Don't let anyone push you in a direction you don't want to go."

"No one's given me a choice in a long time." Desi covered her face with her free hand and sobbed.

"You had the strength to survive, and I know you have the courage to say *enough*." She continued speaking softly until Desi faced her again.

"Trust me, there's nothing courageous about me."

"I can't fathom what you've been through, but I don't think this was a first-time thing." She gripped Desi's hand. "No one has a right to do this to you, and it's up to you to demand different. That's a first step to peace."

"Thank you."

"You're welcome, and all this, as well as your injuries, will get better. All you need is faith." She squeezed Desi's fingers before standing.

"I'll try my best."

"I know you will, and you won't have to do it alone."

Harry left to do rounds, but her thoughts stayed with Desi all day. She couldn't imagine what it had been like to live with that fear, to become so beaten down and lost. And she couldn't imagine what life was going to be like having Desi around all the time.

❖

"She has to be there," Byron Simoneaux said to the receptionist at University Medical. He'd been out of jail for a few days and had been sleeping at his brother Mike's house, ignoring the police that kept stopping by and banging on the door.

Spending a night in lockup was enough to convince him he didn't want to go back, and the cops looking for him meant he was going back. All he had to do was find the bitch he was married to and explain a few things in a way she'd understand perfectly, and then the cops would back off.

"She had surgery and was discharged that night," the woman said for the third time. "I have no idea where she went, and I don't know how else to explain it to you."

Fuck. He didn't want to cause a scene, so he moved to the side and called his brother. "Did you go by my place like I asked?"

"What the hell happened in there? There's blood on the floor and stuff's everywhere."

"Forget that shit. Desi and that bitch Rachel haven't shown up?"

"Place was locked up, and no one's there. She's not at the hospital?"

"Not anymore, and the old fucker at the desk won't tell me where she is. Call me when you get home, and tell me if those cops are there."

He sat in the big lobby beating his fist against his knee and looking around.

"You still there?" Mike asked.

"Let me call you back." He hurried to follow the guy in scrubs pushing a wheelchair. He'd seen this guy before, and the hospital credentials around his neck were a way to get answers. "Hey, man."

The guy stopped and stared for a bit before smiling. "Hey. Bob's Bar, right?"

That's where he'd seen him. "Yeah, and maybe you can help me." He explained what he needed, and his new friend didn't appear reluctant. "I'm so worried about her after the accident, and no one here is telling me shit."

"I'll try, man. Come on."

Forty minutes later his new friend found what Byron needed. Desi had herself moved as a way of hiding from him, of that he was sure.

"I owe you." He slapped the guy on the back and headed out to the car he'd borrowed from his dad's garage.

He'd have to play it cool at the next place, but finding Desi was important. All he had to do was remind her what was going to happen to her and her mouthy sister if she decided to talk to the police. That was the best way to keep Desi in line, and it'd worked from the time Clyde had started using it back in high school.

The cafeteria at Baptist wasn't crowded, so he sat and waited for the visitors to start to thin. He didn't want to talk to too many people, but the lady at the register told him most of the orthopedic patients were on the third floor.

He apologized to the patients he walked in on, but finally he stood in the doorway of the last room on the hall and stared at Desi as she slept. No matter the passage of years, Desi stayed pretty, but nothing he'd ever done for her had softened her heart when it came to loving him. The ungrateful little bitch had never learned that she belonged to him and she should be thankful she did.

Desi was completely relaxed, giving him the chance to walk in and stand next to the bed. Her leg was in a brace and her face had been stitched up, but she appeared fine despite the horrid bruise. The urge to touch her made him decide to start with her hand, and he wrapped his fingers around her wrist and squeezed, hard.

"Miss me?" he asked, smiling when her eyes grew wide with fear. "Make a noise, and I'm going to slit your throat and walk out of here and do the same to your slut sister."

"Byron, please." Desi appeared terrified, and that turned him on more than anything she could do for him. "I didn't say anything."

"Yeah, I'm sure that's why they locked me up and keep coming by the house. You're going to tell these people you're ready to come home. We need to have a talk about how you can't seem to learn anything." He stopped before his voice got any louder and someone came in. "You know I don't mean to hurt you. You know that, right?"

"Yes."

He barely heard her and could see her hands trembling. "It's you doing stupid shit that makes me do that." He made a fist and beat it into the mattress, getting Desi to flinch. "I'm so tired of your dumb ass."

"Please, Byron." Desi moved back as much as she could, and the sudden expression of pain made him smile.

"You're like a fucking anchor, and it's time to let go." He moved fast before she could scream and wrapped his hands around her throat. If Desi was dead, she couldn't testify against him. No more trying to get her to understand. "Fucking die."

Desi hit against his arms and moved the leg that wasn't in a brace, but she wasn't strong enough to stop him. He increased the pressure, feeling a sense of freedom that was close to euphoric. There'd been a time he couldn't wait to get his hands on the beautiful woman who'd never given him a glance, but that'd been a mistake. It hadn't taken long for him to figure out Desi was disgusted by his touch—not that it had stopped him, but it had fueled his anger. Granted, she took care of the house his father had given them, and she cooked, but she was no wife. The memory of the truth of that made him tighten his grip, and Desi finally stopped fighting.

He laughed again. "Bitch." She was a dog that needed to be put down, and it would free him to find someone else. He smiled at that and tightened his grip. A noise made him look up, but then there was shooting pain and nothing but blackness.

CHAPTER EIGHT

Harry shook her hand out, not caring if she'd broken her fingers. All that mattered was the asshole she assumed was Byron Simoneaux was unconscious on the floor. She pressed the call button and demanded security as well as the police, as she moved to Desi's side. Her heart hammered in her chest as she took in Desi's pallor, the bruising coming up around her neck, and the fact that she couldn't see her chest moving.

"Desi." She carefully moved Desi's head, so her airway was open, hoping it was enough to get her breathing again. The slight cough almost buckled her knees in relief. "Open your eyes for me, sweetheart."

"Harry?" Desi glanced at her and cringed back as if there was still something to fear. "He's here."

"You're okay. He can't hurt you again." She found IV tubing in the utility drawer and used it to tie Byron's hands behind his back. "This should earn him a free pass back to jail."

"Please be careful," Desi said as she rubbed her throat.

"Detective," she said into the phone as she nodded in Desi's direction, "we found Byron Simoneaux for you."

"Where?" Landry asked.

"In Desi's hospital room trying to kill her. When you come, make sure you bring someone who can take pictures of her throat. And where the hell was the officer who was supposed to be outside her door?" The security guards came in and replaced her makeshift bonds with handcuffs.

"Should we bring him to, Doc?" the older guy said.

"Get him out of here until the police arrive. Have one of the nurses look at him, but don't let him out of your sight, and put him in a room where he can't disturb the other patients when he's sure to start having a temper tantrum." One of the nurses came in and moved quickly to Desi's side. "Get someone from respiratory up to look at her."

"You got it, Dr. Basantes."

They dragged Byron out, and she had to take a few deep breaths to calm down. Coming in and finding that idiot trying to kill Desi had sent her into a blind fury that made her punch him so hard she'd knocked him out cold. She turned to Desi. "Are you okay?" It was a stupid question. Desi was anything but okay, but she had to start somewhere.

Desi shook her head with her hands still on her throat. "He's never going to stop," she whispered. "Maybe you should send me somewhere else. Somewhere he can't hurt you."

"The thing about guys like Byron is they're slow learners. At least, they are until someone who hits harder than they do teaches them it's better if they move on." If she hadn't decided to check on Desi one last time before she left for the night, Desi would have died. The thought made the bile rise in the back of her throat.

Harry got a cold compress for Desi's neck and dealt with the uniformed officer who arrived. Landry and his partner showed up soon after and took over. The whole thing took a few hours, and she wanted to know how Byron had found Desi to begin with. The only good news was that the consult she'd requested said Desi's neck was bruised but there was no other damage.

"I can't answer how he got here, Doc, but I'll ask him when I get downtown. We couldn't leave an officer posted on the door forever with all these city cuts. After a few days we figured she was safe and he wouldn't find her." Landry had sent his partner to deal with Byron while he questioned Desi. "This place is compromised, though, so we might need a new location."

"Don't worry about that. We're moving as soon as you're done."

"Skip giving me the address, and I'll call you if I need anything." Landry left, and Harry sat on the bed.

"Nothing I say will change what happened, but you're going to be okay. Right now, let me take care of you."

Desi's mouth seemed frozen, but she nodded hesitantly. Her tears were back, and she closed her eyes when Harry took her hand. Perhaps Desi was right, and this guy would never back down, but she couldn't leave Desi to fight alone. Whatever had happened between them, it didn't rise to the level of forfeiting Desi's life.

She moved to the chair and eventually fell asleep once the nurse checked Desi's vitals. No one bothered them again until the morning, and Harry arranged transport before anyone from Byron's family showed up to finish the job. Rachel was furious that animal had gotten close to her sister again.

"I'll cancel my appointments and come with you." Rachel rested her head on Harry's chest and cried.

"Go to work. I'll take care of her."

"Thank God you were here last night, Harry. If he'd killed her, I would've lost my mind." Rachel hung on to her as she cried, and not for the first time in the last week. Harry felt inadequate to deal with all these foreign emotions.

"I promise I'll do my best to keep you both safe." She put her arms around Rachel and kissed the top of her head. "Go on in and give her a pep talk while I get everything ready."

She wasn't surprised to see Kenneth and Tony waiting for her. They'd both called after Rachel had told Tony what had happened. It had been a long night, and her back ached from sleeping in the chair, but she couldn't leave Desi alone in the state of mind she was in.

"Is she okay?" Tony asked.

"That bastard almost choked her to death." She looked at her phone when it rang, not recognizing the number. "Hello."

"Dr. Basantes, this is Marge from University. We ran the search you requested and found the information was accessed by a transporter. His shift is over, but we're calling him in to answer some questions."

"I'm going to send the police to wait on him. Once he gives his statement, fire his ass. If he didn't pay attention when you covered patient privacy, he can refresh his memory in the unemployment line." She hung up and smiled when Kenneth did.

"Why don't you let us take Desi home for you, and you can get some sleep?" Kenneth massaged her shoulders and she shook her head.

"I cleared my morning, so I'll ride with her. You guys are welcome to come." She noticed the same team that had transported Desi before waiting by the elevator. "This is some shit, huh?"

"Are you okay?" Tony lifted her hand and stared at her bruised knuckles. "Is this okay?"

"Trust me, if I could've broken his neck, I'd have gladly sacrificed some broken bones." She greeted the guys and asked them to wait until she got Desi ready.

She walked in and waited until Rachel and Desi finished talking, their heads close together. At least this relationship hadn't changed through the years, and the sisters still seemed close. From day one she'd known they came as a package deal, and Rachel being there meant Desi always had someone in her corner.

"Hey, come in," Rachel said.

"I think it'll be better if we move you before anything else happens, but I don't want to risk damaging your leg. The ambulance is here, so if you're ready, we'll go."

The ride was as smooth as before, and Harry rode in the back with her. They'd gone out of the service entrance as an extra precaution in case someone was watching.

"Damn, Doc, this place is nice," the driver said as he waited for the gate to fully open.

"Tony knows his real estate," she said, knowing he and Kenneth were in the car behind them. "Stop under the portico, and we'll go through the kitchen. It'll be the easiest route upstairs." Her cell phone rang as the back doors opened, and she figured her clear morning was about to get complicated.

"We have an industrial accident en route, Doc," the emergency room nurse at University said. "A section of scaffolding fell, and we need you in surgery. We're waiting on at least fourteen, maybe more."

"Call everyone in and start prepping three rooms. I'm ten minutes out." This could take most of the day depending on the severity of the injuries, but it would give Desi the chance to settle in. "Tony and Kenneth will stay with you until Rachel gets back. She shouldn't be more than a few hours."

"Don't worry about me. I can stay by myself, so no one has to go to any trouble." Desi held the edge of the green sheet and stared at her feet.

"You can't even walk on your own yet, Des. The boys don't mind, and later Mona can help Rachel with whatever comes up." She loosely held the side rail to keep the guys from moving the gurney.

"Mona?"

"She pretends to be my housekeeper, but she's an open communication line back to my mother. She's got three days off to visit her family, but she never lasts the whole time and always comes home early." She smiled, trying to ease Desi's tension. "Don't let her give you a hard time, and she knows how to contact me if something goes wrong."

"Thank you. I don't deserve your kindness." Desi didn't lift her head, and she had to go, so there was no choice but to walk away.

"Jesus. What exactly did this guy do to you?" she whispered as she walked to her car. That was a mystery she didn't know if she wanted an answer to.

❖

Desi watched Harry walk away until she was out of sight, then smiled at Kenneth when he stepped up beside her. She remembered both men from high school and some of the things they'd done together. She and Harry should've had years of good memories to share with them, but at least Harry had a piece of what had been stolen.

"You holding up okay?" Kenneth said in that soothing voice she also remembered. "Give us a minute, and we'll get you squared away and comfortable."

"Thank you."

"Darling, you've been through enough, so no need to thank us," Tony said as he unlocked the door. "Come on."

She tried to relax as she looked at the parts of the house they were passing. The place was beautifully decorated, and the kitchen was an awesome place to gather a family. It was strange that Harry didn't have one, considering how often they'd talked about that.

The thought of Harry alone made her take a shuddering breath, as she tried not to cry.

"Are you hurting?" Tony asked from behind the guy at her feet.

"I'm okay." She closed her eyes to fight the slight nausea and her mind flew back to all those long talks.

One day during senior year, it was too cold to go out to their usual spot in the yard, so Desi followed Harry up to the attic. Harry had made a spot for them behind the Christmas decorations, complete with a heater so they could get naked.

Desi was straddling Harry's lap enjoying not only the feel of her skin but the sensation of her tongue in her mouth. It was getting harder to be apart, but the weekends were their best chance to be alone. From their first night together as lovers, they'd learned so much about what felt good and what would be the biggest turn-on.

"You feel so good," Harry said, putting her hands on her ass and holding her even closer. "I missed you this week."

"It's all those practices you have to go to. My dad's always home before we finish our homework." She ran her hands down Harry's back, moaning when Harry kissed her neck. "I'd complain, but you look so good in those soccer shorts that I can't."

"I can go put them on if you want," Harry teased.

"You're not going anywhere until you touch me." They'd spent time after dinner playing a board game with Harry's parents, but now she was so wet she was close to begging.

"You want me, baby?" Harry squeezed her ass, and she was sure Harry's abdomen was wet from her sex.

It sometimes started slow like tonight but always built to this overwhelming need that drove her mad until Harry took her to the places she only wanted to go with her lover. They might've been young, but they both understood what passion was and how to build it up in each other. "Yes. Please touch me."

Harry laid her back and hovered over her. "You don't ever have to beg me for that." She kissed her way down her body and put her mouth on her.

She placed her feet on Harry's shoulders and moved her hips to the rhythm Harry set, sensing the now familiar tightening in her stomach. The orgasm she desperately wanted was right at the cusp of her consciousness, but she tried to hold it back. "Go inside, baby. I need you inside." Talking to Harry while they made love was new, but Harry had broken through her inhibitions like a hammer through eggshells, and her words drove Harry insane. She'd quickly figured out she liked Harry insane.

"That's good, baby." The way Harry's fingers moved in and out, along with her tongue flat on her clit, made it hard not to give in, but she bit her lip and tried her best. They were on the opposite side of the house from Harry's parents, but there was no reason to chance it.

All the small discreet touches all night and the kissing in the kitchen when they were fixing everyone drinks made it impossible not to come. She had to—needed it like she needed air in her lungs to survive, and she swallowed the scream she wanted to let out as Harry pushed her over the edge.

"Do you think our kids will mind going to bed at five in the afternoon so I can drag you to the bedroom?" She traced small circles on Harry's chest as she daydreamed out loud once Harry had come up and held her.

"You better pray they're all like you then. The only way I'd do that for my mom would involve a tranquilizer gun."

"I want all our kids to be like you, baby." She lifted her head and kissed Harry, already wanting her again.

"How many kids are we talking?" Harry rolled her onto her back and put her hand between her legs.

"Four or five at least." She closed her eyes and bit her lip when Harry squeezed her clit between her fingers. "It's a good thing you can't get me pregnant, or we'd be on our way to number one by now."

"We should keep practicing." Harry made her laugh, but she knew when they did start their life together, children would be part of it.

"Every chance we get."

"She'll be over there," Tony said, pointing to the right. "The room at the end of the hall."

"If you're busy, I really don't mind being alone," Desi said as they locked the gurney's wheels. The big room was as gorgeous as the bed they were getting ready to put her in.

"Girl, you know that isn't going to happen, so smile. You're stuck with us until Harry gets home, but it won't be horrible." Tony folded the blankets back and stepped away as the medics expertly moved her to the bed. "It'll give us a chance to catch up."

"You look happy, and it's nice to know you and Kenneth are still together." She placed her hands flat on the mattress and took a deep breath. All the jostling and Byron's visit had left her leg and body aching.

"Thank you, guys." Tony placed a metal frame over her leg and covered her as Kenneth led the medics out. The frame kept the weight of the blanket off her leg. "How about a bowl of soup, so you can take another pain pill?"

"That would be great."

"Don't move, and I'll be right back."

She concentrated on her breathing when Tony left her alone. Everything that had happened in the last week was hard to put into perspective. There was no way she could have imagined that Byron's usual behavior would put her back into Harry's life and into her house.

The room she was in reminded her of Harry, with the dark wood, pale blue walls, and fireplace. Harry's parents had taken them on a vacation once, and they'd made out in front of the fireplace in their room. That's when Harry had said they'd have to have one in their bedroom when they bought a house.

This place certainly appeared to be the space Harry had talked about. "The only thing missing is me," she murmured to the empty room.

God, why did all this still have to hurt so much? She was tired of crying, but her tears were the only things left that were completely hers. Everything else, including her freedom, had been ripped away.

"Hey, don't cry. You need to eat a little, and then you can take a nap."

Tony put a tray down, and she didn't argue with him. Explanations had to come with sharing what was bothering her, and she wasn't ready for that at all.

"Rachel and I got you some stuff you'll need, so we'll change you once you're done."

"You didn't have to do that." She stopped with the spoon near her mouth. "There's no way for me to pay you back."

"Put it on, and don't worry about owing anything. The fact that Rachel loves to shop as much as I do is payment enough." He placed a chair close to the bed after getting a bag from the closet. "This will keep you warmer and feel nicer against your skin."

She ate methodically, more to please Tony than to satisfy any hunger, and she studied the room to keep from talking. The antique pieces were beautiful, as was the original art, but she kept going back to the fireplace and her memoires. Her gaze landed on the framed photo that sat on the right edge.

"It clashes with everything in the house, but she's kept it all these years." Tony followed the direction of her gaze. "It's also been her excuse to never move on. That's my opinion, anyway."

The picture was of her and Harry in their caps and gowns right after graduation, and in her mind, it captured a perfect moment in time. Harry had her arm around her with a wide smile that mirrored her own as she gazed up at her lover. If their time together had been a fairy tale, this was the last page before the story ended with no happy ending.

"I know what you think, but I've never forgotten my time with Harry." The proof that Harry hadn't forgotten either gave her equal parts grief and happiness. "I don't blame any of you for hating me, but I didn't let go easily."

"No one hates you, Desi, least of all Harry. You broke something in her that has never healed, though, and here you are again." He moved to the bed, and she finally blinked and looked at him. "When she asked me to get this place ready for you, it didn't surprise me."

"Why not? It surprised me."

"Because even though she's pissed and has been for so long, that part of her that loved you, craved you, is still alive and well. You're the key that fits perfectly in the hole in her heart." He sighed as he touched her arm. "I can see it wasn't easy for you either, but if you aren't planning to stay, I need you to tell me. Kenny and I'll be happy to have you and Rachel stay with us, even though it will be a little cramped, but Harry won't get her hopes up for nothing. She won't survive you twice."

"The last thing I ever wanted was to hurt Harry—not then and not now." She tried not to lose her composure but couldn't stop her chin from quivering. "Believe me, I've paid over and over for what I did to Harry, but she was free and safe."

"I'm not blind, sweetie. What you've suffered is plain, but I love Harry. You aren't a prisoner, so this time, talk to her before you go."

"I promise, but there isn't a place for me anywhere, not anymore. Byron wants me dead, his family is scary, and Harry got pushed into this." Once she was on her feet, she'd be out on the street, but it was what she deserved. "You and I both know she needs better than me and my pathetic problems."

"You have plenty of time to readjust your view of things because Harry thinks no such thing. Take the time to heal and talk to her, but if you want her to move on from her anger, you need to open up. Tell her the truth of what your story is, and I mean all of it. This isn't the time to hold back. At the very least, give her a way to heal so she can move on."

"Harry is so lucky to have you."

He smiled and puffed out his chest. "You're damn right. Without me there'd be a recliner and a massive television in every room. I set her straight, and I love her. That she still loves you is plain to me as well."

"I doubt that." This conversation wasn't easy, but she appreciated him for trying. "I'm grateful for everything, but I'm the last person Harry wants. I'm damaged goods, and nothing will change that."

"No one is that far gone, and I'll be here every day to remind you of that." He smiled again when she squeezed his fingers. "You're safe here, and I'm easy to talk to, so I promise to listen."

"Thank you." She gladly hugged him when he came closer, and that's how Kenneth found them.

"Hey, ready for a pain pill?" Kenneth held up a pharmacy bag.

"Can I try without one?" She relaxed against the comfortable pillows. "I hate how they make me feel."

"Give them a chance for three days or so, and then you can stop. Right now, they help with the healing process." Kenneth handed her one with a glass of juice. "Later on, we'll start your antibiotics."

"Are you a doctor too? Do you work with Harry?" She swallowed the pill and tried to keep her eyes open.

"No, Harry picked gore and glory. I'm a pediatrician, which is fun, but a good reminder of why our border collie is enough kid for both of us."

"I'd love to work with kids." She did her best to stifle a yawn, but she was exhausted. "Have you heard from Harry?"

"Don't wait up for her. From experience, she's going to be late. Try and get some rest, and we'll be downstairs if you need anything. Please keep us on Harry's good side by not trying to move by yourself."

"I promise, and thank you both for everything." She closed her eyes, but knew sleep would take some time in coming no matter how tired she was.

Tony was right that she was safe here, but for how long? Her life was like running a deadly gauntlet every single day, and every day she ran slower. Lying here made it easy to pretend what it would've been like to live here with Harry.

"Don't be an idiot." Fantasies were only dreams little girls had that were soon crushed under life's boots time and time again.

She stared at the picture and thought back to life without Harry. The nightmare had so many chapters she had a hard time centering on one, but Kenneth's admission of not wanting children made her settle on that subject. She drifted into memories she would rather have forgotten.

"Byron's coming home soon, so I have to hang up." Desi stood at the sink filling a pot with water, getting dinner ready for their fifth anniversary. She was having a hard time hearing Clyde with the bar noise on his end, and Clyde's coughing wasn't helping. She hadn't considered him a parent in a long time.

"He told me the last five years have been the best of his life."

At least one of them was happy. She gripped the phone, fighting the urge to run and not look back. "That's great to hear." She'd learned to lie well. Clyde and Byron's dad had drinks a few times a week, and Clyde kept no one's secrets.

"Do something nice for him—he's been good to you, girl. How about that baby he wants bad?"

"Yeah," she said noncommittally about the one thing that would truly tie her to Byron forever. "I have to go." She didn't often allow herself the luxury of anger—that emotion always ended in a beating—but she seethed with it for Clyde.

Her life had become mechanical, moving from one chore to another to keep from straying into his path. No matter how well she did those things around the house, she got hit, and Byron enjoyed that more than anything. Having a reliable punching bag was why his life was so great.

"You done good for yourself, girl, so you better start thinking about pleasing your man." Clyde's threats were clear. "He married you even though you're a pervert. You're lucky he loves you." He had to stop because of the coughing fit that seemed to get worse by the day. "You're so ungrateful for everything I did for you."

She hung up, unable to lie and thank him like she usually did. Clyde always called on her anniversary to remind her what a great thing he'd done, but basically this day was a reminder of something completely different. This was the day Clyde had traded away her happiness for this hell.

Leaving, though, would put Rachel in more danger now than whatever Clyde had planned. The leash that kept her tethered to her husband was his constant threat to kill her sister. Her plan to bide her time until Rachel was old enough to get away from Clyde had blown up into this existence.

"Five years, honey. Do you still think about me? Would you even recognize me and the joke I've become?" She didn't speak out loud to an imaginary Harry often, but she hadn't forgotten her. The door slamming behind her meant her little indulgence had been overheard.

"You think your life here is a joke?" Byron screamed so loud the veins in his neck stood out. "Are you too stupid to know I was the best you were going to get?" He picked up a container full of cooking utensils and threw it at her. "Clyde said you were fucked in the head, and he was right."

"All I was doing was cooking you dinner." She tensed, waiting for him to move, and trying to think of her escape route.

"Oh, right," he said sarcastically. "You're in here crying over nothing? Is that what you're doing?" He threw a chair next. "I get to put up with my dad calling me stupid all day, and then I come here and find you crying over some asshole who forgot you before she got to LSU." He moved too fast for her. "It's more than a man should have to put up with."

He struck out blindly in a frenzy, and she was in a ball on the kitchen floor before his anger burned out. She stayed there until the next morning when he demanded breakfast after an insincere apology. He'd ordered her to stay inside until the bruises faded, considering she had only herself to blame.

She'd nodded to appease him, but nothing would ever be different. *Byron's shortcomings would always be there, as would her father, his disappointments, and her tears.*

CHAPTER NINE

The house was dark when Harry stopped under the portico and let her head drop back before getting out of the Yukon. She loved what she did, but days like today took their toll. Most of the injuries would heal, but the youngest worker's leg was too far gone to save, so she'd had no choice but to amputate.

Explaining things like that to the parents and girlfriend of a twenty-year-old didn't get easier with experience, but he was alive and would walk again. That had brought things into perspective when it was reported three of the crew hadn't made it. She stretched and stopped in the kitchen for a Yoo-hoo before a shower.

Standing for sixteen hours had left her starving, but she was too tired to think about fixing anything. Right now, all she craved were a shower and sleep. She finished her drink and dropped the bottle in the trash as she stripped off her scrub top and left it on the counter.

Having houseguests made it a bad idea to strip outside her bedroom, but it was so late she doubted Rachel or Desi was awake. She left her shoes at the foot of the stairs and dropped everything else along the way so she was naked except for her underwear by the time she entered the master bedroom.

"I hope Mona's in the mood to make waffles tomorrow," she said when she closed the door. Talking to herself was a habit she'd formed to combat the loneliness of a big house.

She stretched, hearing the slight pops as everything went back into alignment. She considered skipping the shower, but hot water made her feel better and relaxed her into a better sleep. She could stay in tomorrow since her residents would cover rounds. If anything came up, they'd call, so she tried her best to clear her head as she adjusted the shower. Surprisingly, the thoughts of patients, the hospital, and surgery slipped her mind a lot more easily than thoughts of Desi ever did.

The image of that asshole with his hands around Desi's neck made her livid, but the question of why still lingered. How had they gone from what they had to Desi ending up with Simoneaux? It was like trying to shove a crawfish back into its shell.

Her knuckles were still sore and had made a marathon day of surgery no fun, but she'd promised herself to try and be the friend Desi needed. "That's all she probably wants." Right now, Desi deserved patience and a shoulder to cry on.

Then Harry could finally let go and move on.

"Oh my God," Desi whispered when the bathroom door closed, but not before she got a good look at a naked Harry outlined in the bright light.

The thrill that Harry had come to check on her died quickly with the realization of where she was. "Tony, what the hell were you thinking?" The water started in the shower, giving her a short window to fix this.

"The picture." It finally made sense. This room reflected Harry down to the old memory of the picture because it was Harry's room. She glanced to the other side of the bed and saw the stack of books, which wasn't much different than in Harry's old bedroom.

They'd spent a lot of nights reading before sleep, and she knew Harry loved it and obviously still did. Once they'd shut the light off, she'd snuggle with her head on Harry's shoulder, and she'd fall asleep to Harry's fingers trailing up and down her back.

"Stop daydreaming, idiot." She needed to call Rachel, but she doubted she could get to another bedroom before Harry was finished, even with help. As if conjuring up the worst, the water stopped.

"Great, just great." All she could do now was apologize and pretend she'd been sleeping the whole time. "Please be wearing pajamas." This was embarrassing enough, but that short glimpse of her was enough to remind her how stunning Harry could be.

The bathroom light clicked off, but there was still enough light to see the light blue T-shirt and dark sleep pants. The way Harry walked made her think she was tired, and she indulged in how good it was to be this close to her. Harry must've been exhausted since she walked to the other side of the bed, lay down, and seemed to instantly fall asleep.

"Harry," she whispered, but all she heard was deep steady breathing. "Harry," she tried again, lying still so she wouldn't startle her.

The bed was big enough that they weren't touching, but she doubted Harry'd be thrilled to wake and find her lying next to her. She took the opportunity to study Harry as much as she could in dim light. She seemed to carry a bit more muscle than the last time they were this close, as if she found the time to work out. There was also a scattering of white along her temples, and her dark curly hair was much shorter than she'd worn it in high school. But her gorgeous face had hardly changed.

"Desi." Her name spoken in a whisper made Desi stop breathing, but Harry didn't move. She had to be dreaming…about her.

"It's okay, sleep." She stayed still and stared at Harry's face. "I never thought I'd be this close to you again." It didn't take long for her to fall asleep, and it seemed like she hadn't been unconscious long when she woke to Harry snoring and the sound of someone's voice in the hallway.

"How many times have we been over this?" An elderly African American woman came into the room, and her aggravated tone made Desi almost levitate off the bed. "I'm not spending my golden years picking up after your messy ass, Harry." Despite her words, she was doing just that. "Are you this messy in surgery? You probably left your socks in somebody's chest. It's a miracle you haven't been sued."

The woman had a bundle of clothes in her hands, and she picked up the briefs with her fingertips. "Then that Tony finds you the biggest damn house in New Orleans, so I can hunt your underwear in thirty rooms instead of the ten we had before."

"Hi, you must be Mona." She spoke softly, not wanting to wake Harry, and not to freak the woman out.

The woman startled and looked up from her armful of laundry. "Hey, sorry, I didn't notice you. You can lose a horse in here with the mess that one likes to make." Mona dropped the pile next to the door and came closer. "Who might you be?"

"I'm Desi."

"Yes, of course. Harry mentioned you'd be staying with us. Can I get you anything?" Mona lifted her eyebrow to an impressive height, but it was probably over their sleeping arrangements.

"I really have to go to the bathroom, but I'm stuck. Could you get my sister? Maybe the three of us can figure out how to get me in there without breaking my other leg." She was trying to lie still, but she was about to embarrass herself.

"No need to wake Rachel. That girl sleeps like the dead, so we'd all end up with a broken leg. We'll get the big moose to help you."

"Oh no," she said, but Mona's hand came down on Harry's forehead with a light smack.

"Goddamn it, Mona. What the hell?" Harry sounded whiny as she lifted her head a few inches and squinted in the direction of the french doors.

"Harry, what have I told you about taking the Lord's name in vain in my house? Do I need to cut me a switch from outside for your misbehaving butt?" Mona pointed at her, and Desi almost laughed. "Get your lazy ass up, and help your friend to the bathroom."

"Have you finally driven to crazy town? What are you talking about?" Harry closed her eyes and relaxed against her pillow. "Give me a few more hours. I was in surgery forever yesterday."

"Harry, don't make me haul you out of there by your ear. Desi has to go."

Harry turned her head and opened her eyes, then frowned. "Hey, what are you doing here?"

"I'm so sorry, Harry. Tony didn't tell me this was your room. I assumed he put me in a guest room. If you help me, I'll move."

"Hey, slowpoke," Mona said, following up with a poke to Harry's forehead. "These are your favorite sheets, and the pretty girl's about to start an elaborate pee-pee dance."

"A call to a maid service would end all this grief, you know." Harry got up and quickly moved to Desi's side. The light blue T-shirt and navy pants really showed off Harry's body in the light of day, and Desi tried not to stare. Passion wasn't really something she experienced anymore, but Harry could make a nun want to touch and be touched. She tightened her hands into fists at her sides, not wanting to overstep what she knew in her heart Harry wanted from her.

"No sane person would put up with your ass," Mona said, turning the bathroom light on.

Harry carefully pulled the blankets back and removed the metal frame Tony had set up. "This is looking better."

"It's hideous." The row of staples down her leg was hard to look at.

"I'm a doctor, and this is healing nicely." Harry rubbed her hands together and glanced at her. "I need you to hang on to me, relax, and let me do all the work." Harry knelt on the bed and slid her arms behind Desi's back and under her knees. "Put your arms around my neck." Harry lifted her slowly and walked her into the bathroom. "I'm going to put you down, so rest all your weight on your good leg." Once she was on her feet, Harry lifted the back of her nightgown. "Keep your leg straight out," she said as she lowered her. "Call me when you're done."

Desi looked around the large bathroom, noticing the shower chair in the corner and hoping it was for her. After a week, she was ready to be clean, at least. There was also a big clawfoot tub, and she wondered how many women Harry had shared that with. Long-dormant jealousy flared to life.

"You okay?" Harry called from outside the door.

"I'm done, thanks, and sorry to be so much trouble."

"You aren't any trouble, and in a couple of weeks you'll be able to get up on your own." Harry picked her up and started for the bed.

"If I'm not too heavy, you can put me in with Rachel."

"You aren't going anywhere," Mona said, fluffing pillows. "Tony put you in here because this bathroom is the best one for your needs."

"Now that the ruler of the house has spoken, let me take another shower, and I'll get out of here. Mona can help you with a sponge bath today, but we'll figure something out so you can take a shower."

"Thank you, that'd be great."

"And I know it's not the best, but if Tony or I aren't around, you'll have to use the bedpan."

She nodded, not able to stop the heat spreading across her face. Mona got her settled and opened the doors to the balcony, cooling the room a little. "I will, I promise."

"Harry, when you're done, Serena's here, and she has Albert with her," Mona said from the door. "Enjoy the fresh air, Desi, and I'll fix you some breakfast."

"Thanks, Mona," Harry said, coming out of the closet with some clothes in her hand. "I'll be down in a minute, so keep my little buddy entertained."

"What in the hell was that girl thinking, naming that sweet child *Albert*? Might as well tape a note to his forehead the first day of school with *I'm Albert, please feel free to beat the crap out of me and steal my lunch money.*" Mona shook her head.

"Albert is Serena's father's name, and she figured he became a federal judge with it, so how bad could it be? But everyone in school will call him Butch, even if I have to go with him every day and do some coaching. He can go back to the stuffy name when he gets appointed to the bench. The Honorable Butch doesn't sound official if he takes after his grandfather."

"Thank God for you and those two boys being in that child's life. He wouldn't have any friends without the three of you," Mona said, then mumbled something when Harry threw her pajamas toward Mona's head from the safety of the bathroom.

Desi smiled and listened to the running water when Mona left. It didn't take long for Harry to walk out wearing perfectly pressed chinos and a button-down shirt. Harry looked like all the other yuppies she'd seen going into the better restaurants and stores in town whenever Byron let her out to run errands.

She often spent those times walking close to the places she and Harry used to visit, dreaming of running into her again. She'd never spotted Harry out, and after a few years she'd convinced herself that Harry had moved away from the city and started over somewhere else.

"How about some coffee? Mona's a pain in the ass but makes the best coffee," Harry said with a smile.

"I heard that," Mona yelled from somewhere outside.

"As I was saying, Mona's a pain in the ass but makes good coffee. Would you like some?"

"I'd love a cup. Could I have some toast too?" she asked. "Sorry, only if it's not too much trouble." The morning had made her forget her place. She wasn't to ask for anything.

"One toast and coffee coming up, and as an extra treat, I'll provide a nice breakfast companion to share it with."

Harry left her to wonder who that was, but she smiled when she heard the delighted squealing of a child right after Harry left. "That must be Butch," she said to herself as her eyes drifted back to the picture on the mantel.

She was staring at it when Harry came back in.

"Uncle Harry, who's that lady in your bed?" the little boy partially hidden behind Harry's legs asked.

"That's Uncle Harry's oldest friend, buddy, and her name is Miss Desi. I bet it'd make her feel better if you go and say hello." Harry tilted her head in the direction of the bed and waited. "Be careful, though— Miss Desi has a big owie."

The little boy stared up at Harry with his head cocked all the way back as if thinking about Harry's request. It didn't take long for him to walk to the bed with purpose and hold his hand out. "Hi, I'm Albert Hubert Ladding III. It's really nice to meet you."

Desi shook his hand, smiling at his impeccable manners and his outfit. The button-down blue shirt, chinos held up by a brown belt, and the bucks on his feet were a perfect match to what Harry was wearing.

"Hello, Albert, I'm Desi, and it's great to meet you." He was a beautiful child with blond hair plastered down and combed to the side, giving him a mature appearance.

"Miss Desi, my friends call me Butch. Will you call me that?" He gazed at her with such earnestness she couldn't help but smile and nod. "Great, but don't do it in front of my mommy. She yells at Uncle Harry."

"I promise I won't."

"It's a deal," Butch said, then spit in his hand and held it out to her.

"Did Uncle Harry teach you that too?" She glanced at Harry, who was looking at Butch adoringly.

"Yep, my Uncle Harry's the best."

"I think so too." She put a lot less spit on her palm before shaking his hand and getting him to laugh.

Harry smiled at the exchange before placing the tray across her lap and handing her a napkin for her wet hand. They watched Butch go to the other side of the bed and try to climb up. The bed was too high for him, so Harry picked him up and helped him off with his shoes.

"You promise—no jumping. Miss Desi's leg is hurt, so you need to be careful."

"Okay, I'll sit and have my coffee with Miss Desi. Granny Mona made me some to go with my cinnamony toast." He picked up the glass that appeared to be more milk than anything.

"Mona spoons in some coffee," Harry whispered when she leaned in to arrange the stuff on the tray and handed her a cup of coffee. "You guys going to be okay? I'm going down to talk to Butch's mom, but if he gets rowdy, fling him out the window."

"Uncle Harry," Butch said, laughing.

"We'll be okay, Uncle Harry." She watched Harry walk away, trying not to think of who Butch's mother was to Harry. She had no right, but she couldn't stop the dread that Harry had found a way to heal what she'd done to her. And that healing came with a precious bonus named Butch.

CHAPTER TEN

How do you manage to look this sexy no matter what time it is?" Harry stopped at the door to the sunroom and stared at the gorgeous blonde by the window, drinking coffee.

This was the only woman Harry had ever considered making a life with. Serena was stunning, with her pale blue eyes and gorgeous body. That's what had attracted her to Serena at first, but it hadn't taken her an hour to figure out that she wasn't simply beautiful, but smart, funny, and a compassionate soul.

She'd asked Harry for her number and hadn't wasted time before calling her. They'd shared a few dates before she figured out Serena had a bit of baggage, but by then she was willing to help carry it.

Serena's abusive prick of a husband had disappeared when Serena filed paperwork to leave him. He'd left her in debt and pregnant, but to Serena it'd been worth it to not have to deal with him again. It'd been easy to stay with Serena through the bad times, and with Kenneth's and Tony's help, they'd gotten her life back in order.

Their romantic relationship hadn't worked out, but she'd fallen in love with Butch. Harry had been there when he was born, and she'd vowed to always be a part of his life. That Serena would remain in her life as well wasn't a hardship. Solid friendships weren't something to be sniffed at.

"It's a good reminder of what you're missing out on. You could've had me, but you passed." Serena put her hand on her hip, and Harry didn't need any refreshers of how beautiful Serena was. "And Albert comes as part of the package, but you're too dense for words."

"You don't ever fight fair, sweetheart." She bent and kissed Serena hello.

"No, but no matter what I try, I can't convince you to bite." Serena kissed her again and led her to the couch. "But it's all or nothing, which raises the stakes. At least you're always honest. I forgive you because Albert loves you so much."

"I love him and his mother, even if you don't believe me."

"Oh, I believe you, but I wanted to be your wife, not your sister." Serena pulled the hair at the back of her head and laughed. "So, tell me why I'm here this early. I was out on a date last night, which ran late, so make it good."

"Wait, you're giving me a hard time when you've gotten over me already?" She pouted. "You're killing me. Is this idiot even worthy of you, and can they be trusted around Butch?"

"Will you stop calling him that? Albert Hubert is my father's name, and it's perfectly lovely."

"Having a lovely name isn't what the kid will be going for, babe. Besides, everyone calls your father Hubbie, and you know it—though, I'm not sure how that's better. Now quit complaining, and let me tell you a story." They sat close together while she updated her on Byron's latest attempt on Desi's life.

"How this guy got bail is a mystery to me. It took me hours to fix the damage he did the first time." She was getting agitated, but Serena put her hand in her shirt and scratched her stomach to calm her down, and it was working. "I say the first time, but I know there were plenty of others before. So just the first time this week."

"You should come to court with me. Your friend's story is horrible, but I've dealt with much worse." Serena kissed her cheek. "I have a good feeling about this case. The fact that she wants to press charges—that she's willing to do that, is major. If she doesn't change her mind, and that happens more than you think, we have a fighting chance. Juries have little patience when women change their minds about their abusers."

"I don't know her well enough anymore to promise that she won't backpedal. She barely looks at me when we talk."

"That's not uncommon either. I don't know how long Desi was with her abuser, but the one thing that anchored her to him was fear. She's felt that for so long that it's hard for her to trust there's no reason to be afraid anymore."

"What do you think?" She was at a loss with all this—nothing in her experience would help her understand. Real men—and real women—didn't use their fists on the women they supposedly loved.

"I think this meeting is a good idea, and that you're a good friend.

You'll need to be, to get her through this. There's still plenty of people who don't think this is a crime."

"Are those people idiots?" The memory of Desi wouldn't let her be objective. "That's ridiculous."

"I'm not disagreeing with you, honey, but domestic violence isn't an in-your-face kind of crime. It happens mostly behind closed doors, and it's not often seen or acknowledged. Once the woman shows an ounce of compassion for her abuser, it's all over."

"Like I said, I wish I could tell you that wasn't going to happen, but I'm not sure. There's no way to know what the hell this guy did, but he did a good job of breaking her. She's not the girl I knew." She gazed at Serena, knowing she'd been there once upon a time. Finding an asshole to share your life with wasn't a choice restricted to the poor and uneducated.

Serena smiled at her as if realizing where her mind had gone. "I'm okay, and Desi will be too. You know there isn't anyone who can convince her how important it is to see this through like I can."

Harry cupped Serena's cheek, remembering the night Serena had told her about her ex-husband and all he'd done. But she couldn't find the words to go with how she'd felt that night.

"I can't promise we'll win, but trying will go a long way toward building her confidence."

Harry closed her eyes when Serena leaned closer in and kissed her again. "Thanks, and thanks for agreeing to come over here. I think she'll be more comfortable in less intimidating surroundings."

"It sounded important to you. Is Desi important to you?"

Harry sat still, not knowing how best to answer the question. "A long time ago we were good friends, and one day we weren't anymore."

"One day?" Serena put her hand back in her shirt and drew lazy circles on her stomach. "What does that mean?"

"She disappeared from my life, and I haven't seen her since that day. I never knew why." She had to confess how skillful Serena was at getting information. "I'm not expecting special favors, but it'll make me feel better if she leaves here and goes as far from where I found her as we can get her. Do you understand me?"

"I do, and that's understandable, so wait down here while I talk to her. Trust me, she's not going to open up if you're in the room. There's always a fear of judgment."

"I do trust you, but call if you need something."

Serena gave her another quick kiss and stood. "We'll be fine, and

I'll send Albert down here to keep you company. You can get out that insipid gaming system I don't know anything about and rot his brain some more."

"Studies show it's good for hand-eye coordination. He can't be LSU's quarterback if he's clumsy."

"You're a riot, and I promise I'll come get you if I run into a roadblock." Serena walked with her to the stairs. "And Albert's going to be the president of the chess club, so get football right out of your head."

"The boy's going to have no friends if I let you have your way." She smiled when Serena laughed.

Whatever happened next was out of her hands, but she'd have a clear conscience. And maybe, just maybe, the old Desi would have a chance to come back to life.

❖

Desi enjoyed Butch's total attention as she told him one of the stories she used to tell Rachel when she was a toddler. His laugh lightened her heart, and she listened to him tell her all about his uncle Harry, and from his excitement, she could tell how much he loved Harry.

She stopped talking when she noticed the beautiful woman leaning on the doorframe. "Hi," she said, seeing where Butch had gotten his good looks.

"Hi." The woman winked at her, dropped her briefcase, and came in. "Have you been a good boy, Albert?"

"Yes, Mommy. Miss Desi tells the best stories. I ate all the cinnamony toast Granny made me, and I finished my coffee." He glanced back and patted her good leg. "And I didn't move much like Uncle Harry told me."

"You're the best boy." Serena came in and kissed his forehead. "Uncle Harry's waiting for you to play your secret game. Do you want to tell me what that is?"

Butch swallowed hard while shaking his head. "No, Mommy, I promised Uncle Harry I won't tell, and if I tell, we can't save the world."

"I don't want to stop you from doing that. Go on."

Butch got on his knees and hugged Desi, kissing her cheek. "Thanks for my story, Miss Desi. See you later, okay?"

"I can't wait."

He jumped down and started down the stairs like someone was chasing him. "Slow down, Albert, before you break your leg," Serena yelled while shaking her head. "Sorry, sometimes I can't help channeling my mother since Butch came along. I'm Serena Ladding— it's nice to meet you." Serena shook her hand before sitting in the chair next to the bed.

"I'm Desi Simoneaux." This woman was gorgeous, and her clothes were like nothing she owned. "I thought you didn't like anyone calling him Butch."

"It's good to keep Harry guessing, so I don't tell her everything." Serena's smile never faltered as she shrugged. "You can't let her get too smug."

"I guess," she said, not finding any reason to dislike Serena even if that was her instinct. "Harry said you work for the district attorney. Is that how you met?"

"No, we met at a party for Children's Hospital, and she was the sexiest thing I'd ever seen." Serena fanned herself at the memory, and it made Desi ill. "My asshole ex-husband had disappeared after hitting me for the last time, and I'd just found out I was pregnant. Harry was there for all of it, and she helped me find my way back to myself."

"What do you mean?" She couldn't blame Harry for falling for Serena. She was beautiful, had a career, and came with a cute kid.

"Sometimes we ignore plenty because we convince ourselves this person we love can't be all bad. He hits me, but then he says I'm sorry and he loves me." Serena sobered and folded her hands together. "After it happens enough, you think of ways to change *your* behavior, so you don't get hit again."

"Part of that is true."

Serena nodded and took a deep breath. "That's how I handled it, but everyone's story is unique to them. The only thing we have in common is that it's not our fault. You're a survivor, and you're ready to say *enough*." Serena stood and moved the tray off Desi's lap so she could sit closer. "My hope is you're ready to say *enough*."

She nodded slowly, but agreeing was like standing at the edge of a cliff with a rushing river below. Jumping might or might not kill you, but you had no other choice but the abyss. "All I want is peace. I haven't had that in so long. It's hard to remember what it's like not to be terrified all the time."

Serena plucked some tissues and handed them over. "You have

every right to that and so much more." She held her hand and waited for her to regain her composure. "Remember that I'll be with you through the entire process, as will Harry. She told me what happened at the hospital, and I want you to know Byron has been arrested and is in jail."

"He was arrested after breaking my leg. No offense, but I doubt anything will happen to him."

"I'm not here to lie to you or try and sugarcoat anything by saying this is going to be a breeze. Your husband doesn't want to go to jail, and his family probably wants it even less."

"His father is probably madder than Byron is." Big Byron, as everyone called him, was almost scarier than her husband, and he was the one who taught Byron how to treat women. "He's a scary man."

"Abusers raise abusers, Desi, so I'm not surprised. If you keep in mind that he doesn't want to pay for his crimes with jail time, you'll be better prepared for what comes next." Serena put her fingers under Desi's chin and gently lifted her head. "If he hires a good attorney, you'll be on trial as much as Byron. If his attorney is really good, the jury will gladly break your other leg."

"That's encouraging," she said and laughed humorlessly. "Where do I sign up?"

"It's only fair to warn you, but that's the defense side of things. This is going to sound obnoxious, but there's no one in the DA's office better at prosecuting abusive assholes than me. That's what I do best, and this time I want to put Byron Simoneaux away for a very long time for what he did to you." Serena appeared so intense she had a hard time looking away. "Is that what you want to do?"

"The truth is, I've been trying to get away from Byron from the day I met him, but I had nowhere to run where he wouldn't have found me and killed me." She was so tired of running, and of fearing what the day would hold. Even now, her sleep was riddled with waking up at every little creak. She doubted she could ever leave that reflex behind, or the overwhelming apprehension that was her constant companion.

"It's up to you to take that first step, and only you. But you have to be the one to decide to move forward." Serena waited as if really giving her the option to choose.

"What do I need to do?" She really didn't have a choice. There was no going back, but the future was just as terrifying.

"Let me get my pad so I can get some information." Serena sat back in the chair with a yellow legal pad in her lap. "Are you still in love with this guy?" She tapped her pen against a blank page and cocked her head slightly. "I start with that because if you are, all this is a waste of time for me and everyone who cares for you. Don't interpret that as me not wanting to help you."

"You're really blunt." This wasn't what she expected, and it sounded like a cruel joke.

"It's ripping the bandage off quickly and not meant to be rude. If you're not resolute about this, and you're waffling, we'll be back here in six months." Serena put her finger up before Desi could respond. "I should say—I'll be here in six months. If you go back, there's a chance you won't live long enough to try this again."

She chose to let the words out, words she'd been careful to keep locked away for a long time. "I don't love Byron—I never did. That's why he hits me, I think. He knows. You probably think I'm weak and stupid, but I didn't pick this life." She lifted her hands and let them drop. "My plans were different than this." She pointed to the cut on her temple.

"I understand you better than anyone, Desi, and I'm going to battle for you."

Now that the words were out, she couldn't seem to stop them. "Some days I wonder how this became my life. I'd sit and wait for him, trying to guess if the man who walked in would be the guy who tried to romance me on my daddy's porch even when I told him to go away, or the guy who liked to hit me. At first, he liked to put the bruises where they wouldn't be seen, but that didn't always work out. And then he stopped caring about that altogether."

Serena moved back to sit on the bed and took her hand. "I get that. My husband was the perfect guy while we were dating. He planned romantic dinners, got me little gifts, and made me feel special. That lasted through the proposal and the wedding. When we came home from the honeymoon, I met a completely different guy, and he made his point with his fists."

"You married someone like Byron?" That surprised her, considering how confident Serena seemed.

"He never hurt me this bad, but he did hurt me. I was married to him, and now I'm not. That's the most important part of my story." She squeezed Desi's fingers and smiled. "My experience is what makes me fight so hard."

"Thank you. Is there anything else you need to know?"

They spent thirty minutes going through her history. Serena would take care of getting the wheels of justice turning. Desi's job was to be ready to go once they got a court date. The main thing Serena wanted was for her not to change her mind.

"You're a brave woman, and I'm proud of you," Serena said once they were finished. "Everything is going to be okay."

"I don't know about that. I have no idea what I'm going to do next."

"From where you're sitting, I'd say you're off to a good start. That has to count for something."

"I don't think so. I have no skills, and I have enough scars that I'll never forget this."

"Girl, you're still young, and with a bit of calm you'll forget Byron and his family."

"Sure, it was easy for you. You have a family, Butch, and Harry. All I have are the choices I've made and Rachel. And God knows, she deserves her own life, away from all this."

"Wait." Serena leaned back. "Do you think Harry belongs to me?"

"She doesn't?"

"Granted, I wish she did, but Harry is a confirmed bachelor. There've been plenty of women who've tried to change her mind, but she's firmly in the available column." Serena laughed and tapped her on the nose. "There's only one woman in her bed, so maybe start thinking about ways to reel her in."

"If she didn't fall for you, there's no way she'd be interested in me. I mean, look at you…And we have history, but it's not good." Admitting that was like running her tongue over her razor. "I hurt her, and this is charity, me being here. It's just because she's a good person."

"It'd take me a day in the mall to make you look better than me, so follow every real estate agent's mantra—location, location, location. And you're in a great location." She patted the surface of the bed and wiggled her eyebrows.

"She's never going to forget what I did." She'd seen a softening in Harry, but any romantic feelings were a long way off.

"Wait. You're the girlfriend from high school, aren't you?" Serena pointed at her.

"Harry talked about me?" She felt the heat rise in her face, thinking of what Harry had probably said about her.

"No, never, but you've met Tony, haven't you? He didn't go into detail, but he gave me the wide brushstrokes." Serena stood and paced a little. "I was asking for advice on how to get her to commit because I'd struck out badly. It was either consult a voodoo priestess for a love potion or kidnap her, but nothing broke through Harry's very solid brick wall."

"You never asked her about the picture?" She pointed to the reminder she'd stared at all day.

"This is the first time I've breached the inner sanctum." She walked to the picture and studied it closely.

"You never slept with her?" That was hard to believe, and probably none of her business, but Serena hadn't held back on embarrassing questions.

"I didn't say that, but this is the first time I've been in her bedroom. And I've never seen her smile this wide." Serena tapped Harry's face. "Don't be jealous. We met, had an instant attraction, and when I wanted more?" She shrugged and walked back. "That's when Harry decided we should be friends for Butch's sake." She tilted her head and studied Desi. "I decided friendship was better than nothing."

Desi wished she'd had that option, but now, she didn't have any. "Harry was always my choice, but my father couldn't accept that. I did let her go, but it killed something in me, and nothing is going to revive it."

"Don't be too sure about that. Harry's been waiting for someone, and here you are."

They heard running on the stairs, which meant their talk was over, but she wished for a few more minutes. Serena had answers to questions she didn't even know how to ask.

CHAPTER ELEVEN

If you break something, I'm taking it out of your hide," Mona said loudly.

"Sorry, Granny," Butch yelled.

"I'm not talking to you, sweet boy. It's that overgrown piece of trouble chasing you," Mona said, coming in holding Butch under her arm.

"Ooh, you're in trouble, Uncle Harry."

"Story of my life, buddy." Harry put her hands in her pockets, hoping she hadn't come up too soon. "You two need more time?"

"We're done. It was nice meeting you, Desi." Serena put her hand on Desi's shoulder. "Don't hesitate to call if you have any questions or if you hear from Byron's family. I'll be in touch with the next steps."

"Thanks for talking with me."

"No need to thank me, and remember everything we discussed."

"Do you need anything?" Harry asked Desi.

"I'm good."

"I'll walk Serena out, so yell if you do."

Serena smoothed her skirt and followed her to the door. Butch laid his head on Harry's shoulder and breathed against her neck on the way down. He'd told her how much he liked Desi and wanted to stay for more stories.

"Mommy, can we stay with Uncle Harry?"

"We're having lunch with Grandma and Papa, so we have to go. I promise we'll come back soon." Serena combed his hair with her fingers when Harry put him down.

"We're going to the place with that good stuff, Uncle Harry, but you're not going." Butch sounded down about that. "Mommy won't let me lick the plate if you're not there."

"Mommy, life's too short not to lick the plate." She squatted to his level and held her hand out. "Tell Papa, and he'll help you out."

"By the time he's twenty we won't be allowed in any restaurant in the city because of you. Between you teaching him to spit in his hand and licking plates, I'm going to cut you off." Serena shook her finger at her.

"No way," Butch said loudly. "Uncle Harry's my best friend, and I have to see her."

Mona came in and waved to Butch. "Come on, and I'll pack up some cookies for Papa and Grandma."

Serena pulled her close when they were alone. "That's a special but fragile woman up there, Harry. The coming months are going to seem worse than living in a hurricane, but we need to get her into court before you take all that stuff off her leg."

"He really hurt her," she said, wanting to know what Desi had said, but she wouldn't pry.

"She's more upset about hurting you than about what happens to Byron. Don't make it worse by keeping your distance." Serena put her hands on her chest. "Find a way to forgive her. She's going to need you more than I did when we met."

"I'm not throwing her out, but you don't know what you're asking." Everyone kept telling her to give Desi a chance, but none of them understood what she'd gone through after Desi had deserted her.

Serena moved a hand over Harry's heart. "Believe me, it's killing me to admit this, but you've been waiting for this woman a long time, and the picture proves that. Don't throw away the chance to be happy over your pride."

Harry dropped into a chair and Serena sat in her lap. "I am happy."

"Your job, Tony and Kenneth, and this house aren't going to keep you warm at night, honey. I would have, but you took a hard pass on that," Serena joked. "If she wasn't important, you'd have forgotten her by now."

"I haven't forgotten, which means I haven't forgotten what happened." She wasn't going to give in so easily.

"You're good at your job because of your compassion. Desi could use some of that right now." Serena kissed her and moved her mouth to her ear. "Remember the old saying—holding on to anger is like drinking poison and expecting the other person to die."

"You're getting philosophical before lunch?" She laughed as she held Serena closer. They might not be together, but Harry treasured the companionship and connection Serena offered.

"It's true—it's time to come in from the cold, baby. If I can't have you, then I want Desi to get a shot. She's got a story to tell, and it's up to you to find out what it is." Serena kissed her again and stood as Mona and Butch came back.

"Hey, buddy." Harry picked Butch up and hugged him. "Do me a favor, okay? Be good for your mommy and skip licking the plate. I promise we'll go, just the two of us, so we can do it together."

"Deal." Butch kissed her cheek and took Mona's hand when she joined them.

"Come on, and I'll strap you in the car," Mona said.

"Thanks, Mona," Serena said, turning to Harry. "Don't run scared. I have faith in you to do the right thing."

"I love you. You know that, right?"

"I do. Albert and I love you too, and I'm always going to be your friend."

Harry held her and kissed her in a way that she hadn't in a long time. It was intimate, but it was the easiest way to finally put to rest all the things they'd never have together. There was a small part of her heart that wished Serena could be the one. They could've built something that didn't have a foundation of mistrust and pain. But she simply wasn't the one, and Harry didn't want to settle for *good enough*.

"That makes me a lucky bastard, and I'll always be here for you and Butch. I'm not sure how our talk took such a serious turn, but I don't want to lose you."

"You won't. Now let me go, so my son can scandalize everyone with his questionable table manners."

She walked Serena out and waved to Butch until they turned onto St. Charles. Mona patted her on the side as she headed to the kitchen. They'd been together from the time she was six. Mona was the one person in her life who knew her best.

"Harry, you must've died some horrible way in a past life, like being burned at the stake for a crime you didn't do." Mona piled ingredients on the counter for lunch.

"What do you mean?" She gazed out at the yard and wished she had some pressing matter at the hospital to escape to without guilt.

"I've never seen anyone in this world so blessed to be loved by so many special women." Mona stood at the sink filling a pot with water.

"Serena loves you, but she's somewhat settled with a family and good friends to support her." The water stopped, and Harry startled when Mona gripped her by the bicep. "That young woman up there is lost, though, and she needs you more than anyone."

"You were there, Mona," she said, hugging Mona no differently than she would her mother. "How can you say that?"

"I say it because me and your mama didn't raise a coward. Punishing Desi now for something that happened years ago would amount to nothing but cruelty." Mona patted her back and hummed. "You, my precious child, will never be cruel, and if you are, there's a big spoon in the drawer with your name on it, and I won't hesitate to take it to your backside."

She smiled and held Mona tighter, kissing the top of her head. "Thanks, and I love you too."

❖

Desi dozed for an hour and smiled when she found Rachel lying next to her when she opened her eyes. "Hey, you're finished with work?"

"I am, but today was my blue hair brigade day, and I hate when it ends. They have the best gossip on everyone in town." Rachel took Desi's hand and kissed her fingers. "How was your day?"

"I talked to Serena Ladding from the DA's office and agreed to press charges against Byron." She told Rachel everything she talked to Serena about and what came next. "He's going to go ballistic when he gets out, but you're right. I can't go back."

"He deserves to be buried to his neck in hot lava and forgotten for the years of hell he's given you. Promise me you won't change your mind."

She nodded slowly. "I will, if you promise to be careful. You know how Byron's family can be, and his father must be in a wild rage by now."

"It's a shame you can't talk your mother-in-law into coming with us. That poor woman has had a shitty life, and it's only going to keep being crappy unless Big Byron drops dead." Rachel threaded their fingers together and shivered. "You'd think the big slob would've already, but life isn't fair."

"That's kind of what Serena said, but nothing will change unless

I'm willing to take the steps to do it." She was tired of just lying there, but her leg was throbbing.

"The whole family's screwed up, and if neither of us ever sees them again, I won't shed any tears over it." Rachel rolled to her back and closed her eyes. "Have you and Harry talked any?"

"This morning a little, but Serena visited longer." Her slight hesitation made Rachel turn her head and stare at her. "She told me they dated."

"Harry told you she slept with this woman?"

"No…no." She didn't want Rachel hunting Harry down. "Serena told me when I asked." The story about where Harry slept last night would have to be part of the narrative. "She was really nice, taking me to the bathroom when we woke up, and setting up that meeting."

"Why would Harry sleep with you? I know you guys got horizontal every chance you got in high school, but this is fast."

She pointed to the picture. "Tony put me in her room instead of one of the guest rooms, so I'm the one who doesn't belong." They both stared at the picture, and she had no doubt Rachel remembered everything about that day, as she'd been sitting with Harry's parents.

"I was embarrassed Clyde didn't take off to see you graduate," Rachel admitted, "but we had Harry and her parents."

"I wasn't embarrassed. I had everyone who mattered there, and it was a great day. Better, really, without him there. There were so many dreams I had then." She dropped her attention to her leg. "But Byron didn't want a dreamer."

"Byron was like his father—he wanted a slave and a punching bag. Don't ever use him as a gauge for what your life should be."

She nodded and jumped a little when she heard the knock. Harry stood outside, which seemed ridiculous since this was her room. "Hey," she said softly, trying her best to maintain eye contact. If she couldn't do it with Harry, she'd never make it through a trial.

"I don't want to interrupt, but it's a nice day outside." Harry looked strangely shy. "Would you like to sit on the veranda?"

"If you want, you can move me in with Rachel and take your room back. I keep telling you I don't want to be any trouble." She couldn't seem to get her voice to work at a normal level whenever Harry was in the room, and from the way she came closer, she was having trouble hearing her.

"That wasn't my question, and you don't want to put me in Mona's doghouse, do you?" Harry sat next to the bed and cocked her head. "This is the best bedroom with the easiest access to the bathroom, and anywhere else, you'd miss out on the great view outside. Now, how about a change of scenery?"

"Sure," she agreed, if only to keep Harry talking to her like she wasn't angry.

"Give me a minute, and it'll be the same drill as this morning. Speaking of, do you need a bathroom run before we head outside?" Harry lifted her hand before she could say anything. "Don't turn me down because you think you're pestering me. How about we call a truce?"

"What do you mean?" She wanted an answer, but she also needed to go to the bathroom, now that she'd mentioned it.

"We were friends once, so maybe we should try that route again." Harry stood and, with Rachel's help, pulled the blanket back. It didn't seem like a hard thing for Harry to pick her up and carry her like before. Although, like before, it was just as embarrassing.

This time Rachel followed them and stayed with her while Harry went to get the veranda ready. It was a miracle that Harry was trying, and having Harry as a friend would be nice. And having Rachel in the bathroom with her was way less humiliating.

"You guys ready?" Harry asked as Rachel finished helping her clean up. Every movement, every tiny twist hurt, and by the time they were done, she was exhausted again. "Your chariot awaits."

The veranda had a covered section and a semicircular open area that overlooked the garden at the side of the house. Harry had fixed a chaise longue with pillows and blankets to keep her warm from the slight chill. The spot was beautiful and peaceful, and it brought on more tears.

"Hey, you okay?" Harry carefully put her down but appeared concerned. "Are you in pain?"

She shook her head as she took some breaths trying to calm down. There was no easy way to explain to the person who'd always loved doing special things for her that she'd settled for someone else, who didn't believe in frivolous things. When you caused so much pain, there was no way back to the one person who made life worthwhile.

"Come on, tell me what's wrong." Harry sounded so compassionate, so genuine. "You're safe here, and you know I won't let anything happen to you."

"Why?" She had to ask, even if the answer scared the hell out of her, and she had no idea how to handle Harry's compassion.

"Why what?" Harry reached out a tentative hand and wiped the tears off her cheeks.

"Why would you do that for me after everything? I don't deserve you being this nice to me."

Harry sat back on her feet and sighed. "I'm sorry—I'm not sure how to answer that. We don't have to talk about it, but I'm sure you had your reasons. Whatever those were, you've paid enough of a toll in pain, and I'm not going to pile on to that."

"You deserve to be happy with someone like Serena—and Butch." She noticed that Rachel had disappeared sometime after she started talking to Harry and wondered why. "She fits with you."

"Did she tell you that?" Harry sounded more curious than angry, and it gave Desi some courage.

"No," she said quickly.

"Serena's a good friend, and I love that little boy, but we don't fit as anything but friends. You don't have to worry about stepping on any toes here, Desi. I chose a job that thrives on its unpredictability. That's the commitment I made, and it hasn't left room for anything else." Harry moved to sit across from her. "Up to now, it would've been selfish to try."

"Serena said all that, but maybe you should try and work it out. Butch loves you, and she sounded interested enough." She stopped when Harry shook her head. "I'm sorry, I didn't mean to tell you what to do."

"Let's set some ground rules." Harry leaned forward, tapping her fingers together between her knees. "Stop apologizing for things that aren't your fault, and start asking for the things you most want."

"You don't...what I mean is...I'm not going to take advantage. Once I get better—"

"Let's take it slow." Harry smiled and shook her head some more. "I don't want you to rush and mess up my repair job." Harry stopped and lost her smile, and she appeared to have thought of something that drained her good mood. "I'm not keeping you from something, am I? Do you and Byron have children? I'm an idiot for not asking before now."

"No," she said more emphatically than she meant to. "I never wanted children with him. I took birth control religiously to prevent that mistake. There was no way I would've given him another target to hit, and I would've let him kill me before that happened." It was blunt, but true.

"I'm not sure what to say, but not being tethered to him by children will make it easier to leave him behind." Harry brushed Desi's hair back, keeping her hands at the back of her neck. "You're still young enough to start over, Desi, and you deserve that."

"It's not something I ever thought I'd get the chance to do. Starting over is a foreign concept at this point." She stared at Harry, trying to figure out what she was thinking.

"You have a chance now, and you also have people who'll help you along the way. I'll keep telling you that until you believe it."

"Harry?" She wanted to talk to Harry about all the stuff between them but didn't think she could come up with the words. "You asked me why."

"I did, but take your time. The last thing you need is someone pushing you, so I'll give you some space to make that decision, and I'll be okay even if the right time never comes." Harry slid her hands back into her pockets. "If you need anything, let Mona know."

"Thank you, but I'll be happy to move if you want your space back."

"Circular conversations are never fun, so just accept you're in the right place, and we're doing this. I'm only going for a run, so you're free to stay out here, or I can take you back in."

"I'll stay."

Harry finally gave her the kind of smile she remembered. "That's good news."

CHAPTER TWELVE

Mona and Rachel came out and sat with Desi, bringing a pot of tea with them.

"What are you thinking so hard about, baby?" Mona asked, putting a cup in her hand.

"Nothing." She wasn't used to having anyone but Rachel to talk to, so the days since the assault had her saying more than she had in years. Silence and obedience had saved her plenty of beatings because they'd made her invisible. "It's good to finally meet you. I heard about you for years, but surprisingly we never crossed paths."

Mona sat close to her and held her hand and didn't seem to mind her changing the subject. She seemed so kind, and being with her brought back vague memories of her mother, but those were like trying to hug air. Nothing concrete ever formed. The only parent she could remember was Clyde, but him she wanted to forget.

"You and you"—Mona pointed to Rachel—"mostly came to the house on the weekends or at night when I was gone. Rosa, Harry's mama, always insisted I take the weekends off to be with my kids. I've been chasing Harry and her brother for years, and they took tons of patience, but they're like my own."

"It's wonderful you're still with her," Rachel said, taking Mona's other hand.

"Yeah, once they both left for all that schooling they got, I figured Rosa would let me go, but I kept coming, and she kept welcoming me." Mona shook her head and smiled as if enjoying all the reminiscing. "I missed Harry something awful when she left for school, but she came home at least twice a month with a bag of laundry."

"She brought her laundry?" Rachel asked, laughing along with Desi.

"Girl, she did her own laundry, but I'd come over and help her fold and listen to what was happening. We did that until she came home for her residency. Once she started working, Dr. Francisco was ready for retirement, and Harry asked me to come live with her." She squeezed her hand. "My girls were gone by then, and Harry bought a place close to here."

"You didn't want to retire as well?" she asked.

"Retirement was boring as hell, and it was nice to have my girl back."

"Thank you for taking such good care of her." Desi looked at Mona and choked up. "I'm sure she told you—"

"Forget all that now, baby. You had your reasons, and from what Harry's told me about you from the beginning, it had to have been something important." Mona glanced between her and Rachel and didn't let go of either of their hands.

"It was," Rachel said.

Desi wasn't ready to talk about it and simply traced the pattern in the blanket.

"That's good enough for me then." Mona took her empty cup and tucked the blanket around Desi's legs. "Let me go check on my gumbo, and you two take it easy. Oh, and if you have any laundry, leave it out tomorrow. I'll do it with Harry's when the maid cleans upstairs." Mona spread her arms out and snapped her fingers. "This place is huge, and Harry says she don't want me doing anything but supervising in my own house."

"She always had a good heart, and she still does."

"Harry's my family, and my girls think the same thing." She grinned, the lines around her eyes deepening. "She thinks I don't know, but she's paying for my grandkids to go to private school. Public school was good enough for her, but my babies are wearing fancy uniforms and working their way to college."

"That's nice of her, and thanks for the laundry offer, but we don't want to put you out." Rachel said what Desi was thinking.

"It's more in line with putting your dirty drawers out, sweetie, and someone puts them in the washer. This is your home now, so live with the fact that it comes with some perks. Your laundry and housekeeping duties are behind you." Mona slapped her thighs and stood. "Now relax and enjoy the nice view while I take care of dinner. I'm making Harry's favorite, so hopefully everyone's in the mood for pork roast and lima beans."

"That sounds delicious, but I don't remember that being Harry's favorite," Rachel said.

"Harry's smarter than your average honey bear," Mona said winking. "Everything I make is her favorite according to her, but I think she says it to keep me cooking."

"That's hilarious." Rachel moved to the seat Mona had vacated when Mona walked off. "What's going on in your head?"

"Nothing." Desi ran her hand along the soft blanket and didn't look up.

"Excuse me, but that's an answer you give someone who doesn't know you. That is in no way me, so cut the shit and talk to me."

The best reward for all her sacrifices was seeing what a confident woman Rachel was. Her quick wit and bold personality were the reasons she was booked solid months out—it was like her regulars loved sitting in a chair being told off by her beautiful sister as she did their hair. Despite what they'd lived through, and Rachel staying with her and Byron, she'd made a success of herself.

"Being here is every wish I have ever had come true, but it's also fate's worst joke." She glanced out at the expansive yard, further proof of Harry's success and the very different lives they'd led.

"That makes no sense."

"The day we graduated was the beginning of a new life for us. Harry and I had plans," she said, thinking of all the nights they'd talked about what came next. No more hiding what they meant to each other, no more sneaking around to be together, and the rest of their lives to build on the love they'd found early. "She'd go to school, I'd go to work, and we'd live for the weekends. I'd go up whenever I had the chance to watch her play, and we'd get to spend time together. Once she came back to the city for medical school, the three of us would get a place until we could buy our first home and start a family."

"And if it hadn't been for your pesky little sister, you would've had that." Rachel's tone was, as always, remorseful when it came to this subject.

"That's not what I meant, so *you* cut the shit." That made Rachel laugh. "I had something to look forward to back then, but instead I stood still—actually, I regressed. Harry, though…" She didn't know how to articulate it.

"Harry moved on? Is that what you're saying? She moved on and left you behind."

"That's the easiest explanation. I used to fit into her life, but now the gap is too wide to cross." She laughed at the absurd thought. "Listen to me. The last thing Harry's going to do is fall in love with me. I'm an embarrassment to myself, and I would be to her. Add to that how upset she is with me, and I doubt we'll come out of this as friends, even if she's the one who raised the possibility."

"I hate to be the one to break it to you, but I seriously doubt Harry ever stopped loving you."

"Don't talk crazy."

"The blue hair brigade, at least some of them, have daughters and granddaughters. Today when I brought up her name, some of them were more than happy to dish on the charming but elusive Dr. Basantes."

"What does that have to do with anything?"

"I'm sorry, but are you blind? Harry's a catch, and there's been plenty of interest in bagging her into a happily ever after situation through the years." Rachel seemed to get into the gossip as she leaned forward. "It sounds like she turns even the straightest of heads, but Harry is a perpetual dater. Commitment isn't in the cards no matter how hard those women try."

"And you think that's because of me?" She laughed at how ludicrous that was. "We've covered this subject, and nothing's changed to make the story turn out any differently. She simply hasn't found the right person yet."

"Stop with the pessimism, babe. Start finding the glass half full. Hell, start with finding a glass in general. We'll worry about how full it is once you've got one. You're the worst when it comes to seeing what's right in front of your face." Rachel kissed her cheek and stood. "Let me go get our laundry together, and I'll come back out. Take a nap while I'm gone, and dream of good things. You look tired."

"Thanks for trying to make me feel better."

"Did it work?" Rachel put her hands on her hips.

"It did, and I love that you're my sister." That was the thing she'd built on. No matter what happened next, she had Rachel, and that would be enough.

❖

"Hey." Harry spoke softly, trying not to startle Desi. She'd watched her sleep for a few minutes trying not to remember how many times she'd done that in the past. That, along with everything she tried not to do when it came to *not* thinking about Desi, was futile. Her mind had given itself free rein, and the memories were bombarding her.

"Hey." Desi blinked a few times as if chasing sleep away and smiled at her.

"You ready to head inside?" She squatted next to the chair and felt an overwhelming urge to protect this woman who'd done more damage to her heart than anyone in her life. Desi, she had to admit, was the definition of defeated, and it wrecked her to see what someone so special had become.

"Yes please. It's starting to get chilly out here." Desi pulled the blanket under her chin and shivered.

"Give me a second to grab a clean shirt, so I don't get you all sweaty."

"That's okay, I don't mind." It was like Desi was forcing herself to keep eye contact and it made her think of Serena when they'd first met.

"You deserve better, so hang tight."

She'd run the track in Audubon Park twice before stopping and watching the ducks. This was one of the first days she'd taken off in two months, and the downtime had given her nowhere to hide from all the crap running amok in her head. Everything Serena had said resonated, but really it'd been her early days with Serena that had made her think.

If she did it once, she could do it again. She'd helped Serena, and she could help Desi. Mona was right—she was neither cruel nor a coward. She stripped off her wet shirt and changed, determined to try and let go of the anger when it came to her past.

"If you like it out here, let me know, and I'll set you up whenever you like." She knelt and picked Desi up, pressing her against her chest. "I don't want you to go stir crazy inside."

"Your yard is beautiful," Desi said. It wasn't much better than talking about the weather.

"Just wait until spring. There are enough bulbs out there to carpet the yard with color." She walked them inside, and gently put Desi down, slowly pulling her hands free. "Need the restroom?"

"Not yet."

"I'll grab a shower, then have Mona and Rachel come up and help you with a sponge bath if that's okay with you."

"I don't—" Desi stopped talking when Harry lifted her hand.

"Sorry, I don't want to be rude and interrupt you, but we agreed—no more apologizing." She smiled to take any sting out of the statement.

Her life revolved around being focused in all things, and these awkward stilted streams of conversation were something she was ready to be done with.

"Okay, sorry," Desi said clearly unable to help herself, but she did laugh along with Harry.

"It'll get easier." She headed for another shower but didn't linger, and Mona and Rachel were setting up when she came out. That gave her the opportunity to escape to the office downstairs to check in with the hospitals she split her time between. She spent the remainder of the afternoon reading medical journals and dictating patient notes.

"Stop hiding and help us carry stuff upstairs. I don't want Desi eating alone." Mona clapped her hands when she didn't stand quickly enough.

Dinner was a bit more relaxed but only because Mona peppered the sisters with questions about their childhoods. The great talent Mona had that led the long list of things she was good at was getting people to talk about themselves. Granted, Rachel carried most of the conversation, but Desi wasn't completely quiet.

"Thank you for this, Mona." Desi pointed to her empty plate. "It was delicious."

"Yes, Mona, thank you," Rachel said. "I'll do the dishes since you cooked."

"That's the kind of help I won't turn down." Mona grabbed their plates and followed Rachel out.

They were left alone, and Harry went through what would become their nighttime routine. "It's getting late, so let me get your meds, and you can get some rest."

"I've napped all day, and I'm still tired."

She looked it, but Harry wasn't about to say that. "You've been through more trauma in a few days than most people experience in a lifetime. Give your body a chance to heal by not pushing it." She handed over two pills and got the blanket settled around Desi's legs.

"Thank you."

"I'll be right next door if you need anything. Don't be shy about calling if you need to get up." Harry smiled and grabbed her pajamas.

"Are you sure you don't want me to move? I hate that I'm putting you out."

"You're still stubborn," she said and chuckled. "I've learned to sleep anywhere, so stop worrying. We both need some rest, so close your eyes and count sheep."

"Good night, and thank you for everything."

The old house creaked in the night, and to Harry it sounded like someone trying to deal with old joints. There was still plenty of life left in the place. Having to put up with the few headaches that came with an old house was better than settling for a new one with no character. Listening to the noise that broke the silence was how she went to sleep most nights, but all she could do now was stare at the ceiling.

Confusion in her personal life was something she wanted to leave in her past. She'd been there, and it'd taken a lot of work to straighten herself out when Desi had disappeared. She had no desire to repeat the process. It wasn't that she was unfeeling when it came to Desi's problems, but to her, this unexpected tableau was simply an exercise in patience.

If she took this one day at a time, it wouldn't be long before daylight would be visible in the dark tunnel she was stuck in. She punched her pillow a few times and rolled onto her side. "Stop with the overthinking," she whispered as she closed her eyes.

She had no sense of time when she woke up again, and she rubbed her face with her hands, trying to figure out a noise that was different from the normal house sounds. It was faint and she couldn't pinpoint it, so she got up and opened her door.

"What the hell?" The moaning had to be Desi, and she barely second-guessed herself before opening the door.

Desi was moving her head from side to side, but it didn't appear to be from pain, since she was still sleeping. At least, she thought Desi was sleeping when her hands came up as if she was trying to protect herself from an invisible attacker.

She debated for a moment about waking Rachel, but instead she moved closer and took one of Desi's hands to keep her from injuring herself. She wanted to gently wake her, but she let go when Desi's eyes opened, and Desi shrank away from her as if she was terrified.

"Please," Desi said, sounding like a wounded animal. "Please… don't hurt me anymore."

The pleading was heartbreaking, and the need to make it better took over. "Desi, it's okay. It's Harry and you're safe." She didn't touch Desi again, but she didn't move away either. "Wake up. I don't want you to move wrong and injure your leg."

Desi blinked furiously and stopped moving. The death grip she had on the blanket slowly relaxed. "Harry, I'm so sorry I disturbed you."

"Forget about that. Are you okay?" She sat on the bed just able to make out Desi's features in the low lighting coming from outside. There was a craving in her to take away the pain by holding Desi, but she resisted. Desi was in pain, but so was she, and she was loath to let hers go. Holding on to the memories no matter how hurtful had saved her from adding to the misery of the past.

"Nightmare." Desi took a deep breath and looked at her. "He kept getting closer, and I couldn't get away."

"Right now, there's no way he can get anywhere near you, and I'll help you do what you have to, so that'll be true forever." Harry stood and adjusted the blankets, mostly because she wanted to reach for Desi and needed to do something else with her hands. "Dreams are hard to run from, but try and get some sleep."

"Thank you." Desi seemed better. "Could you…"

"It's okay to ask. Please," she said, needing Desi to ask for something. She was aware that the desire was ridiculous—she was aware of that, but it didn't negate the truth of it. She'd spent years trying to vilify the memory of this woman, but it was turning out she couldn't.

Desi's demeanor wasn't some ruse to soften her up or to gain sympathy. No one could fake this abject fear. It was time to bring her in from the cold. If she could do that, it'd finally be Desi who'd warm the parts of her heart she'd abandoned.

"You don't have to, but would you sit with me for a little while?"

"That's an easy request." She sat on the bed but didn't touch Desi, not wanting to push things. "Do you want to talk about it?"

"It's weird to dream about him, but it's even harder not to."

"What do you mean?" She noticed Desi wasn't making eye contact again, so she moved to the vacant side of the bed to get out of her line of sight and make it easier on her.

"That was my life for so long that my dreams were the only place I could get away from him. It's the only place where…"

She was getting used to Desi's voice fading away, but this time she wanted to know. Desi's story was one she needed to hear to make sense of all this. "Where what?" she asked softly taking her hand. "I won't judge you, and it's okay to tell me."

"It's the only place you were." Desi's admission came in a rush. "He always won, though. Then my memories of you, of having someone to help me, faded too. I was stuck there, and all I could do was wait to die."

"Will you do something for me?"

"If I can." Desi turned her head, and she appeared almost hopeful.

"Tell me why. Please, I want to understand."

Desi stared at her for the longest time, and it seemed like she was making some life-altering decision. "Do you remember the day we graduated?"

"Yes," she said, because that day was by far her worst, even if it hadn't seemed like it at the time.

Desi took a deep, shuddering breath, her fists closed around the blanket, and she started talking.

It was graduation day, and she couldn't have been more excited. "Are you sure you don't want to come over tonight?" Harry asked as they got dressed.

They'd spent the night together at Harry's house with Rachel in Harry's brother's old room. Her mom had given Rachel the space so she could study for exams, but they were all taking a break for her and Harry's graduation later that afternoon. Desi was glad to be done with school. She'd been searching the classifieds for a job that would pay more than minimum wage, so she could start saving for school.

"Rachel has school tomorrow, baby, and Daddy's not coming to graduation because we're here so much. He's already complaining about me not being there to cook for him. Let's not push it." She put her arms around Harry's neck and pulled her head down. "You could always come over once we're through with dinner with your family and keep me company."

"I'd love to. It's making me nuts that I won't see you for days at a time," Harry said and kissed her, picking her up until her feet left the ground.

"Don't remind me, but let's get dressed before anyone comes looking for us."

Their graduation ceremony was long because their class was huge, but the best part was watching Harry give the commencement speech. She looked good in the dark blue cap and gown, and Desi daydreamed about seeing her in the deep purple and gold of LSU when she attended Harry's college graduation.

Rachel and the Basantes clan cheered when she walked across the stage, having graduated with honors with Harry's help, and they all had dinner at Blanchard's to celebrate the day. She'd blushed when Harry's mother handed over a jewelry box with a circular diamond pendant on a gold chain as a thank you for being the person who made Harry's life complete. They hadn't told Harry's parents just how complete she'd made Harry's life, but she figured Rosa Basantes was no fool. Harry being gay wouldn't be an issue, but Cuban mothers weren't big on their kids having sex, so they'd kept it subtle.

"We only have a week before you go," she said to Harry as they sat outside on their porch swing. She'd turned off the light outside so she could sit in Harry's lap.

"Why don't you ask your dad, and you and Rachel can come with me when I move into my dorm room. My parents can drive you both back, and you can see where I'll be living." Harry kissed the side of her neck as she ran her hand up and down her thigh. "You're the poet in this relationship, and I'm sure my description won't be very good if I put it in a letter or something."

"I'll ask, but right now all I want is for you to kiss me." They had a few hours before her father got home, and she didn't want to waste any time.

Their touches and kisses got more heated than they should've, but both of them had their impending separation on their minds and nothing else. Harry finally pulled away and pressed her forehead to hers. "Honey, I either have to carry you inside and strip you naked or go."

"Will you come by in the morning and get me once Rachel heads to school? We can check out some jobs I have in mind, and then we could go somewhere private, so think of someplace."

"You got it. I love you."

She kissed Harry again and held her tight. "I love you too, and I'll miss you." Harry waved one last time as she drove off, and she caught sight of movement on the sidewalk. The sight of her father made her feel like someone had injected her with cold water. How much had he seen?

"Daddy, what are you doing here so early?" Even in the low light she noticed two things. There was vomit on his shirt and rage in his eyes. As an answer he hit her so hard it knocked her off her feet, and then he dragged her inside by her hair.

For the first time since she could remember, her father had left work because he was sick, and he'd stayed in the shadows until Harry had left. Rachel tried to intervene, but he slapped her away and kept at Desi until her eyes had swollen shut and she could taste the blood as it pooled in her mouth.

"You're going to keep your ass in this house, and if you see that bitch again, I'm going to kill you and your sister, and then I'll go after that bitch," Clyde screamed, hitting her one more time.

Rachel tended to her wounds that night, and neither of them made a sound when Harry knocked the next day and talked to her father. From the way he'd lost control the night before, Desi had believed he'd kill them all, and she loved Harry too much to lose her to her father's bigotry. Clyde might've only been a bartender, but he worked for Big Gino Bracato, the head of the Bracato mob family, doing more than pouring drinks. No one, not even the police, could help them if her father really wanted to carry out his threats.

He kept them locked inside for days, and every day Harry called and came by as if knowing something was wrong. The school demanded Rachel's return or they'd have to fail her for the year, so Clyde let her go with plenty of threats to keep her mouth shut, and he made sure she went to school and came straight home, even calling in sick to work so he was there when she was done. He threatened to kill Desi if Rachel tried to contact Harry or anyone else, and there was no question he'd follow through, so Rachel avoided everyone, especially Harry. Once Rachel was finished with her exams, he sent her to stay with his mother so he could deal with Desi alone. He continued to beat her to the point everything hurt, and he stayed put to make sure she had no contact with Harry.

He answered the phone and sounded nice as he put Harry off again. "If I catch you crying over that big bitch again, I'm going to give you good reason to cry, you understand me?" Clyde said as he slammed the phone down. "No fucking kid of mine is going to be some queer, so shut the fuck up. I'm tired of hearing you go on about the great love of your life. What a damn joke."

"I promised you I wouldn't see her anymore, but let me just talk to her and explain," she said. Clyde slapped the side of her head so hard it made her ear ring.

"I give you this, Desiree—you're a slow learner, so let me explain something to you." Clyde smacked the top of her head. "If you want to be with her that bad, get the fuck out of my house, but Rachel stays with me. Once you go, you'll be dead to me, but she's too young to leave without me calling the police."

"What are you talking about?"

"I'll tell the cops Rachel's a runaway, and they're going to side with me. You and your bitch can live happily ever after, but I'm going to make sure Rachel knows what's expected of her. I'm going to teach those lessons personally, and there's shit you can do about it. I'll make goddamn sure she knows what a woman should be."

The thought was sickening. "I promise I won't see her again, but Harry deserves to hear it from me," she said as she stood, her legs shaking.

"No, Desiree, you promised a clean break, and I'm going to keep my eye on your ass. If I catch you going behind my back, I'll either beat this sick shit out of you, or leave with your sister to where you'll never find either of us," Clyde said as he slapped her to the floor again. "Once I'm through with that stupid sister of yours, she'll know what it's like to have a real man. Hell, it's something I should've taught you once your mama was gone. I should have put a stop to you spending time with that uppity family years ago too. You stay away from her, or I'll make sure she never makes it to that fancy school."

"Please, Daddy, I gave you my word."

"Stop whining, and get your ass up. I told you—Byron's picking you up at six to show you a good time. You want me to leave your sister alone?" He stood over her and she nodded. "Then take that boy up on his offer. He even came by and asked for your hand. That's what real men do."

Byron showed up at their house and gladly took her out, even with the bruises and cuts on her face. She'd wondered what kind of person ignored that, until she didn't answer one of his questions fast enough and learned the truth. She never told her father that Byron hit even harder than he did. Her father and Byron had the same ideas about women. They thought if you hit hard enough, and often enough, women would follow their rules.

"Please, I'll do whatever you want, but I'm not ready."

No one got married after two weeks, there was that, and also she loathed Byron Simoneaux as much as she loved Harry, but Clyde didn't care. Clyde's reaction to her relationship with Harry seemed over the top, but he had always been an angry man whose wife had died, leaving him with her and Rachel. That had been a responsibility he didn't seem to want. His rage left her with no doubt he'd gladly kill her and dump her somewhere without any guilt or remorse, rather than live with the shame of a gay kid. She'd shivered when he'd told her about the times he'd done jobs like that for Big Gino, and he hadn't gotten caught yet.

They'd never had a close relationship, but it hadn't taken her long to learn to totally fear him. She'd been afraid of him as long as she could remember. Harry, she knew, would give her a place to stay to keep her safe, but she believed him when he threatened Rachel. She could leave, but it'd be at the sacrifice of her sister, and she couldn't do it. Rachel wasn't to blame for her choices, but she'd pay the price for them.

"You think I care if you're ready?" Clyde took a step toward her and she lowered her head, prepared to protect herself. "I want you out of here but close enough I can keep an eye on you, and Byron's willing to take you, so you're to do what I say. Or I could make your sister marry him…"

"I can stay and take care of both of you." She tried again. "If you want, I can even get a job to help you out with money, but I don't love Byron." The pain of the punch to her ribs taught her that agreeing was the only way to keep him from hitting her, so that's what she'd done from that day on. At least Rachel would be safe, and when her sister was old enough, they would both find Harry and beg her to take them back.

If she lived that long.

❖

"I didn't know what else to do," Desi said, finishing her story through her tears. "I was completely trapped, and if I reached out for help, I could get us all killed. I never told you who Clyde worked for, but Bracato was a scary man, and I believed Clyde when he told me exactly what some of his job duties were."

Harry had stayed quiet, not wanting to add any pressure, but the guilt was starting to choke her. "You went through all of that because of me? Oh my God." She pressed the heel of her hand to her forehead. "I shouldn't have walked away. I should have kept pounding on that door until I knew what was going on."

"Harry, no." Desi wiped her face with one hand and grabbed for Harry's hand with the other. "What I finally had to accept was the only person to blame was Clyde. When he died, and I still stayed…That's on me, not you. None of this is your fault."

"The hell it isn't. I shouldn't have had my hands all over you out there, so don't tell me it's not my fault." She'd been so busy blaming and vilifying Desi when all she'd done was try and keep her safe. Desi had sacrificed so much to keep Clyde from coming after her. She couldn't help the tears that started out of shame.

"It's not, though." Desi tugged on her hand. "The truth is it never made any sense to me. It's not like he ever cared that much about either Rachel or me, and I never understood why he gave a damn. It's like a switch flipped and he went crazy." Desi sandwiched her hand between hers and it made her smile. "You have to know how much I loved you, but I couldn't do that to Rachel, or to you."

"He put you through all this just because we loved each other?" She wanted to run and hit something, but she wouldn't do that to Desi. "I'm so sorry, Desi."

"You have nothing to be sorry for except maybe meeting me in the first place." Desi shook her head and went on. "And he didn't do it just because we loved each other. I don't really understand what pushed him over the edge, but I'm sure it was more than you and I being together." She shrugged slightly. "I know how badly I hurt you, but Clyde made it impossible for me not to believe his threats. If anyone has to be sorry, it's me."

"No, honey. You're the hero in this story." She put her arm around Desi when that made her cry harder. "If you let me, I won't allow anyone to hurt you like that again."

"Don't you see, though?" Desi cried against her chest. "I knew back then you'd keep us both safe, but I was too afraid to even try. You and Rachel were my only family, and I left you behind."

"No," she said softly but adamantly. "I remember what a crappy parent he was, and Rachel's your sister. Keeping her safe isn't something I'm going to hold against you."

"You don't have to forgive me, Harry. I can't forgive myself for how I treated you, but now that the thought of talking to you—of seeing you again, someday—kept me from going insane." Desi lifted her head and really looked at her. "I never forgot you, and you were the love of my life. You probably don't want to hear that, but it's true."

"It's me who needs to ask forgiveness. I've wasted so much time being angry when I should've been looking for you and Rachel. I shouldn't have stopped until I knew exactly what had happened." She wanted to laugh at her mom's voice in her head, reminding her there were always two sides to every story.

"Harry, when I saw you in the emergency room, I thought I'd woken up from a nightmare. Like with Rachel, all that mattered was that you were okay. I wouldn't change what I did if I had to make the same choices for the same reasons again."

"You didn't deserve all this, and I should've known. There's no way I would've left you there." That Desi thought she had to endure what she had for the two people most important to her was going to be hard to live with.

"I know that, but really the most important thing to me is that you believe me. After what Clyde made me do, I didn't think you'd forgive me."

"That's not an issue, but I'm really sorry for the way I've acted from that first moment." She shook her head, trying not to cry. "No, I was a complete ass, and I'm sorry."

"You haven't been any such thing, and you took us in even though you were mad. It makes me happy that you're still the caring soul I loved."

Desi squeezed her hand, and Harry couldn't help but notice the fading bruise on her temple. It was in that yellow-green phase, but it didn't take away from Desi's beauty.

"You've suffered more than anyone should, but you aren't alone anymore." She hugged Desi closer, still angry, but more because of everything that had been stolen from them. "If you want, I'll stand by you for the duration."

"That's too much to ask, but thank you." Desi laid her head against her chest. "Anything worth having is worth all the pain you have to endure to keep it safe, but I have to admit I couldn't handle it anymore."

"Then we'll do whatever it takes to make sure you'll be free of all that. All I need is your promise to talk to me whenever you need to." There was no way she'd lose Desi again to the built-up despair of what she'd lived through. "We have the time to be friends again, and I want that more than anything."

"You do?" Desi glanced up at her. "Think about what you're saying."

"There's nothing to think about."

Desi's eyes were wide, her voice high when she said, "I wasn't exaggerating when I said Byron wouldn't let me go. I couldn't handle it if you got hurt, not when I've protected you for this long."

"Battles are hard when you fight them on your own, but you have plenty of people who care about you. Byron can try whatever he wants, but I'm not backing down again." She cupped Desi's cheek and smiled. "The only thing that'll make me do that is if you ask me not to."

"I don't think I can."

"Good." Happiness infused her soul when Desi rested her head back on her chest. "It's time to start over."

CHAPTER THIRTEEN

"All rise," the bailiff said, and everyone in the crowded courtroom who stood didn't appear happy to be there. "The Honorable Judge Jude Rose presiding." It was plea day, so the onlookers were almost equal in number to the lawyers and defendants, and Serena knew from experience this wasn't Jude's favorite day.

The judge had told her on numerous occasions that the longer he sat on the bench, the harder it was to tell the attorneys from their clients, and Serena agreed with that assessment at times. Despite his griping, Jude was a fair judge who knew the law better than anyone she'd worked with.

"Have a seat everyone—we have plenty to get through," Jude said, staring at the pile Serena had given to his clerk. "Are you keeping me here past lunch, Ms. Ladding?"

"Most are pleading out with agreements to enter appropriate programs, Your Honor, and only four are choosing to go to trial. The pleadings need your signature, so that shouldn't take too long." The television to Jude's left came on, showing a white wall. Prisoners were seldom brought to the courtroom for the preliminaries, so the closed-circuit system was used. "We have to think positive, sir."

"I love your optimism, Ms. Ladding, but you're usually full of surprises, so we'll see about the time." Jude stood, turned his back to the gallery, and appeared to adjust something under his robe.

Serena smiled, knowing it was a pistol he kept holstered in a custom-made alligator skin holster. It was always loaded and ready for action. Jude had fired it only once from the bench, and the story of that would live on way after they'd all retired.

"Let's hear our first case," Jude said, sitting back down and putting on his reading glasses.

"Yes, Your Honor." She opened the first folder as the defendant took the stand to answer questions about whether he understood what was expected of him by entering a guilty plea while receiving no jail time. The other eight went through the same process. They were all first offenders in domestic violence situations. Serena was always hopeful avoiding jail time and getting counseling would set them straight on how to act around women, but she was often disappointed.

"Impressive," Jude said as some of the gallery cleared out. "One more to go."

"The People request remand for this one, Your Honor. Mr. Simoneaux was granted bond after his first arrest and abused the court's generosity to visit his wife in the hospital, where he tried to strangle her."

"That's a damn lie," Byron said as he stared into the closed-circuit camera from jail.

"Mr. Simoneaux, don't make this worse than it has to be by speaking," Jude said.

Serena glanced briefly at the television before looking at Byron's attorney in the courtroom. "Due to the viciousness of the unprovoked attacks, we'd like him held without bail."

"He attacked his wife in the hospital?" Jude asked, staring at the television momentarily as if daring Byron to say something.

"Yes, Your Honor." She referred to the file on the case. "Mrs. Simoneaux was in the hospital from his first attack, and because of this second attack, Mrs. Simoneaux had to be moved to a secure location. Her recovery will be long and painful."

"Will she press charges?" Jude asked.

"Her statement is in the file, and she plans to testify. Both attacks rise to the level of attempted murder, and those charges are in there as well." She glanced at Byron's attorney when he tapped on the table. She couldn't wait to hear what bullshit he was getting ready to spin. She'd never met him, but he seemed nervous. "Mr. Simoneaux is a danger to Desiree Simoneaux, so I'd ask you to seriously consider the State's request."

"Your Honor," Byron's attorney spoke loudly and laughed, "Mr. Simoneaux is a law-abiding citizen with no criminal record of any kind. The man doesn't even have a traffic ticket, and it's a travesty to hold him on these bogus charges. All this boils down to is a larger alimony check because Mrs. Simoneaux wants out of the marriage even though her husband still loves her. Don't be fooled by all these theatrics."

The creak of Jude's chair sounded especially loud when he swiveled forward and rested his elbows on the desk. His expression telegraphed his displeasure, and Serena exchanged a look with the bailiff. Lessons were going to be taught in this courtroom, and they were entertaining as hell when they weren't directed at you.

"Who might you be?" Jude sounded like an old Southern host welcoming a guest to his home.

Serena almost laughed when the young man smiled and puffed his chest out as if he'd been given a ribbon for being the teacher's pet. "Bradley Blum, Your Honor. Mr. Simoneaux is my client, and—"

"Mr. Blum, have I asked you anything but your name?" Jude narrowed his eyes with his index finger up.

"No, Your Honor, but—" Bradley swallowed hard when Jude slammed his hand down.

"Why are you still talking? This isn't debate club, it's my courtroom, and people only speak when spoken to." Jude was almost on his feet, and Bradley appeared ready to run, but Serena gave him credit for standing firm.

"I meant no disrespect, You Honor, but my client is innocent. You deserve to hear our side before you make any snap judgments."

Jude was on his feet now, and Serena lifted her hand to her mouth to hide her smile. "Are you accusing me of impropriety, Mr. Blum?"

"No...no, Your Honor."

"You're talking again, Mr. Blum," Jude said, making Bradley's name sound like *fuck you*. "You should take Ms. Ladding's example and show some courtesy. Do you understand me, Mr. Blum?" Jude seemed to be memorizing the name, and Serena knew that wasn't a good thing. The judge was fair, but that didn't mean he wouldn't make you work for it in the future.

Two minutes passed, and the room was deadly quiet. "I asked if you understood me."

"I'm sorry, Your Honor, but you told me not to speak." Bradley removed the decorative handkerchief from his jacket pocket and wiped his forehead.

"When I ask questions, that's your cue to open your mouth. That's how this works."

"Yes, Your Honor, I understand you."

"Good." Jude sat down and took a few deep breaths. "Ms. Ladding, what is the extent of Mrs. Simoneaux's injuries?"

Jude stared up at the light fixture as she read off the list Harry had given her as well as the procedures it'd taken to repair the damage. She referred him to the pictures in the file before going on to the second incident that had gotten Byron rearrested.

"Thank you," Jude said. "Let's hear from you, Mr. Blum."

Bradley listed all of Byron's supposed wonderful qualities, and Serena watched the smug asshole nod on the TV screen as Bradley droned on. Byron looked horrible in an orange jumpsuit, but he also appeared arrogant. An older man seated in the courtroom behind Bradley wore the same expression, and the family resemblance was undeniable. This had to be Big Byron, the father of the asshole in prison.

"Is that it?" Jude asked.

"Yes, Your Honor." Bradley pointed at Byron. "All this has been a terrible set of misunderstandings, and my client's innocent. He deserves to be sent home to his family, so he can prepare a vigorous defense. Remember, Your Honor, my client has no record whatsoever."

"You're absolutely right, Mr. Blum, and in deference to that, I'll give Mr. Simoneaux a chance at bail." Jude wrote something as he spoke, and Serena wanted to slap the gloating smile off Bradley's face. "Bond is set at four million dollars." Jude slammed his gavel down and stood again. "We're adjourned."

Serena wasn't thrilled but figured having to put up close to half a million dollars would keep Byron where he was.

"What the hell just happened?" The old man behind Bradley grabbed him and turned him around forcefully.

"I explained this was only the first step. Once we go before the judge who'll hear this case, we'll ask for a reduction of this crazy amount." Bradley was talking fast as Serena packed up her files. "The upside is, going forward we won't have to deal with Judge Rose again."

"You think I'm stupid?" The man hadn't let Bradley go and glared at Serena as she turned to leave. "You promised a whole lot and ain't one thing come through."

What a charmer, Serena thought as she stepped through the hinged door in the railing separating attorneys from spectators. She smiled at the petite meek-looking woman in the first row, and her heart ached for her. If she was Byron's mother, she was in the same situation as Desi, only she'd had plenty more years of misery under her belt.

She headed to her office and called Harry's house, then dropped into her chair. "Hey, I wanted to update you and tell you the judge did set bail, but it's high. If he wants out, Byron will have to put up close to half a million, and I don't see that happening."

"What happens now?" Desi asked.

"We set a trial date and hope Byron's attorney does as well there as he did today." Serena slipped her shoes off and sighed. "This will be over soon, and you will make it real for the jury."

"Thank you for telling me, and I'll do my best to be ready." Desi hesitated before going on. "Is it okay to tell Harry and my sister what you said? Harry gave me her cell number in case I had to call her."

The question and needless explanation were something Serena understood well. Women like her and Desi had learned, rather violently, to never assume they could just make any decision without permission. To defy that rule meant more violent lessons.

"I'm sure Harry and Rachel will appreciate the update." She made a quick decision to mention the in-laws so there'd be no surprises later. "The other thing is Byron's family. If they somehow try to contact you, you have to let me know."

"They were there?" Desi sounded panicked.

"They didn't introduce themselves, but the family resemblance was hard to miss. His father was there with a woman who looked scared and small."

"That sounds like Big Byron and his wife. As bad as I've had it, Miss Tammy's had it worse. She's had a miserable life."

"Worry about you right now, Desi. It's okay to be selfish for once."

"Do you think they'd come after Harry?" Desi took a breath. "If I've put Harry in danger, I'll never forgive myself. And they all know where Rachel works."

"If the Simoneaux men are smart, they'll stay the hell away from Harry and Rachel. Harry's an excellent surgeon, but she's good at breaking bones too. She studied martial arts in college, and she knows just how to cause damage. As for Rachel, maybe have a talk with her, and convince her to take some time off."

"Okay," Desi said softly. "Thanks again for your call."

"Is something wrong?"

"No, just tired. I'll talk to you soon," Desi said and hung up before she could ask anything else.

"Please, Desi, don't run now." Serena stared at her phone and inhaled deeply. "You do and you'll never be able to stop."

CHAPTER FOURTEEN

Desi held the phone to her chest and stared at the blanket covering her leg. Serena's words ricocheted in her head like a pinball off bumpers. The thought of Harry hurting anyone was so foreign she couldn't picture it, but maybe people changed. Maybe pain and hurt drove a person to a different way of handling life's problems.

She reached for the card with Harry's information on it and thought about dialing. They'd woken up together, and Harry had stayed to have coffee with her, but she'd left early with a mention she'd be late. Serena's news was a good reason to call, but she decided against bothering Harry with more of her problems. She called Rachel instead and warned her about Byron's father and brother. Rachel promised she'd be home as soon as she finished her appointments and would make sure no one followed her.

After that conversation she spent some time trying to convince herself Harry couldn't have changed that much, eventually tiring herself into a nap. The sound of a door opening and closing made her anxious. It was three thirty in the afternoon, too early for Rachel or Harry, and she knew Mona was down the hall watching her soaps, so she held her breath, thinking the worst. Had Byron already found her? Her hands shook, and it became hard to breathe. The heavy footsteps on the stairs made her freeze, and she could barely hold back the scream settling on her lips.

"Hey, how are you feeling?" Harry asked, walking into the room with shopping bags.

"What are you doing here?" She blinked repeatedly, trying to calm down, and looked to the clock, thinking it had to be wrong. She slowly unclenched the blanket and tried to breathe calmly again.

"I live here," Harry said and laughed. "If you want, I can leave and come back tonight."

"I'm sorry." She pressed her hands so tight around her phone it creaked, but it was hard to beat back the fear once it took hold. "I wasn't expecting you so early."

"I should've called." Harry dropped her bags and seemed to be studying her. "Are you okay?" She clearly figured it out and closed her eyes and dropped her head forward. "Sorry, I didn't mean to scare you. I wanted to surprise you."

"Don't apologize. It's your house, and I'm being an idiot." She smiled, trying her best to make Harry relax. "And you're a good surprise."

"Thanks." Harry took her shoes off and threw her socks close to the bathroom door. "We have days full of gremlins, and days when everything goes perfect. Today everyone was early, the difficult parts were done by two, and the rest will be good experience for the residents with an attending supervising."

"I'm glad you came home."

"Me too, and like I said, I have a surprise for you." Harry picked up one of the bags and handed it to her.

This reminded her of all the times Harry thought to get her something to make her smile. They were always little things, but they'd made her feel cherished. "It's been a very long time since anyone's surprised me like this." She held the bag and gazed at Harry, trying not to cry.

"Don't." Harry sat next to her and cupped her cheek so tenderly it did make her tears fall.

It'd been even longer since anyone, aside from Rachel, had touched her like they cared for her. She'd gone so long without it, she hardly thought it was possible. The sobs came not from pain, but from the wonder of feeling the warmth on her cheek. When Harry came close and held her, she lost complete control.

Harry didn't let her go until she was calm again, and she couldn't come up with the words to explain what had happened. "Harry, I—"

"Sometimes the best thing to do is release all that stuff we have pent up inside and have a friend offer a shoulder to make it easier." Harry rubbed her back as she spoke, and it was like heaven. "But if you feel better, we can get on with what I had in mind."

"Thank you."

"Anytime." Harry tapped the bag as if trying to get her mind on something else.

She opened it and found a sports bra, a nice fleece pullover, a pair of jogging pants with snaps all the way up the sides, several pairs of cashmere socks, and a warm hat.

"How about a trip to the park to feed the ducks?"

"I'd love to go with you, but I don't think I can." She pointed to the oversized boot that came up over her knee, and her lip started trembling again.

"I didn't ask you if you could—I asked you if you wanted to. Now do you want to?" Harry put her fingers under Desi's chin and gently lifted her to meet her eyes. "Do you?"

"Yes, you know I do, but—"

"No buts. Let me change, and we can enjoy the afternoon." Harry stepped into the closet, coming out in sweatpants and a fleece top. "You and me have a date to fatten up the local fowl."

"If you say so, but I'm not sure how I'm supposed to do that," she said, knowing Harry always had a plan.

"Have some faith, my friend. Now, do you need help putting that gear on?"

"I think I can manage with the top, but I'll need you to help with the bottom." She held up the sports bra with clasps in the front, and Harry turned around to give her some privacy. That made her feel better since her body wasn't something she was proud of, thanks to Byron's souvenirs.

She pulled her nightgown off and struggled to get the sports bra on as her ribs protested the movement, but she got that and the fleece top on before she asked Harry to turn around. "How do you want to do this?"

"Let's start with the good leg," Harry said as she placed her nightgown across her waist and put the unsnapped pants on the bed next to her. "I'll lift you on three, so try to keep your legs straight." She lifted her carefully and placed her butt on the pants. Then Harry snapped up the side of her good leg, and Desi snapped around the crotch, her face heating with embarrassment. Harry pulled the material over her injured leg, snapping around her ankle to keep it in place, then placed the warm socks on her feet. She swallowed and then gave her a quick smile, and Desi wondered what was going through her head.

"Ready to go?" Harry stood and slapped her hands together.

"I'm not sure how we can, but I'm ready," she said as Harry leaned over her and picked her up. She put her arms around Harry's neck as they walked down the stairs, and Harry stopped at the bottom, gazing down at her.

"Want a tour?" Harry asked.

"Are you sure I'm not too heavy?"

"You aren't, and it'll give you and Tony something to talk about tonight at dinner. He insisted on coming over and cooking for us, which is something he loves doing, but he loves talking decorating even more." Harry carried her around the first floor, ending up in the great kitchen Desi remembered. "If you want to befriend him for life, suggest some changes."

"I'd never do that. He did a beautiful job."

"He did, but he never thinks any space is finished, and he'd love that you understand that."

Mona opened the door for them and followed Harry to open the car door as well. Harry placed her in the back so she could stretch her legs out, and she enjoyed seeing the houses they drove by as they headed to the park. Dream homes, as far from her daily life as it was possible to get. The park wasn't far from Harry's place, and she hadn't been there in years, but this had been one of their favorite spots when they were growing up. She remembered sitting by the duck pond while Harry ran the two-mile track, then going home and trying to find some privacy to make out.

Harry parked close to the golf course and opened the back before getting her out. She wheeled a chair with a leg rest to accommodate her boot next to the door.

"It's a variation on a regular wheelchair with thicker wheels, which ought to make any bumps along the way manageable." Harry locked it and lifted her out and onto the seat. "How about a walk around the park before we feed the ducks?"

"I don't mind waiting if you want to run." She accepted a blanket and another bag from Harry.

"There's always time for that, but right now I'd rather spend time with you and relax." Harry started for the track. "If this doesn't cause you any discomfort, we can come again."

She nodded as they started down the track, relaxing as she stared up at the canopy of oak tree limbs that completely covered almost the entire circuit. This sense of peace was hard to accept, but in that moment, she enjoyed the familiar surroundings with someone she hoped was becoming a good friend again.

The blanket on her lap kept her warm, and the silence between them wasn't uncomfortable. There were a few people who ran by them, but none of them said a word as Harry made her way around to the duck ponds.

The cold weather had killed off most of the vegetation around the waterways, but the air was crisp, and Harry was right behind her keeping her safe. Harry slowed and took the slope down to the water carefully, and she smiled at the way the ducks were already swimming toward them. "Looks like they're still spoiled," she said as Harry took the blanket from her and spread it on the ground.

Harry picked her up and set her down, then joined her. "It's a wonder they can still swim, the porkers."

"They're cute." She accepted a bag of seed from Harry. Once the food hit the ground, they attracted a large flock of ducks, and they made her laugh. By the time the bag was empty, it was hard to hear anything over the quacking.

"Hey," Harry said as one of the ducks pecked at her sleeve, "you have any more, and there's a stomachache in your future." The duck stopped, then went right back to pulling on Harry's sleeve. "You ready? I don't want to keep you too late."

The sun was setting, and the temperature had started to drop, and Desi nodded then hung on as Harry lifted her. Harry's gentleness reminded her of the call from Serena and what she'd foolishly thought when she'd hung up. She lowered her head when Harry put her in the seat, and she tried to look away when Harry crouched next to her.

"Are you hurt?" Harry rested her hands on the arm of the chair and whispered the question.

She shook her head and placed her hand on Harry's arm. "I'm so sorry," she said as the damn tears started again.

Harry had put a lot of thought into their afternoon, and she was ashamed she'd painted Harry with the same brush as Byron. Terror and anxiety were cruel even when there was nothing to provoke either because it was hard to change your mindset. Letting go of the constant vigilance was also terrifying because that attention to her surroundings had kept her alive.

"Hey, tell me what's wrong?" Harry leaned in closer and reached for her hand. "It's okay to just tell me. Let me help you work through it."

She turned and pressed her face to Harry's neck, crying when she felt Harry's arms come around her. "Don't let me go," she said, holding on to Harry with all her strength.

"I'm right here, but let me get you back to the car." Harry wrapped the blanket around her and headed back at a much faster pace.

She tried to stop the stupid outburst and was grateful for the few moments Harry held her as she lifted her back into the car. The chair stayed outside as Harry sat beside her and put an arm around her. They didn't speak until the tears stopped, and she was glad for the time.

"Feel better? You're not in pain, are you?" Harry brushed her hair back and looked at her.

"No, that's not it." She took a breath and tried to find the best way to explain that wouldn't break the fragile bond between them. "Serena called today before you got home."

"Is something wrong with the case?"

"I don't think so. Byron got bail, but she said it's so high she doubted he'd come up with the money." She rested her hand on Harry's chest, making it easy to feel the deep inhale.

"Does it bother you, him stuck in jail?" Harry seemed afraid of her answer.

"No." She pressed her hand down harder, wanting Harry to feel her. "God, no."

"Did Serena say something else that bothered you?" Harry's soft voice made her feel unworthy to be her friend. "Tell me."

"She told me about Byron and his parents, and then she started talking about you." Her throat closed and she had to stop.

"Please, Desi, don't cry anymore. You can tell me anything. That hasn't changed between us."

"I was afraid for you. Byron's family is so crazy, and I thought they might hurt you if they found out where I was." She was miserable having to deliver the explanation. "Then Serena told me not to worry because you'd taken these martial arts classes."

Comprehension seemed to hit Harry like a frying pan to the face. "And you thought I'd hit you?" Harry's smile was so slight it was as if she didn't have the strength to lift her lips any higher.

"I was being a fool. I know you'd never—" She stopped when Harry pressed a finger to her lips.

"I'm not mad, and thinking that is totally understandable, so stop punishing yourself." Harry wiped her tears, but there was no hiding the sadness in her eyes. "Stop torturing yourself for things that have kept you alive. If you hadn't, I would've never gotten you back, and my life would be poorer for it."

She let out a sob at the words, not believing Harry had said them. "Do you mean it?"

"From the moment you told me what happened, what Clyde did, I've been trying to wrap my head around the whole situation. We had such sure feelings for each other growing up, and they died that day." Harry stopped and wiped her own face. "Without warning, my life, at least the life I knew and wanted, was gone."

"I'm so sorry."

"How can I blame you for something that wasn't your fault?" Harry caressed her cheek and kept talking. "I've buried all those feelings, dreams, and love for so long it changed me. Your loss left me with a sense of despair that almost broke me."

The words hurt, and she hated that she'd left Harry to feel that way. "You have to believe I would've never done that if Daddy hadn't forced me. If I'd thought there was another way—"

Harry lifted her finger again and shook her head. "Please let me finish. I need to tell you this."

She reached up, hoping Harry wouldn't mind, and pressed her hand to the side of Harry's neck. "You can tell me anything."

"It took seeing you again to realize I never got over what you meant to me. I didn't make a life with someone because I couldn't trust my heart. That acute pain was too much to ever live through again."

Seeing Harry's tears was killing her, and she pulled her closer. "I'm so sorry. You never deserved this, and you don't deserve to become a target because of me."

"No." Harry's voice rose, but she wasn't yelling. "We grew up together knowing what we wanted, and we lost out on that. Rachel keeps telling me it's fate that we found each other again, and maybe she's right."

"Careful or she'll wrap you in crystals next," she said, trying to make Harry feel better.

"I'll keep that in mind, but she's right. This time, though, there's no Clyde, and we're not seventeen anymore."

"What are you saying?" She held her breath and focused so she could memorize Harry's words.

"That this time, we take it slow and become friends again, so we can explore where we go from there. If you don't want anything more than friendship, that's okay, but don't disappear without talking to me first. That's all I ask."

"Are you sure?" She didn't want any misunderstandings that would drive them apart again. "I want to be sure of what you mean."

"I didn't move on, Desi, because I couldn't forget you. I was devastated, but I couldn't forget you. What's important now isn't how we got here, but *where* we go from here."

"Hopefully, I'm not dreaming," she said, her lips next to Harry's neck.

"You're not, and you're safe with me. I trained in martial arts only to be able to protect myself and the people I love."

Desi shook her head. "You don't have to explain."

"I'd never hurt you, and the only thing I ever hit is the bag in the gym." Harry stopped when she pressed her thumb over her mouth.

"You don't have to explain yourself to me." She rubbed her thumb across Harry's lips as she moved her hand to cup Harry's cheek. "I let my past taint you, and I'm really sorry. You never were—and could never be—like Byron."

"Let's concentrate on the good and forget all that for now." Harry kissed her forehead. "You work on getting better and making choices about Byron and his family. If you want out of that relationship, I'll do whatever I have to so that happens."

"All I want…is to be with you." It took every bit of courage she had to say that out loud.

Harry smiled and appeared relieved. "No matter what you think, you're a remarkable woman who's more courageous than anyone I've ever known."

"No, I'm not."

"You are, and I'll remind you every chance I get."

"You were always a gift, Harry, and I'm glad you haven't changed. Thanks for today."

"We have plenty of days to enjoy, and all we have to do is practice asking for the things we want."

"You promise?" She wanted this more than anything in life.

"With all my heart."

Any thought she'd had about finding relief in letting go in the infinity of death evaporated in the deep blue of Harry's eyes. "I'm so glad I found you." It was like finding salvation in the most familiar of places, and only a month ago, she would've thought that was lost to her forever.

CHAPTER FIFTEEN

"Did you have a good time, baby?" Mona asked Desi as she tapped a cooking spoon against a pot simmering on the big stove.

"It was wonderful getting out of the house." Desi stripped off her new hat and laid it on her legs. Harry pushed her to the kitchen table, and she was glad she wasn't going upstairs just yet.

"I'm glad, but bonehead should've known better than to keep you out there too long in this cold."

"I was okay." She folded her hands over the hat and smiled at Mona. "My doctor took good care of me."

"Kept you warm, did she?"

Harry smiled at her as the heat swept across her face, a sure sign she was blushing. "She did, and it was nice being back there. Do you remember all our days in the park?"

"I remember plenty of them. It's a miracle we didn't get killed by a golf ball." Harry sat next to her and took her hand. "The best times were after we finished our homework, and we'd lie back and watch the clouds go by."

"Those were special." Desi gazed down at their hands, thinking of how the differences in them magnified their different paths in life. Harry's were still soft, while hers were a mess from housework and trying to protect herself. "There were so many times when we were out there that I wanted to blurt out how I felt about you." Desi felt the heat on her face again and stopped talking. "Is this okay, me talking like this?" she finally asked.

"I never needed your words to hear what your heart was saying. That one, though, I didn't figure out until you were gone. The collage of my memories was what convinced me," Harry said, tugging on her fingers. "And you go ahead and tell me whatever you want."

Desi took a breath to control her emotions, but she was all over the place. "I thought about you every day, and after so many years I was almost convinced you were someone I'd made up to survive. You seemed too good to be true."

Harry glanced back at Mona and lowered her voice.

"All you need to do is live a day at a time talking to me, Rachel, Mona, and the guys. Think of this as your home, and eventually the sense of safety will crowd out the bad stuff. Once it does, that'll be your new normal." Harry wiped under Desi's eye and combed her hair off her forehead. "If you believe that in your soul, then it'll be easy to believe I don't blame you, and I want you here. That's the truth."

Mona stepped out to answer the doorbell, but Harry never took her eyes off Desi's.

"It's so hard not to think of this as a soap bubble. Once you realize how broken I am, it'll pop, and I'll be back there, and you won't have been real after all." It was pathetic, but that *was* her truth.

They were alone. Whoever was at the door had stayed in the front of the house, and Harry took one of Desi's hands and placed it over her heart. "Do you feel me?" Harry asked.

"Yes. I'm sorry, I shouldn't be doing this if you have people waiting on you."

"Forget about all that right now. It's just you and me here, and I want you to know that I want you in my life. You're not only safe with me, but you have a place with me."

"I'm so scared," she said, glancing at her hand on Harry's chest.

"Tell me." Harry wasn't running.

"I'm not enough for you, and you deserve better. What'll happen when you finally figure that out?"

Harry leaned in, careful not to go anywhere near her leg, and Desi stopped breathing. It'd been over sixteen years since Harry had kissed her, and her lips felt as good now as they had on Clyde's porch. She closed her eyes and immersed herself in the joy that exploded inside her.

"Never think you're not enough." Harry moved only slightly back. "You've always been the one girl who fit."

"Oh, Harry. That last night in your arms was the last time I felt cherished by the only person I wanted this kind of attention from." Her hands were on Harry's shoulders, and she wanted everyone to go away. Being this close to Harry gave her the strength to finish her story and erase all the secrets between them. She needed to do that before Harry made promises she wouldn't hold her to when she saw shame or pity in her eyes. "He—"

"You don't have to say anything else. I believe you about Clyde and what Byron did, and it's enough."

Desi took Harry's hands and held them. "Please listen. I want you to hear it from me and not in front of strangers when I testify."

Harry nodded and locked their fingers together. "You don't need to do this for me, but I'll listen to whatever you want to say."

"He was nice to me at first." Her heart and lungs felt tight, like someone was squeezing them in a vise. "He liked to talk about how he could've gone to college on a football scholarship, but his dad thought it'd be a waste of time."

"Why did he need his father and yours to arrange a marriage for him? I vaguely remember him from high school, and the star quarterback never seemed to have girl issues."

"That's easy. In high school he came close to going to jail in our junior year for putting his girlfriend in the hospital. It took a big check from his father to make the charges go away." She laughed at how Clyde hadn't been bothered by that. "But the recruiters lost interest."

"Jesus, Desi, I wish I would've known all this. Nothing Clyde threatened would've stopped me from getting you both out of there."

"My father was not only crazy—he was a cold bastard. I couldn't chance him following through on his threats when it came to you." She stopped and took a breath. "I never said anything, but growing up…" She couldn't quite think of how to put it. "He wasn't a nice man to either me or Rachel. I guess you'd say he was emotionally abusive. He only hinted at the things he did for the Bracato family, but I believed him when he said he was good at making problems disappear. All Clyde wanted from us was to do as we were told and to fear him. We did. I just never said anything because I didn't want you to decide it was too much to deal with and leave."

Harry appeared to be in pain. "I knew something was wrong. I was trying not to push you, to not make you uncomfortable. I failed you from the very beginning. How in the world will you ever forgive me for that?"

"That's the last thing you did, Harry, and what's done is done. We can't change it, but I'm here, and you don't hate me." She smiled to make Harry feel better. "Back then the bruises Byron gave me were hidden by the ones Clyde delivered after he saw us together, and a wedding was my price to protect you and Rachel. Before that, all his threats were verbal." She squeezed Harry's hands to center herself. "He and Big Byron agreed they had two problems in their houses, and the best solution was to put us together."

"That's barbaric," Harry said.

"It was, and I couldn't understand how everything had gone so wrong. Clyde didn't care that Byron was getting a punching bag who wouldn't press charges. As a bonus, Clyde got to feel better about himself—he didn't have a gay kid." She lowered her head and fought to finish. "It didn't seem real, but Clyde was always there, threatening what he'd do to Rachel or to you if I didn't play along. That last night we had together made him crueler than he'd been before, and he started hitting Rachel too, and I was desperate to make it stop. That was one of the reasons Rachel came with me."

"So you gave in," Harry said in a raw voice.

"I almost left once, but Clyde convinced me you'd moved on and wouldn't want me. I fought not to believe him, but you'd stopped coming and calling, and I had nowhere to run. I believed you were better off without my drama in your life. In a way I still do."

Harry tilted her head back as if to hide her tears, but they fell fast and steady. "I'm so sorry." The words were emotional and stuttered. "My God, what in the hell did I do to you? There's nothing I can do or say to make up for that. It's a miracle you don't hate me."

"No, Harry, no. If I had to do it all over again, I would—gladly. My life was horrible, I can't lie about that, but you and Rachel were safe. Whatever sacrifice I made was worth everything because you two had the chance to live in peace. Or as much peace as we could manage. I was lucky—I was Byron's only target, but I'm sure Rachel has suffered as much as I did, having to witness it all." She put her hands on Harry's cheeks and shook her head. "The rest is my fault."

"Don't say that," Harry said, sounding broken.

"It's true. Once Clyde was dead, I should've gambled and run with Rachel to find you. She kept pushing me to do it. She said you'd understand once we explained what happened, but my fear damned us all. I was just…frozen."

"Don't you dare blame yourself for anything. It's the rest of us who failed you. Me most of all. I supposedly loved you, and I ran like a petty little shit." Harry's head dropped as if she couldn't look at her. "Don't make excuses for me."

"You can choose to feel this way, but I'm never going to blame you. And God, we were kids. Teenagers shouldn't face that kind of stuff. Wasn't it you who said the only person responsible is Clyde?"

"That miserable son of a bitch. How could he have done this to you?"

"I have no answer for that, but you?" She moved her hand into Harry's hair, encouraging her to look up. "Harry Basantes, you're who kept me alive. What you meant to me, how you loved me, and my love for you were the things I hung on to no matter how bad it got."

"All that's over now. He's never going to touch you again."

"I believe you, but listen to me. Byron is an angry, violent man. I know you'll protect me, but you need to be careful. I don't want anything to happen to you because of me."

"I'll be fine, but you need to be careful until all this is over. We have a second chance, and I don't want anything to happen to you before we enjoy it."

"This is a weird time to talk about all this, but I'm glad we did." She laughed, glad to have Harry do the same. "And I'm glad we have one more chance to get it right."

"I'd give everything I have to change what happened to you."

"Even if this is all we get, it's enough," she said, thinking of Harry's kiss.

"We'll have more than one talk and kiss in the kitchen," Harry said, running her thumb over her lips. "So much more if you let me in."

"Everything okay in here?" Rachel asked, her question not making Harry move back.

"She's always had the worst timing," Harry said, kissing her forehead before leaning away from her. "Are you alone, or is there a crowd in the other room?"

"I'm not a crowd," Tony said, making an entrance with his hands over his head. "You're gorgeous, and it's good to see the ogre has freed you from the bedroom." He kissed Desi's cheek and winked at Harry. "Now I know it's safe to take you shopping."

"Don't forget—I love to shop," Rachel said, sitting in Harry's lap and pressing a bunch of kisses on her cheek.

She was jealous of Rachel's mobility and her choice of seat, but she smiled when Tony touched her hand. He'd volunteered to help the physical therapist she'd start with tomorrow, but his friendship was more important to her. The doorbell rang again, and she didn't know who else it could be.

"If you both love to shop, we'll never get rid of him," Harry said.

"You're so not funny," Tony said, sticking his tongue out at Harry.

"Hello, everyone," Serena said, coming in with Kenneth and Butch.

Desi smiled at the little boy in the peacoat and boots. He could've been a model, and he was overjoyed to see Harry, but he quickly came over and kissed her cheek when she leaned down.

"Hey, Miss Desi," he said as he tried to undo the buttons on his jacket, seeming glad when she took over.

"Hey, I'm so glad to see you again."

"Let's get Desi to the dining room, big guy," Harry said, getting Butch to help her push the chair.

They spent the next few hours around the big table enjoying Mona's shrimp and okra gumbo. Rachel had quickly charmed Butch, and he'd spent most of the night on her lap. He smiled when she combed her fingers through his hair, and he listened intently to whatever she was whispering in his ear.

"Mona, that was delicious," Harry said after her second bowl. "I thought you were supposed to be cooking," she said to Tony.

"I had a board meeting with the group that helps LGBTQ homeless youth, so Mona bailed me out. She knows my rain check is good."

"Uh-huh, slacker," Harry said, and everyone laughed when Tony stuck his tongue out at her again. "You ready for your meds?"

"Two more days and we won't have to worry about those," she said as Harry stood and squeezed her shoulders from behind.

"Be right back." Harry started out of the room, and it didn't surprise her when Serena went with her. It was hard to miss how Serena's eyes stayed on Harry when she thought no one would notice. Maybe all those old feelings Serena told her about weren't so ancient.

She felt better when Butch went as well, and Rachel moved to sit by her while the guys helped Mona clear the table. "Who's the blonde in love with Harry?"

Rachel seldom missed anything, no matter how subtle, but in this case, it was pretty blatant. "Not right now, but they're old friends."

"Blondie hasn't gotten the friendship memo." Rachel wasn't being loud, but Desi glared at her to shut her up. "What? I'm not blind."

Neither was she, and it'd been an effort not to chuck her bowl at Serena to get her to stop. Harry, though, seemed oblivious as she included Desi throughout the night. It was hard to be upset when Harry gave her such a sense of place. After a lifetime of trying to be invisible, she was seen again, and it was nice.

"Neither am I, but I trust Harry." And she would. She was done running.

❖

Harry took pills from two bottles after turning the bed down for Desi. "Thanks for calling Desi today and keeping her in the loop."

"No problem," Serena replied, "but who's the cute redhead?"

"Don't play her unless you have more than a night in mind." She closed her fist around the pills, keeping her voice light for Butch's sake.

"Babe, you left me, remember?" Serena winked at her and smiled sweetly. "Besides, it's a simple question."

"Don't give me that smile and try to make me feel guilty. You've dated plenty since me, and the redhead is Desi's sister, Rachel. They've both been through hell, so don't do anything to add to that."

"Ooh, it's good to see you this overprotective. It's refreshing, and it really was a simple question. I'm seeing someone, but she *is* cute."

"If you don't want me to teach Butch to pee in the yard, behave yourself."

Serena shivered from either the mental image or from Harry whispering in her ear, but it ended in a slap to Harry's stomach. "Ew, tell me you don't do that."

"Only when the call of nature moves me," she said, laughing.

"You're disgusting, and I get the message. Stay away from the redhead." Serena followed her out and carried Butch down the stairs.

Harry handed over the medicine and smiled at Desi. "You're right, only two more to go."

Desi nodded as she swallowed and seemed happy to take her hand when she sat back down. "If only this part would be done in two days." Desi pointed down to her leg.

"Don't rush it, sweetie," Tony said, beating Harry to it. "Your doctor knows nothing about fashion, style, or decorating, but bones she knows. Believe me, you'll be okay with me pushing you around until you get your stamina back. Then we can shop for days."

"God help us," Kenneth said, making Harry laugh. "If he gets any more stamina, I'll have to get another job at Starbucks to pay for everything he wants."

"Kenneth Jerome Reynolds, I know you're not complaining about my stamina. If you are, you can work on yours while you park your ass on the couch."

"Your middle name is Jerome?" Harry asked Kenneth.

"He changes it every time he feels the need to add a name to make the threat more credible."

Everyone laughed, and Harry followed Mona into the kitchen to help get the coffee and dessert Mona had made. They continued to joke until Butch fell asleep on Rachel's lap, and Serena announced it was time for her to get him to bed. Rachel helped her by carrying the little boy out, and Tony and Kenneth helped Mona finish up in the kitchen while she carried Desi back upstairs.

"Damn," she said, looking at the clock next to the bed. "I'm so glad I don't have an early morning tomorrow."

"Harry, go on and grab a shower if you want, and I'll help Desi get ready for bed," Mona said as she came in with Desi's nightgown.

"I'll help you." Rachel sat next to Desi and kissed the top of her head.

When Harry came out of the shower, Desi was in her nightgown and alone. "You have everything you need?"

Desi simply stared at her as if trying to work something out in her head. She'd woken up that morning with her arms around Desi, but she'd sworn to herself she'd go slow. No one lived through the trauma Desi had without some personal space issues, and they'd have to work through them. Whatever was on her mind appeared to have beaten Desi when she lowered then shook her head.

Harry sat on the bed and waited. She didn't have any experience with this, but giving Desi the chance to make even the smallest of choices like raising her head seemed important. A little nudge wouldn't hurt, though, and she reached for Desi's hand.

"Do you need anything?"

"I don't…I don't want to be alone."

Harry walked to the other side of the bed, lay down, and opened her arms. "You don't have to be if that's what you want. I didn't want to be presumptuous."

Desi moved until her back was resting on Harry's chest. She couldn't sleep on her side yet, so this was a good way to be close. "Thank you for today, Harry. You can't know how much it meant to me. It's a hard thing to trust, but you've finally given me something back I'd never thought to have."

"What's that, honey?" Harry closed her eyes and tried not to get lost in the sense of how she'd failed this fragile woman who'd given her more than she'd ever thought possible.

"Hope."

It was a simple word, but she knew it meant the world. All she had to work through now was if a lifetime would be enough to make up for the existence she'd left Desi to.

"I'm glad, sweetheart."

CHAPTER SIXTEEN

Two weeks later Desi sat in the waiting room of Harry's private practice with Rachel, Tony, and Mona, since all three of them had insisted on coming with her. Mona had even come home early from visiting her family to make sure she'd be on hand for the appointment, and to give Tony directions when he carried her down to Harry's car.

The room was big but crowded, which gave her an idea why Harry came home so late on some nights. "Did you decorate this place?" she asked Tony. The walls had quite a few framed autographed jerseys and other sports memorabilia, as well as a large display case with helmets, balls, and caps.

"I had to go to the spa afterward and detox all the sports machismo out of my pores, but yes. Harry loves it, but I drew the line on any of this coming home with her." Tony put one hand on his chest and fanned himself with the other.

"She could make a fortune on eBay," Rachel said.

"Hey, Mona." A nurse came out and walked toward them. "You guys ready?" She unlocked the chair and invited everyone to go in. "Can I get you some water, a soft drink, or a cappuccino?"

"What? That's great service," Rachel said when they were placed in an exam room. "We're good," she said when they all shook their heads.

"Yell if you change your mind. Dr. Basantes should be back from rounds any second."

Tony and Rachel sat together while Desi studied the pictures hanging in the room. Harry was in all of them with different smiling people. Not all of them looked like athletes. She was about to ask about them when a woman knocked and stepped in.

"Hey, Tony. Are you here to do some redecorating?"

"I'm letting Harry and the rest of you recover from our last go-round, so I'm only playing escort today."

"Hello, I'm Julie, one of Dr. Basantes's nurses. You must be Desi, and I'm dying to know what your blood pressure is," Julie joked as she wrapped the cuff around her arm. "How's your pain level today?"

"Okay enough to skip the pain pill." She smiled at Julie and thought about what a minor miracle it was that Harry was still single. She certainly didn't lack for beautiful women in her life.

"Dr. Basantes shouldn't be too long." Julie finished with her vitals and placed her chart in the holder on the door. "Actually, here she is."

Harry grabbed the chart and entered wearing a pristinely white starched lab coat over navy blue scrubs. "You guys do okay getting here?" She squatted next to the wheelchair and gave Desi a quick kiss.

They'd spent a lot of time talking and sharing a few kisses, but Harry never pressured for anything more. It was comforting, but the part of her that'd missed who Harry had been in her life wouldn't have minded a little more.

"You look nice," she said as the skin around Harry's eyes crinkled from her smile.

"I have to look the part, or Mona won't believe I'm a real doctor."

"Hush up, you," Mona said.

Harry winked and kissed her again. "Let's get some X-rays and see where we are."

"Is this how you treat all your patients?" Rachel asked, puckering her lips. "You're so gorgeous in that lab coat that I might fling myself down the stairs if it is."

"Sadly, no, so try not to do that." Harry motioned for them to stay put as she rolled Desi down the hall to imaging. She lifted her onto the table and allowed her radiology tech to take a series of angles.

Back in the exam room, Harry checked the incision below her knee and smiled. She sat at a computer and looked over her X-rays and smiled wider. "You're healing nicely, and you're moving without pain, but let's give it another week before I put you in a permanent cast. I could do it today, but your incision is still in the itchy phase, and that'll be murder if a cast is in the way."

"Can we keep it in this the whole time?" she asked as Harry redid the straps on her boot.

"The cast will make it easier for you to move around, and after a few more weeks, you'll be able to put weight on that leg."

"That'll be nice." She put her arms around Harry's neck when she lifted her to get her back in the chair. "Will you be late getting home tonight?" Being able to say that to Harry was surreal, but it made her happy.

"I have appointments this afternoon, but I cleared my schedule to take everyone to lunch." Harry stood and placed her hand on Desi's shoulder. "If you give me a second, I'll change, and we'll take off."

"Are you sure you have time? There's plenty of people in the waiting room." She covered Harry's hand with hers and looked up at her.

"My partner's also seeing patients today, and I'm sure."

"That'd be great," Rachel said, as Harry left to change. "Stop obsessing over what you're wearing," Rachel whispered in her ear.

"She's right," Tony said. "Little sis and I picked that out for you, and you look gorgeous in it, so bring your freak level down a few notches."

The green cashmere sweater felt nice against her skin, and the pants were like the ones Harry had brought her the day they went to the park. She'd thought it was ridiculous when Rachel had done her hair and makeup, but a glance in the mirror surprised her. The bruises were gone, and she hadn't looked like this in years.

"Face it, babe, you're beautiful." Rachel fluffed her hair and winked.

"Mona, how about lunch with Kenneth and me?" Tony asked, and Mona stood immediately.

"Why don't you want to come with us?" Desi asked.

"My big guy becomes a madman if he doesn't eat, and you two need to bond with your big guy. You have to start working on that, and we get to see Kenneth, so it's a win-win." Tony kissed her cheek and waved, and Mona followed suit.

Rachel explained where Tony and Mona had gone when Harry came back. The slacks and white shirt Harry wore looked fantastic on her, and while Desi knew she loved Mona and Tony, Harry appeared happy it was only the three of them.

"Do you want to stick close, so we don't keep you too long?" she asked Harry when she started pushing her toward the exit. "It's nice when you come home early."

"I have a surprise for you two, and it's not too far." Harry lifted her into the car and gazed at her before closing the door. "I'm an idiot for not mentioning this earlier, but you look beautiful."

"Thank you." She gently touched Harry's cheek. This was love, and it beat back Byron's shadow from her head. Although she couldn't help being on the lookout for Byron whenever they were out in public, being with Harry made her feel safe.

They didn't drive long before they stopped at Blanchard's. The last time she'd been there was to celebrate their graduation with Harry's parents. "If you want to go someplace else, I'm okay with that, but I thought it'd be nice to revisit some of our favorite places. The old memories are good, but it's time to make some new ones."

Harry had one of the valets carry the wheelchair up while she carried Desi up the back steps to the garden room. Their table by the floor-to-ceiling windows gave them a great view of the courtyard below them, and the waitstaff was as attentive as she remembered.

"Dr. Basantes, welcome." The waiter unfurled everyone's napkin and laid them across their laps. "Is the table location satisfactory?"

"Perfect, thank you. I wanted my girlfriend out of the main traffic, so no one would run into her leg."

"Can I get some drinks started?" The waiter was talking but all Desi could concentrate on was the word *girlfriend*.

They all ordered iced teas and listened to the specials as Rachel glanced around the restaurant. Desi was instantly ready to bolt when it looked like Rachel recognized someone. They ordered and she raised her eyebrows in Rachel's direction in a silent question as to what was going on. Rachel smiled.

"Isn't that your friend?" Rachel asked, pointing discreetly behind Harry to the main entrance to the room.

"It sure is," Harry said, taking Desi's hand.

Desi smiled at Serena's date who had her arm looped through Serena's as they walked. Maybe she was over Harry after all. "Who's that with her?"

The young woman seemed as tall as Harry but thinner and younger. Desi waved when Serena glanced their way.

"Hello, everyone. It's good to see you out, Desi."

"I had a doctor's appointment, and my doctor invited me to lunch." She liked the way Harry smiled at her.

"Who's your friend?" Harry asked, and Serena's face became almost expressionless.

"Brenda's a law student at Loyola, and she's thinking of an internship in the DA's office this summer." Serena glared at Harry when she opened her mouth.

"That's so nice of you. So you're like a mentor, like in the Girl Scouts?"

"I'm only answering serious questions, Harry, so stop while you're ahead." Serena appeared uncomfortable, but Harry seemed more amused when Brenda tightened her hold on Serena's arm.

"I'm being totally serious, and your…student looks so eager," Harry said with a huge smile.

"Harry, don't make me stab you with a fork," Serena warned.

Desi took Harry's left hand and pulled her index finger. "Hi, Brenda—I'm Desi, this is Harry, and that's my sister Rachel."

"I've heard all about the three of you, especially Harry, from Albert. No one can get him off the subject of his perfect Uncle Harry when he gets going." Brenda looked like she was trying to squeeze the words through clenched teeth, which of course seemed to perk Harry up.

"Maybe Albert's figured out you're more interested in his mother's—"

"Desi," Serena said, loud enough to make people around them look. "Desi, have you heard from Byron's parents?"

"No, but they don't know where I am. Rachel was the only person whose exposure worried me, but she took some time off for now." She'd tried to put what came next out of her head, but seeing Serena brought it front and center.

"While we're waiting for a court date, why don't you get a divorce attorney? The judge and jury will see a pending divorce as proof of how serious you are about not going back."

"I'll help with that, and we don't want to keep you here talking shop when you're otherwise engaged," Harry said with a sweet smile.

"Call me if you have any problems, and that goes for you too, Rachel. It was nice seeing you all, but we'll leave you to your lunch." Serena smiled and almost lost her footing when Brenda grabbed her by the wrist and led her to their table.

Harry laughed when they were alone, and Desi shook her head. "Miss Brenda seems a little possessive, so I hope Serena knows what she's doing."

"I'm sure she does, and Harry loves poking the bear as much as I do," Rachel said.

They enjoyed the rest of lunch, laughing and talking about old times until more than a few of the diners stopped by their table and pantomimed different movements to show how much better their tennis and golf swings were after Harry's care. Harry seemed as amused as she and Rachel were, but through it all, Harry held her hand and introduced her as her girlfriend.

It was an amazing feeling, being at the center of Harry's attention, and being respected was like a healing balm. In all their married life, Byron had never shown her this kind of attention. It'd be hard to put the nightmare behind her, but now all she wanted to do was remember that she'd survived. He'd tried, but he hadn't defeated her.

Even as her mind wandered, it was hard to miss some of the envious glances from more than a few women when Harry picked her up and carried her out. That was way out of her norm, and if any of them realized where she'd come from, they'd all line up for their chance at Harry.

"What's going on in that beautiful head?" Harry asked when they waited outside for the car.

"Are you sure?" she asked, looking into Harry's eyes. "About me, I mean."

"There've been plenty of books written about how there's only one perfect fit in the universe for you. Sometimes it takes a lifetime to find that person, and some people never do." Harry tilted her head and kissed her. "I was very lucky—I found the one girl put here just for me in the third grade. I'm going to spend years proving to you how true that is."

"You're the answer to every prayer I've ever offered up." Not everyone got one more chance to get it right, but it was time to take hers and hang on no matter what.

CHAPTER SEVENTEEN

W ait," Desi said when Harry turned down a narrow street close to the house. "You cook? Are you being serious?"

"Yes, I'm being serious. I've developed some new skills since high school." Harry stopped at a small specialty grocery and smiled into the rearview mirror.

"I'll just bet," Rachel said with a slight sarcastic edge.

"I took cooking lessons, wiseass."

"I tried giving you cooking lessons, and you almost blew up your mother's kitchen," Desi said laughing. "You were the most inept person to ever turn on a stove, no offense."

"That's very true, but Tony and I took lessons at LSU so we wouldn't die from each other's cooking, and because Tony's idea of a meal back then was tuna casserole. There's something about hot tuna from a can that makes me nauseous." Harry parked close to the door and turned to face her. "I'm not a gourmet chef or anything close to that, but I can debone a chicken faster than either of you."

"You're a surgeon, babe, so I'm sure you could debone us with no problem," Rachel teased.

"You're not funny. I'll be right back."

Harry left the car running, and Rachel glanced back at Desi. "She hasn't changed all that much in a fundamental way, but she's completely different. Do you know what I mean?"

"I do," she said, her eyes on the door. "Most days I keep waiting to wake up and find all this will disappear—that how she is with me will go away."

"You're wide awake, and that isn't happening." Rachel snapped her fingers to get her attention. "It might take her some time to admit it, but she's still in love with you. Don't be some selfless idiot and pass up the opportunity once she does. You mess this up, and I'm going to date her, and you can visit us on weekends."

"Am I crazy for wanting this? Is it fair to her?" That's the one thing she couldn't deny feeling. Maybe if she'd been braver, challenged Clyde on his threats, and gone to the police things would have been so different.

"Crazy and unfair are the last things this is." Rachel sounded so sure. "Let me ask you this—was she unforgiving when you told her what happened? Did she say thanks, but it's too late?"

"No, but—"

"Let me finish. You've given me so much for so long that I'm never going to be able to repay you. Now it's my turn, so let me help you build some happiness by being honest." Rachel reached back for her hand. "If you love her like you did back then, don't hold back. Show her all of you, even those parts you think are ugly and embarrassing. Like I said, fundamentally she's the same. She's not going to put you out because of what's happened to you."

"My head knows that, but my heart isn't so sure."

"The most important first step is wanting it. You deserve this, but do you want it?"

"I do want it, but I'm terrified of what comes next with Byron. You know how his family is, and it won't matter if he's locked up or not. If his dad and brother are out, Harry's never going to be safe." There was nothing in Harry's life that could prepare her to deal with the Simoneaux family.

"They all deserve to be caged, but if you keep going over all these what-ifs, you're never going to be happy. Try and forget all that, and enjoy today." Rachel leaned forward and kissed her hand. "You saw and heard her today. Harry wants this too."

"I don't want to lose her, but I want her to be safe."

"Broken records have nothing on you," Rachel said and laughed. "Start playing a different song."

"It's hard to believe she waited for me. According to Tony there's been plenty of women, but no one stayed long." That bit of information surprised her. Harry had never been a player, but she'd also been single, so she wouldn't judge her.

"You're staying, and all you need to do is one simple thing." Rachel put her finger up and Desi shrugged. "Be the woman in her life who plans to stay."

She watched Harry walk back with a bag and a smile. "All set?"

"What's in the bag, Dr. Harry?" Rachel asked, putting her seat belt back on. "It's not one of those prepared meals you're heating up later so you can brag about your cooking, is it?"

"You're such a smart-ass, and no. It's veal. I'm cooking fettuccine Alfredo." Harry opened the back door and put the groceries on the floor. "You'll be impressed enough to kiss the cook, and Mona says I look great in an apron."

She and Rachel laughed as Harry wiggled her eyebrows. Harry backed out and drove back toward St. Charles, and she couldn't help but notice Rachel grab Harry's bicep as if something had scared her.

"What's wrong?" Harry asked, beating Desi to the question.

Rachel pointed to the truck in front of them. "That's the tow truck from Simoneaux's garage."

That brought on an instant bout of fear that made it hard for Desi to form words, and she prayed whoever was driving the truck wouldn't notice them. Why would they? They didn't know where she and Rachel were, and they wouldn't think to look for them in Harry's car.

"Breathe," Harry said. "It's not Byron. That much we know for sure, and he's driving slow, so maybe he's looking for an address." Harry reached back and touched her leg to reassure her.

Harry slowed down, and they all watched the driver slow at every driveway as if indeed searching for a specific place. There was an empty space in front of a house, so Harry pulled over. "Let him get ahead of us, and we'll be fine."

She wanted to relax, but then instead of continuing down the road, the tow truck's brake lights came on, and the driver reached up and adjusted the rearview mirror. It was clear who he'd been searching for.

"Hang on," Harry said as she pulled out and turned on the next street.

Desi looked behind them and saw the truck back onto the neutral ground and follow them with no problem. "Maybe we should keep going until we reach the police," she said as Harry pulled over again.

"Stay in the car," Harry said as she got out and started for the end of the driveway with her phone in her hand, as though she was headed toward the house. The truck wasn't far behind them and thankfully didn't stop, but the driver slowed going past them, then sped off when Harry seemed to head for the door of the house. Harry pulled a pen from her shirt pocket and wrote something on her palm. "Who was that?"

"That was Byron's brother, Mike," Rachel said.

"He was looking for us, wasn't he?" Desi asked, every one of her fears springing to life. Her palms were sweating, and she couldn't get her voice above a whisper since it felt like someone was choking her.

"Whatever he was looking for, all he found was a mountain of trouble," Harry said. She placed a call and put her phone on speaker, so she and Rachel could listen in. "None of these idiots will get near you again, so let me take care of this."

"Hello."

"Serena, it's Harry." Harry went on to explain what happened and asked what they could do about it. Serena asked her to hold, got the detective on the phone, and patched him into their call.

"Dr. Basantes, are Desi and her sister okay?" Roger Landry asked.

"They're okay, and I'd like them to stay that way. Can you get a restraining order on this guy?"

"He didn't approach them, so I doubt any judge is going to order that, and our hands are tied until they try something. I could question him, but he'll say he was there for work, and there's nothing to say he wasn't."

"So we wait for these crazy assholes to screw up before you can do anything about it? Is that what you're telling me?" Harry asked as she gripped the phone and shook her head.

"He's right, Harry. We don't get to make the law up as we go. It's frustrating, but I'll do my best to try and get a protective order." Serena tried to sound soothing, but no one in the car was calm. "We need to wait these guys out but put some legal protections in place."

"If any of these idiots get within a hundred feet of either Desi or Rachel, I won't need the police." Harry sounded dead serious, and that only worried Desi more.

"Harry, please, that's not helping. You need to let Landry and his crew handle these guys, so we don't do anything that'll impair their prosecution if it comes to that."

"You know as well as I do, by the time the police get to us, these morons will—" Harry stopped, as if realizing what she was saying. "I can't let that happen, and you can't ask that of me."

"No one is telling you not to protect your family, Harry, but we need to be involved. We start by putting the Simoneaux family on notice that if they're trying to intimidate Desi or Rachel, that will not be tolerated." Serena sighed and seemed to pause. "Roger, is there anything you can do?"

"We can talk to them, but it'll have to be a friendly visit. This guy didn't actually approach you, so we can't lean on them too hard, but that doesn't mean I don't want to."

Serena said, "Have you given divorce any more thought? That might make it easier for me to get a restraining order."

"I'll do whatever I can to get free of Byron and his family and keep Harry and Rachel safe. Why don't they just leave me alone?" It wasn't like she and Byron had shared some great love affair.

"If you give me your attorney's name, Desi, I'll give him the police reports from both incidents," Roger said.

"His name is Jerry Castle, and Serena can give you the contact information. I don't want to wait until we get home to start all this," Harry said.

"It's going to be okay," Landry said, "and all you need to remember, Desi, is that by standing up to Byron and demanding peace, you take the power back from your abuser. We'll all be with you until you're done."

"Thank you, that means a lot. But you'll protect us, right?" Desi asked.

"I promise I will, Desi. No matter how long it takes, I want Byron to pay for what he did to you," Landry said.

Harry hung up and got out of the car and opened the back door to get closer to Desi. "Are you okay? I didn't mean to get all caveman on you, but I can't stand back and let anything else happen."

"All I want is to be free of all of them." She clung to Harry and had the urge to go somewhere and hide, but that's what had gotten her here. Hiding from her feelings for Harry, hiding from Byron's and her father's anger, and most importantly hiding inside herself because she didn't know what else to do.

"I'm glad you said that." Harry gazed down at her and smiled. That one simple act warmed her more than anything in her life ever had. "Because I'm ready to be happy with you. I don't want to own you, Desi, but you're mine."

"I don't want any of this anymore, but I also don't want it to hurt you." She put her hands behind Harry's head and brought her head down and kissed her. "The smart thing would be to let you go to keep you safe, but I can't do it." She didn't want to cry, but the thought of leaving Harry again was like facing death when there was so much more life to live.

"Let me help you."

"I will, because the best time in my life was when I belonged to you, and I'm ready to claim what's mine," she said kissing Harry again. "With you I can be strong enough to face anything."

Rachel drove them home so Harry could sit in the back with her, but all of them kept a lookout for Mike, not wanting to lead him to their door. She hung on when Harry carried her upstairs and got her comfortable so Harry could change into her scrubs and lab coat, and then Harry called her friend Jerry Castle and asked him to come by the house to talk to her about starting the process of legally separating from Byron.

"I called Mona and told her to come home and bring Tony with her. I'm setting the alarm, so please tell Rachel to stay inside with you." Harry held her and spoke softly. "I feel like an ass for leaving, but I have a full afternoon of patients. I promise I'll be back as soon as I can."

"We'll be okay." She kissed Harry again and pressed her hand to her cheek. "I'll be here."

❖

"It's a big house right off the avenue." Mike talked fast as he tried to backtrack to where he was supposed to be to tow the car. If that big bitch who'd headed right for him had called the cops, he didn't want to be anywhere around her and Desi.

It'd been one lucky break after the other after first spotting Rachel and Desi, and he'd ended up right behind the SUV he was following. Once it was a given they'd spotted him, he'd had no choice but to commit and follow them home.

"Who are they with?" Big Byron asked. His father had been calling him from the moment he'd hung up.

"I ain't ever seen her, but she got out of that car looking like she wanted to beat the shit out of me." He laughed at the memory of the woman. "She stared me down like she could do it too."

"The day you get beat by some woman is the day you ain't my son no more." Big Byron laughed as if that was the most absurd thing he'd ever heard. "Do you remember where this place is?"

"Yeah, but that house and the woman look like money, so I think maybe we should lay off for now. Remember what happened to Byron when he pushed too far," he said, not wanting to end up in a cell with his idiot brother.

"The day you start doing my thinking for me is the day you fucking put me in the ground." Big Byron was loud enough to make Mike take the phone away from his ear. "If you're scared of some bitch, then it's too late for you already."

"You know I want to help Byron, but whoever that woman was, she didn't show any fear. You know Desi told her who I am." He was tired of the daily beatdowns, but showing fear wasn't the way to handle this. "What do you want me to do?"

"Forget about those sluts for now and get your ass over to the jail. I put up the business and the house to get your brother out, so grow a pair and help him finish this."

"I don't want to end up in that cesspool if something goes wrong."

"Listen to me, you chickenshit. The sooner we get Desiree back, the sooner this'll all be over. I want you there so Byron doesn't get crazy and screw this up."

"I'm not sure that's the way to do this. Byron got himself in this, and you should let him get out of it. What's the good of all of us going down with him?"

"Stop before I take you out with that little bitch who started all this. She needs to come back and drop the charges. That's all you need to get in your head, so I can get my business back, and all this goes back to normal." There was a large crash—his father must have hit something. "I might break that little bitch's other leg when all this is done."

"I'm sorry, Daddy, but ain't no telling who this woman is and why Desi is with her, so I'm out after I pick up Byron." He'd get Byron, but if their father thought he needed help, he was going to have to go with him.

"You're going to do whatever the fuck I say, when I say it, boy. Now go get your brother. God knows what the perverts in there did to him."

He hung up and drove to the jail and met with the bail bondsman to present the paperwork. The room they sat in was full of miserable looking people waiting for either the release of or a visitation with a prisoner.

When the metal door in the corner opened, everyone's head turned, then dropped when it wasn't the person they were waiting for. Byron was the third person out, dressed in the clothes he'd been arrested in.

Mike stood and noticed a guy in a suit who stood too and walked toward Byron.

"Byron Simoneaux?" the stranger asked as he held his hand out.

"Yeah," Byron said, ignoring the guy's hand.

"The Byron Simoneaux married to Desiree Simoneaux?" The young man's smile never faltered, and he stood like he had all day. "These are for you. Have a nice day."

"Wait, what the fuck is this?" Byron held the envelope as if he wanted to give it back.

"You've been served. Those are divorce papers and a restraining order from Desiree Simoneaux. You and your family members are ordered to stay a minimum of five hundred feet from Ms. Simoneaux or face legal consequences." That was the only explanation the guy gave before he waved and disappeared out the door.

"That fucking bitch. That piece of shit." Byron crumpled the envelope and threw it as far as he could, as if the papers could burn him. "There's no way she's going anywhere until I fucking say she can go."

Mike grabbed him by the arm and squeezed as hard as he could. "You want to shut the fuck up before they arrest both of us?"

The police officer behind the glass partition tapped on the thick glass with his key to get their attention. "Keep it down or get out, but if you keep screaming, you're going back in."

"Shut up and start walking," Mike said. "If you get clipped again, Daddy's going to let you die in here."

"There's no way she's leaving me. No fucking way. I'll break her in half before that happens."

"You broke her leg, so it shouldn't shock the shit out of you that she wants out," he said, wondering if their father had hit Byron in the head one too many times. "Then you followed that up by trying to kill her. And you're surprised she wants a divorce? C'mon, man."

"Why don't you go out and find yourself a girl before you give me shit about mine. I'm the best thing that happened to Desi, and she owes me." Byron sat in the passenger seat of the truck and glared out the window. "No one else wanted anything to do with her, so she owes me."

"Well, I found her today." He spoke without thinking and was rewarded with a sudden sharp pain in his upper arm. Byron had punched him hard enough to bruise him. "Fuck you, asshole."

"You waited until now to tell me that?" Byron sat up and seemed interested in what he had to say. "Where is she?"

"I think we need to wait until they forget about us." He headed back to the garage, not wanting his father to get any more pissed than he already was. "You just got out. Do you want to go back in? I mean, fuck, they *literally* just gave you papers saying you have to stay away from her."

"I'm not going anywhere until I get my hands on Desi, and she fixes this. If she's lucky, she'll still have teeth when she goes down to the police station and drops the charges." Byron balled his fist again, which made Mike put his hand up to keep Byron from hitting him again. "Tonight, you're driving me wherever she is, and we're going to check it out. Is this someplace that dyke got for her?"

Mike knew that was what Byron liked to call Rachel, and telling him about the woman he'd seen today was a bad idea right now. "I think it must be a friend of theirs, or maybe she's a friend of Rachel's, but I've never seen her before."

"It's a woman? At least Desi's smart enough to not completely piss me off. If it was some guy, I'd have to rip his balls off."

Big Byron gave them a lecture on what had to happen, and how important it was not to get caught. Now they were gambling with his business and house, and mistakes would lead to him cutting them off. They took one of the cars they'd finished repairing, so they wouldn't be recognized. Byron was quiet as they drove down one of the prettiest streets in New Orleans and turned three blocks before Tulane University.

They parked across the street from the large house surrounded by a cornstalk fence, and from closer inspection, Mike figured it took up more than half the block. "Do you know anyone around here?" he asked Byron, who appeared ready to storm the place.

"Yeah, Mike, I come here all the time for champagne and hot dogs." Byron moved down in his seat and hit his thigh with his fist. "Fuck no, I don't know anyone anywhere around here."

The lights downstairs were all off, but the corner room was lit up, and they saw two people moving around. He had to hold Byron back when they embraced. At least that's what it looked like from the silhouettes.

"What the fuck are you up to, Desi? I'm your husband, and there isn't anything in this world that'll make me give you a divorce, baby. Until death do us part is what the guy said, and that's how it's going to be. The only way out is in a pine box, and I'll be happy to fit you for one if you don't change your mind."

"Byron, man, the smart play is to wait." Mike tried reason one more time, but he could see that something in Byron had snapped, and the bastard was crazy.

"Get me the fuck out of here," Byron growled. "We'll wait a few weeks until the heat is off and then come back. If you have the balls, we're going in there and taking Desi back home."

"Keep your mouth shut about me if you want me to help you."

Byron laughed as he glanced back one more time. "Didn't think the stupid little bitch had it in her, but I'm going to beat that newfound courage right out of her first chance I get."

CHAPTER EIGHTEEN

Harry got ready for bed, nearly asleep on her feet. She'd been in surgery for hours at University with some difficult cases. It had taken some convincing by the medical school to get her to accept a teaching position, but she'd come to enjoy it as she rose through the academic ranks. She'd had to cut back on her private practice, but so far, the only big sacrifice she'd made was her time.

Tonight, she saw the drawback to the hours she put in. She'd missed dinner with everyone, and she needed to get some sleep so she could repeat her day tomorrow. That left no time for Desi, so there'd have to be some changes going forward. She didn't want to get Desi back only to spend all her time at the hospital.

"Hey," Desi said, watching her pace.

The disconcerting feeling of restlessness had been building during the two weeks since they'd found out Byron had been let out on bond, but really that was only a small part of it. She was confident she could deal with Byron, but holding back from Desi was getting harder. She wanted what she'd had, but she also wanted to go slow to make sure Desi felt comfortable with their pace.

"Come here," Desi said when she didn't respond quickly enough. "Everything okay? You're a little hyper tonight."

"Just a long day. When I have to concentrate for so long it wires me up." She sat facing Desi and took her hand. "You need anything?"

"No, but I wish this cast was off already." Desi took her hand and smiled.

She was happy to see Desi somewhat relaxed and slowly coming out of the shell she'd built for herself. The pressure of what they were facing meant Desi wouldn't ever let her guard down completely, but she was a different woman from the one she'd met in the emergency room, and she was happy she'd had something to do with the transformation. The more time they spent together, the freer Desi seemed, and that made her want more. The only tension between them came from waiting on what Byron's next move was going to be. She couldn't convince Desi not to worry about that, since she was fearful for Desi and Rachel but tried not to show it.

"It won't be long." She placed her hand on Desi's cast and tapped her fingers against it. "You'll be joining me in the park for runs before you know it."

"Harry, I've never run in my life, and I'm not starting now," Desi said, laughing. "If I could kneel, though, I could give you a massage."

"I remember those with great fondness." She wiggled her eyebrows, getting Desi to blush.

"Stop it, you." Desi lowered her head, but it seemed from sudden bashfulness rather than submissiveness.

"Did Rachel make it home for dinner?" she asked, giving Desi a break. She knew Tony and Kenneth had invited her to give them haircuts to help with the boredom of being home all the time.

"She got home right after Mona helped me with a bath, and they changed the sheets for us while I was up. I'm going to get lazy after all this forced lying around."

"You'll never be lazy, but I'm glad they're getting to spend time with you and taking such good care of you." She leaned in and kissed her, enjoying the emerging passion that built fast and hot. "You sure smell good," she said kissing Desi's neck.

"Tony brought me a bottle of perfume when he came over today. He's so nice." Desi ran her fingers through Harry's hair and kissed her again. "I've missed you for years, but I missed him and Kenneth too."

"He quit painting when you weren't around anymore, but he got some of that back with all the decorating."

"All those art classes we took together were fun, and I'm glad he was able to forgive me." Desi went willingly when she held her. "So much stuff got messed up, huh?"

"It's hard to forget, but try to put that behind you." She held Desi and rubbed her back. "What I'm asking is impossible, I know that, but pain recedes when we give it the time to heal. We have all the time we need to make that happen."

"When you say stuff like that, I totally believe you."

"Good, and I think we need a break. How about a weekend trip with just the three of us? We could go somewhere relaxing, like a resort on the beach."

"I'd love that, but I'm not sure how much fun I'll have if I can't get wet." Desi blushed harder after saying that.

"Sitting and listening to the waves is all I want. We can stop and visit my parents, then hit the lounge chairs in the sand and have a good time."

"That sounds nice," Desi said in a way that sounded like she was forcing her to spend the weekend having a root canal.

"What?" Harry leaned back and tried to look Desi in the eye.

"I remember your mother, and I'm sure she won't be thrilled that we're here." Desi plucked at Harry's T-shirt and seemed to lose all her good humor. "I'm sure she won't be quick to forget what I did."

"My mother is a unique person, I'm not denying that, but she does want to see her children happy. You make me happy, and that's all that's going to matter." Harry kissed Desi's hand and pulled her forward again. "The only thing to remember is she and my father loved you, and they'll fall in love with you again. I wouldn't suggest going if I didn't believe that."

"You might be slightly exaggerating, but if you think it'll be okay, I'd love to go with you. Rachel will start packing the minute you mention it." Desi ran her hands through her hair again and kissed her cheek. "Is there some reason your hair is still this wet?"

"She was just following orders," Rachel said, coming in with her bag. "I'm cutting her hair. I'll have a whole new set of clients when everyone sees how fantastic she looks."

"Her hair is perfect now," Desi said as Rachel pointed to the chair she'd set up.

"Sorry, but in my professional opinion, it could be better." Rachel shook out her cape and crooked her finger at Harry.

"Don't cut too much off," Desi said. "Unless that's what you want, Harry." She looked down and bit her lip.

"Desi, do you want your surgeon's hair falling in her eyes while she's doing a spine transplant?"

"Your knowledge of new and innovative medical procedures is astounding, and Desi has last say," Harry said as she sat in the chair.

For the next hour she sat and smiled as Desi, Mona, and Rachel argued about every strand of hair that came off. She came close to having to separate Mona and Rachel when Rachel suggested Harry color away the gray at her temples, but that argument died when Desi said she liked the added color. Life wouldn't be boring in the future, she thought, as Rachel pulled out the hair dryer.

"You look good," Desi said when Harry joined her on the bed, and they got in their familiar sleeping positions.

"I hope you think so." She kissed the top of Desi's head and closed her eyes.

"Serena called again. Byron's attorney found a way to push everything back again. Something about unsigned paperwork or something."

Harry sighed and held Desi tighter. It was the second time this had happened, and waiting for the final bell was irritating. "We'll get there, and eventually he'll run out of places to hide."

"There you go, Desi. This will be much more comfortable." Harry's nurse finished wrapping the new smaller cast and smiled up at her. "You'll be much more mobile in this one if you promise to use your crutches."

It had been over two months since that last catastrophic night with Byron, and Harry's care had gotten her back on her feet like she'd promised. The latest X-rays were great, according to her good-looking doctor, and she was happy to be able to get up and around again. "Thank you, Beth, and hopefully in a couple more weeks, I'll be free."

"We'll be happy to see Dr. Basantes relax a bit once that happens."

"Speaking of, is she around?" She'd gotten a ride from Tony, but Harry was bringing her home.

"She's working on patient files in her office. We locked her in there to keep her from hovering. The doc is making everyone nuts when it comes to you, so thanks for healing so quickly."

"She's good at hovering, but I don't mind. How about handing over my crutches, and I'll go surprise her."

"She'll be thrilled," Beth said, making sure the crutches were at the right height. "The girls and I wanted to say how happy we are you're here."

"I'm happy to be here too. It always means I'm a little closer to wearing both shoes."

"That's true, but we meant how much happier and mellower Dr.

Basantes seems since you've been around." Beth put up her hands and laughed. "Not that she wasn't great before, but she was a tad intense."

Desi felt her face heat at the compliment, but that was nice to hear from someone who knew Harry well. "Thank you for saying that. It's nice to be here, and I'm glad she's happy about that too."

"You make a cute couple, and she'll be thrilled to see you on your feet, so let's go surprise her. If we take too much time, she'll work herself into a frenzy with too much coffee and worry."

She stood and held Beth's hand to get her balance. For some reason, the thought of Byron's foot coming toward her leg dominated her thoughts, and she had to close her eyes and take a breath to dispel the dark place her mind had gone to. Everything had been so good, and it was hard to not think of it all being snatched away. She was finally back on her feet, but one wrong move and she'd be knocked down again, only for good next time.

"You okay? Do you need to sit again?" Beth's voice made her shake her head and open her eyes.

"Sorry, maybe I need to eat something." She tried to shake it off, but that sense of dread wasn't going without a fight. It was like an omen in her gut warning her not to let her guard down because someone was close and meant her harm.

She'd wanted Byron out of her life for years, and now that he finally was, she worried constantly about where he was. After his release he'd disappeared, but she knew him too well. Everywhere she went with either Harry or Mona she was on the lookout for him. She'd never seen him or Mike again, but that didn't mean they'd forgotten about her.

"Are you sure you're all right?" Beth asked, not leaving her side. "You're a little pale."

"If you give me a minute, I promise I'll be fine," she said, placing the crutches under her arms while she leaned against the exam table.

The only good news she'd gotten lately was from Jerry Castle, the attorney Harry had hired, who said the divorce was going smoothly, and they hadn't gotten a counterclaim from Byron. Jerry had filed her paperwork with no request for spousal support. He thought she deserved it, but Harry had backed her up on that. It was better to have him out of her life completely.

After a long talk one night, Harry explained that while she wasn't super rich, she was comfortable enough to support both her and Rachel forever. The last thing she wanted was to be a long-term burden, but Harry had been persuasive. What had finally convinced her was that by accepting Harry's help, she not only severed her ties to Byron but also gutted his argument that she'd lied to the police about the assaults to sweeten her divorce settlement.

Harry had taken those burdens off her soul, and all she wanted now was to be on equal footing with Harry, as her partner. She wanted to take care of Harry's needs and make her happy about sharing a life and home together.

The next step to that was rekindling the intimacy they'd once shared, but her injury and marital status had put the brakes on that. Harry was the noblest and most patient person she knew. She didn't push, and she'd allowed Desi to get there in her own time. Finally, she felt like she was just about there.

Now with the lighter cast and legally separated, she could maybe do something about moving them forward. "Okay, I'm ready," Desi said to Beth, balancing herself to start moving. They made their way to Harry's office, and she tapped on the slightly open door with her crutch. "Hey, are you up for some company?"

Harry's smile was immediate and infectious, and it made her forget all her gloomy thoughts. "You look good and happy." Harry waved her in but kept her seat when Desi motioned for her to stay put. "It's good to see you walking around, but promise me you'll be careful."

"You worry too much."

"That's my job, but if you're good I'll take you out to dinner." Harry leaned back, making the leather of her chair creak.

"That's my job too, but you tell me not to worry all the time. And it's great to be back on my feet. I plan on taking advantage of that, but I promise I'll be careful." She stuck her tongue out at Harry, liking that she could make her laugh.

"So how about it? Would you have dinner with me?" Harry stood and smiled.

"Would that be like a date?" The last time she'd been on one was with Harry, and she was looking forward to the process again, even if she was over thirty.

"It's definitely a date, and I'd be honored if you said yes," Harry said, bowing with her hand out.

"Would you sit for a second?" She rested her crutches on the side of the desk and sat in Harry's lap when she did as she asked. Harry hadn't woken her up when she'd left that morning and she'd missed her. "Thank you for my freedom in more ways than this spiffy cast, and thank you for being so sweet." She kissed Harry, trying to pour everything she felt for her into it. "Tony will be thrilled if I can go shopping with him for the changes we're making to the house too."

"I'm sure he will, but let's not talk about him right this second," Harry said, kissing her again.

"I missed you today. I hate when you leave before I wake up."

"I missed you too, but there's no reason for both of us to suffer. Right now, I'm ready to have you all to myself. Any requests on where we go?"

"You pick," she said as she ran her finger down Harry's neck, making her shiver.

Harry's cell rang, and Desi reached for it and handed it over. When Harry saw the readout, she put it on speaker. "Hey, Jerry. Have you called to tell us you found some obscure law that grants Desi a divorce today?"

"I wish," Jerry said, sounding as upbeat as he always did. "Do you know where Desi is, by chance?"

"She's sitting here with me," Harry said, winking at her.

"Good, and hey, Desi."

"Hi, is something wrong?"

"I wanted you to know I tried Byron's attorney today, and he still isn't taking my calls. You should know that the judge ruled on the paperwork we filed and has agreed to designate the day you were rushed to the hospital as the date of separation. That makes the end of this less than two months away."

"That's great," Harry said. "Right, honey?"

"Yes," she said, but she didn't trust Byron not to do something before then. "Are you sure Byron can't stop this?"

"Byron keeps insisting through counsel that you two are working it out. I explained to the court that's not at all the case, so everything is on track. Are you worried about anything specific?"

"Byron can convince himself of anything, and if he finds out about Harry, I'm afraid he'll try something to hurt her." She put her head on Harry's shoulder and sighed. "I know him better than anyone, and he's not going to disappear without a fight. He handles things by balling up his fists and lashing out. I don't want Harry exposed to that."

"We're prepared for everything, Desi, so believe what I'm saying. The next time you see Byron or anyone in his family will be either at his criminal trial or for your divorce proceedings."

"I want to believe, but it's hard," she said, taking Harry's hand.

"Think of it this way—if we're patient and do everything correctly, there's no way you're not getting what you want. I know Serena is doing the same thing on her end, so breathe, and know this will all end sooner than you think."

"We'll be careful until he's put away. Being stuck inside hasn't been fun, but it makes me feel better," Harry said.

"Thanks for the update, Jerry," Desi said.

"I'll keep you in the loop, but call me if anything changes."

"I'm sorry about all this," Desi said, not lifting her head. Who needed this kind of drama in their life?

"I'm not," Harry said, kissing her forehead. "What happened was horrible, but the one thing we can celebrate is it brought you back to me. This time I'm not giving up without a fight."

"That's the last thing I want, but promise you'll be careful too." She gladly accepted Harry's kiss and tried to get them back to the flirting they'd been doing. "Are you ready, or do you have more patients?"

"There's one more, but this guy wants to meet you. Are you a Saints fan?" Harry helped her to her feet and they walked slowly to the exam room at the end of the hall.

"I think it's a requirement if you live in New Orleans."

Harry let her go in first, and the biggest guy she'd ever seen was sitting in the exam room with a huge smile on his face. "Hey, Doc, is this your girl?"

"She is, and if you make it through the exam without crying, she'll hand you a lollipop." Harry explained he'd broken his ankle in a freak fall, but he was almost healed. "And I wanted her to see that eventually the cast does come off." Harry knelt to examine the ankle.

They joked back and forth until the guy put his shoe back on and shook Desi's hand before Harry's, and then he left whistling.

Desi waited for Harry to take the lab coat off and followed her to the elevator. "Are you sure I don't need to change?" She'd worn a comfortable long skirt that made it easy to dress without worrying about the cast.

"You look beautiful as always, so let's go get some Chinese food and call it a night. I want to go out, but I'd really like to be alone with you as soon as I can manage it."

"I like the way you think."

They talked about nothing important until they reached Five Happiness restaurant, and she remembered coming here with Harry's family. The attractive hostess hugged Harry and kissed her cheek as soon as they entered, and it made her laugh and arch her eyebrow. Any jealousy she felt vanished when Harry introduced the hostess and her husband as the owners.

Harry ordered some appetizers when they got a table, and she told Desi to order the rest. They were quiet until the food came out, and Harry put an eggroll on her plate. She was glad to be here, but the conversation with Jerry hadn't completely left her mind.

"Harry?"

"Did I skip something you wanted?"

"No, I just wanted to ask you a question."

"Ask away, I'm an open file."

"When do you…" She was having a problem finishing her question, since she wasn't sure she wanted the answer. "Do you want Rachel and me to move out?"

"What are you talking about?"

"I know you didn't ask for us to get dumped on you like we did, and now that I'm more mobile, it'll be easier for me to get a job and find a place. Just because we're trying again doesn't mean we have to live together yet." She stopped when Harry put her fork down and put her hand up. She'd opened the door to this conversation, and it would kill her if Harry pushed her right through it now that she'd given her the opportunity. But it was only fair to ask.

"You aren't moving, and neither is Rachel. I take that back— Rachel is free to go if she wants to be on her own, but you're not going anywhere unless you want that too." Harry pointed at her. "You're right, we don't have to live together yet, but in my mind, it's your home as much as it is mine, and if you want a job because you're bored or there's something you really want to do, then wait a few months and go for it. Just don't feel like you have to because of me."

"You can't support me forever. That's not fair, and I can't expect you to do that for both me and my sister."

"That's easy. You didn't ask me, I offered. There aren't any strings you're not seeing, and I want you with me. From experience I know Rachel is part of the deal. She's been with you from day one, and I wouldn't want that to change. I just want her to stick with us until all this is over, and then she can make her own choices." Harry stopped and put her eggroll down. "Wait. Do you not want to live with me? Am I pushing you too fast?"

"You know I do, but it shouldn't always fall on you to take care of us. You've been doing it for years, and it's time for me to contribute something." She spoke faster when she saw Harry combing her hair back like she was worried about something big.

"I think if you stay and we make a life together, that *is* you contributing. There's no way anyone can have a relationship alone." Harry reached for her hand, and she was quick to give it. "Besides, you and Rachel do plenty to take care of me, so it was never one-sided."

"We don't do that much, and you know it."

"First off, if I have to pay for another haircut in my life, I'm going to be a little peeved, and you did a good job of looking out for me before. That's not going to change, is it?" Harry asked and she shook her head. "Good, partnerships are built on more than money, and that's not what we're about. You can live on your own if you want to, of course, but I don't see any reason to go backward."

"I don't want to leave. I want to take care of you. All I want is you, and for you to be proud of me." She gazed at Harry and wondered what her life would've been if she'd never found this amazing person.

"I'm already proud of you. All I want is for you to be happy and find the things in life that'll keep you that way. Along the way we'll have each other to lean on. That's what I want, but don't be shy if I left anything out."

"You forgot the chicken in garlic sauce."

"No, I didn't. You were so busy worrying over nothing that you didn't hear me." Harry kissed her hand and laughed. "Life's been tough enough without you, so please stay. You know Mona will find a way to blame me if you don't."

"I didn't want you to think I was taking advantage." She smiled when Harry pressed her hand to her cheek. "Did you really mean it, that I could get a job?"

"That's up to you. If you want one, then go out and get one."

"I don't have any experience doing anything," she said, leaning back when the waiter put some dishes on their table. "Byron wouldn't let me go to school once we got married, saying it was a waste, so all I have is a high school diploma. I doubt that'll get me very far."

"Is school something you're interested in? It's not too late to pursue a degree." Harry sat back as Desi filled two plates and handed her one. "If college isn't what you want, maybe work with Rachel, and see if that's something you'd enjoy."

"I'm not sure. No one except you has ever asked me what I want."

"The most important thing is it should make you happy. You also don't have to decide this second what that is. You can take all the time you want to think about it."

The more they talked, the more her doubt melted away, and her thoughts bounced from one subject to another as they ate. Life was so much easier when you had someone who believed in you, someone who enjoyed talking about whatever came to mind. They packed the leftover food, and Desi was happy she could sit up front with Harry, thanks to the smaller cast. She held Harry's hand on the way home and didn't look away from Harry's profile.

"It's a shame you got rid of that old two-seater," she said.

"We had some good times in that thing, but the back seat in this one will be more comfortable if we ever go parking." Harry smiled at her, making her laugh.

"That might be fun if you're game."

"That's like asking me if I'm up for chocolate ice cream." Harry turned into the driveway and followed her to the stairs. "Let me give you a hand." She carried Desi up and set her on the bed.

Desi and Tony had redecorated the master bedroom. The formerly blue-gray walls were now light cream, the comforter was now silky, and the sheets had gotten an upgrade. Tony had found an antique dresser for Desi's things, and Mona had rearranged the closet for them.

Harry had taken all the changes well and had encouraged her and Rachel to do whatever they needed to feel more at home. The house was comfortable, but she wanted to do whatever she could to make it a home for all of them. She'd always thought of Harry as family, and now she was getting to live out her dream with the woman she loved.

"I'm going down for your crutches," Harry said, taking her shoes off and untucking her shirt. "Do you want anything while I'm downstairs?"

"Want to open a bottle of wine?" she asked in a low voice. Tonight, she wanted to show some of the newfound courage Harry had nurtured in her. "We could relax and talk before bed."

"That would be nice. Anything else?" Harry asked, gazing at her in a way she hadn't in a long time.

"That's all." Harry started walking, and she had one more request before she was too far away. "Could you close the door for me?"

"No problem," Harry said, cocking her head to one side as if that was a strange request, but she did it anyway.

"If that's your answer for everything tonight, we'll have a wonderful night." Once she was alone, Desi limped to the dresser and took out the nightgown she hoped would show Harry she was ready for that next step. "Now if only I can convince myself."

❖

Harry shook her head as she descended the stairs, perplexed at Desi's sudden need for privacy. Not that she begrudged her the opportunity to be alone, but this was the first time she'd asked for her to close the door. She'd take her time going back up, and she'd ask Desi if she needed to be alone.

She found Rachel in the kitchen leaning against the counter eating a sandwich in large bites. "Are you hungry or in a hurry to get somewhere?"

"I'm hungry, tired, and pissed."

"That doesn't sound like a good combination. Rough day?" She took a bottle of white out of the wine cooler and reached for two glasses.

"It was more of a bitchy day than rough. You ever have one where everyone complained about everything? If I have to look at another strand of hair before tomorrow, someone's getting their head shaved." Rachel took another bite out of the sandwich like she was taking her frustrations out on it.

"I promise I'm perfectly happy with my hair and there's no one upstairs expecting you to mess with theirs." She searched the drawers for the opener after kissing Rachel on the top of the head.

"What are you doing down here besides planning to get drunk?" Rachel bumped her hip with hers as she worked on the cork.

"Your sister asked for wine and conversation, so I'm getting one part of that list." The cork gave way so she picked up the glasses and bent so Rachel could kiss her good night. "We're going to bed, so unless you fall and break your leg in the shower, I'll see you in the morning."

"Wait up." Rachel grabbed the back of her shirt. "Do you mind some advice?"

"Sure. Is there something wrong?"

"No, I just want to talk to you before you go back up there." Rachel lowered her head and took a deep breath.

"Hey." She put everything down and put her arms around Rachel. "Talk to me."

"I want you to be—" Rachel stopped, blushed, and didn't display any of her usual sarcastic bravado.

"What?" Harry pulled her closer to see if not having to look at her would make it better.

Rachel exhaled, and Harry felt it against her chest. "Don't think I'm accusing you of anything, or that I believe you'll do anything wrong. That's not it, but you need to know some things before you scare my sister off."

"I'd never—"

"Harry, I know that. Like I said, it's just advice, so promise you won't be mad."

"Okay, go ahead."

"I know you guys had an intimate relationship that started your senior year." Rachel rested her head on her chest as she spoke. "That's the last time she had that kind of bond. Since then, she's had a hard time with intimacy, so be gentle, and go slow if she's willing to try."

"You know I will."

"I know that too." Rachel finally looked at her. "With Byron, let's just say I tried to stop what he was doing. Actually, I thought of killing him more than once. When I interfered, though, it only made it worse for her."

Harry held Rachel tighter when she started to cry, and she tried hard not to join her. "I'm not going to push her into anything, if that's what you're worried about."

"That's not what I mean at all, so don't take this the wrong way. That's the last thing I want. I see how happy she is with you, and I'm thrilled her confidence in herself is slowly coming back. All that's because of you, but please don't do anything that'll send her running back into her shell."

"I haven't said it to her, but you know how long I've loved your sister," she said, wiping Rachel's face with her fingers. "Those feelings never died, which means I'll go at her pace. And when she does decide she's ready, then I'll show her how much I love her."

"I believe in you, Harry. You're the only person the two of us have ever known who's true to her word."

"You love your sister, and I'm glad you've been there for her your whole life."

"I don't think I've done a very good job of protecting her. First Clyde, then Byron, and I did nothing. All I did was stick around to make sure he didn't kill her. I know she's told you about Byron, but if she hasn't told you about Clyde, then give her time. Desi's the sweetest person I know. She's got a big heart, but aside from you, there haven't been many happy times." Rachel sniffled but seemed to feel better after unburdening herself.

"If Clyde were still alive, I'd find him and kick the shit out of him. She never said anything back then, but I knew there had to be something off."

"He snapped after that night and was quick with his fists. Desi got the brunt of it, but I wasn't immune. That miserable bastard died alone and in pain, and that was still too good for him. I try never to waste my time on hate, but I still hate Clyde and everything he did to us."

"It's good to get all that out, but concentrate on the future when it gets to be too much. I promise—it's brighter."

"Thanks, and could you…" Rachel stopped as if she didn't have the right to ask any more.

"This talk is just between us, sweetie. Don't worry about that." Harry patted her on the back. "And whenever you need to talk about anything, I'm available."

"I love you, Harry, and more importantly, so does she. Good night and good luck." Rachel laughed as if she'd gotten her good humor back.

"It's wine and conversation. Not much to it that I'd need luck for." She picked up the wine and glasses and started out the door.

"If you say so." Rachel laughed again as if she knew something Harry didn't.

Wine and conversation would be perfect, even if she missed the feel of Desi's body under her hands. Holding her every night was bliss, but she couldn't deny the way her body was on fire every morning, either.

CHAPTER NINETEEN

Desi tweaked the navy-blue silk material of the nightgown that came to right above her knee and hoped the cast didn't detract from the look. She thought its message was a little too blatant, but Tony warned her if she didn't buy it, he would, so here she was. Seduction wasn't at all in her wheelhouse, but Harry had found her attractive once and, with any luck, would again.

"Come in," she said when she heard the soft knock. Harry seemed cautious after her request to close the door.

"Hey, I—" Harry entered and dropped the glasses on the floor. "I...ah..." Harry opened and closed her mouth like a beached fish, her gaze traveling the length of Desi's body.

Desi smiled, amazed they didn't have to stop to sweep glass off the floor. "Why don't you change and get more comfortable? Or you can come sit over here." Harry just stared at her and acted as if her feet were glued to the floor. "Are you all right?"

"I'm...ah...I'm okay," Harry said. She ran her tongue across her lips, then smacked them together as if trying to get them to start working again. "That's new," she said, pointing at her.

"You don't like it?" she asked, crooking her finger at Harry.

"I love it." Harry took a step forward, but it appeared more like she was trying to keep her balance from the way she was swaying. "You look beautiful."

"Thank you." She smoothed the material down again. "Tony talked me into it, and I'm glad to see you're not running for the exit."

"If I can get my feet to move, it'll be more like I'm running toward you," Harry stepped closer and put the bottle down. "I dream about this all the time, so no one better wake me up. If I'm not dreaming, remind me to buy Tony the washing machine he wants in the morning."

"I'm glad he was so insistent." She raised her hand and offered it to Harry. "Want to come closer?"

Harry stared at her as if having trouble understanding her, but she nodded before dropping down on the bed with the grace of a drunk person. "What did you want to talk about?" Harry asked, swinging her legs onto the bed.

"You know I love talking to you, but I had something else in mind for tonight," she said, pulling her toward her. "Do you remember all those nights we spent in that spot in the yard, or in the attic?"

"Yes," Harry said, sounding hungry enough to devour her.

"I remember them too," she said, running her fingernail up Harry's shirtfront until her hand went under the collar. "I think about them a lot, and I also think it's time to add new memories."

Harry closed her eyes at her touch, but they flew open again when Desi started unbuttoning her shirt. "Are you sure? I don't mind waiting, so don't do this because you think I expect it."

"Baby, you have to know me better than that," she said, kissing Harry's neck.

"Just know you're precious to me, and I'll never do anything that would hurt you."

"I want you to touch me. I want you to erase the time we've been apart, and I want to start on the life you promised me." She pulled Harry closer with each word. "I want to feel like a woman you find desirable."

The kiss that followed had a different feel to it, but at the same time, it felt so familiar. It was a reminder of those electric times when they'd learned what they liked and how much they loved each other. She pressed her tongue against Harry's lips, thrilled when Harry moaned.

Harry caressed her skin as she lowered the strap of her nightgown.

"Your hands feel so good." Desi gladly rolled to her back, giving Harry more room to touch her.

"Surgeon's hands, baby," Harry said as she lowered the other strap.

Desi closed her eyes, and her breath caught when Harry palmed her breast. Her nipple tightened and it ignited her passion, long-buried to protect her soul from fracturing. But that part of her that burned for Harry came out of hibernation.

"Look at me, baby," Harry said as she flattened her hand.

"I know I don't look like I did." There was no way the excitement of being together again could make her self-doubt disappear. She was waiting for Harry to come to her senses and realize their one chance had passed.

"You don't have anything to worry about," Harry said, taking her shirt off. "But I do want you to tell me if you need to stop."

Harry lowered the nightgown and exposed Desi's breasts, and Desi watched her expression. One of the things she'd loved about Harry was how she couldn't hide her emotions. The way Harry's eyes took her in, and the way her nose flared, told Desi what she needed to know.

"You're so beautiful," Harry said as she circled her nipple with her index finger. "From the time I was old enough to know what it meant to touch you, I never wanted to stop."

"I've never thought of myself as beautiful, especially lately." She hesitated to touch Harry, so Harry placed her hand on her chest and kissed her again.

"The only thing that matters is you and me." Harry lowered her head and ran her tongue over her nipple.

It was like the damn thing was on fire, and it made her clit start pulsing, ratcheting up her need. She needed to be naked and feel Harry on her, loving her, and making her believe she did desire her. The want in her protested when Harry moved off her, but she smiled when Harry took off the rest of her clothes. She took the opportunity to get naked as well, and she came close to tears when Harry lay back down.

"It's like coming home," she said before Harry kissed her and ran her hand down her body. It felt so good, and she was having trouble breathing, but it wasn't enough. She wanted it all. "Touch me, honey." She sounded strange to her own ears, and everything in her was laser focused on Harry's hands. "Please."

Harry moved her hand over her abdomen to the middle of Desi's thigh and squeezed. "Tell me what you want." She encouraged Desi to spread her legs and moved her hand higher. "Whatever it is, I'll give it to you."

"Please...I need you to touch me. I want you to." This was how it'd been with Harry from the very beginning. She had a way of making her crave her hands, and the insanity of it wouldn't stop until Harry filled her and made her come. "Make love to me."

Harry gently bit her bottom lip as her hand moved again until she was cupping her sex. She covered Harry's hand with hers, and the heat of Harry's skin didn't burn as intensely as her sex. There was no turning back, and that Harry wanted her this much meant there was no looking back.

"Can I touch you?" Harry asked, holding still.

"I'm yours, and I want you."

Harry dipped two fingers into her opening, then dragged them over her clit. She lifted her hips as much as she could and pressed her head into the pillow. Everything in her had narrowed to that one spot between her legs.

"Tell me what you want," Harry said.

She opened her eyes and reached for Harry. "You…only you." That's all she could say when Harry slowly slid her fingers in and put her thumb on her clit. "Oh God." Everything in her body electrified as Harry moved her fingers in a gentle rhythm.

"So good," she said as her body demanded more. "Give me… more, baby—harder." She held on to Harry's shoulders as she turned in to her. "I want you." The start of her orgasm made her want to stop to savor it, but she wanted to reach that peak more. "Oh, Jesus—don't stop. I…oh, I need to come. Don't stop—don't—yes, honey, yes. I'm coming." She could no more stop the pleasure that engulfed her than the words spilling out of her mouth.

"Wait," she said, and Harry stopped but didn't move her hand.

"You okay?" Harry asked lifting her head.

"I am now." There was nothing that compared to this. "I missed you so much…so stay where you are," she said when Harry was about to pull out. "I've dreamed of this more times than I can count, and it was better than any fantasy I ever had."

"I missed you for a lot of reasons, but wanting to touch you was always a big one." Harry kissed her. "Being with you like this was always my honor." The next kiss was to the side of her neck, and it sparked her desire back to life.

"Come here," she said so Harry would lie over her. "I want to touch you." She surprised herself with her sudden forwardness as her hand went down Harry's back to her butt. Harry was careful of her leg as she straddled Desi's thigh, trapping her hand between Desi's leg and her clit.

"Do you want me to touch you?" she asked.

"Yes," Harry said, but her hand had started that delicious cadence again and it was hard to think.

They moved together, and she held on to Harry as the fire that had burned to an ember flared into an inferno, and she pressed her leg against Harry. Neither of them said a word but moaned as their movements got more frantic. She'd forgotten how freeing this act could be. It was the ultimate act of loving someone.

The only sound for a long while was skin against skin, but Harry went rigid right before her. "Wow," Harry said as she edged off her, her fingers still inside her.

"That was pretty spectacular," she said, hissing softly when Harry pulled out.

"Trust me, if you give me the chance, I can do so much better." Harry laughed.

"Whenever and wherever," she said, combing Harry's dark hair off her brow. "I might not let you out of this room, and I hope Mona and Rachel didn't hear us."

"Don't threaten me with imprisonment if you don't mean it, and knowing those two, they're at the door with my stethoscope."

She laughed, and it felt so good to not only feel sated, but cherished. It felt good to be loved.

❖

Byron stared at the house trying to tune out Mike's heavy breathing next to him. They were silent as they watched the house go dark one room at a time. He hadn't seen Rachel, but he figured she had to be in there as well. His first mistake had been letting that bitch stay in his house. Rachel had been a bad influence on his wife, so if she was there, he'd take care of her too.

He'd bided his time, hoping Desi and Rachel had dropped their guard about him and Mike. His father had made him stay around the garage and work, but he'd waited long enough. The cops had stopped by after Mike had followed them that day, but they hadn't done shit. He was here to get what he'd been dreaming about since that first night in jail.

He could've had anyone, but he'd wanted her. He'd picked her— Clyde had given her to him, so she belonged to him. There was going to be no divorce—period. His father was right about so many things. The most important was that she was going to pay for all this independent thinking she'd displayed. Tonight, it was her choice. She either came back and submitted, or she wasn't going to see the morning.

"It's not too late to change your mind. Why not quit and cut a deal?" Mike spoke in a whisper as if he was afraid he'd wake the people inside the house. "This sounds easy, but I got a bad feeling it ain't."

"Daddy told us what to do. The plan is solid, so quit being a pussy." He grabbed Mike by the bicep and squeezed. "Remember, if you don't, you'll be looking for a new job."

Mike yanked his arm away from him and lifted his fist. "Quit acting like some big man," Mike said, making him laugh. "It's so funny, but you keep needing backup. That ain't something a man needs."

"Shut up, or you're going in there with a bloody nose." He put his head back and closed his eyes. "Let's give it another hour. If they're dead asleep, they're not going to know what's going on. That way the woman who owns the house won't get a chance to call the police until we have Desi. Whoever she is, I might beat the shit out of her for taking my property."

"If all this is about getting Desi back, then concentrate on that. Leave everyone else out. You don't, and you're going back to jail. Only this time it's going to be for a long time. You think they won't know it's you if you do shit, when the cops have been sniffing around? C'mon, man. Think."

"What the hell happened to you? You're afraid three women are going to fuck you up." He had to calm down, or this was going to blow up into a shit storm. His problem was that he couldn't do this alone, not with other people in the house. "Okay, we only take Desi. She's going to pay for putting me in jail, and you can't stop me from doing that."

"You get caught doing something to Desi again, and they're going to bury you in that jail before they let you out. Why don't you wait until after the trial is over? Is it worth years of your life?"

Mike tried to sound reasonable, but he could hear the slight tremble in his voice. He didn't want to do this.

"Forget all that, and pay attention." He was sure Desi was in there even if he hadn't seen her, Rachel, or really anyone else. He believed Mike, and there was only one question he wanted answered. Who did the big house belong to? He'd driven out alone on the nights he couldn't sleep, but everyone was already inside.

"Let's go if you're not changing your mind. I'm tired of sitting out here." Mike reached up and turned off the dome light. He was willing to help, but he seemed not to want to take any chances.

"I'll go in first and grab Desi," he said as they climbed over the fence in the front corner where it was the darkest. "You watch my back, and keep anyone who tries to stop us away from me."

"This is making me fucking sick to my stomach," Mike said as he landed in the yard.

"Place like this probably has a fancy security system," he said, looking at all the utility boxes on the outside of the house. He started cutting wires, wanting to seize the advantage. "You understand?" He didn't want to cut the main power line and kill himself, so he flipped the main breaker.

"Yeah, I understand that this is going to land me in jail. Let's go."

"Go check the panel by the back door, and see if the light went out," he said. There were two more boxes he wasn't sure about, so he cut them to be safe.

"It's out, so let's go."

He cupped his hands and pressed them to the glass to look inside. The kitchen was dark, and what he'd done so far didn't seem to have woken anyone. This was going to be like cutting through warm butter. "Okay, get ready." He wrapped his jacket around his hand and smashed through the glass.

They waited to go in, making sure everything was still quiet. Ten minutes crawled by, and there was no movement. Mike walked to the front of the house and opened the gate. That was good planning for when they'd need to run out.

His heart hammered as they walked into the kitchen that looked as expensive as the house. Where would Desi or Rachel have met somebody with this kind of money? Next to the kitchen was an office with lots of built-in shelves lined with books. The artwork on the walls looked expensive as well, and he hoped whoever owned it didn't own a gun.

They reached a staircase like something from the movies, and they walked slowly in case any of the steps creaked. The long hallway at the top went both ways, and he wondered who was in the other rooms, but he was sure Desi was in the one on the end from all the nights he'd watched the silhouettes. She was in bed with whoever owned the house, and that enraged him.

"Watch my back," he whispered.

The old wooden door opened soundlessly, and he waited just outside the room to make sure Desi and her bedmate were sleeping. His breathing was too fast and shallow, but he shrugged off Mike's hand, needing to finish this. He was tired of feeling like a failure, and he couldn't live the rest of his life with his father telling him what an asshole he was for letting some little woman beat him.

He balled his fists and walked in, stopping in the middle of the room. The electricity was off, but there was enough light from the street to see the two people spooning on the bed. It was clear they were naked, and it made it clear why Desi wanted the divorce. It had nothing to do with him hitting her and everything to do with this old motherfucker holding her like he owned her.

Where Desi had found a lover who looked old enough to be her father was a mystery. He closed his eyes and clenched his teeth together from the pain in his chest that reached into the middle of his skull. The best thing to do was kill them both right here, but he had to have Desi one more time. She'd come to see the mistake she'd made right before he choked the life out of her.

He gulped in air and held it. Desi's shoulder-length hair was fanned out on the pillow, but her face was under the blanket. He couldn't hold in the anger choking the life out of him. "You fucking bitch," he screamed, loud enough to wake the people next door. The people on the bed startled and got tangled in the sheets.

Mike was right behind him when he yanked off the sheet and wrapped Desi in it. When it came off the bed, the smell of sex hit him like a shovel to the face, so he let go of Desi and punched the guy hard enough to knock him off the bed. He'd never wanted to kill someone so much in his life, and the thought of spending the rest of his years in jail didn't bother him. It'd be worth it.

"I should fucking kill you," he screamed as he picked Desi up and threw her over his shoulder. He started walking when the old man got up and headed toward him naked. He dropped Desi, hearing the groan of pain when she hit the floor hard. The old man took a swing at him and missed, so he punched the old fucker again, following him to the ground and hitting him a few more times. "Stay down if you're smart." He hit the guy one more time, and he slumped back with his eyes closed.

He went to pick Desi up, but she'd tried to unwrap herself. She screamed when he covered her head again, picked her up, and positioned her like he had before. They were on the stairs when she got an arm free and hit wherever she could reach. What didn't make sense was the way she was screaming back. That was new.

"Let me go, asshole," Desi said as she grabbed onto the banister and hung on with a strength she'd never shown.

The move threw him off balance, and they both went down together with her landing on top. He moaned as his ankle throbbed. "Are you crazy?" he asked when he sat up, pushing her off. That's when he looked into the face of a stranger. "Who the fuck are you? Where's Desi?"

The woman surprised him by driving the heel of her hand into his nose, making it bleed in a steady stream. He put one hand over his face and slapped her with the other. That pushed her back, but he slipped and landed on his stomach. That gave the woman the chance to free her hands completely from the sheet and hit him again. The old man was on the stairs, and he had no choice but to run. Mike shot out the door in front of him and jumped into the driver's seat, his breath coming in hard rasps.

"Gun it," he said when he got in the car. "Fuck." He looked back as they sped away. The sound of sirens was getting closer, and he told Mike to pull over. They ducked as the squad cars raced past.

"I told you this wasn't going to work."

"There's no way they're going to know it was us." He looked in the side mirror as the flashing lights stopped in front of the house, and Mike slowly pulled away, lights still off. "No way in hell."

CHAPTER TWENTY

B asantes."
         "Harry, it's your Uncle Jude." Harry's family had been lifelong friends with Judge Jude Rose from almost the moment her father had moved to the city from Miami. Jude had met the excellent doctor when his daughter had fallen and hurt her arm, and the two families spent so much time together, their kids considered them family.

"Hey, are you okay?" Harry went from groggy to completely alert.

"I hate bothering you this late, but it's Monica. We had an incident over here, and she fell down the stairs. Could you come over and examine her? That'd make me feel better."

"I'll be there as soon as I get dressed."

"Thanks, Harry, and ignore the police when you get here. If they give you any problems about coming in, call me."

"Okay," Harry said, stretching out the word.

"Trust me, it's a long story."

"Who was that?" Desi asked placing her hand on Harry's back.

"Jude Rose, and his wife fell down the stairs. I'm going to run over there and check her out, so go back to sleep. This shouldn't take long unless I have to run her to the hospital."

"Be careful and hurry back."

"I hate to leave you especially after such a great night, but he wouldn't have called if he wasn't worried."

The closest parking spot Harry found on the street was a block away from the house. She grabbed her bag and wondered what was going on. When Jude had said *incident* and that Monica had fallen down the stairs, nothing computed.

"I'm Dr. Basantes," she said to the uniformed officer by the front gate. "Judge Rose called me."

"Harry," Detective Sept Savoie said from the front door. "Come on up."

"Wow, it must be serious if you're here." She shook hands with Sept before they embraced. They'd known each other for years. Harry was also a favorite of Sept's six siblings, when it came to setting bones.

"This is plain bizarre, and there's going to be hell to pay once we find these idiots. Rose is pissed, but I don't even know where to begin. Home invasions usually involve robbery, but the two guys who did this were only interested in taking Monica."

"Damn, that's scary." She walked into a room full of police taking fingerprints and dabbing at a small pool of blood close to the stairs. She'd been here plenty of times and loved the house, but never imagined this happening here. "Uncle Jude," she said, hugging him. "Are you okay?" His face was swollen in multiple places, and his eyes were turning a nice shade of purple-black.

"I'm fine, but I need you to check Monica."

She opened her arms to the beautiful woman Jude had married and held her for a long moment. "I'm so sorry this happened to you. Is there a room that isn't being processed?"

"Let's go up to one of the guest rooms," Monica said with her arm around Harry's waist.

She gave Monica an exam before turning her attention to Jude. Both of them appeared battered but thankfully nothing was broken. "Once all these people clear out of here, I'd like you to come to my office and get some X-rays." She put everything back in her medical bag and sat with them. "It's only a precaution, but I don't want to miss anything."

"This might take a while," Jude said.

"Uncle Jude, you know I'm not going anywhere, so let's go see what Sept found."

"You know Sept?" Jude asked, holding Monica's hand as they headed down.

"New Orleans sometimes feels like a small town. Sept and I have been friends for years, and she's the best person for the job."

The house was still just as crowded, so they sat in the dining room to stay out of the way.

"So, you woke up, and these guys were in your room," Sept started.

The story was told by Jude first and then Monica. Harry thought it sounded bizarre and was thinking of ways to improve her alarm system at home when the words out of Monica's mouth hit her like a bundle of bricks.

"The only thing he said that might lead you somewhere is the name *Desi*. That's who he was looking for, and believe me when I say he looked baffled when he saw it was me under that sheet."

"Oh my God," Harry said, loud enough for the others to stop talking.

"What?" Jude asked, and Monica took her hand.

"Did you get a look at this guy?" Harry asked.

"Stocky build and blond hair," Monica said, closing her eyes. "There were two of them, but I didn't see the other one, I just heard him shouting at the one who'd grabbed me."

Bile rose in the back of Harry's throat, and her pulse started to race. "The guys you want are Byron and Mike Simoneaux. He was in your court recently on attempted murder and domestic violence charges." She had to get home. Desi and Rachel weren't safe if these morons tried this.

"That's really specific," Sept said, writing the names down. "Do you know these people?"

"Desi Simoneaux is staying with me," she said. "I need to get to her."

"Harry, wait," Sept said after instructing two of the units to head over to Harry's and keep an eye on the house. "If Desi is with you, how did they end up here?"

Guilt made her drop back into her chair, and she closed her eyes, not wanting to face people she cared about. "This is my fault. I'm so sorry."

"I doubt that, but explain," Jude said.

She told them about Mike following them and where she'd stopped to confront him. "All I could think was to keep the girls safe, but I stopped in your driveway. He must've assumed this was my house."

"Harry, we don't blame you," Monica said.

"Your Honor, I need to go and talk to Desi Simoneaux to get the information about where to find these two. I'll be back before the guys wrap this up," Sept said, motioning Harry toward the door.

"Uncle Jude, I never meant to put you or Monica in danger. Please believe that."

"Go on. No one is blaming you. Tell Desi I'd like to meet her as well, and Rosa will be thrilled to see you this protective of someone. She must be special."

"She is, but we need to get Byron out of her life for good."

"That isn't going to be a problem if I have anything to say about it," Jude said firmly.

And she believed him. He'd assaulted a judge and his wife and by doing so had made it a hell of a lot easier to put him away. She just had to keep Desi safe in the meantime.

Harry waited for Sept to get out of her car and had her wait in the kitchen while she went to talk to Desi. She took the stairs slowly, trying to think of the best way to tell Desi what had happened. All her promises to keep her safe gnawed at her.

"Sweetheart," she said softly as she ran her hand gently over her leg. "Wake up."

"Harry." Desi blinked up at her and smiled. "Is your uncle okay?"

"He's fine, but you need to get up and get dressed. There's a police officer downstairs, and she needs to talk to you." She told Desi what had happened and held her when she started crying. "It's going to be okay, but Sept needs a clue about where to start looking for them. Think you can do that?"

Desi put her nightgown and robe on and held on to her as they joined Sept. She took plenty of notes on all the home addresses Desi gave them as well as the other places the brothers liked to hang out. "Once you find them, they'll deny it. They'll also have an alibi in their father."

"Leaving your DNA at a crime scene will trump any alibi, so don't worry. You might not realize it yet, but you have some influential friends who'll carve this guy out of your life." Sept patted Desi on her good knee. "The only thing you'll need from now on is help with this one. She's barely housebroken."

"Why are we friends again?" Harry asked, glad that Sept's joke had made Desi smile.

This was what she wanted for Desi. People in her life who cared about her. The thought of Byron getting to her and hurting her again made her nauseous. "You'll call us if you find him, won't you?"

"I sure will," Sept said, taking Desi's hand. "Trust me, I will find him. I do a pretty good imitation of a bloodhound."

She saw Sept out and made sure the gate was closed before going in and setting the alarm again. "Come on, let's go back to bed."

Desi was tense when she picked her up, but she couldn't blame her. "He'd have killed both of us if he'd come here. I can't believe he did this." Desi's words were broken by her tears. "If he'd found us in bed together, we wouldn't have survived. He always went on about how relationships like ours were perverted."

"Listen to me." She put Desi down and moved to hold her. "I'm going to do my best to protect you from anyone or anything that means you harm. The only thing I ask is that you don't run, thinking it will keep me safe. We're stronger together."

"I'm running because it's the best thing. You can't keep me here any longer. Think of Mona if he somehow figures out where we are." Desi was starting to sound hysterical. "I want you more than anything, but I can't live in a world that doesn't have you in it."

"You love me?" she asked, gazing at Desi's face with a smile.

"Concentrate on the rest of what I said," Desi said, kissing her shoulder.

"Uh, no. You can't throw that in there and expect me to let you go. Will it make it easier to convince you of what I'm saying if I tell you I love you too?"

"Are you saying it to make me stay or because you mean it?"

"Loving you has never been about trying to gain something you're not willing to give, and it never will be." She kissed Desi and wiped her tears with the corner of the sheet. "Loving you is the easiest thing I've ever done, and nothing has ever brought me this kind of happiness. I want you here, and I'm not letting go easily."

"I love you, and I need your word that you won't do anything stupid because of me. You don't know Byron like I do. He's an animal with no conscience. Maybe I could leave until he's caught."

Harry stared at Desi and shook her head. "Life is many things, but when it comes down to the truth, it's about surviving every day that's given to us. That's what I've done for years because I never expected you to come back." She blinked when her tears blurred her vision. "I lost you, so I went to class, studied, and counted the days. It's like a blur now—graduating, going to medical school, and starting a practice. At the center of all that, in the deep parts of my brain, there was always you. The girl I loved and always would, no matter how hard I tried to erase you."

"I'm so sorry, my love." Desi brushed her cheeks and kissed her again.

"You've always been my hope, baby. I love you, and you can't ask me to let you go. I can't. Not again."

"Please don't cry—I promise, I'm not going anywhere," Desi said, running her hands through Harry's hair. "And I'm glad you never gave up on me. I'd be lost if you had."

"I never did, you know. The day I found out I'd passed my boards, I went to your house. It was stupid, but I thought you'd want to come and celebrate with me. You're the first person I thought of, and I hoped if you saw me again, maybe you'd forgive me for whatever I'd done."

"You did?" Desi asked and she nodded. "What happened?"

"Your father told me you were married and deliriously happy. That I should understand that and leave you be." Harry laughed bitterly. "He slapped me on the back, saying how proud of me he was, and how different our lives had become."

"Clyde was a bastard. There's no denying that."

"He was so convincing when he told me all you wanted was to be a good wife and mother. That you didn't have children yet, but you had one on the way."

Desi placed her hand on her cheek. "Oh, honey, I'm so sorry."

"He said it with such a straight face, it was like a knife through my heart. There was nothing left but work, so that's what I did. I worked, worked out, and fucked around. That was my life."

"I wish I'd had more strength. I wish I'd seen you that day. I wish…so many things."

"What I'm telling you is we're better off together. We *are* happy together, so don't throw that away. Don't let him win."

Desi didn't hesitate to kiss her with the kind of passion that made Harry glad to be alive. She reached for the hem of Desi's nightgown and pulled it up until she could put her mouth on her nipple. "It's been you—always you."

"Touch me," Desi said as she spread her legs and pushed Harry's hand down. "Let me feel you over me, loving me and making me yours."

"Are you sure?"

"Yes," Desi said as her hips bucked up to meet her hand. The one-word answer was firm and broke through her restraints to be gentle and go slow. Desi was wet and sounded like she knew what she wanted.

She lifted her hips to fit her hand between them and put two fingers in. The feel of Desi's fingers on her clit made her lose focus for a second, but she wanted Desi to get lost in their passion and put her past to rest.

"Does that feel good?" Harry asked as she pulled out and slammed her fingers back in. This was how it had been in the beginning. She wanted to make Desi forget everything but her.

"Yes, don't stop," Desi said, her fingers moving fast and hard over her clit. "You make me feel…oh God," Desi said, her hips coming up to meet hers. "Baby, please, harder. Yes, like that." Desi put her free hand behind Harry's head and pulled it down. "I love…damn, oh, oh…the way you touch me. More, baby, more." Desi moved her hand down to her ass and squeezed. "I'm coming. Don't stop, I'm coming."

Harry concentrated on her hand, wanting to see Desi reach her peak. Before she could act, Desi pushed her onto her back and moved down her body. "Do you want me, baby?"

"Shit, yes," she said, putting her hand behind Desi's head and holding it between her legs. It was like a lightning strike that electrified her body when Desi sucked her in. Whatever they'd been worried about emptied from her brain as Desi's relentless mouth never let up. "So fucking good." She wouldn't last much longer as Desi entangled their fingers and glanced up at her. "Fuck," she said as the orgasm hit her when Desi flicked her tongue rapidly until she'd drained her.

"I love you," Desi said, coming back up and lying over her.

"I love you too, and that was fantastic."

"It was, and you're right. I'm tired of apologizing or being afraid of what I want. You're mine, Harry, and I don't want to lose you."

"That's the last thing you're going to do. We started out together, and that's how we'll finish."

❖

Desi woke to an empty bed and lifted her head in search of Harry. "Where'd she disappear to?" After a night of making love she was a little hurt Harry would've left without saying anything. "Harry? Where are you?"

Harry stepped out of the bathroom, still naked, and stretched.

"Sorry, I had to go." Harry put her arms around her when she climbed back into bed and kissed the side of head. "Go back to sleep. It's still early."

She put her head on Harry's shoulder and ran her hand from her neck to the top of her sex. She'd loved touching Harry from the first time they'd gotten naked together. "You feel so good," she said, repeating the move but going lower this time.

"I'll feel *really* good if you keep that up." Harry's hand landed on her ass and she smiled when Harry rubbed it.

"I remember sitting in English class with you and having the urge to put my hands in your pants and over your butt. Remember the day we knew we were alone in the house for a few hours?"

"That kitchen counter was hard to say goodbye to when my parents sold their place."

"Having you between my legs with your pants around your ankles while you made love to me is one of my favorite memories." She moved her hand over Harry's sex, not surprised to find her hard and ready. "You made me crazy once I knew I could have you any way I wanted."

Harry moved her so she was on top, her legs spread over Harry's thigh. She smiled when Harry moved her fingers from her ass down to her sex. After last night she shouldn't be this ravenous, but they couldn't stop now.

"You make me fucking crazy," Harry said as she lifted her hips a little, chasing her fingers.

"It's mutual, baby. I'd keep you in bed if I could, but that's never stopped you before." She thought of all the places they'd fooled around because they couldn't wait anymore. "So, we're okay?"

"Not as okay as we will be when we finish what you started," Harry said, rolling over and putting more pressure on her clit. "Right now, I don't want to talk."

"Uh, uh, like that, baby. Like that," she said, lifting her ass to give Harry better access. "That's so good."

"Yeah," Harry said, her fingers sliding alongside her clit and squeezing hard as she moved them up and down. "You're so wet," Harry said, quickening her movements. "I love when you get this wet for me."

"Honey, don't stop. I need more." She wanted to protest when she stopped stroking and moved her fingers, but like last night, everything flew from her mind when Harry filled her up and drove her need for an orgasm. The relentlessness of her passion made her feel like she was coming apart, but it all concentrated in her groin as she climbed the peak Harry was leading her to. "Yes...yes...oh God, yes," she screamed as she came. Harry wasn't far behind as she came on her thigh and trembled as she tried to hold herself up.

"I love you," she said, rubbing Harry's back. "And I thought of something to do."

"Something to do?" Harry asked sounding confused as she rolled off her.

"You know. Like a job," she said, moving so Harry would spoon against her back.

"That's good news, and you're amazing if you can think of future career prospects while we're making love. My IQ drops to my shoe size," Harry said, putting her hand flat on Desi's stomach. "Is it a secret?"

"No, and I wasn't exactly thinking about it right then. It was your hands that reminded me of the idea Tony gave me. It's something we can do together."

"You and me, or you and Tony?" The way Harry spoke to her made her feel human. It was such a strange sentiment, and she was getting used to it in the best way.

"You have a job, love." She ran her fingers along Harry's forearm and smiled.

"Did you fall asleep to keep me in suspense?" Harry kissed her neck and tickled her middle when she didn't answer. "Whatever it is, will it make you happy?"

"Yes," she said, clearing her throat. "I was thinking of becoming a potter." She spoke fast, trying to remind herself this wasn't Byron.

It was a craft she'd learned as a child and had Harry's mother to thank for. When she'd shown interest in developing her talent, Rosa had paid for the lessons. She'd become friends with Tony when he took art classes alongside her. Desi loved it until she'd graduated from high school. Magazine Street with all its boutiques full of pottery made her think she could make a living at it. At least, she could contribute to their life together.

"A potter?" Harry sounded confused.

"A person who makes pottery. Remember, I used to do that when we were growing up. I thought I'd gotten pretty good, and with a little practice maybe I could again. Tony could help me think of designs and sell what I make." She started to slow as her idea fizzled out. "Do you think it's stupid?"

Harry came up on her elbow and waited for her to look back at her. "I'm sorry, have we just met?"

"What do you mean?" Her insides trembled as she waited for the letdown, to be told her idea was ridiculous and not to be naive.

"You can't think I'd ever consider anything you want to do stupid." Harry leaned down and kissed her. "You can do anything you set your mind to. I've known that since grammar school, and you've survived something and come out the other side. That means you can do anything you set your mind to. If this is what you want, then what do you need to get started?"

The trembling feeling in her stomach took a moment to settle, and she waited until she could breathe past it again. "Are you sure? It might take me some time to save to buy what I'm going to need."

"Let's not worry about that now. Tell me more about the pottery." Harry rested her head on her palm and seemed interested.

"Tony said there were a few stores always looking for new stuff. If I come up with some new designs, maybe they'd carry them." She shrugged, a little overwhelmed now that she'd voiced something she really wanted. "If I was good enough."

"If you want my opinion, you're going to be great at this. You aren't going to forget about me when you become famous, are you?" Harry chuckled and it lifted a weight off her chest. "Tomorrow we'll figure out how to get you started. Mona will be thrilled, since this is something you can do from home. We'll also have to set up one of the guest rooms for when Tony moves in."

She turned on her back and put her arms around Harry. The burn between them started again, but this time it was slow, and they enjoyed each other until they were sated. She loved the small caresses and kisses as they talked until it was time to get up.

Her heart had finally come home.

CHAPTER TWENTY-ONE

Byron and Mike sat behind the dumpster next to the convenience store close to their parents' house and looked around the corner. The sun was coming up, and they'd missed the chance to sneak inside in case anyone came looking for them. After driving down all the side streets, they'd ditched the car and found four police units parked in front of the house.

"Look," Mike said, pointing but staying out of sight.

The front door opened, and they saw their father in his T-shirt and work pants standing on the porch. "Maybe they're getting ready to leave. All we need to do is say we were at your place watching a movie, and we fell asleep."

Mike glared at him like he was totally insane. "I'm sure they've been by my place already. How did they find us so soon? How'd they ID us?"

"This can't have anything to do with what happened. Those people didn't know us."

"I'm beginning to think you're fucked in the head. Who else are they here for? No cop sits on a house unless they're looking for two dumb bastards who tried to kidnap some woman and beat up some old man." Mike punched his legs as if he was in pain.

"We're not going to find out what it's about by sitting out here. If we go over the fence in the back, we'll be home free." He stretched out his legs to get the circulation going again and almost cried at the sensation of ants and pins.

"We are so fucked. This was a stupid idea from the beginning." It was the fifth time Mike had said that. "The only difference now is I'm going down with you."

"You keep forgetting that you're the asshole who fucked up the address. Shut it, or I'll do it for you."

"Aren't you forgetting something, brother? I'm not Desi. Try it, and I'm going to beat your ass to death." Mike shoved him hard enough to slam him into the wall. "The only thing we can do now is get out of here and wait these assholes out."

"What are you talking about?" He rubbed his shoulder from the shove and calmed down. There was no way he could do this without Mike.

"We need to leave town, but we need money." Mike stood but stayed bent at the waist.

"Let's go get the car, and we'll call Daddy. He can meet us somewhere and tell us whatever this shit is about."

They jumped a few fences to stay behind the houses where they'd parked the car. Byron was about to walk out when Mike pulled him under some bushes. There were a few plainclothes cops surrounding the vehicle they'd used. "Fucking great, there goes our ride," Mike said as a cat came near them, meowing.

They were under a clump of bushes on the side of an abandoned home. That gave Byron an idea. Once the cops took the car, they could break in and hide out. "Don't panic. We're too smart to get caught. We practice the same story and come back in about a week or two. They can't prove we weren't out with friends."

"These guys found the car, and they're at Daddy's. The only way they're going to stop looking for us is if we disappear forever." Mike pointed to the tow truck. It was a competitor's, and it was probably there for the car. "We could give up and tell them we lost our minds."

"I have to be in court in a month. If we don't find Desi, then that bitch from the DA's office is going to hang an attempted murder charge around my neck like a weight and drown me. I take that back. It's *two* attempted murder charges." He grabbed his crotch but kept his voice down. "If you think I'm going to put my dick on the block and let that slut cut it off, you're the one who's fucked in the head."

Mike closed his eyes and sighed like he'd given up. "My problem is you haven't been right yet."

"We got the wrong house. The people who saw us don't know us from Joe Blow. But yeah, she saw my face, so you're right." He put his hand on Mike's arm and shook him a little. "There's nothing wrong with a vacation, and when we come back, we look for Desi."

The cops towed the car and cleared out. A tall woman with white hair and a badge on her belt stared into the yard, and he held his breath. It was like she was looking right at him, but she made a circle motion with her finger and they all took off.

Byron hit speed-dial on his phone. "Daddy," Byron said, not moving from the bushes. "We need some help."

"You two are bigger fuckups than I thought." Big Byron sounded like he was just getting started.

"We got the wrong house." He explained what happened. "You need to get us some money and a way out of town. We'll come back when things blow over."

"You sound like some gangster movie, but the cops have a hard-on for you. Turn off your phone, and go to your grandmother's old place. I'll send one of the guys from the neighborhood to get you what you need."

"Come on," he told Mike, crawling to the backyard. Their grandmother used to live a few blocks away, and Big Byron loved talking about that old house.

It took a few hours, but a kid showed up with a nondescript sedan and two thousand dollars. Their father had included an address in Pensacola. That way he could call them on the landline.

He let Mike drive and they didn't talk much as they hit the interstate. Their father had told the cops they'd been gone for two days, which would hopefully throw them off the scent.

"Did you say something?" Mike asked.

"A little fun in the sun, and then I'm coming back for her." He laid his head on the door and let the wind blow his hair back. "She can't hide forever," he whispered as the wind whipped along his face.

❖

"How did I not know Judge Jude Rose considers you his niece?" Serena asked as Mona put a plate of pancakes in front of her. "His clerk called and said we had to be in court at one concerning the Simoneaux case, but he didn't say why."

Harry had just explained her relationship with Jude. "He and my parents are old friends. I've never been in trouble with the law, so I'm sure it's not widely known that we're close. Why? Is that going to be a problem?" Harry had just gotten off the phone after moving patients around to clear up her morning. There was no way she was letting Desi meet with Serena alone after what had happened last night. "He's not presiding over Desi's trial, so I don't see any issues that'll set us back."

"No, it's not an issue for the actual trial. If Blum got wind of your relationships—with Desi, as well as with Judge Rose—that might be a problem. It could be a basis for asking for a reduction in bail, if he can prove prejudice."

"We're in trouble? After what Byron and Mike Simoneaux did last night, I'd think Uncle Jude would be interested in other things," she said as Desi took her hand, instantly calming her down.

"What are you talking about?" Serena said with her mouth full.

"You must be so charming on dates with manners like that." She tilted her glass at her. "Byron and his brilliant brother broke into Uncle Jude's last night. He beat the hell out of him and tried to kidnap Monica. As of this morning, the police haven't found them."

The pancakes appeared ready to fall out of Serena's mouth when she opened it in shock. She swallowed hard. "Are you being serious right now? And how do you know they haven't been found?"

"Serious as a heart attack. I know because Sept Savoie called me and gave me an update."

"If Rose can ID the brothers, the shit-ton of bricks about to fall on the Simoneaux family is going to crush the life out of them," Serena said with a wide smile.

"You mean he can still do something to Byron?" Desi asked, nodding to Mona when she served her breakfast.

"Jude Rose has a tough reputation on the bench, but now that he's personally involved in this case, he'll have to recuse himself. The bricks I'm talking about come in the form of Monica Rose. She's a partner in one of the most successful civil litigation firms in the city. If there's a way to strip Byron's family of all their worldly possessions, Monica will find it and gleefully execute her plan."

"I doubt she'll get much. Byron doesn't own anything, including his truck. It's all in Big Byron's name," Desi said, tapping her finger on the handle of the mug.

"Trust me, she has a talent for finding the deep pocket and picking it clean." Serena took another bite of pancakes and appeared ecstatic.

"What's the next step?" Harry asked, pushing Desi's plate closer and pointing at it. "You need to eat, even if it's just a little."

"That depends on the mood Judge Rose is in," Serena said thoughtfully.

Harry could guess what both he and Monica looked like this morning, and it would not make for a good mood. "If there's one person in this world Uncle Jude loves, it's Monica. She had a bruise in the shape of a hand across her face when I left last night, so I wouldn't count on a sunny disposition."

Desi lowered her head when she said that, and she stopped to kiss her.

"It's my fault," Desi said, tears in her eyes.

"Did you sneak out last night and attack the Roses?" Harry asked.

"No, but Byron and Mike were there because of me."

"They were there because they're both as smart as slugs," Serena said. "When people do stupid shit, it's on them. Period."

"What happens today?" Desi asked.

"Let me consult my crystal ball," Serena said, waving her hands like she had one in front of her. "Bradley will be sweating by the time Rose shoots down every one of his motions, and then he'll recuse himself from the case because of last night. Bradley will be thrilled for about a second before wishing for the devil he knew."

"In English please," Harry said as Desi pressed against her.

"I'll bet my pathetic salary that your darling Uncle Jude will have something to do with whoever takes over. If I'm right, the new judge will fast-track your trial, Desi. That means your case will come up before the month that was scheduled. If Byron doesn't appear, he'll have officially jumped bail."

"Which helps us how?" she asked.

"His father put up everything he owns, including his bank account, to get him out. Once the new judge labels him a fugitive, old man Simoneaux will be the big loser," Serena said as if that would explain everything.

"I still don't understand how that hurts Byron," Desi said.

"To be a successful fugitive takes money. Once the bail bondsman freezes Big Byron's assets, that's going to be a problem. He either gives up his sons or his business. Those are his only choices."

"Karma, it's truly a bitch," Harry said, and Desi smiled. "It took forever, but it's nice to see life giving them shit instead of the other way around."

"Karma in this instance will teach a valuable lesson," Serena said.

"What's that?" Desi asked.

"You should never piss off one of the most powerful people in a judge's robe. The city might be famous for its voodoo priests, but Jude

Rose can fuck you up with a nod of his head and a slam of his gavel."
Serena winked.

"I hope you see why I was worried about Harry and Rachel. These people are dangerous and even more so when cornered."

Serena reached for Desi's hand and held it tightly. "This isn't all about you anymore, sweetheart. What he did last night landed him in a world of hurt that'll be hard to come back from. Touching Monica Rose in any way just blew up any chance he had at a short prison sentence."

"I'm so sorry that happened to her," Desi said.

"We've been invited to dinner. That means she's not holding a grudge," Harry said, kissing Desi's temple.

"Go ahead and eat, Desi. Everything is going to be okay. I'll call you as soon as I'm out of court, and I'll give you an update." Serena kissed them both and followed Mona to the door.

"Sounds like Santa came early this year," Harry said when they were alone. "This will ensure they're out of your life for good." She tapped her fork against Desi's plate and started eating herself. "Eat up, so we can enjoy the day."

"I know you said not to apologize—"

"That's still true."

"But I'm sorry for all this. Everyone in your life shouldn't have to suffer because of me." Desi pressed her hand to Harry's cheek. "You know what, though?"

"What?"

"I'd do it all again without hesitation if I found you waiting for me at the end of that road. I love you." Desi leaned in to her and kissed her.

"That hard road is permanently closed, my love. Now finish those, so we can take a walk. You've been here for almost three months and haven't seen the yard. If you hate it, we'll get another house so Mona can stop complaining about the size." They laughed and finished, telling Mona where they were going.

"Don't step beyond that yard, Harry. With all these crazy people running 'round, I don't want Desi hurt," Mona said.

"See, she likes you more already. I promise we'll stay put."

"We're not really selling the house, are we?" Desi asked as she followed her outside.

"I want us both to be happy, so I'm serious about that. There's also something I want to show you that's not visible from the veranda."

She was happy to play tour guide as they walked to the back gate. The yard was huge for a house within the city limits, and there was a place she seldom went. The reminder inside was too much to take. The Realtor had shown it to her when she was thinking of buying, and that was the last time she'd seen it.

"You can start using the pool to strengthen your legs once it gets warmer, and we can use the outdoor kitchen. On nights with no moon, I'll be happy to sit in the hot tub naked with you."

Desi laughed. "It's beautiful back here."

"It's also private. The tall brick wall must've cost a fortune to put in, but it makes it perfectly private. We only have one set of neighbors, but I think they travel extensively for work." She led Desi down a brick path to a small building at the back of the property.

"Is that a garden shed?" Desi rested her foot when they stopped to look at it.

"No, this place was built by the previous owners. They raised their family here and retired to Florida when they were done. Sound familiar?" Harry asked, putting her arm around Desi.

"Is it a guesthouse?" Desi made a face as she asked. "If someone like your parents come to visit, honey, we can't stick them way out here."

"It's an artist's studio, which the woman who lived here received as an anniversary present from her husband. He joked it got him their dining room back. From what Tony tells me, she had a successful career as an artist."

"Does Tony use it?" Desi stared at the structure with its cute front porch and flower bed.

She laid her hand on the small of Desi's back. "No, I don't think it's been open since I signed the mortgage papers." There must have been something in her voice that made Desi turn and put her arms around her.

"Are you okay?"

"She was working on a large canvas when I came in here and I admired it. At the signing she told me she'd finished it and left it as a housewarming gift. I appreciated her gift, but I hung it out here and haven't looked at it again."

"Why?"

"After Tony had it framed, I couldn't look at it." She tilted her head in the direction of the door and they went inside.

"Oh my God," Desi said, leaning heavily on her crutches.

The old cypress frame set off the work beautifully, and it still touched something deep in her soul when she looked at it. The house the woman had used in the painting could've been any shotgun house in the city. The color and yard, though, bore an uncanny resemblance to the place Desi grew up, down to the swing at the corner of the porch.

"Mrs. Emerson told me she spent hours out here creating the pictures in her head, and this one she started when they placed the house on the market. She told me her garden outside was home to strong creative spirits that were wonderful muses."

"It looks so much like…" Desi said as she moved closer to it.

"Her hope was that I would share this place with a creative soul who'd keep the spirits happy. This was one of the last she did."

"But why? She's so talented."

"The arthritis in her hands makes it painful to hold a brush, so she decided to give pottery a try. This place has been waiting for you, and I think Mrs. Emerson's creative spirits are thrilled."

"You're like a dream," Desi said, dragging her eyes away from the painting to Harry's gaze.

"My hope is to be your reality. Whenever you're ready, you can work out here and create whatever you like. It's a little dusty, and it needs some updating, but we both know a good decorator." She put her arms up when Desi dropped her crutches and fell into them. "My dream is that you're as happy here as Mrs. Emerson, and for as many years."

They both cried after the gentle kiss, but for once, the tears stemmed from joy and not pain. Happiness was the greatest healer.

CHAPTER TWENTY-TWO

A ll rise," Jude's bailiff said as Jude took the bench.

Serena glanced around the almost empty courtroom before turning her attention to Jude. The few people in attendance let out a small gasp. Jude Rose's face was a mess, and from Bradley Blum's expression, it was a total surprise.

She smiled when there'd been a hint of glee on Jude's marred face when he sat down, and she guessed it was from the fact that Bradley was alone. The young attorney was already sweating and pulling on his tie as if it was trying to strangle him. Maybe it was, since his face was red. The guy really needed to go up a shirt size if he was going to survive the pressure.

"Your Honor, we're set to hear the defense motion filings for docket number LA6689. There are twenty-eight, unless Mr. Blum has anything else to add," the bailiff said.

"Mr. Blum, are you and your client ready?" Jude leaned back in his chair and glared at the man over the rim of his glasses. He was an impressive sight even if one of Jude's eyes was swollen shut.

"If Your Honor would be so inclined, we'd ask for a couple of days' delay so we can be better prepared," Bradley said.

"I'd like to hear that from your client," Jude said, his facial expression not changing.

"Actually, Your Honor, I wasn't able to reach my client. His father informed me this morning that Mr. Simoneaux is out of town on a short vacation. He can't be reached but should be home in a couple of days." Bradley smiled when Jude leaned forward and didn't say anything for a long while. "We have the next month, sir, so I don't see the rush. I'm also missing an important court appearance for this, which I told your clerk."

"Jefferson Parish gave you problems?" Jude asked.

To Serena it sounded like the first crack in the ice, and Bradley was about to go under. No one was obligated to inform Bradley about what had happened the night before. Once they caught Byron, the police couldn't question him without his lawyer present, but Bradley seemed to have no idea what was about to happen, and obviously Big Byron hadn't mentioned it.

"No, Your Honor," Bradley said slowly. "I'm sorry, Your Honor, but are you all right?"

"We're not here to talk about me and my health, Mr. Blum. To answer your question, no, I'm not all right."

"Car accident, Your Honor? We don't mind giving you more time to heal."

"Mr. Blum, I'm beginning to think you skipped some crucial days in law school. Are you aware that as a stipulation of the bond I set for Mr. Simoneaux, the court has a right to know where he is at all times?"

"Yes, Your Honor, but—"

"Considering the charges Mr. Simoneaux is facing, I would have expected him to display a different kind of behavior. I'd think he'd be at home practicing being contrite as he prayed the rosary." Jude's voice started to rise. "That would be my way of handling things, but I'm not Mr. Simoneaux. So unless he's in the tundra of Alaska where there is no phone service, you can get in touch with him. Where is he?"

"Your Honor, you sound as if Mr. Simoneaux has already been proven guilty. We need the trial to determine that." Bradley grimaced after he finished speaking, and from Jude's face, it was a grievous mistake.

"Thank you, Mr. Blum, but unlike you, I actually showed up for all my classes in law school. Unlike you, I'm well aware of that." Jude slammed his hand on the desk. "Do you need a refresher on the rules I set about when to speak, and how to answer a question?" Bradley wisely only nodded. "Appearing when ordered to do so is the first thing you should've told your client. Appearing or not appearing isn't *voluntary*. Do you understand that?"

"Yes, Your Honor."

"Do you think the court will accept his failure to appear because you couldn't reach him as sufficient enough reason to grant a continuance?" Jude asked.

"No, Your Honor?"

Serena was starting to get worried about how red Bradley was getting, and how vigorously he was pulling on his collar.

"You got one right, Mr. Blum. The court will go on without him. Now, if you or Mr. Simoneaux don't agree with my decision, there's always the state appellate court. They might be more understanding of his need for a vacation." Jude pointed at Bradley when he opened his mouth. "Ms. Ladding, would you like to enlighten Bradley about that avenue of thought?"

"In twenty-two years, Your Honor has only been overturned on appeal once." Serena stood and answered respectfully.

"What was the reason for the one time?"

"Your Honor was on his honeymoon and someone else filled in for you."

"Thank you, Ms. Ladding, you're prepared as usual." Jude smiled at her and lost it when he stared Bradley down. "You'll be happy to know I'll be recusing myself as of today." Jude delivered the news in his usual blunt style, and Bradley smiled at her for the first time that day.

"Thank you, Your Honor. I'm sure my client—"

"You're talking again, Mr. Blum, when no one of importance has asked you to do so. As I was saying, I'm recusing myself but have made arrangements for this case." Jude stood and held the gavel up, ready to recess the proceedings. "We're all in luck, and Judge Reaper is waiting in my office to deal with your twenty-eight motions, Mr. Blum. I'm impressed, and I'm sure he will be too."

"Judge Reaper, sir?" Bradley asked in a way that sounded like his mother had told him she didn't love him and never had.

"Did I stutter?" Jude asked but didn't give Bradley a chance to answer. "If there's nothing further, we're adjourned. I trust you have nothing further, Mr. Blum?" Jude's expression dared him to say something.

"No, Your Honor, we're ready," Bradley said with a firm nod.

"Good, we're adjourned."

The clerk told everyone to stay put and they'd reconvene in ten minutes without having to move across the hall to Reaper's courtroom. Bradley nodded even though he appeared ready to bolt.

"All rise," the clerk said, and Carlton Reaper took Jude's seat less than two minutes later. He was younger and, in Serena's opinion, tougher than Jude, which was bad luck for Bradley.

"Mr. Blum, you have quite the workload for me," Reaper said, opening a file. "Let's get started."

"Yes, Your Honor." Bradley tapped nervously on his file, his gaze flitting from the judge to Serena.

"The last motion is denied," Carlton said after ten minutes, banging the gavel down as if beating all of Bradley's work to death.

Serena could've predicted the outcome after her conversation with Desi and Harry that morning, but Carlton had sound case law to back him up. Bradley was shoving things into his briefcase as if dying to get out of there, but his day was far from over. She also suspected Bradley had no idea what was about to happen. She stood again when Carlton glanced her way.

"Ms. Ladding, thank you for appearing today on such short notice. Are the people ready to proceed with their case against Mr. Simoneaux?" Carlton's demeanor completely changed when he addressed her, and it made Bradley glance up from his packing.

"Yes, sir. I've been ready for weeks. Desiree Simoneaux is here and ready to testify, as are the police who were there that night," she said, glancing at Bradley. "Had it not been for the number of filings by Mr. Blum, we'd be finished by now. We're prepared to begin." She smiled at Bradley, and he answered by pulling on his collar. "Do you have a date available?"

"I do indeed. Tomorrow morning at eight sharp," Carlton said. "Will that be a problem, Mr. Blum?"

"I might need more time, Your Honor. My client isn't due back for another two days." Bradley sounded ready to cry.

"I'm sorry, while I was reviewing this case this morning I missed where Judge Rose gave your client permission to leave town. Can you point that out?" Carlton waited and Bradley said nothing. "Good, tomorrow morning. Don't be late."

When Carlton cleared the door that led to Jude's private offices, Bradley turned and glared at Serena. "The Grim Reaper is going to hear this case? What did you have to do, sleep with the old bastard Rose to get that?" he asked in a low voice.

"Let me fill you in. Judge Rose is happily married to a lovely woman, and I'm gay. It was pure luck that landed us Judge Reaper—he hates that nickname, by the way. If he catches you using it, the only thing dead will be your career." She smiled again and closed her briefcase. "I'll be happy to share your thoughts on the assignment the next time I'm having lunch with Jude. I'm sure he'll appreciate your admiration of his sex appeal. See you tomorrow," she said in a sugar-sweet voice.

"You wouldn't." Bradley was back to his usual panicked self. "Please don't."

"I like you so much I'll keep my mouth shut, and I'll give you some advice as a bonus. Pull the police reports for last night, and then up your retainer."

"Why? I don't have time for that."

"It's free advice, Bradley. Take it or leave it, but don't complain I never did anything nice for you." Serena walked out, wondering if she should have simply told him about Byron's newest fuckup. But the judge hadn't asked, and it was obvious Blum didn't know where Byron was, so asking him if he knew his client's whereabouts so they could arrest him was obviously out of the question. And she didn't owe him anything.

"Eight o'clock tomorrow. Don't be late if you want to practice in New Orleans after this case," she said from the door after blowing him a kiss.

❖

"Any more days like this, and I might have to retire," Harry said. They were lying on the floor of the studio naked, staring out the window at the garden.

After Desi had gotten over the shock, she'd given Harry a special kind of surprise. The spontaneous lovemaking session had left them covered in dust, but it'd been worth every second. It was Desi who'd made the first move, and Harry counted it as progress.

"If that's a threat, I'm all for it. I love spending my days with you." Desi lifted her head and looked down at her. "And getting you naked is also a favorite, so you won't get an argument out of me." Desi kissed her before relaxing again and sighed. "Thanks again for this, honey."

"You're welcome, and all we have to do is find a way to get back in the house without Mona seeing us. I can't deal with her teasing us all night." She sat up, taking Desi with her. "Then we'll call Tony and have him plan a shopping trip for all the stuff you'll need. It can be installed once the cleaning staff finishes."

Desi draped her arms over her shoulders and smiled at her before kissing her like she wanted to repeat everything they'd done in the last hour. "You're hard to let go of."

Harry moved her hands down Desi's back. "You ready for a shower?"

"No, but I'll let you up. I know you have to go to work."

She stood, helped Desi to her feet, and got her crutches. "You're so beautiful." She cupped Desi's face and kissed her again.

Desi smiled up at her, and it made her want to take the rest of the day off, but she couldn't do that to her staff. "You're gorgeous all the time, but I love it when you're naked."

Harry laughed and turned around as her phone started ringing in her pants. "Thank you, my love, but you're the good-looking one in the couple."

"I'm losing you sooner than I thought, huh," Desi said when Harry retrieved the phone to see who it was. "Is this where the term *medical widow* comes from?"

She held her finger up and answered. "I had something come up this morning, but I can get there in fifteen. Tell the staff to start working him up and I'll deal with that right after the knee replacement I moved back today."

"You want to run ahead?" Desi said with a slight pout. "I don't want to slow you down."

Harry stared at her standing with the sun streaming through the windows. There would never come a time that she wouldn't find Desi attractive, but moments like this made her want to stop the world. "I love you, and I'm not leaving you behind. Let's share a shower, and then I'll be gone four hours, tops. There's only two people waiting on me, so I'll be home to have dinner with you."

"I'm being selfish, but I'm not ready to let you go. I shouldn't, considering you put me back together, but I don't want to share you today."

"Spending the rest of my day naked with you is better than whatever is waiting for me, so I'd stay if I could." She pressed their bodies together again and whispered in Desi's ear, "After dinner I'll be happy to make it up to you for having to leave." She kissed Desi's neck and went back to her ear. "Do you want to know how I'm going to do that?"

"Yes," Desi said and held her breath when she reached down and cupped her sex.

"I'm going to start right here, but we'd better stop before I can't. There's no way I have that kind of willpower."

"Jesus," Desi said and laughed as Harry put her pants on.

"Having to choose between a naked you or a knee replacement is cruel. Put your clothes on before I go blind." She pulled her shirt over her head and helped Desi with the rest of her clothes. "Tonight I'm taking you out to dinner, and then we're coming home and taking our time. Lots and lots of time."

"Get going then." Desi started for the door, stopping to kiss her. "The sooner you leave, the sooner you come back to me."

Harry carried Desi inside to save time, and Desi sent her into the shower alone. "I'm not in the mood to behave, so go ahead."

She finished and came out of the bathroom in scrubs. "I'll see you in a little while."

"Can you send Mona in if she's not busy? I don't want to slip and break something else. And wear a jacket. It's cold out there."

"Okay to both things," Harry said after a quick kiss. "And take a nap after your shower. You're going to need it for later."

"You promise?"

"With all my heart."

CHAPTER TWENTY-THREE

Desi stripped and dropped everything in the hamper. With any luck she didn't reek of sex and wouldn't be giving Mona a reason to tease her for the rest of the afternoon. She was putting her robe on when she heard Mona come in.

"Hey, sweetie," Mona said, heading for the bathroom. "Let me get the shower chair ready."

"Do you think we can wrap my cast well enough to try the tub? I've been wanting to try it out, and I think my leg is strong enough to climb in." She smiled when Mona turned on the faucets. The old refurbished clawfoot tub was something she wanted to share with Harry once the cast came off.

"Harry said you two are going out," Mona said, helping her with her robe. "Where's she taking you?"

"My date wouldn't give me a hint except to say jeans were out. That means I have to find something to make me look halfway decent." She held on to Mona as she stepped in and rested her leg over the side with more difficulty than she anticipated. "Did Rachel say what time she was coming back?"

"Girl, you worrying for nothing. I could cut holes in a garbage bag, and Harry would still be gone on you." Mona fussed with her hands on her hips. "Sit in there and think about how Harry feels about you. I'll be back in thirty minutes. You going to be okay?"

"Thanks, Mona, and for more than this. Feel free to kick me in the ass whenever you think I need it." She sat back and closed her eyes, doing a mental check of her wardrobe. The knock came before she could get settled. "Hey," she said to Mona. "Did you forget something?"

"No, and I hate to bother you, but Serena's here. She says it's important she talk to you."

"Could you give me a hand?" Mona helped her out and held up a towel. "Thanks. Could you tell her I'll be down in a few minutes?"

She put on a pair of sweats Harry had gotten her and the shirt Harry had thrown on the bed that morning. She'd rather soak in the hot water than face Serena and her news, but maybe the police had found them. Maybe this time they'd rot in jail for good.

She used the stairlift Harry had temporarily installed to keep her from tripping on her crutches and met Serena in the sunroom. Any dread she felt about this meeting disappeared when she saw Butch.

"Hey, Miss Desi," Butch said, running and hugging her good leg. "Wow, you're walking. Is my Uncle Harry here?" His eyes were the same shade of blue as Harry's and she almost laughed at how easy it would be to believe Harry had fathered this beautiful boy.

"Sorry, buddy. She had to go to work, so you're stuck with me and Granny Mona." She pointed Butch toward the sofa and sat with him. Serena chuckled as she gazed at them. "Is something funny?"

"I'm not laughing at you, Desi. It's just that every time I see you, you're a different person."

"I don't get how that's funny." She couldn't help but be on the defensive. Serena had it all, and feeling dumpy next to her was easy, especially without Harry there.

"Come on, don't take that the wrong way. It's just that I see you now and compare it to the first time I saw you, and you're worlds apart, like there's been a heavy weight lifted off your shoulders, and it's a good thing."

She backed down and took a deep breath. "I can thank Harry. She's been a rock from the moment she saw me again."

"Take some of the credit. You did what I told you and let the fear go. That's allowed you to come into your own, as they say." Serena sat across from them and smiled. "At our first meeting it was easy to see you were a beautiful woman, and I was right."

"Thank you."

"But now I see from the way you treat my child that you're as beautiful on the inside. Harry's a lucky woman."

"Thanks for saying that," she said, holding Butch's hand. "That feeling is mutual. After getting to know you, it's easy to see why Harry loves you."

"Harry's in love, and you have dibs on that."

"She loves you and my buddy here," she said and tickled Butch. "There's no need to hide that it's mutual. It makes me feel better that she had such a good friend when I wasn't here. With time, hopefully you and I will become the same."

"We will, I have no doubt." Serena smiled and held her hand out to Butch. "Hey, would you mind visiting Granny while Miss Desi and I talk? I promise not to keep her too long."

"Can I have a cookie if she has any?"

"One, Albert, and I mean it." He ran out with Serena shaking her head. "He'll be a better attorney than me, and he'll be filthy rich with those negotiating skills."

"It's those good looks that'll slay whoever he's up against." She folded her hands in her lap and waited.

"Let me tell you what happened today."

Serena gave her a rundown, and she was relieved things appeared good for her, but also terrified Byron hadn't been found yet.

"What happens tomorrow?" she asked, wishing more than anything that it would simply be over.

"I talked to the police, and Sept's guess is Byron and Mike skipped town. She thinks it's their way of trying to establish a concrete alibi. The problem with that is how much evidence they left at the Rose house last night, not to mention that they were identified." Serena took her hand. "They're looking for them as a top priority."

"They'll lock him up when they find him?"

"Judge Reaper will issue another warrant, and the service that posted his bond will send out their own search party. My best guess is it'll be Big Byron who turns them in."

"He'd die first," she said with conviction.

"When the bond guy shows up and slaps a For Sale sign on everything Big Byron owns and drains his accounts, he might change his mind. Money is sometimes the greatest motivator."

"They can do that?" she said and had to smile at the thought.

"If Byron doesn't show up, that's what's going to happen. You don't know Jude Rose, but Byron dragged his naked wife out of bed and slapped her a few times. There are mistakes you regret, and then there are mistakes that obliterate your life." Serena made a check motion. "Byron checked the *My life is over as I know it* box with that move."

Desi lowered her head and sighed. "I feel horrible that happened to them because of me."

"Your soon to be ex-husband is an animal with no forethought. He went in there last night without thinking and screwed up big time. That's on him, not you. The bonus here is, his screwup will make it easy to prove your case." Serena gave her a one-arm hug. "He's going away for a very long time, and once he does, you'll be a single woman."

A cold sensation went through her body when she thought for the thousandth time what would've happened if he'd gotten the right house. "You're right. Byron always led with his fists, but he rarely thought anything out. As for being single, not really," she said with a smile.

"Ah," Serena said and laughed. "See, I told you." Serena tightened her hold on her. "Congratulations, my friend. If I had to lose out to someone, I'm glad it's you."

"Reaper. That has to be the best name for a judge ever," she said as the phone rang. "Sorry. Hello, Basantes residence." There was music playing in the background, which made her smile.

"Hey, baby," Harry said, and the music stopped. "Just wanted to tell you I'm heading in to our second surgery, so I'll be home in a couple hours." Harry grunted a few times and Desi heard some other undistinguishable sounds.

"Are you okay? What are you doing?"

"Getting some new scrubs." Harry's voice was muffled. "Everything okay?"

"Serena came over and let me know what happened today." She smiled at Serena and gave Harry a quick rundown.

"Man, it sounds like this is moving at top speed now. How about we cancel on my parents this weekend in case they need you to testify? We can have everyone over, and we can cheer on our favorite prosecutor." Someone was yelling behind Harry. "I have to go, but hang in there, and I promise a hug when I get home."

"I can't wait, and I miss you."

"I miss you too, and I'm sorry I'm not there. You sure you're okay?" Harry said after telling someone to be quiet.

"I'm fine, and I want you to concentrate. Serena and Mona are here keeping me company. Would you mind if we had company tonight?" It was nice to be talking about such mundane things like having friends over.

"I love being alone with you, but I don't mind the right company."

"There's someone here who can't wait to see you." Desi smiled at the way Butch's face lit up when he ran back in the room. "I bet we could talk them into coming with us."

"Is my favorite person under six there with you?"

"That he is, love, and he'll be waiting. Call and add two more to our reservation." She put the phone down and lifted Butch on her lap. "Want to have dinner with Uncle Harry?"

"Aren't you coming?" he said sounding disappointed.

"Of course, I am," she said, and he gave her one of his tight hugs.

"Good, Aunt Desi." He turned to Serena and seemed to be trying to figure out if she was on board. "We're going with them, Mommy." There was no question in his mind.

"We are, but we have to go change, so say your good-byes for now," Serena said, standing and holding her hand out to him.

"See you soon, Aunt Desi."

"Yes, you will."

"You're in now, Aunt Desi," Serena said and winked.

"That's the best news of the day." They left, and Desi sat on the couch for a while, thinking about how vastly her life had changed. As her body healed, her mind did too. She wouldn't suddenly become a different person, but at least she could work on being the one she wanted to be.

❖

Desi settled for a shower and Mona helped her on with the dress she'd picked out with Tony on their last shopping trip. How they'd gone from bed linens to the women's section was still a blur, but the little black dress was now part of her wardrobe. He'd proclaimed an LBD was an essential part of any closet, so she was glad she was living up to his standards.

"Does it bother you that she slept with Harry?" Rachel asked as she did her makeup. She opened her mouth and Rachel put up her index finger. "Don't tell me she didn't, because I know she did."

"Then why ask me if you have all the answers?" She fidgeted with her fingers, not comfortable with the line of questioning.

"I'm not saying you should set strict ground rules for Harry," Rachel said, going back to putting on eye shadow. "But you should set some strict ground rules for Harry."

"I trust Harry implicitly." She closed her eyes, making it easier to talk about this. "Does it bother me? Yes, but Harry loves me. She wouldn't have lied about that, and she doesn't need ground rules."

"I'm not saying she does, but you're tempting the love fates by inviting Serena to spend so much time with you guys. Think about it,"

Rachel said, moving to her cheeks next. "I'll be the only one at the table tonight who hasn't seen Harry naked."

"You're not making me feel better, sunshine. I realize she's gorgeous and everything I'm not, but she's Harry's friend. She's also been nice to me and is in charge of my case." She puckered her lips, mimicking what Rachel was doing. "I don't want to alienate her by getting possessive." She didn't mention how defensive she'd been with Serena earlier. It would only make Rachel's point.

"Sis, Harry is completely in love with you, so don't make unnecessary comparisons." Rachel massaged her shoulders before starting on her hair. "But there's no reason to chance something stupid happening."

"It's not like I'm not hearing what you're saying. Serena and I talked about it, and she's happy for us," she said, staring at Rachel in the bathroom mirror. "Part of me wants to tell her to stop looking at Harry when she stares a little too long. As a mature adult, though, I also understand how Harry feels about Butch. I can't deprive her of that relationship because I'm an insecure mess."

"Babe, you need to open your eyes and start noticing what the rest of us do. You're gorgeous, and you have nothing to worry about when it comes to our charming doctor. Harry loves you, and she's going to make you a happy woman." Rachel finished the twist she put her hair in and stepped back. "That doesn't mean I won't be keeping an eye on Serena. I've waited as long as you have for you and Harry to get back together, and nothing is messing this up."

"Thanks, and I love you for listening. It's hard to believe it's happening, but I want this."

"You deserve the life that Harry's going to give you, so enjoy it without driving yourself insane."

They arrived at the Palace Café downtown, and she had to laugh at Rachel's version of keeping an eye on Serena. She came close to snorting when Harry wiggled her eyebrows at her because of all the flirting going on at their table that had nothing to do with Rachel keeping an eye on things.

Dinner was excellent, and she and Harry paid extra attention to Butch, who'd been a perfect little gentleman the whole evening. Harry was the kind of person you wanted to have a child with, and it made her consider her biological clock for the first time in forever.

"Can we order our special dessert, Uncle Harry?" Butch asked, getting out of his chair to stand next to Harry. His blue blazer, bow tie, and slicked back hair made him appear like a mini adult, but he was the cutest thing Desi had ever seen. "I finished all the stuff I ordered."

"We *have* to order that, buddy. Are you up for a special job?" Harry asked, picking him up and setting him in her lap.

"What?" he asked hopping a little in her lap.

"How about a bathroom break and we'll talk about it?" Harry's question got an immediate nod, and they excused themselves.

Desi watched them stop and talk to their waiter, and she smiled when Butch looked back at her and held up his thumb. Once they disappeared around the corner, she concentrated on the other side of the table. Rachel's plan to keep tabs on Serena was going well, considering they were close enough to share a chair. Her sister was a notorious flirt, and it was serving her well tonight.

It was funny that Serena's relationship with Harry bothered Rachel, but trying for one of her own wasn't taboo. She shook her head and studied the large murals of famous New Orleans musicians painted on the walls. This was fun, but she was ready to head home and spend some time with just Harry.

She noticed Harry and Butch on their way back, following two waiters carrying trays to their table. Harry had told her the restaurant was known for their white chocolate bread pudding that was served covered in a cream sauce. It looked delicious, but Harry held up a hand before anyone took a bite.

"May I have everyone's attention," Harry said, tapping her spoon on her coffee cup. Butch sat in his chair with his spoon at the ready as if waiting for a starter gun. "Butch has something important to say."

"You have to finish if you want the best part," Butch said, taking a big bite.

Serena and Rachel separated long enough to finish their desserts and joined in the conversation until everyone was done. Butch was hopping in his seat again.

"This is the best part, Aunt Desi. Uncle Harry taught me," Butch said, putting his hands on his plate. He lifted it and gave it a lick from bottom to top.

Serena groaned and dropped her head when Harry did the same, and it was hard to miss the laughter from the tables around them. She was about to laugh but held it in when she saw the pride on Butch's face as he introduced her to the fine art of plate licking.

"Hey," Rachel said as Harry paid the bill. "Would you guys bring Butch home with you?"

"If it's a problem, we'll take him," Serena said. "I wanted to take Rachel to this jazz club I like, but we'll skip it for a night I have a sitter."

"We'd love to," she said, pinching the top of Harry's hand. "Be good," she whispered in Rachel's ear as they stood to leave. "And awesome job keeping an eye on her."

"She's not so bad," Rachel said, laughing.

"Desi, I need you in court tomorrow," Serena said. "Maybe we should postpone the club."

"How about we take him, he spends the night, and Mona will keep him if we have to go?" Harry said holding Butch's hand.

"Perfect," Rachel said, waving and dragging Serena to the stairs.

They enjoyed putting Butch to bed in the room next to theirs and reading him a story. Harry helped her get undressed when they were alone, and she laughed when she sent Harry to the closet to hang everything up.

"But you're naked," Harry said as she held her dress up.

"And I still will be when you finish putting that on a hanger."

"I saw you putting some weight on your foot tonight. Did that cause any pain?"

"I've been trying to behave so my doctor doesn't fuss." This was a strange change of subject.

"Tomorrow after court, let's swing by the office and get you out of that cast and into something lighter. That'll give you more freedom to move around, but I'm not making any promises until I examine you." Harry still stood with her dress in hand, and it was time to get her moving. "You've healed beautifully."

"It's all because of my brilliant doctor. My plan is to run away with her if she finishes her hanging duties." She stood naked next to the bed and smiled. "If she does that, maybe there's something else she'd like to examine."

"That's a lucky son of a bitch," Harry said, running for the closet. When she came back, she picked her up, kissing her until her legs wrapped around her waist.

"I'm the lucky one," she said as Harry laid her down. "Hold me."

Harry gently loved her while telling her all the things she needed to be reminded of. They fell asleep with Harry still holding her, giving her a sense of safety that reached all those places that still hung on to the fear.

Tonight she'd reveled in what it was to love Harry and be loved in return. "Tomorrow will come soon enough," she whispered as she closed her eyes and kissed Harry's chest.

CHAPTER TWENTY-FOUR

"You ready?" Harry asked as they entered the courthouse. Today would most probably be a wasted effort, but Serena told them if Byron showed up, they'd begin her case, so they had to be there as a sign they were ready to proceed.

Desi had never been in the building, but it radiated desperation and something sinister. She gazed at Harry and nodded. "You look good in that suit, honey."

Harry had on a navy pinstriped suit with a white shirt that made her eyes appear bluer. "I wanted to make sure I did my best to keep up with you, gorgeous," Harry said, putting her hand at the small of her back.

She'd worn another dress Tony had helped her pick out, and she'd felt worlds away from her life when she'd seen her reflection that morning. There was no doubt she loved Harry, but Tony had also become an important part of her life. Her new best friend had helped build her self-esteem while educating her about fashion and style.

Harry held the door for her, and she wasn't surprised Byron's parents didn't acknowledge her as they headed for the front of the room where Serena was standing.

"You're coherent enough to keep up, aren't you?" Harry asked Serena in a low voice. "Rachel got back way past her bedtime, so if you break her curfew again, I'm banning you from any future playdates."

That made Desi laugh, a sound out of place considering where they were.

"We had one drink, and I had to drop her off after my boss called. It was way too early to call it a night, but I had to be here at the crack of dawn this morning for a meeting with my boss and the police chief."

Serena poked Harry in the chest and scowled. "I'm sure I could sleep through the five minutes this is going to take and still win."

"Why?" Desi asked.

"I'm sure Uncle Jude is in there giving the Grim Reaper a pep talk. After that it's going to take less than five minutes for him to revoke Byron's bail and send whatever law enforcement is needed to hunt them down." Serena smiled, looking thrilled with the world. "The word is they're the prime suspects in the Rose case, and there's so much evidence, my boss is convening the grand jury today. Translation, they're up to their eyeballs in shit."

"You have such a way with words," Harry said, and Desi laughed again.

She sensed someone standing too close to her, but before she could say anything, Harry moved to stand between her and Big Byron.

"Desiree Simoneaux, have you lost your mind? Are you happy? It's about time for you to remember your place and stop acting and looking like some whore. You need to come home with us after you tell these people you lied about it all." His tone, as usual, held menace that he didn't bother to hide. "You look so much like a bitch in heat that I didn't recognize you." He moved so fast Harry couldn't block him, and Desi grimaced as he squeezed her bicep. The sudden pain made her forget everything she'd accomplished from the moment she got away from Byron. She froze as the fear took over, and in her mind, she was right back where she started.

"Let her go," Harry said, her voice sounding like ice. "I said, let her go." Harry encircled Big Byron's wrist with her hand, and Desi saw her knuckles were white from the pressure.

"I don't know who you are, but fuck off." He didn't let go, but Desi could see the signs of pain on his face. His expression broke through the fog she was in.

"Let her go, or I'm going to rip your arm out of the socket and wrap it around your neck." Harry's voice got lower.

"This is family business, so back off before I hurt you," he said, but he let go of Desi's arm.

"You couldn't hurt me if you hired someone to help you," Harry said, and Big Byron grabbed her.

Desi wasn't sure what Harry did, but Big Byron dropped to his knees and pawed at Harry's arm, trying to stop whatever it was. She didn't care for violence, but it was satisfying to see the bully brought down.

"If you keep fighting, I'll make it hurt twice as much," Harry said as the bailiff hurried over. Serena held up her hand to get him to wait, and it didn't seem to take much convincing.

"Let me go, bitch." Big Byron's face was getting red, and he couldn't seem to get away from Harry.

"Listen to me," Harry said softly. "The next time you lay a hand on her, or come anywhere near her, I'm going to make you sorry. Understand, big man?"

"You threaten me and it's you who'll be sorry." It was like he couldn't get his voice above a whisper.

"I'm not threatening. I'm promising," Harry said, moving her hand slightly, and Big Byron stopped struggling. "Try this again, and I'll break every one of your fingers and name the bones as I do."

"He's not worth it," Desi said, putting her hand over Harry's. "Let him go."

Harry let go, and Big Byron fell back, holding his wrist.

"Behavior like that isn't okay. I'm not going to sit back and let anyone treat you like that." Harry stared him down. "And it'll never happen again."

Big Byron got up with Tammy's help and cradled his hand against his chest. "You know I'm right, Desiree. Byron didn't mean anything, and he's sorry. You're a Simoneaux, girl, and it's time to start acting like it."

Desi stared at him hard enough to make Harry put her arm around her waist. This reminded her of that bus stop all those years ago. She had the right to stand up for herself, and Harry would keep her safe. She swallowed against the tidal wave of fear and lifted her chin.

"I do know what Byron's like, and I've had enough. That was never my home, and it will never be again. I'm leaving your name and family behind. I'm never going back." She straightened her shoulders and didn't break eye contact.

"You never know what's going to happen, girl, so don't count on that." Big Byron spoke with that condescending smile but lost it and took a step back when Harry took a step toward him.

"Maybe you should concentrate on your family and the world of trouble they're in," Harry said. "If you threaten her again, you're going to pray the police get there in time to save you from me."

Serena cleared her throat as if to stop this from escalating, and the bailiff appeared relieved as he ordered everyone to rise. Judge Reaper waved everyone down and called the first case. Desi stood, her trembling hand in Harry's, and she released the breath she'd been holding. She'd stood up to a bully and could have wept with the feeling of it, but instead she held it together and concentrated on what was going on. The judge was handsome, Desi thought, but that passive expression on his face changed when he stared at the man sitting at the table next to Serena's.

"Good morning, Ms. Ladding. Are the People ready to proceed?" Reaper focused solely on Serena.

"Yes, Your Honor. In the interest of time and justice, we waive a jury trial if the defense is so inclined." Serena glanced at Bradley, who was tugging on his collar and seemed to be turning a sickly shade of red.

"A couple more minutes and that guy's going to need a doctor," Harry whispered in Desi's ear.

"Thank you, and the court will take that under advisement. And you, Mr. Blum?" The leather chair creaked as the judge turned to Bradley. "Are you ready to proceed?" Judge Reaper stopped and leaned forward as if just noticing something. "You look so lonely, Mr. Blum. Where's your client?"

"Your Honor, we beg the court's indulgence. I know you said for Mr. Simoneaux to be here, but he's out of town and couldn't be reached. He can't be held accountable for something he knows nothing about. He has a right to be present."

"Is he dealing with a grave family emergency?" the judge asked with a wide smile.

"No, Your Honor."

"A business engagement he couldn't get out of?"

"No, Your Honor."

"Do you think Mr. Simoneaux's absence stems from being wanted for questioning in another unrelated matter? Does he think the judicial system is as clueless as he is?" Reaper's voice rose until Desi was sure he could be heard all the way to the street.

"No, Your Honor," Bradley said with his hands up.

Judge Reaper tapped the desk. "Unless you have trouble understanding the written word, Mr. Blum, you should've advised your client of a few things. The most important is he's not to leave the area without a way for the court to contact him. The reason for those stipulations, Mr. Blum, for future reference, is for times like this."

"But, Your Honor—" Bradley tried.

The judge put his hand up and Bradley wisely shut up. "I don't want to hear it. Everyone is ready to proceed, and your client isn't here. Do you know what that means, Mr. Blum?" Judge Reaper asked, and Desi was sure no one in the courtroom would ever forget Blum's name, the judge had used it so much.

"He's to be remanded back into custody as soon as he's apprehended."

"Exactly, Mr. Blum, good for you. He has until nine o'clock this morning to report, and if not, bail is revoked. We're adjourned, ladies and gentlemen," Reaper said as he rapped his gavel and left the room.

"Aren't you glad you're not Byron?" Harry asked, smiling. "That was damn entertaining as well as a step in the right direction." Harry stood and offered her a hand up.

"It's that last step I'm looking forward to," she said as she kissed Harry's knuckles. The only thing that made her happier than the dressing-down the attorney had gotten was the look on Big Byron's face. He didn't have to say a word for her to understand what was going through his head.

Her father-in-law believed a lot of things that proved his ignorance on a variety of subjects. She'd been subjected to his views every time they had to spend time with him and Tammy, and he'd gotten worse with age. Gay people, though, were at the top of his list of people God got wrong. Leaving his son for Harry was tantamount to a crime against not only nature, but him.

"You're almost there, love."

"Thanks for sticking by me." She kissed Harry's hand again before facing Big Byron and straightening her shoulders. It was time to stop hiding from who she was and who she loved. "I love you for it."

CHAPTER TWENTY-FIVE

Desi appreciated Harry's hand on her shoulder as they left Byron's father behind, arguing with his attorney. She was still surprised and happy with herself for standing up to him, but everyone had their limits.

Harry opened the car door for her and put her crutches in the back. They were free for the rest of the day since the court proceedings hadn't lasted long, but Harry hadn't said much once they were done. From the tight set of her jaw, she was mad about something.

"Honey?" She reached for Harry's hand and entwined their fingers. "I'm sorry for all this. Please don't be mad."

"The thought of hurting someone, I mean really hurting them, never crossed my mind until today. I'm angry, but not at you." Harry smiled at her briefly. "What gives him the right to touch you like that?"

"If you wouldn't have gotten in trouble, part of me would've loved seeing you break his hand. That man deserves to be taught a lesson." She didn't move away from Harry, but it was embarrassing to have her see what her life had been like. "He taught his son well."

"His behavior, as well as Byron's, has nothing to do with you. He raised men who have no respect for women, much less themselves. What you should think about is how fast your relationship with these people will come to an end." Harry ran her hand through Desi's hair. "It may take a little longer than we'd like, but the plus side is once they're caught, they won't be a problem. If they're in jail, they can't bother you."

"They won't be locked up forever, so will it ever truly be over? It's like Clyde cast this shadow over me, and I'm never getting rid of it." She gazed at Harry and wished things weren't so complicated. "The worst part is that I'm bringing all that to your doorstep."

"My love, the only thing that worries me is that you understand our home is ours. It's a place that'll keep you safe from people like Byron and his family. You're never going back to that life or to them. Even if you decide not to stay with me, you're never going back." Harry touched her cheek and smiled. "Do you believe me?"

"I want to, but it's so hard when I have to face them like that."

"Eventually you'll see what I do," Harry said as she looked her in the eye. "You're a strong woman who can stand on her own. With what you've been through, that's going to take time to absorb, but no matter what you decide is best for you, I'm here. All you need to do is believe me." Harry cupped her cheek. "Let me help you cut these people out of your life forever."

"You've been taking care of us for what seems like my whole life. This time, though, I can't bring all this into your life. What happened to us wasn't something either of us wanted, especially not something I would've chosen, but Byron and his entire family are dangerous," she said as her bottom lip trembled.

"Do you want to go back to that life?"

"No," she said, louder than she meant to.

"Then right now what I can offer you is a way to make it to the life you want. A place where you can stand on your own and be proud of the woman you are. If there's a place for me once you get there, I'll count myself lucky, but don't ask me to walk away because these guys are dangerous." Harry pressed her lips together as if trying to keep her emotions in check.

"What? You can tell me."

Harry took a deep breath and released it slowly. "Don't disappear and sacrifice yourself to keep me safe."

"You're all I thought about every single day we were apart. Sometimes all my reasons seem like such stupidity when I look back on them, but I panicked, and then I was trapped. Eventually, I became such a pathetic thing that I almost lost hope, but there was always you." Her vision blurred as tears filled her eyes. "You were that voice in my head and in my heart telling me to get up and live one more day. Now, though, I don't know if the cost of something happening to you is worth the gamble. You saw what his father is like. Byron isn't much better."

"I can offer you a way to cut those ties, Desi, but the final decision is yours. The best proof that you're ready for that is how you stood up to that idiot today and said *enough*. You started claiming your future when you did that." Harry pointed to the courthouse. "That's something you can take pride in. Those guys tried to break you, but you survived long enough to stand on your own."

She nodded and laughed despite her tears. "That felt really good."

"I'm sure it did, so now all you have to do is convince yourself that I'm not going anywhere. What we have is solid. That's the last time we have to talk about that because it's simply the truth—just like you don't have to apologize for anything ever again."

"I know, and I want to believe that. Why you'd still want me is what I can't understand."

"In my life, I've loved only one woman. I've only ever wanted to share my life and all that I have with one woman. That's you, and our future is something you can count on as real. Nothing in this world will ever change my mind about that."

"I love you so much," she said, leaning in and resting her forehead against Harry's. "You can't know how much I want all that."

"Then accept it. Being happy and looking forward to what comes next doesn't erase the past, but it does put all you went through *in* the past."

She tilted her head slightly and kissed Harry for her sweetness. "Thank you. It's going to take time for me to have your courage, but I don't want to lose you. I don't have much, but I'll gladly share what I have with you."

"That makes me richer than anyone I know. It's an honor that you picked me to love, and I'll do my best to not ever make you sorry you do." Harry kissed her again, and the darkness faded a little more.

"Let's go home," she said and laughed. There was nothing holding her back except herself. "I want to spend the rest of the day enjoying all the happiness you bring into my life."

They drove home, and Harry took a different route, checking often to make sure she wasn't being followed. What had happened to Monica was fresh in her mind, and there was no way she wanted a repeat if these guys knew where she lived. She was glad to see the marked car of the security company she'd hired parked by the gate, and the guy waved as they turned in.

"Who's that?" Desi asked waving as well.

"I hired a security service to keep a couple of guys posted so I don't drive myself insane when I'm at work, worrying about you, Rachel, and Mona. They'll be here until the Brothers Dumb are caught."

"Thanks for thinking of that," she said as Harry moved around to open her door.

From outside they heard Butch's excited chatter and it went into overdrive when they walked in. He was on one of the high stools at the counter with Mona at his side, having waffles. Rachel was nowhere in sight, making her think Serena had done more than take her to a jazz club.

"Hey, buddy," Harry said. "Mona made you waffles? Are there any left?"

"Uncle Harry!" Butch said loudly. His face was pure joy at seeing her. "You're home and it's the daytime." He drummed his hands on the granite.

"I'm home for the whole day, and we're going to have fun," Harry said, picking him up and kissing his cheek, then holding him out so Desi could do the same. "What do you want to do?"

"Granny Mona said you put on the hot water thing, so I want to swim." He was always quick with an answer if there was something he wanted. "You can come too, Aunt Desi."

"That does sound fun, but I still have a cast. How about I watch you guys from the side?" She combed his hair back and smiled at him.

"Our first stop is going to be my office then," Harry said. "It's time to set you free, baby." Harry sat him back down and grabbed a juice out of the refrigerator. "After that, we're going shopping."

Mona stood and took a thermometer out of a kitchen drawer and headed to Harry with it. "You better put her to bed, Desi. She's delusional with fever if she's volunteering to shop for anything. Usually it takes threats to get her to agree."

"You better be nice to me, or I won't buy you anything," Harry said, laughing. "You two get ready while we go change. It's crazy warm today after yesterday's cold front, so we'll be swimming when we get back."

"What are we shopping for?" she asked Harry as she held on when Harry carried her to save time.

"We're getting you out of this cast first," Harry said, putting her down and watching her closely. "Does it hurt to walk?"

"No, just uncomfortable to limp with this thing on." She hobbled to the closet and waited for Harry to unzip her. "What are we shopping for?"

"That's a surprise."

"What are you up to?" She wrapped her arms around Harry after she'd taken her jacket and shirt off. "I think spending the day in this room would be surprise enough, but we'll be good and go out and play."

"I'm up to nothing, and as soon as we get all the people coming over later out of here, we're not leaving this room. Right now, though, you're going to love where we're headed."

"Are you sure you don't want to give me a hint?" She encouraged Harry to lower her head so she could suck on her earlobe.

"I'd tell you to behave, but I don't have that much willpower," Harry said, lowering her hands to her ass and picking her up.

This close, she couldn't help but suck on Harry's neck, and she didn't let up until she was flat on her back on the bed. "Do we have time?"

"We'll make time."

They were done and showered in forty minutes, and her face flushed when they saw Mona in the kitchen with her arms crossed. Mona shook her head and laughed when all Harry did was wiggle her eyebrows. That made her face hotter than it was before.

"Were you having trouble with your shoelaces or something?" Mona asked, carrying Butch on her hip.

"No, it was the zipper on my pants. Ah-ah-ah," Harry said, pointing to the door. "No more comments are necessary. Everyone get in the car." One of the security cars followed them out.

Harry's staff played with Butch while Harry cut the cast off her leg, revealing horrible looking skin. After some more X-rays, Harry recommended a lightweight boot for when she was going to be on her feet for long periods of time, but she wouldn't have to wear it all the time. "Don't push it, and you won't need my services after a couple of weeks," Harry said.

"Bite your tongue, lover," she said and pressed her hands to her face when her ears got scalding hot. "Sorry, I'm not sure what's wrong with me today."

"I do, and I totally feel the same way. Let's go. We've got another stop to make."

Harry stopped and picked up Tony, who gave directions as Harry drove. They were headed out of town and Desi wasn't sure what the business was from the nondescript name.

"Let's go, people," Harry said opening her door. "You sure you don't want the boot?"

"Not yet." She got out with Harry's help and put both feet on the ground. "What's Dixie Supplies?"

"Aunt Desi, this place is the best," Butch said, clapping his hands and pulling Mona along. It was obvious he'd been here before.

"Come on, baby, let's go shopping," Harry said, and they entered the largest art supply place she'd ever seen.

It took two hours to find everything on Tony's list, and the guy promised they'd have it delivered in a day. Her new studio would be ready as soon as they unboxed everything. She helped Butch pick out a new easel, smaller than the one Tony got, and she looked forward to spending time with them in that space.

"The cleaning crew said they can't make it until next week," Mona said.

"We'll get it done," Harry said as Butch ran between them. "I don't mind a little dirt."

They worked together for the rest of the day to get the studio cleaned. Even Butch pitched in, not minding that they'd skipped the swimming. The equipment arrived just as they finished, which surprised Desi, but the delivery guys just shrugged. Harry tipped them, and the delivery guys were happy to assemble all their purchases.

By nightfall the studio was done, and Harry grilled steaks to give Mona a break. Rachel joined them for dinner after much teasing about how late she'd gotten home, and Serena called after they were done and asked if they'd mind keeping Butch one more night.

"We'd love to," Desi said as Harry put a movie on for Butch and set him up on the sofa. "Do you need anything else?"

"The grand jury true-billed the case against the Simoneaux brothers, so I'm slammed with work. They accepted all the charges the DA filed, so the police have stepped up their investigation. Once we get them in court, they're going away for a long time."

"Thank you for all your hard work, and don't worry about Butch."

"I know that, Aunt Desi," Serena said. "He'll make a good juror one day. You won't find a better judge of character, and he loves you, so I know he'll always be okay with you."

"Thank you."

"All set?" Harry asked when she hung up.

"This has been a great day," she said. They sat on the floor of the den and enjoyed the fire Harry had kindled, while they kept an eye on Butch. He was engrossed in the movie, with his head in Harry's lap. "I love you. Thank you for being you."

"You're welcome, and I can't wait to see all the stuff you'll create." Harry kissed the side of her neck and leaned back more. "As for the rest, promise me you'll talk to me throughout the process. Don't ever think you're alone, or that I don't want to hear it."

"I promise." She kissed her. "It's almost bedtime for cute little boys," she whispered.

"Five more minutes and I'll carry him up." Harry smiled and kissed her hand. "Then I don't want to share you for the rest of the night."

"Where's Rachel?" She hadn't seen her sister after dinner.

"She was going to watch some show with Mona, and then she was going to bed. The late night must've done her in." They shared a smile at that and turned to watch a few minutes of the film.

"You ready for bed, little man?" Desi asked as she ran her hand through his hair.

"Would you read me a story?" Butch sat up and put his arms around them.

"I'd love to, and I'll get Uncle Harry to help. You want anything before we go up?"

"A cookie?" he asked.

"Nice try, buddy, but a story, then sleep." She waited for Harry to move and help her up. She'd been walking most of the day and surprisingly her leg didn't hurt. "I'm sure Mona will make up for the cookie with a treat for breakfast."

"That's good," Butch said, happy with his story and a kiss from each of them.

"Will you hold me tonight?" she asked Harry when they finally went to bed.

"Tonight, and all the ones yet to come," Harry said.

"You're my miracle, Harry, and I'm so glad you found me. So glad."

CHAPTER TWENTY-SIX

Harry spent the morning at the hospital seeing patients and arrived home early enough to grill dinner. She watched as Desi and Rachel entertained Butch with a card game and smiled when Serena arrived as Mona came out with a salad. Then her phone rang but she didn't recognize the number.

"It's not the hospital, I don't think." She answered since she was on call. "This is Harry Basantes."

"Hey, Doc, it's Detective Landry. I hate to disturb you."

She moved a little away from the noise of everyone greeting Serena. "Hey, Roger, you have news about the Simoneaux brothers?"

"No, but I'm hoping soon. I'm actually trying to get in touch with Desi, but the number you gave me for her just rings."

"Sorry, we've been outside. Do you need to talk to her?" Whatever this was about, it wasn't going to be good.

"Maybe this would be better coming from you," Roger said, sounding tired. "Byron Simoneaux Sr. beat his wife to death tonight."

"What?" These people were nonhuman, and she was lucky to have gotten Desi back alive.

"The bail bondsman came and took his shop, and it set him off. He went home and took it out on her, and then the asshole sat and ate the meatloaf she'd made him before calling 9-1-1. She was long dead by the time the paramedics got there."

"Jesus Christ," she said with such disgust that Desi headed toward her.

"Pretty much, but there's still no sign of Byron and Mike. I realize this has nothing to do with her case, but I thought Desi would want to know. At least one of them is in jail and isn't going anywhere."

"Thanks, and keep in touch."

"Harry?" Desi said putting her hands on her waist.

A fist of fear gripped her chest at the thought it might have been Desi. One more day with Byron, and this could've been the outcome. They'd just seen that small terrified-looking woman the day before, and now she was dead.

"Tell me what's wrong," Desi said, holding her.

"Mona," she said. "Could you go inside and get his special cup, please? We'll come in when we're done." Mona didn't need any more hints and she shooed Butch ahead of her.

"What's wrong?" Serena asked when it was just the four of them.

"Big Byron beat his wife to death today," she said, and Desi tightened her hold on her.

"God." Desi put her head on her shoulder. "We were never close, but she was always nice to me. At least she's at peace. She led such a horrible existence."

Rachel stood at Desi's back and cried. "You'll never know how many nights I went to bed praying I'd see you in the morning. Or how many times I went to work waiting for the call that I'd lost you." She cried harder and Harry put her arms around her too. "It's too late for Tammy, but thank God it's not you. That's a horrible thing to say, but it's true."

"Let's go inside and have something to drink. You might not be hungry, but you two need to eat something." Harry helped Mona put out all the food, but none of them ate much. "Serena, why don't you stay tonight? I'm sure Rachel would like that." She put her arms around both Desi and Rachel. "Come on, let's go inside and get everyone settled," she said. "None of us should be alone."

"He killed her?" Rachel said, shaking her head as if still not believing what Harry had said. "I don't think we ever had a long conversation, but she was a nice woman."

"She was," Desi said, holding her hand out to her sister. "It makes me sad that all she ever knew was Big Byron. They got married when she was only sixteen, and her parents weren't much better before that. How sad that all she ever knew was violence and fear."

"I remember her saying she loved being a mother in the beginning. Taking care of them when they were babies and toddlers, she said, made her thankful that God had given her that gift," Desi said. "It makes me wonder what she would've been if she'd found someone who really loved her."

"She would've been what you and I are. Survivors," Serena said, leaning in and putting her hand on Desi's and Rachel's knees.

"I can't help but feel that it's my fault. I goaded him in the courtroom, and poor Tammy paid the price," Desi said, shivering and praying that at the end, it had been quick. Tammy had suffered enough.

"No, love. This in no way is on you," Harry said.

"She's right," Serena agreed. "Big Byron will pay for this with his freedom, and he'll have to spend the rest of his life locked away with people who will make him seem tame. To me, that's the best justice. Having him live in fear until he stops breathing will show him what it's like."

"You're right about that," Harry said, kissing Rachel on the head, then Desi, more intimately. "Let's get some sleep, and we'll deal with laying Mrs. Simoneaux to rest in the morning if she has no other family to do it."

"You don't have to do that, honey," Desi said.

"I know, but she's the only person from your past who deserves our compassion."

They walked up the stairs, and she let go of Desi and hugged Rachel before she headed down the hall. She and Desi took care of putting Butch down with another story. All she wanted after that was to hold Desi and reassure her of the future. "I'm sorry this is so hard."

"The poor woman never knew kindness or love. That makes me so sad for her." They undressed and went to bed. "I love you so much, and I'm happy that's not my life. Not anymore."

"No, it's not, and it sounds so simple, but it'll be better in the morning." She held Desi and let her cry. "Tomorrow we'll spend the day doing nothing but celebrating life."

She closed her eyes and gave thanks for Desi's broken leg. It had taken a while to heal, but without it, they'd never have seen each other again. Desi had traded a bad injury for a life cut short, and how empty her own future would've been if things had been different.

"I love you," she whispered, kissing the top of Desi's head. "And I promise I'll take care of you."

❖

They spent the morning painting the studio and getting Desi's space ready to use. Serena had stayed, and Tony had dragged Kenneth along to help. The project had taken Desi's mind off Tammy's tragic end, though it still came crashing through in the quiet moments.

Detective Landry had swung by before lunch and told them the search for Byron and his brother was still ongoing and that Big Byron had refused to speak to anyone. She got the feeling Landry had put more of himself into her investigation than most, but she wasn't complaining. Harry hired another security guard to stay on the grounds until this was over.

Mona was reluctant to leave to visit her family, but Harry had talked her into at least going for the day. With Tony and Kenneth there, they'd made lunch a group project, with even Harry pitching in.

"The master chef is requesting more cheese," Desi said as she emptied the grater.

Harry lifted the platter with all the meat going on the grill and pointed one finger at the refrigerator. "Look on the bottom shelf. Mona usually has a stash in there."

She bent to check the spot Harry had mentioned and heard the platter being put down. Harry walked up and pressed her crotch into her ass, and she forgot about the cheese. She didn't resist when Harry turned her around and kissed her like they didn't have people waiting on them outside.

"You're driving me insane in this outfit," Harry said, biting the skin of her neck with gentle pressure.

She'd borrowed the shorts and tight ribbed top with spaghetti straps from Rachel, and she'd smiled at Harry's expression when she first saw her. It was the same look she was giving her now. "Honey," she said, tilting her head to give Harry an invitation to keep going. "Everyone's going to go hungry if you don't stop."

"Let them," Harry said, picking her up and setting her on the counter.

She wrapped her legs around Harry and gave in to the affectionate mood Harry seemed to be in.

"I can't be expected to sit on my hands when you're this beautiful," Harry said before kissing her.

"I wouldn't want that," she said, licking the length of Harry's bottom lip. "But I'll be happy to sit on your hands." Harry's groan made her tighten her legs, bringing her closer, but Tony interrupted all her plans.

"I figured you'd be in here making out. I'm hungry, so leave all the sexy talk for later when I'm not here," Tony said from the door.

"Besides, I'm the only one out there not making out with someone, and I'm getting lonely. That means cool it before I have to turn the hose on all of you."

"We were just coming," she said, smiling at Harry.

"I'll just bet, so I'm glad I got here before that," Tony said, laughing. "Should I wait, or can you two be trusted?"

"Can you blame me for wanting her?" Desi asked, moving her hands through Harry's hair until they landed behind her neck. "Look at her."

"Harry is a nice specimen if you're into that kind of thing." Tony snapped his fingers. "Now move, so I can eat before my blood sugar goes crazy."

She tightened her hands behind Harry's neck and moved off the counter, making sure her body slid along Harry's on the way down. It was frustrating as hell, and she could see Harry was in the same state. Feeling the length of Harry had made her nipples rock hard, and there was no hiding them in this shirt.

"I'm so wet right now I'm about to go insane," she whispered into Harry's ear. "But come on. It's time to be hospitable." She put her hand in the waistband of Harry's shorts and pulled her along, stopping at the platter so she wouldn't forget it.

"Here," Harry said when they got to Tony. "I forgot something in the pantry."

"Do you want me to get it?" Tony asked, smiling sweetly.

"If you tried, you'd need surgery to repair your nose," Harry said, taking Desi back inside and slamming the pantry door behind them. It didn't take long to get them both what they needed, and they laughed as they helped straighten one another's clothes before going back out.

"Uncle Harry, I missed you," Butch said when they made it outside as Kenneth was taking food off the grill.

"I missed you too, but I don't have to work tomorrow either, so let's do something fun," Harry said. "Now come over here and let me teach you how to eat meat like a caveman."

"Harry, do not teach him any more bad habits. Once you two have kids, I'm coming over here often to show them the joy of coloring on the walls or something else equally obnoxious that'll make us even."

"Our kids will know everything Butch does, and if we're lucky, they'll be just as perfect."

The *our* part of Harry's teasing remark got Desi's attention. She'd never wanted children with Byron, but that didn't mean she didn't want to be a mother. She wanted that, but with the woman who owned her heart. She stepped next to Harry and put her arm around her waist so she could get as close as possible.

"I think you're perfect too, my love," she said as she stood on her toes and kissed Harry's cheek. She laughed when she heard Tony making retching noises.

"Keep it up, sugar pants, and I'm throwing you in that pool," Harry said as she flipped everything on the grill.

"Not in these pants," Tony said, placing his hand on his chest for dramatic effect. "And that's not my nickname."

"I can come up with something better," Harry said.

The laughter and lighthearted conversation continued, and Desi took in the warmth and safety around them. Rachel looked relaxed and happy, something that had been a long time coming, and there was no question about the status of the growing attraction between her and Selena. This felt like…like family. The thought nearly made her weep with the beauty of it all, and when she caught Harry's small, intimate smile, she knew she didn't need to explain.

CHAPTER TWENTY-SEVEN

"Where do you think they are?" Mike asked as he sat in the attic of their parents' house with Byron.

The money had run out after they'd hit the strip clubs, and there was no way to call and ask for more, so they'd had no choice but to come back. The house was empty, and they'd gone straight up to the attic to avoid being seen. There was still a marked car in front of the house, but the guy sitting in it appeared too bored to pay attention. Their time away had done nothing to calm Byron's anger at what had happened to his life, and all he could think about was finding Desi.

"Who knows? Pop is probably in one of his moods and dragged Mom along for the ride." There was still enough light to see what was stacked around them. "Mom put my yearbooks in a box with my name on it and stuck it up here. We need to find them. I want to know something."

It took a couple of hours and pawing through four boxes of all his old school stuff, but they finally found his old yearbooks along with some trophies and ribbons he'd won for the sports he'd played. The memories of who he'd been back then came to him as he cracked the spine and saw himself in that letterman's jacket. He was a winner destined for more than pumping gas and fixing cars. The girl who'd charged him with assault was to blame for bringing all that to an end. In fact, all the women in his life were to blame for how he'd ended up.

"Start with my junior year, and see if you recognize the bitch Desi was with the day you saw her."

On the tenth page of his senior yearbook there was a large picture of Desi standing next to a tall girl with sharp features. "I remember you," he said, tapping his finger on the girl's face on the page. "Is this her?"

"She doesn't look like that anymore, but I'm pretty sure that's her." Mike stared at the image and nodded. "Who is that?"

"Let's get out of here," he said. "Where's the phone book?"

"I don't think they make those anymore, but Mama keeps an old one in the cabinet in the kitchen."

He slid his finger down the *B*s. There was only one *Basantes* in the book. The number listed was for a medical office, but *H. Basantes* had to be the one Desi was staying with. "Desi's found an old friend, but her running days are over."

"Leave that girl alone, man," Mike said. "It's over. Accept it. We just need to figure out how to get on the road and get out of this mess."

"The only way I'm leaving it alone is if I'm dead." He tore the page out and stuffed it in his shirt pocket. "Get some sleep. We move in the morning."

"What's your plan?" Mike asked, following him down the hall.

"It's not hard. We wait outside her office and follow her home. This time we get it right."

"There's no way we're doing that again." Mike stopped halfway to the stairs and glared at him.

"You're in this now. Remember what Pop said. We need to finish this, and you have to help me."

Mike's jaw worked as he glared at him, and then he closed the door to his old room and Byron headed toward his, praying he could go to sleep. This space hadn't changed from graduation, and it was a shrine to who he used to be. The star he'd been on the field had died when he agreed to what his father had set up for him. His explanation had been that marriage would keep him out of trouble. It seemed like the less complicated route, but that hadn't worked out. He couldn't breathe and had to get the hell out of there, but he wasn't leaving without Mike, so he headed for the bottles of whiskey in the cabinet over the kitchen sink.

He moved the dirty plate someone had left on the table to the counter, surprised his mother had left the kitchen in this condition. There was always a first time for everything, but in Desi's case, she'd gone back to the old tried and true. He opened his senior yearbook and flipped through it, finding Desi's smiling face more than once. When was the last she'd smiled at him like that? Had she ever smiled at him like that?

Harry Basantes. He should've guessed this years ago. This was who Desi had been crying over when she should've been making him happy. The solid fact was Desi was his, and that wasn't going to change. "I won, asshole, and she's mine." He spoke to the picture as he stabbed it with the knife on the table.

Why in the hell was this happening to him? He'd taken care of Desi the best way he knew how, and it was going to cost him everything, including his freedom. That had never happened to his father because his mother knew better. He'd done what was expected of him as a man, but fucking Desi never appreciated anything. She couldn't because of fucking Basantes. That woman was to blame, and it was time she died for everything she'd taken from him.

"She's mine, and I'm not giving her up." He slashed through Harry's picture before ripping it out of the book and crumpling it in his fist. "I'm going to kill you and make you watch, Desi. They might lock me up, but you're never going to be free of me."

The alarm went off the next morning, and Desi reached for Harry when she rolled over to turn it off. "Can you stay home?" Desi asked.

Harry had taken a couple days off to help her through everything she was feeling because of Tammy's death, and it had been heavenly. Everyone had left early the night before, and Harry had taken her to bed and made love to her until they'd tired each other out.

"I wish I could, but we both have dates with lumps of clay today," Harry said, putting her arms around her.

"You're giving up your practice to make pottery?" She kissed Harry on the throat and loved the feel of warm skin against hers.

"No, it's more like you have actual lumps of clay waiting, and I have my residents who act like lumps of clay at times." Harry moved her hand down her back and caressed her butt. "Remember, though, it's your first day, and I don't want you to get carried away. You're healing well, but don't wear yourself out."

"I'm just going to play around and get used to everything again."

"You're going to be great," Harry said as she moved to hover over her body. "I'm so confident that I'm taking you to dinner to celebrate. How about a date later?"

"No matter what, I'm not saying no to anything with you."

"Good, I'll try to finish early. Mona won't be back until tomorrow, so I'll try not to mess up the kitchen any more than I have already."

"I'll be happy to cook if you want to stay in. I'll even clean up."

She touched Harry's face, still in awe that life had taken her to this place.

"I love you, and I'd love to take you out. Enjoy yourself today," Harry said, putting her hand on her breast, making her nipple hard and sensitive. "And I can't get enough of you."

Her nipple hardened to the point she craved Harry's mouth on it. "Don't tease if you really have to go, honey."

"You think I'm teasing?" Harry's hand went lower. "This is my incentive to come home early."

Her hips came off the bed when Harry touched her sex, and she wanted it to last. Harry went slowly and drove her to the brink before she kissed her and brought her over. She closed her eyes and moaned as the final spasms went through her body, and she smiled when Harry held her.

"You make it hard to let you go," she said. Her arms were on Harry's shoulders, and she wanted to laugh at how good she felt. "And I can't wait for tonight. I can thank you for this morning if you have time."

"Tonight I'm all yours, but I can't be late." Harry kissed her again before rolling away from her and off the bed.

"I'll go start the coffee and get you something to eat. Anything you really want?" Desi put her robe on and stood in the doorway to the bathroom.

"I can't have what I really want, so anything fast would be good," Harry said from the shower.

She hummed on the way down the stairs, missing Mona and her usual advice on all things. But being alone in the house for a couple of days a week gave her the chance to take care of Harry's needs. That was the job she wanted for the rest of her life, but she was sure Mona would be happy to share.

"If this is all a dream," she said as she scooped coffee into the machine, "I hope I never wake up."

❖

"I understand you, sir," Harry's receptionist said for the fourth time. "Dr. Basantes isn't in today, but I can set you up with another doctor if you like."

"I need to talk to her."

"Our first available appointment is next month. I can get you in earlier if you have a referral," the woman went on as if she hadn't heard a word Byron had said.

"Look, I don't need an appointment. It's important I talk to her as soon as possible," he said, trying not to stay on the phone much longer in case the police were listening in. "Is there any way you can tell me where to find her? We went to med school together, and I'd love to see her while I'm in town."

"I'm sorry, I misunderstood. Can you give me your name again?"

"Richard Bailey." He gave her the first name that came to mind.

"I'm sorry she's going to miss you, Dr. Bailey, but she's in surgery at University Medical all day."

He hung up before the woman could bore him anymore. His father's extra set of keys were in the drawer by the door, and he fisted them as he slipped his shoes on.

"What are you doing?" Mike asked, coming in scratching himself. He still appeared half asleep.

"Get dressed," he said, getting a beer and cracking it open. Their parents weren't home yet, and he was curious about where they'd disappeared to. "I found that bitch and need to get in place to follow her home."

"Where do you think Mom and Dad are?" Mike searched a few cabinets before settling for a beer.

"I'm not worried about that now." He guzzled the rest of the bottle he'd opened and slammed it on the table. "I need to finish dealing with my shit before I worry about anything else."

"We coming back here?"

"I saw more cruisers pass by this morning, so I sure as hell can't go home. As long as we keep going out the back, they won't see us."

They'd have to walk to the garage and grab a truck, since they couldn't use the one out front. They didn't talk as they walked, and he thought of the best way to grab Desi if she was with this Basantes.

"What the hell is that about?" Mike asked, pointing to the For Sale signs.

The padlocks meant they weren't getting in, but there were some cars in the back. "I'm not sure, but spot me," he said, breaking a window. This was some weird shit, and an itch started under his skin like it did when things were about to go sideways, but he had to go before he missed Basantes. This business was his father's life, but if he could just get to Desi… Thoughts crowded his mind, and he knew deep down his problem wasn't fixable. But that one thing he could do, and maybe Daddy would forgive him if he could just fix it.

They took the small car closest to the fence and headed to the medical center. He drove around until he found the parking lot reserved for staff and figured they'd have to wait until the afternoon to spot anything. There was a fruit vendor close to the entrance, and the guy was putting an assortment of fruit in small bags.

Byron's head came off the headrest when he saw a dark SUV come into the parking lot. The driver lowered their window, and the woman he recognized as Harry Basantes leaned out and held up a five, getting the fruit guy to hustle to the car. The guy nodded at whatever Basantes told him and waved when she pulled away to park.

"That's her?" he asked Mike.

"She's the one with Desi and Rachel that day. What now?" Mike put his hands on the dash and they watched Basantes until her car disappeared.

"Now we wait and see where this bitch lives. We do that, and we find Desi and her piece of shit sister." He put his head down again and closed his eyes. "She'll be here all day, so relax. You need to be rested for what comes next."

❖

Harry grumbled as usual as she tried to navigate to a spot. The new garage was built by someone with no concept of how large even the smallest car was. Maybe it was time to give Desi this vehicle and get something smaller for herself to make her life easier.

Her assistant was waiting at the entrance and handed her a lab coat. "Are we ready to go?" She took the list of patients and figured it'd be a busy day.

"You have three ORs ready to go. All I need is who you want to start with."

Harry studied the list. "Go with the fusion, and we'll start everyone else once we finish that one. There's nothing else too complicated, so I should be able to float between rooms."

"I'll let them know."

She was in surgery for the next four hours and was pleased with the residents' job. They did rounds after that, and she gave out assignments for the rest of the day. Her shift was finally over, and she took her phone out. "Hi, love." She took her keys out, grateful the lot was close to empty and she wouldn't be delayed by any last-minute conversation. "How's it going?"

"Hey," Desi said, sounding excited. "I have a present for you, but it's still cooling. I made my first vase, and it's yours. It only took twenty pounds of ruined tries before I finally got the hang of it again."

"Twenty pounds isn't bad, and I can't wait to see it."

Desi laughed and Harry imagined the size of her smile.

"It was good practice, and I should have the basics down again in about a week."

"Take your time. I'm proud of you," she said, waiting for the arm on the gate to go up. "But I already have your first creation. It's sitting on my desk at the office close to the house."

"You do? I don't remember what it was."

"It was a small dish, and you put your fingerprints in the bottom. Your name is along the edge." She laughed at the memory of a young Desi handing it over bashfully. "I put candy in it."

"I'll have to take a look the next time I go by."

The sound of Desi's voice was grounding her. Their last surgical case that morning was a woman who'd had her jaw broken in a domestic violence incident, among other injuries. The events of the last months came rushing back, and she'd had to take a minute before starting.

"That's sweet you kept it," Desi said, and it was quiet on her end. "Now you'll have two originals, but right now I need to know where we're going, so I can get dressed."

"Are you telling me you're naked right now?" She sped up to make the light.

"I am, but I'd like to get dressed so I don't keep you waiting. Knowing you, there was probably no time for lunch today, and you're starving."

"Hmm, it might take me a little while to remember where I had in mind. I could speed up and help you get dressed. If that's the case, I'll even spring for dessert."

Desi laughed again and made a kissing noise. "If you buy dessert to go, you can come home and lick it off me."

She waved to the security guy by the gate and was stealing a glance up at their bedroom window when she heard Desi clear her throat as she got out of the car. Desi smiled down at her and leaned over the rail wearing a robe. "Are you naked under that?"

"You're going to have to come up and see for yourself." Desi blew her a kiss and walked back inside.

She ran up the stairs and found Desi's robe over a chair and Desi on the bed in a lace bra and matching panties. It took a millisecond for her to get naked and make it to the bed.

"God, I missed you today," Desi said as she put her arms around her. "Would you like to see how much?"

All she could do was nod like a simpleton and roll to her back when Desi pushed on her to move. Desi straddled her and pressed her sex down on her abdomen, moaning when she squeezed her ass. "Yes," Desi said when she sat up and kissed her hard.

"You're so beautiful, baby," Harry said, kissing Desi again.

"I've been thinking about you all day. Feeling that wet clay made me think of your hands on me, and how you make me feel. But it really made me think of my hands on you." Desi grabbed her hands and put them over her head. "Can you keep them there for me?"

"Yes," she said, totally breathless and all thoughts of work banished from her head.

Desi leaned down and ran her hard nipples down her body. She made her way down slowly, and Harry saw her smile when she knelt between her legs. "I love you, and I want to make you feel good." Desi spread her sex with her index fingers and put her mouth on her.

"That feels so good." She went to put her hand on the back of Desi's head but remembered her promise to keep them above her head.

"You're so hard for me, honey." Desi went back to what she'd been doing with the tip of her tongue, and Harry threw her head back and tried to hang on.

Desi put her fingers in and by the second stroke that was all she could take. The muscles in her arms were straining to keep from moving, and she felt every ounce of self-control ebb away until she couldn't hold back. "Yes," she said as the orgasm hit her like a wave, and as it rolled away, it pulled the day's stress out to sea with it.

Desi kissed her sex one more time before moving back up, and she rolled over again and pinned Desi underneath her. She kissed Desi before moving down and sucking in her nipple. She moved her hand down until she reached the elastic of the pretty panties.

"Don't tease me, baby," Desi said as Harry put a knee between her legs.

"I'm not teasing you," she said as she closed her eyes at how wet Desi was. Desi stopped her when she went to move down.

"No, honey. I want to look at you when you make love to me tonight. I need to see how much you want me."

She shifted to get Desi naked and put her hand back on her sex. Desi moaned into her mouth when she kissed her as she put her fingers in and held them still to let Desi feel the fullness. Desi put her feet on her butt and her hands on her back.

"I need you to make me yours," Desi said as she started moving her hips.

Harry moved her fingers in a slow cadence as her thumb massaged Desi's clit. "Let me hear you," she said as she started going faster.

"Yes, like that." Desi's nails raked up her back. "Harder, baby, harder." Desi clamped the walls of her sex around her fingers and she kissed her. "That's so good," Desi said as her hips came up to meet her strokes. She screamed as she reached her peak, and Harry stilled her hand.

"You okay?" she asked as Desi held her wrist.

"I'm perfect," Desi said, spreading her legs so her thigh landed between Harry's legs. When Desi rocked her hips, Harry was ready to go again.

Harry rode Desi's leg, turned on by how Desi was moving with her, her hands squeezing her butt. She lifted up at the last moment to put more power into her thrusts, and Desi was right there with her. "Come with me, baby," Desi said, really digging her fingers in. "Oh God, oh God…"

They were both breathing hard when they finished, and Harry moved so her deadweight wasn't on Desi. "That's the way to welcome me home, but any more and I might not be able to walk."

"Try and find some energy because I'm starving. Especially after that." Desi moved to lie on her back and kissed the back of her neck. "You know how to build an appetite in a girl."

"You're not kidding," she said as Desi slapped her ass. "Are you sure you don't want to order in?"

"You promised a date, so we're going out."

"Strange time to ask, but do you want to ask Rachel to come with us?" Harry exhaled deeply as she turned her head.

"She's helping Serena with a playdate she set up for Butch. Maybe next time."

Harry got up and got the shower going, leaning in to adjust the water temperature. When she stepped in Desi pressed against her back and reached for the soap. "Am I dirty?" she asked as Desi's soapy hands ran down the slope of her butt.

"Filthy," Desi teased. "And you're incorrigible. So behave, and hands off. I'll never get anything to eat if you don't." Desi washed her back and then the front when she turned around.

"It's a good thing you worked up an appetite," she said as she rinsed off. "It's the only way to finish off a Port of Call burger and the baked potato side. I remember how much you love them."

"I love them and you," Desi said, smiling as she ran her soapy hands down her back. "For that meal, I'll have your baby."

"That sounds like a good deal," Harry said, stopping to look at Desi seriously. They'd never talked about anything beyond the day to day, no long-term relationship plans. A family was something they'd never broached, and it was a lifelong commitment. It had seemed like way too big a topic when Desi was only just coming out of something awful, but now that it had been brought up… "Is that—"

Desi put her fingers over her mouth. "Be honest and tell me what you really want."

"I want the whole thing with you, Desi. That means you, a family, and all that comes with that. But there's no rush."

"That's what I want too, and I want it while we're still young enough to enjoy them. I gave you my heart freely, and I love you enough to share that with as many children as you want."

"Really?" she asked, hugging Desi hard enough to lift her off the ground. "You're sure? So soon?"

"Yes," Desi said, kissing her cheek. "I see how you are with Butch, and I want to see that with our children. I dream about a baby that's part of us both."

"I guess I'll have to have a talk with my brother so we can get started." She'd already thought about how that would work, should the right woman ever come along.

"Good. I don't want to wait."

"Are you sure you don't want to take some time?" She didn't want Desi to feel pressured.

"I'm as sure as I am about wanting to go out with you tonight," Desi said as she put her arms around her waist. "I've always wanted children, but they had to be your children. I have you now, so it's time."

"You do have me, and I'm not going anywhere."

"That is what makes me want a long and happy life. You're the one person in the world made just for me, and I'm going to spend years making you happy."

"That you've already done." Harry swept her into a hug that could never be tight enough to convey how overwhelmed with love she was.

CHAPTER TWENTY-EIGHT

Byron watched the driveway where Basantes had turned in and cursed at the security car that wasn't moving. "That's going to be a problem," he said to Mike.

They'd driven by the gate entrance but hadn't wanted to go too slowly and tip off the security guy. From the little he'd seen, there was a large yard, with an equally large house. Places like this had good alarm systems, and the guards were the giveaway that was what was waiting inside. Extra muscle meant Desi and Rachel were there. They pulled over down the street while he tried to figure out what to do.

He lifted his head when he saw the SUV come back out, but this time Desi was next to Basantes. They headed downtown, and he motioned Mike to get going. If they were going out to eat or something, it would give him time to break in.

"Don't let her leave you behind," he said to Mike when another car got between them.

"I'm not losing them, so relax."

Basantes drove through the Quarter and parked a block from Port of Call. Mike pulled in across the street so they could watch. Desi waited for the bitch to come around and open her door. She pulled Basantes in for a kiss, and he wanted to throw up.

They were laughing and holding hands as they walked toward the restaurant, and if he could've, he'd have run them down and been done with this whole thing. She'd never done that with him, and she'd never thrown herself at him like she had with Basantes.

"I'm a fucking idiot," he said as he got Mike to drive them back.

"What are you talking about? Not that I'm disagreeing with you."

"Here I am missing Desi and doing all this stuff to get her back, and she's a fucking pervert." They turned a block before Basantes's place, and he had Mike park. "Stay here and wait for me. Don't leave me hanging."

"What are you going to do?" Mike said sounding like leaving was exactly what he was going to do.

He put a pair of bolt cutters, a glass cutter, and the one thing he'd stolen from his father under his coat. "I'm going to wait for them and have a little talk when they get back."

"Don't do anything more stupid than what I'm thinking."

"I'm not going to jail for some dykes," he said, getting out and pointing at Mike. "Not in this lifetime, so don't leave." He moved toward the house, his vision tinted red. Jealousy swam through his veins, and the only thing that would make it better was making someone else hurt. He'd figure out the rest of the mess when it was over.

"I haven't been here in years," Harry said as they left the restaurant. She groaned as she put a hand over her stomach and held Desi's hand with the other. "I'm stuffed."

"I remember the last time we came here," Desi said, moving closer to her and looking wistful.

She nodded as she glanced around to make sure they were okay. The neighborhood had changed from that long-ago night. Now the area was crowded with gay bars and restaurants. She was comfortable holding Desi's hand since it was such a common sight.

"I remember that too. That old two-seater was the best when it came to getting you to sit close to me." She kissed Desi's fingers and opened the door for her. "I remember Rachel was with us, and you ate all your food like you did tonight." She pressed Desi to the seat and kissed her.

"You didn't do that last time, but I sure wouldn't have minded." Desi combed her hair back and traced the curve of her ear.

"After your sixteenth birthday it was hard not kissing you. That's why I don't miss a chance now." She stepped between Desi's open legs and took her time. The way Desi's tongue pressed against her lips made her want to rush home. "I have loved you all my life, and I'm going to enjoy doing that until I die."

"You're so good at romancing me, honey," Desi said, pulling her hair to get her to take a step back. "I'm ready to get you home."

She drove back holding Desi's hand and enjoying the comfortable silence between them. Desi was one of the only people she didn't feel the need to make small talk with. They waved to the new guard on the way in and she slowed to make sure the gate closed.

She walked around and opened Desi's door, then fumbled with her keys because Desi was behind her, running her hands between her legs. "You're a tease," she said as the door finally opened.

"Am not," Desi said, wrapping her arms around her neck and her legs around her waist when she bent down. "If you carry me upstairs, I'll show you how much I'm not teasing you."

She moved Desi to the front and smiled when Desi repeated her hold around her neck and waist. They kissed all the way up, and she sat on the bed enjoying Desi on her lap. "I can't get enough of you," she said as Desi started unbuttoning her shirt.

"What is that?" Desi asked, stopping what she was doing.

It was an odd noise coming from the closet, a muted beeping that spelled trouble. She turned from the closet to the bedside table where there was no digital readout on the clock.

"Something's wrong," Harry said softly, her pulse racing as she became laser focused. What had happened at her Uncle Jude's was still fresh in her mind. The area they'd driven through had electricity, but their house didn't. She'd been so involved, she hadn't noticed there were no outside lights on.

They moved to the closet together, and she studied the panel attached to the wall behind her shirts. She turned the alarm off after pressing the panic button that would alert the police. "Someone's in the kitchen," she told Desi. "They came in through the window."

"How is the system still working?" Desi asked as Harry got on her knees by the bed.

"The battery backup works for another two days even without power. Each entryway is accounted for on the panel." She pulled a canvas bag from under the bed and led Desi to the veranda outside, where it was pitch dark.

"What is that?" Desi asked. Her voice shook slightly, and her eyes were wide with fear.

Harry hooked the emergency ladder on the railing and dropped it over the side. "I need you to climb down and run to the studio. Take my cell. I need to know you're safe and out of the way. Stay in the shadows and move as fast as you can into the trees."

"I can't leave you here," Desi said in a full panic.

She pointed to the ladder to get Desi moving. "Don't come back no matter what. Promise me you won't." She helped Desi swing her leg over and get started on the way down. "I love you, and stay safe."

"Please, honey. Come with me." Desi was crying, her breath coming in hard gasps.

"We both know who's down there, and I can't chance him getting his hands on you. If you go alone, there's less chance of him spotting you." She motioned for her to speed up. "You can do it, but I've got to slow him down until the police get here."

Desi whimpered as she moved down the ladder, glanced up, then set off.

She waited until Desi was on the ground and out of sight before she thought of her best move. The quiet around her meant their intruder was perhaps trying to get his bearings. She closed her eyes to acclimate to the dark and to center her emotions. Was he alone? Was his brother with him? She was confident Desi would be safe in the studio, since it was removed from the house and they most likely had no idea it was there.

She took her shoes off to stay as quiet as possible. She walked down the hall, then down the stairs as fast as she could to keep them from creaking.

Her best bet was getting to the sunroom off the back of the house. It was the one room off the kitchen that led to the rest of the house. She moved slowly, making sure her path was clear so as not to take any unnecessary chances. The foyer and den were a clear shot to where she needed to go, so she moved as quickly and cautiously as she could. She heard him from the sunroom before she could see him, and she stopped to make sure he wasn't going to ambush her.

He was breathing hard, but it didn't sound like he was moving. This had to be Byron, and it sounded like he was trying to work up his courage. That seemed funny considering he'd tried to prove to Desi what a big man he was the whole time they were together. Why be afraid now?

She clenched her fists and waited for her chance. All she cared about was that Desi had made it outside. The panic button upstairs guaranteed the police were on their way, but she wanted the chance to get her hands on this guy. How different it would be for him to come up against a woman who fought back and had the same murderous intent he probably was seething with as he stood in her kitchen.

"This is it. Just like before," the man whispered, but he sounded like he hadn't moved yet. "All I have to do is grab what's mine and go." He took another deep breath and took a step forward, the floor creaking softly. "That bitch is all that's between you and Desi."

Byron was a chatty thing who liked talking to himself, and Harry guessed it was the only positive feedback he ever got. It told her he was alone, though, and that was something.

Harry waited, watching the door to the kitchen. Whatever he was trying to work out, he'd done it. He moved with confidence, which probably meant he'd been in the house before they got home. Their problem had been not paying attention to anything but each other when they arrived.

"Hello," she said from the shadows, almost laughing at how he froze with his shoulders up around his ears. His feet seemed glued to the floor, but he swung around, trying to find her. "It's been a long time, but welcome to our home. Most people use the front door, but I'm sure you're good for our broken window."

"Fuck you." He squinted but still didn't seem to figure out where she was standing. "Give me my wife, you fucking pervert."

"I'm sure you've gotten the divorce papers." She edged closer. "She's not going to be your wife for much longer. The truth is, she was never yours, was she?"

"The last thing I'm giving that bitch is a divorce. I took the till death thing to heart."

"You sure about that? The one in danger of dying tonight isn't Desi."

"I don't want to hurt anyone," he said, pulling something from his waistband. His arm shot out, a gun glinting in the dim light. "Give me Desi and I don't kill you."

"You're not a very fast learner, are you?" She pressed against the wall as he continued to search the dark room for her. "You've tried everything you could to keep her with you, but she doesn't want that. You and your sick family are going to be a distant memory soon, and there's nothing that'll ever resurrect you."

"You sick fuck," he screamed. "You've always been there twisting her against me."

"That's because my daddy didn't have to get me a girl. What kind of man needs his father to do that?" She needed him to get mad enough to lose himself. People who were enraged were easier to bring down.

"She married me, asshole, and that's the way it is. You're going to lose again, and ain't nothing you can do to change that. I'm her husband, and the fancy attorney you got her isn't going to cut her loose from my bed." He was shaking as he screamed, and he seemed unhinged.

"How about you put the gun down? You're already in enough trouble without adding to that. Desi isn't coming with you, so think about what's best for her." She tried reason, but the way he was wiping his face meant he wasn't a man to be reasoned with.

"I'm her husband, and I tell her what's good for her. That's how it fucking works."

He swung his arm around in jerky movements, and she was glad it was a revolver with probably five rounds. Any more than that, and she might get shot.

"Did your daddy teach you that?" She didn't raise her voice, and he leaned forward as if trying to hear her. "You and your daddy have something in common. You two can only beat up on women who won't fight back. There's no way you can stand on your own without backup when it's a real fight." She had to press every one of his buttons to make him angrier. "Aren't you a man?"

"Quit talking about my daddy. He is a real man, not some wannabe like you."

The weather was cool, but the sweat pouring off him was dripping in his eyes. He rubbed them with his free hand, and it gave her the chance to shift.

"He taught me how the world works, especially when it comes to my wife."

"Yeah, the big man who knows how to treat women proved that. Your mother was probably getting one of those lessons, but she wasn't strong enough to take it this time."

"What the hell are you talking about?" He swung the gun toward where she was standing, but it only stayed for a moment before he moved on.

It was possible he really didn't know, and this was the key to put him completely off kilter. "He beat your mother to death, then sat and ate dinner. She was bleeding in the front room while he ate the meatloaf she'd made him." She laughed as he bent at the waist a little. "He showed her, I guess, but he's got a big problem now. I mean, he's not going to be able to treat people the same in prison, is he?"

"That's a lie."

"Unlike you, I'm not an asshole. I wouldn't lie about something like that. Face it, he was the real man who did his talking with his fists."

She laughed again, watching his every move, calculating her timing. "You're nothing but a little boy who has to hide behind a gun." She clucked her tongue at him. "Put it down and show me what a man you are. Or are you that pathetic? Is that what your father thought? No wonder Desi wants to be with me."

He screamed at top volume like a wounded animal. "You're lying. You're a pervert trying to get in my head, but you don't know anything about my family, especially my father."

"You're the one who has no clue about his family." She took another step, trying to get behind him. "You don't know your mom is lying on a slab in the morgue, or that your daddy is playing hide the soap with a big dude in lockup." She lowered her voice to try to keep him from guessing where she was. "Your daddy had no idea killing your wife, even if she deserved it, is against the law."

He hit his forehead with the hand he held the gun with. "Shut up."

"Put the gun down and fight me. You aren't afraid of me, are you?" He swung his hand in her direction and pulled the trigger. She'd dropped to her stomach before he'd gotten a good shot at her, but he obviously heard her hit the ground.

"I told you to shut the fuck up, so that was your fault. If you don't want to die, tell me where my wife is." The gun steadied and he kept it pointed in her direction.

Harry lay there trying to think of the best move now. It was obvious he didn't have a problem pulling the trigger. *Forgive me, Desi, if this doesn't work out. At least you won't have to go back.*

She hoped Desi knew how she felt about her and what was in her heart, in case something happened. Making that peace was all she needed to do to make her move. Once she was on her feet and running toward him, he fired again.

Desi stood in the door of her studio gripping the phone. The 9-1-1 operator kept her updated as to where the police were and how long it would be until they arrived. All that mattered, all she could think about, was that Harry was in danger.

"Ma'am, are you still with me?" the operator asked.

"Yes, but you need to hurry. Detective Roger Landry knows how dangerous my ex-husband is, so if you can call him, please do." She heard a whirling noise and saw the yellow flashing lights come into the yard. It was the security guys Harry had hired, and they were driving up to the house.

"The gate is open, and the security guy is in the yard, so please tell the police not to do anything to him." She waited for the woman to relay that message, but the shot that rang out made her start running. "Harry!" She ignored the woman and all her instructions and ran from the studio, terror driving her forward.

Life wouldn't be worth living if something happened to Harry, but if she was hurt, she had to help. That trumped the promises she'd made to stay away. She knew better than anyone what Byron was capable of, and he needed someone to take his anger out on. If there was a sacrifice to be made, better her than Harry.

She didn't hesitate to run through the open back door but stopped when she heard glass breaking. It sounded like it was coming from the back of the house, so she ran out again and pushed the security guard out of the way when he tried to stop her. She stopped and could only watch in awe, her terror receding slightly when she took in the scene.

"Let's see how you like it, asshole," Harry said as she punched Byron in the face.

There was a line of broken windows at the back of the sunroom, but it looked like Byron had gone through first, given the amount of blood.

"This is for her broken leg," Harry said as she hit him again.

"Harry," Desi said loudly, and Byron tried to swing, taking advantage of Harry's flicker of distraction.

"This is how it felt every time you laid a hand on her." Harry hit his nose this time and followed it up with a kick to his side. "Do you like it?"

"She's mine," Byron said as blood poured over his mouth and down his chin. He swung clumsily and howled when Harry grabbed his hand by the fingers and bent them up at an odd angle.

"Hurts, doesn't it?" Harry applied more pressure, and Byron dropped to his knees. Even from where she was standing, Desi heard the bones break. He swayed when Harry let him go, but he didn't go down.

"Desi wants to be with me," he said, glancing her way for a second before looking back at Harry. "You belong with me, Desi. You know that."

"Wrong again," Harry said, landing a punch to the right side of his face. "Desi has the right to make up her mind, and she wants to be here. She knows this is her home, and she knows I don't own her. I'd be devastated if she left, but she's free to do that. Even if that was her choice, I'd never let you hurt her again."

He yelled when Harry grabbed him and lifted his head high enough to hit him again, but now it sounded like a cry of pain. Finally his screeching stopped, and his head dropped back, his eyes closed.

"Please, honey, he's not worth it. That's enough." She moved quickly to Harry's side, adrenaline making her feel ill, and the sight of him this close to her making her tremble, even if he was out cold. "Let the police deal with him."

Harry let her pull her back as the security guard placed cuffs on Byron and asked if she needed any medical help.

"I thought I told you to wait in the studio," Harry said when they walked far enough away to talk privately. She kissed Desi's forehead and held her tight.

"If anyone is getting a lecture, Harry Basantes, it isn't me. He had a gun. What were you thinking? You could've been killed." She grabbed Harry's shirt. "You make me crazy." She shook Harry as much as she could, getting her to smile. "Next time, love, you leave if the idiot is armed. You could've gotten yourself killed."

"I'm okay," Harry said, kissing her.

"Are you sure?"

"I'm perfect, but we need some new art for the wall of the sunroom, and some new windows." Harry held her and made her laugh when all she wanted to do was cry from relief. "It's over, my love." The security guard informed them the police were a block away, and they could head back into the house if they wanted to.

"Thank you," she said, burying her face in Harry's chest. "No one ever stood up for me but you. From that very first day."

"That's what I'm planning to do until my last breath."

"Good." She stood in the circle of Harry's arms until police flooded the yard. They answered questions. Byron was being taken to central lockup, with a detour to the emergency room.

"His brother Mike surrendered when the police got here, so Byron will be joining him and his father as soon as possible," Roger Landry said as he took notes in their kitchen.

"Did his father confess?" Desi asked.

"He did, because he thinks there's going to be no consequence. It was his wife, so it was his life to take." Roger shook his head. "They're a special kind of stupid. But forget about all that tonight. I'm leaving units out front and back, just for peace of mind."

"Thank you for everything, Roger. I'm glad fate put you on my case," Desi said, shaking hands with him. All the men who'd made her life miserable were gone, and for the first time in a very long time, she could breathe freely.

"I'm happy for you. You're a world away from the woman I met at the hospital. Good for you. You need to keep being strong." He shook hands with Harry and stood. "Let this one hold your hand until you're finished with what you need to do, and you'll be fine."

They asked the security guard to sit inside the sunroom until the windows could be fixed and went up to bed. She lay next to Harry and couldn't get her mind to slow enough to find sleep. "Honey?"

"Yes," Harry said and stopped rubbing her back. "Something wrong?"

"Do you think everything will be normal from now on?" She lifted up on her elbow so she could see Harry's face. It was hard to miss the expression of adoration in Harry's expression.

"As normal as things around here get with Mona, Tony, and Butch around." Harry ran her knuckles along her cheek. "As for us, it'll be family dinners, pottery, medicine, and two or more kids."

"Really? You think so?" She wanted to believe. It was a fairy tale of sorts, and those only existed in books. Her knight, though, was real and loved her.

"I do. You and I are going to live happily ever after, and there's nothing standing in our way. Tonight we've swept all the ghosts of the past away, so we can concentrate on what's important to our future."

"What's that?" she said, coming down to kiss Harry. This wonderful partner who'd loved her since the third grade and always would was the center of her world. Of that she had not one doubt.

"You and me, love. That's all that matters." Harry kissed her, and there were no more words necessary.

She'd found her place and her home again, and she wasn't letting go. She'd heal, psychologically and physically, and while she did so she'd be surrounded by people she loved and who loved her in return. It might take a long time to completely be rid of the ghosts of her past, but she had one more chance to live a life of beauty, and she wasn't going to waste a single second.

EPILOGUE

Nine Months Later

Desi admired the flowers blooming outside the studio. She could understand how the woman who painted here loved the spot. In the last year she'd been amazed at the number of bulbs that bloomed at different times of the year. Her days had been full of fun, love, and a sense of permanence, and her nights were full of passion and completion. The nightmares had dwindled, and they rarely surfaced anymore. This was her home, and Harry was her partner for life.

All the evidence of what Byron had brought into their lives—like security guards and fear—was gone. She also let go of waiting for him to pounce when she least expected it. Byron, Mike, and their father were serving their sentences in Angola State Penitentiary, and it would be decades before they'd be released.

That truth, as well as Harry's love, had given her a life and freedom. Byron was gone, and if he survived prison, he'd probably forget them. When he got out, if he got out, they'd deal with it then. Mike had confessed and had agreed to testify against Byron, so they'd given him a better deal.

Harry had sat with her until they'd taken Byron away in handcuffs. He hadn't looked anywhere but at his shoes, and it was gratifying to see him whispering to himself, his head shaking and spittle falling from his mouth as he stayed in his own little world. It was something she'd needed to see to assure herself it was okay to live again. She hadn't wanted to attend Big Byron's trial, but Serena had informed them he was found guilty of murder and had gotten the maximum sentence.

After it was all over, she'd thrown herself into her art and taking care of Harry. The life they'd built was what she'd often dreamed of, and she had to stop and believe she wasn't making it all up. Harry was a remarkable woman, no different from the person she'd been when they were young. The only difference was how much of a romantic she'd become.

Desi had even established a relationship with Harry's mother Rosa, who was standoffish at first, given the way she'd seen Harry grieve when they were teenagers. But their visits to Florida had convinced Harry's parents of her commitment, and they'd been a source of support.

She'd come to love Mona like the mother she barely remembered. They talked and cooked together when Harry left for work, and she listened when Desi had to talk about her past. Rachel joined them when she could, and whatever hurts they had left, Mona had helped them heal in her kitchen. It was a blessing to see Rachel blossom into a happy soul who didn't carry the constant worry of all they'd been through. Harry had freed her sister as well to find the things and people in her life who would make her happy.

"It's about time you quit, baby," Mona said, handing her a glass of milk.

"I'm not a fan of—"

"Don't argue, and drink that."

"Okay, I'll drink it, but all I do is sit all day. I don't need stronger bones for that." She took a sip to make Mona happy. "Is Harry home?"

"Got here forty minutes ago and went up to take a shower. She should be out of your hair while you get ready."

Desi carried her glass into the kitchen and then started for the stairs. "But I like her in my hair, Mona."

As further proof that her life had made a complete turnaround, they were all heading to her debut show for her pottery that night. With practice and Tony's diligence, her pieces had become sought after by a few shops in town. Everyone seemed to love their uniqueness, and she'd found her bank account growing. She'd been working for months to have enough pieces, and tonight would be a first for her.

She made it up in time to watch Harry slip into her shoes. Harry had left that morning, promising she'd be home as soon as rounds were done. The suit Harry had on fit her perfectly, and Desi leaned against the door to admire the view. She swept her eyes over Harry's body and sighed at the brilliant smile directed at her.

"Don't I get a hello?" Harry said, opening her arms.

She pitied the women who looked at Harry and then hated her for taking Harry out of circulation, but only a little bit. "I'm going to be the envy of every woman at this thing. You look good enough to—well, you know." She put her arms around Harry's shoulders.

"I think you need to look in the mirror more often, beautiful. Anyone in their right mind would spot the sexiest woman around, and that's not me." Harry didn't seem to mind the specks of clay splattered on her shirt and held her closer. Harry went to kiss her, and she stopped her by stepping back.

"That suit's too nice to mess up. Stay put, and I'll be right back."

"No way. I don't want to wait to give you a birthday kiss." Harry did just that. "Have you enjoyed your day so far?"

"It's nice that all my days are nice, and the only difference is it's my birthday today. I have you to thank for that, and I love you for it."

"But since today is your birthday, take a shower, so we can get with the celebrating and the gifts."

"You've already given me plenty, honey. Any more, and I might get spoiled." She stripped and liked that Harry never looked away from her.

"Then take a shower so we won't be late." Harry tapped on her watch.

"What are you up to? I know it's something."

"I'm not up to anything," Harry said sweetly. "It's a big night, and I'd like you to enjoy every minute of it. That means shower and get ready. Once you do, I'll be free to kiss you all I want."

She took a quick shower and put on the dress Tony had helped her shop for the week before. It was another simple black dress, but shorter than the others she owned, and Tony had promised it would make Harry sweat. She put on her low heels and the diamond earrings Harry had surprised her with that morning.

Harry was sitting on the railing outside with two champagne flutes, and she walked out to a wolf whistle. "Are you ready?" Harry asked when she stepped between her legs.

"I guess. My agent and business partner tell me most of the stuff is already sold, so this is more for advertising for future sales." She pressed her nose against Harry's neck, enjoying the smell of Harry's cologne. "It's better than having to go around begging people to buy something."

"I'm so proud of you, my love, and I want to toast you before all your adoring fans steal you away for the night." Harry handed her a glass and held up hers. "You are the absolute best thing to ever happen to me, and I'm glad I'm the one you choose to share yourself with."

"Thank you. I love you. I wouldn't have any of this without you."

Harry shook her head and ran her fingers through Desi's hair. "This is the first of many of these nights. I'm sure about that, and I'm sure I'm going to enjoy watching you fly. You're too passionate not to be successful." She pulled Desi forward and kissed her. "So, are you having a good birthday?"

"I got to wake up next to you, I've got beautiful earrings, and I've got you. It's been really good so far." She kissed Harry's chin before moving up to her lips.

"That all sounds great, but wouldn't you like to see your gift?"

"The earrings were my gift, honey."

"Nuh-uh, that is." Harry pointed to the covered space on the veranda.

The swing looked much like the one that had hung on her porch for years. "Is that…?"

Harry grinned and nodded. "In the morning it's getting scraped and a fresh coat of paint, but it's held up well since our homework days."

"How in the world did you—?" She couldn't finish as tears threatened. Everything seemed to make her an emotional mess lately, and Harry wasn't helping with this gift. It was the sweetest thing she could've thought of.

"Hey," Harry said, holding her from behind. "It was supposed to make you happy, not sad. Do you not like it? Oh God, does it remind you of Clyde?"

"I love it." She tilted her head back, trying not to break down and mess up her makeup.

"Let's see if it has any magic left in it," Harry said, leading her to the towel she'd draped over the seat to keep their clothes from getting messed up. "I bought it from the owners of the house and probably paid three times what a new one would cost. Whatever it took, it was worth it." She got the glasses before joining Desi. "Here's to many more happy birthdays, and to the girl I love."

She lifted her glass but didn't drink. "Thank you, but you know what the doctor said."

"It's okay. I chilled sparkling grape juice so we wouldn't kill any of our kid's brain cells."

"Your kid missed you and your sappy songs. I guess that's why he wouldn't stop kicking me today." She rubbed her midsection that now showed her condition and had her out shopping for new clothes.

She smiled when Harry put her hand over hers and appeared as awed as she usually did when she touched the life they'd created together. It was getting harder to push Harry out the door in the morning, and she loved it. As soon as Harry got home it was always a kiss for her, then one for the baby.

Their due date was in a few months, and if she got her wish, they'd come home with a beautiful baby with dark hair and blue eyes. Harry's brother had been thrilled they'd asked, and after seeing his children, her wish wasn't so farfetched. The insemination process had been simple, and she'd gotten pregnant on the first try.

This decision wasn't hard to make once she and Harry had discussed it. Harry was the kind of gentle soul you wanted to bring children into the world with. She'd been so protective of her, and Desi basked in the attention. She was enjoying the pregnancy, and she was ready to meet the little guy.

"Me and baby Basantes love you, honey." She smiled when Harry wiped away her tears. "You always think of what will make me happy, and this is the best birthday since your family took us to the beach that year."

Harry smiled and tucked her hair behind her ear. "You're worth everything to me. And if there's something you need, all you need to do is ask."

"I have you, our baby, and all these people who love me. My life is a miracle now." She handed Harry her empty glass and put her arm around her. "This swing reminds me that not all the things in my past were horrible."

"This thing holds a lot of good memories, and I'll be glad to tell the baby about it when he's older. There's also the chance to make some new good memories out here, now that it's so close."

"Let's not corrupt it right off," she said and smiled. "But thank you for this."

"Don't get upset, but there's one more thing," Harry said, turning and facing her. "My mother will be there tonight, so it's important."

"Honey, it's too much. I don't need anything else."

Harry kissed her to stop her from talking. "There can never be too much when it comes to you. And I was kidding about my mother." Harry dropped to her knees. "I've wanted to give you this for a while, but today seemed like a special day to do it."

"Are you okay? You seem nervous." Desi's heart raced at the sight of Harry kneeling in front of her.

"This reminds me of the night I worked up my nerve to kiss you, but I figure that worked out really well." Harry took her hands and she leaned down and kissed her.

"It worked out pretty good for me too."

"I've known you almost all my life, Desi. We've lived through pain and forgiveness, and we've found love. I want to enjoy the life we have, loving you, raising children with you, and showing you how much I cherish you." Harry took a box from her pocket and opened it. "Will you marry me?"

Her eyes were so full of tears she barely saw the ring. "Yes," she whispered, holding out her left hand.

Harry hesitated and read her the inscription on the inside before putting it on her finger. "Thank you, my love," Harry read, then showed her before slipping it on her finger and kissing her hand.

"Thank you?" She turned her hand this way and that, watching the light reflect on the stone.

"For so long I wished and prayed for one more chance with you. I tried moving on, but my heart wouldn't forget you. So thank you. You came back, and I get that chance to love you forever." Harry kissed her again, and she twisted the ring to prove to herself it was real.

"I love you so much," she said, pressing herself to Harry. Her body felt too small to contain the joy that filled her soul.

"I love you too, but if we're late, Tony's going to break some of your stuff over my head. Ready?"

They walked to the car together, and Mona and Rachel clapped their hands when they saw the ring. "It's about time, bonehead," Mona said to Harry.

"What she said." Rachel pointed at Mona before hugging Desi then Harry.

Harry shook her head as she helped her into the car, and Desi loved that she had the chance to live such a blessed life.

"All set?" Harry asked her before closing her door.

"For this and everything else."

About the Author

Ali Vali is the author of the long-running Cain Casey "Devil" series and the Genesis Clan "Forces" series, as well as numerous standalone romances including two Lambda Literary Award finalists, *Calling the Dead* and *Love Match*, and the novella *On the Rocks* in the collection *Still Not Over You.*

Originally from Cuba, Ali has retained much of her family's traditions and language and uses them frequently in her stories. Having her father read her stories and poetry before bed every night as a child infused her with a love of reading, which she carries till today. Ali currently lives outside New Orleans, Louisiana, and she has discovered that living in Louisiana provides plenty of material to draw from in creating her novels and short stories.

Books Available From Bold Strokes Books

Best Practice by Carsen Taite. When attorney Grace Maldonado agrees to mentor her best friend's little sister, she's prepared to confront Perry's rebellious nature, but she isn't prepared to fall in love. Legal Affairs: one law firm, three best friends, three chances to fall in love. (978-1-63555-361-1)

Home by Kris Bryant. Natalie and Sarah discover that anything is possible when love takes the long way home. (978-1-63555-853-1)

Keeper by Sydney Quinne. With a new charge under her reluctant wing—feisty, highly intelligent math wizard Isabelle Templeton—Keeper Andy Bouchard has to prevent a murder or die trying. (978-1-63555-852-4)

One More Chance by Ali Vali. Harry Bastantes planned a future with Desi Thompson until the day Desi disappeared without a word, only to walk back into her life sixteen years later. (978-1-63555-536-3)

Renegade's War by Gun Brooke. Freedom fighter Aurelia DeCallum regrets saving the woman called Blue. She fears it will jeopardize her mission, and secretly, Blue might end up breaking Aurelia's heart. (978-1-63555-484-7)

The Other Women by Erin Zak. What happens in Vegas should stay in Vegas, but what do you do when the love you find in Vegas changes your life forever? (978-1-63555-741-1)

The Sea Within by Missouri Vaun. Time is running out for Dr. Elle Graham to convince Captain Jackson Drake that the only thing that can save future Earth resides in the past, and rescue her broken heart in the process. (978-1-63555-568-4)

To Sleep With Reindeer Justine Saracen. In Norway under Nazi occupation, Marrit, an Indigenous woman, and Kirsten, a Norwegian resister, join forces to stop the development of an atomic weapon. (978-1-63555-735-0)

Twice Shy by Aurora Rey. Having an ex with benefits isn't all it's cracked up to be. Will Amanda Russo learn that lesson in time to take a chance on love with Quinn Sullivan? (978-1-63555-737-4)

Z-Town by Eden Darry. Forced to work together to stay alive, Meg and Lane must find the centuries-old treasure before the zombies find them first. (978-1-63555-743-5)

Bet Against Me by Fiona Riley. In the high-stakes luxury real estate market, everything has a price, and as rival Realtors Trina Lee and Kendall Yates find out, that means their hearts and souls, too. (978-1-63555-729-9)

Broken Reign by Sam Ledel. Together on an epic journey in search of a mysterious cure, a princess and a village outcast must overcome life-threatening challenges and their own prejudice if they want to survive. (978-1-63555-739-8)

Just One Taste by CJ Birch. For Lauren, it only took one taste to start trusting in love again. (978-1-63555-772-5)

Lady of Stone by Barbara Ann Wright. Sparks fly as a magical emergency forces a noble embarrassed by her ability to submit to a low-born teacher who resents everything about her. (978-1-63555-607-0)

Last Resort by Angie Williams. Katie and Rhys are about to find out what happens when you meet the girl of your dreams but you aren't looking for a happily ever after. (978-1-63555-774-9)

Longing for You by Jenny Frame. When Debrek housekeeper Katie Brekman is attacked amid a burgeoning vampire-witch war, Alexis Villiers must go against everything her clan believes in to save her. (978-1-63555-658-2)

Money Creek by Anne Laughlin. Clare Lehane is a troubled lawyer from Chicago who tries to make her way in a rural town full of secrets and deceptions. (978-1-63555-795-4)

Passion's Sweet Surrender by Ronica Black. Cam and Blake are unable to deny their passion for each other, but surrendering to love is a whole different matter. (978-1-63555-703-9)

The Holiday Detour by Jane Kolven. It will take everything going wrong to make Dana and Charlie see how right they are for each other. (978-1-63555-720-6)

BOLDSTROKESBOOKS.COM

Looking for your next great read?

Visit BOLDSTROKESBOOKS.COM
to browse our entire catalog of paperbacks, ebooks,
and audiobooks.

Want the first word on what's new?
Visit our website for event info,
author interviews, and blogs.

Subscribe to our free newsletter for sneak peeks,
new releases, plus first notice of promos
and daily bargains.

SIGN UP AT
BOLDSTROKESBOOKS.COM/signup

Bold Strokes Books
Quality and Diversity in LGBTQ Literature

*Bold Strokes Books is an award-winning publisher
committed to quality and diversity in LGBTQ fiction.*